*They we
least half
she could speak.*

She didn't want to. She'd rather look at him as he napped.

Sliding back in the cushioned seat, Spence had ceased rowing long ago and stretched his legs out so that his linen trousers molded his thighs and hips. . . .

"You, my Cat, are more beautiful than ever."

She blushed but couldn't move.

"I could feel your eyes on me from across a desert," he whispered. He slid upright. "I have hungered for you every day for the past three years. Now, since your father and Merrick have died, I predicted that you would come out into society again—and soon you'd have other men dancing attendance on you."

"I don't want another man."

"I am ecstatic."

"I don't want you, either, Spence. . . ."

He had her on his lap before she could refuse or run. "The way you stiffen and yield. Always, kitten, you would curl to me like a wild animal. Like now." He brushed his lips on hers. "Like *this.*" He curved her beneath him.

Cat enjoyed his mouth as if he were her sole sustenance. Air. Water. Sun.

But she mustn't have him. The hurt was too wide, too deep. Deeper than this lake.

She arched, pushed, and stood.

He tried to grab her, but missed.

She did what she thought impossible before. She put her fingers to her nose, pinched, and jumped. She had, by God, *left him!*

Booksellers love Jo-Ann Power's
ANGEL OF MIDNIGHT!

Books by Jo-Ann Power

Angel of Midnight
You and No Other
Treasures

Published by POCKET BOOKS

Jo-AnnPower

TREASURES

POCKET STAR BOOKS
New York   London   Toronto   Sydney   Tokyo   Singapore

An *Original* Publication of POCKET BOOKS

A Pocket Star Book published by
POCKET BOOKS, a division of Simon & Schuster Inc.
1230 Avenue of the Americas, New York, NY 10020

ISBN: 0-671-52995-1

First Pocket Books printing April 1996

10 9 8 7 6 5 4 3 2 1

POCKET STAR BOOKS and colophon are registered trademarks of Simon & Schuster Inc.

Cover art by Brent Watkinson

Printed in the U.S.A.

For those who have shared their finest treasures with me—themselves and the stories that define them to make us who we are: the Curtises, the Fletchers, the Lebers, the Pelletiers, and the Powers.

TREASURES

Chapter 1

If money could buy what I want here tonight, I'd empty the last few pounds in my bank account and run home. This *minute.*" Cat met her friend Dorrie in the woman's upper hall and spun at her silent order to turn and let her inspect her new ballgown.

"You've squeezed your last stone, though, Catherine Farrell. You did it for that dress Worth did you the honor to design." Dorrie Billington's eyes danced down the iris silk creation by the noted Paris dressmaker. Cat had depleted her inheritance to pay him, surrendering almost the last of her father's money to buy herself a chance at a rewarding future.

"Honor, my foot." Cat's fingers skimmed her remaining treasure: her family's heirloom amethyst necklace at her throat. "If this gown doesn't help me make an impression, you must realize I'll be *growing* turnips to survive instead of trying to bleed a few here tonight!"

Dorrie chuckled as she looped her arm through Cat's. "Come along and stop worrying. Blanding and I promise you no one will dare be rude to you."

"Facing half of London and most of Kent downstairs in that receiving line and ballroom is my chance to save my school, Dorrie. If I fail . . ." She grimaced.

"You won't." Dorrie patted her arm as they descended the grand staircase of Billington Manor.

"I haven't danced in three years." She was blathering and she knew it but didn't care. "What if I don't remember? Suppose I go downstairs, waltz into that ballroom, and no one waltzes with me? What happens to a twenty-three-year-old jilted spinster who tries to open a school for girls and can't enroll enough students to meet the monthly butcher's bill? Hmmm? I'll be aimless. Idle. Still *poor and* ostracized!"

"Will you please calm yourself?" Dorrie was grinning with her never-ending optimism.

"How can I?" Cat grit her teeth. She had to make the biggest impression of her life on these people tonight. She had to show them she was genteel, capable, *worthy* of educating their daughters. Before she'd gone to Mr. Worth, she'd sunk almost every penny of her father's bequest to her into the Farrell School for Young Ladies. She needed a few more students to operate her first term with a small profit. To flourish, however, her school required that laying on of hands society called *acceptability*. For that, she had to show them she was no oddity. No disgrace.

She would. She had to.

Her own self-respect depended on it. During these past three years, she'd come to know *that* was more valuable than any other prize on earth.

Cat squeezed her eyes shut and summoned courage. Tonight, she needed every ounce. Here—she once more tried to convince herself—she was a hunter.

Not the prey. No one would hurt her here. No one would risk Dorrie and Blanding's wrath, would they?

At her best friends' ball, Cat had to be treated as just another guest. If in reality she was a woman reclaiming her reputation and obliterating the catastrophe of the past three years, few would note it in their public manners. *Would they?*

After all, what she wanted was so simple. Not a man. Not a social life. Just her school and the opportunity to enjoy those simple things money could never buy. Like peace. A job she adored. Children to help and to watch grow into adults.

But to do that the whole of Great Britain had to politely "forget" how Catherine Farrell had been abandoned by her groom the morning of her wedding three years ago. Could they?

The news had been the London tabloids' savory tidbit for weeks. Even now, years later, when Cat's father's fame as an Egyptian archaeologist was recounted in newspapers as background for an agreement Her Majesty's government sought with the khedive of Egypt, Cat knew everyone resurrected details of the scandal that had rocked her world. She had daily proof.

She could not ride into Ashford for a yard of cloth nor up to Canterbury to interview a prospective teacher for her school staff without recognizing how people remembered.

Shopkeepers, who wanted her money, were neutral, if deferential. Those of her own station, who could not avoid her at church or at local lectures, were tolerant. Those of higher rank, whose approval she needed now more than ever, were still too terribly indifferent. She wished people would have outgrown those reactions long ago. But their very longevity drove Cat to a frenzy. Victorian Society ordered itself by donning a rigid social corset. For those who tested the stays, The Proper Set could yank the laces in reproof. If the reprimand seemed ineffective, expiration could be arranged by the artless Slow Death, a series of stifling snubs that cut one's breath, suffocated one's hope, crushed one's heart.

The fact that Cat's hadn't been was what propelled her to Dorrie's house and hospitality. Tonight and for the rest of this interminable weekend, Cat knew she had to brave the treacherous shoals of this social sea—or founder on rocks that could dash her school and her efforts for a life of quiet fulfillment.

Dorrie wrinkled her nose in gaiety as they made the foyer and she described her guests. "We have forty-two staying in the manor for the weekend but half of Kent coming for tonight's ball," she said as she adjusted Cat's roses in her hair. "Relax, dearest. Enjoy yourself. If it's easier for you, pretend they are children—"

"Or naked!"

Cat gasped with Dorrie and watched her husband, Blanding, stride toward them, his butler at his heels.

"What did you say?" Dorrie asked him on a screech.

"Hello, darling. I love the emerald on you. Matches your eyes, don't you think, Cat?" he asked as he pecked both on the cheek. "Lucky man I am this evening. *Two* gorgeous women to work this damnable receiving line."

Dorrie tossed her black curls. "For which you will please imagine we are *not* naked."

"Not a chance." His hand circled her waist. "I use that ghastly image only to get me through these interminable events. Puts a smile on my face."

"I bet," Dorrie chastised him.

"It's a matter of survival. Especially for people like Spence who hate these preliminaries."

Cat turned to stone. *Spence.*

"Well, lord, I put my foot in it. I am sorry, Cat."

"It's fine, Blanding," she told him though she didn't feel it yet. The mention of Spencer Lyonns always petrified her. The very reason she stood here, alone, with this particular problem was because of him, wasn't it?

She picked at her gloves, molding the skintight kid and touching the fifteen tiny pearl buttons individually.

"Don't," Dorrie pleaded. Few had known—only her cousin Jessica and her best friend Dorrie—how deeply Cat suffered after Spence had deserted her. They knew what his actions cost her and understood what her father never could. Indeed, Walter Farrell died last year believing his only child hated the man who had defiled her good character. He never surmised that Spence's golden image strolled her daydreams and danced in her nighttime illusions of what could never be.

How could she ever hate Spence?

Oh, she supposed her initial reaction to his rejection was all of that. But she'd felt it for only a few months after he left her at the altar. Soon after dawned the dreadful but unavoidable realization that they were better parted if he could never love her as much as she loved him. She had seen in her parents' relationship those bounties a mutually affectionate partnership offered a man and wife. She wanted the very same for herself and nothing less. Though she knew now she'd never have that, she would have her name, her pride, and her vocation.

To acquire those, she needed more students. When

she had confided that to Dorrie two months ago, the lady had swung into action. Insisting that *now* Cat must reenter society, Dorrie invited her here for the closing house party of the country season. She'd even enlisted Blanding's support.

Cat had debated, demurred, and finally accepted. Then she'd removed the maudlin purples of her mourning attire and packed them away with her precious memories of her doting father. Withdrawing a sizable amount from her bank account, she'd ignored how small the balance was, taken herself off to Paris, and ordered a few frocks. When she returned, she replaced the fading Farrell family brougham with a black-lacquered coach fit for a duke and practiced quadrilles and waltzes with Jessica in the morning room until she dropped. Now she stood here, hoping someone—please God, *anyone*—would deign to smile at her, talk with her, ask her to dance just one time.

Once.

They needn't fill up her dance card or chatter with her or even escort her in to the buffet supper. Only help her slightly, politely become once more that elusive, priceless commodity: respectable.

"I wish—" she ventured, "I wish one's acceptance came more as a result of what one did with one's life and less as dependence on what other people thought or did."

Dorrie smiled with compassion. "We're here to make that a reality for you, Cat."

"I wonder if we can. Some cannot overlook the past."

"They will." Dorrie squeezed Cat's hand. "Try."

"I will. I am." Dorrie and Blanding examined her as she nodded. "Open the doors, will you? The sooner we start, the earlier we're done. Besides," she said, rolling her eyes at Blanding, "I'm curious about what this year's crop is wearing."

The Billingtons burst out laughing.

"God knows," Blanding sputtered, "I'd rather dance than shake a hundred hands. Carlton," he called to his head butler who stood like a soldier, "let the hordes inside."

But the servant moved like the dead, and Cat thought of feigning a headache, a toothache. Taking a powder . . .

But from far down the gaslit drive, the first carriage in line started forward. That procession became an endless stream of broughams and curricles, coaches, and all manner of conveyances that the local gentry kept to high snuff. Discharging the ladies and gentlemen of Kent in their latest formal dress, the vehicles disappeared around the side where the drivers were welcome to dance and dine in the servants' hall with the few resident staff who were not crazy as old hens with work.

As the first couple walked up the steps, Cat recognized Lord and Lady Mellwyn, minor members of the peerage, but major influences on the social life of Ashford. Lady Mellwyn had not spoken to Cat in three years. Of all the hideous ways to begin the evening, greeting this woman presaged disaster. Cat steeled herself for the blow.

The lady sailed forward, looked Cat squarely in the eye, and, amazingly, smiled. *Smiled!*

Cat's heartbeat pounded in her ears. Why was Lady Mellwyn reaching for her hand, pumping it, saying something innocuous about the weather and her delightful choice of color for her gown?

"The precise shade of your eyes, Lady Farrell. How suitable and charming."

Cat mouthed some inanity.

Lord Mellwyn stood just behind his wife. His hand was bigger, stronger, clumsier. His words as smooth as glass. "So nice to see you, Lady Farrell. You look none the worse for all the work you've put into opening your school. You must need a few minutes of rest. Perhaps you'd take tea with us some afternoon?"

Tea with the Mellwyns? They'd slip a jigger of bromate in the brew and watch her acquire an angry case of hives by which she'd scratch herself to death in ten minutes. They could then claim the glory of having obliterated that sad blot on local gentility, the onerous Lady Farrell.

Dazed by this stroke of good fortune, Cat accepted the invitation, then handed the man on to Blanding, who nodded his head at Mellwyn as if he were approving of something.

"Donald, how good of you to join us. I think I'll have an opening in my schedule soon to discuss your desire to stand for the Ashford seat in Parliament. I have a few insights I'd like to share."

"It will be my pleasure, milord," Mellwyn said, his quivering body stilling to some semblance of quietude.

Cat frowned. Mellwyn *had* been nervous to meet *her*. Yet he had done so chivalrously. She enjoyed the relief but questioned its cause.

"My lady Farrell," crooned the next woman in line, whom Cat recognized as Mrs. Winslow, the wife of the Tuttle church vicar. "How thrilled I am to see you here."

"And I you, Mrs. Winslow." Cat took the lady's hand in frank glee. Her husband came close behind.

"Good evening, my dear," crooned the bewhiskered man as he leaned over conspiratorially. "I'm tickled to see you here. Should have happened years ago."

Then, as if he had passed a benediction over all those who came after him, the terrors of her past three years blew away like so many ashes in the wind. People greeted her as if amnesia had overtaken them *en masse.* For the next hour, Cat stood and shook hands, smiled, conversed, and accepted a few kisses on the cheek from people whom she had hardly seen or thought about for ever so long. The marvel of the evening for Cat was that not one person—not any of the neighbors nor any from the prince's Marlborough Set here for the entire weekend—approached her with anything less than kindness. Many greeted her with downright enthusiasm. In fact, only the adder-tongued doyenne whom many thought was paid by the London tabloids for her gossip, Lady Marietta Hornsby, reacted differently by frowning. But Marietta soon smoothed her features when Bertie, His Royal Highness, the Prince of Wales, descended the grand stairs as the last to arrive by royal prerogative. *He* hailed Cat with a buss on the cheek.

Cat stood, rooted to the marble, dying to throw her arms about the suit of armor in the corner and kiss the steel in glee. But Blanding stopped up her urge as he took her elbow and his wife's and steered them along the hall to the ballroom. With Bertie at their side, Cat felt more ready to meet the world than she had imagined was possible again. She didn't bother to contain her wobbly smile.

As they entered the gold and white ballroom aglow with brass gasoliers and bulging at the seams with more than two hundred people waiting to dance, Cat's newfound confidence cracked like the freshly blown crystal it was.

"Buck up, Cat," Blanding encouraged. "I've instructed the orchestra to begin the first waltz." His gray eyes scanned the crowd as if searching for one person in particular. "Good," he murmured to himself. "Now, listen to me. As is the custom, I shall open the first waltz with Dorrie. Then Dorrie takes out His Highness and I will come for you."

Cat directed her voice so that Bertie might not overhear. "Blanding, really. Lady Hornsby is the most senior of the ladies of the peerage. She takes precedence over me. I'll be blacklisted again."

"No, you won't," Dorrie replied, smiling and greeting those who parted to allow the three of them to walk to the center of the polished floor. "Trust us with this, Cat."

Blanding agreed. "I discussed it with Lady Hornsby and her husband two weeks ago in London. She understands."

Cat croaked on joy and horror. "God, Blanding, *why?*"

He turned eyes dark as storm clouds on her. "Because I said so."

When Blanding looked so fierce, Dorrie said she never argued with him. Cat knew she shouldn't either. Blanding had obviously gone out of his way to make her acceptance a prime order of business and to refuse him was foolish. He was securing for her the very thing she could never beg, borrow, or even *buy* for herself.

She stared at him and slowly smiled. "If one of the queen's favored advisors has said so, then I should put my trust in him as well." She cocked her head to one side and raised a brow. "Will you tell me who then will appear to take the next dance with me?"

"The marquess of Ashford."

Cat fought the urge to gape and chuckled lightly. "Now I know you're suffering from a tropical fever!"

The marquess of Ashford, always to her simply Rand Templeton, did few people favors. He didn't need to. Frank and formidable, Rand Templeton was her neighbor. He was also forever gallant, affable to her here in tonight's receiving line. To dance with the enigmatic marquess would do her some good, even if she quaked in her satin slippers at the mere idea.

Blanding lifted his head in a sign to the conductor to begin and took his wife in his arms.

Behind her she heard murmurs and footsteps as people began to place themselves for entering the waltz. The orchestra leader grinned, raised his arms, and gave a downbeat for the piece Cat recognized as Viennese. Light chords played by ten violins trilled through the crowded room. Heady mixtures of violas and tubas made those behind Cat fall silent as the music swelled and all eyes went to the couple who swirled about the floor. The devotion Cat saw in the Billingtons' grace was a sight others noted with fascination and even envy.

"It's clear when a man adores a woman, isn't it, Cat?"

She glanced up into the sharply hewn features of Rand Templeton. "Yes, very obvious and endearing."

"Blanding counts himself fortunate to have found her, even at what he calls such an advanced age. We all excuse him his obsession because Dorrie is so perfect for him. A man searches for a long time to find the right woman for him. It is such a pity when that union can never be." Rand's midnight blue eyes brooded into hers.

"What are you telling me, Rand?"

He never had a chance to answer. Blanding came forward, took her hand, and swept her off with a style that rivaled the best partners she had had: her father and her former fiancé. She followed him easily, grinning as the guests murmured their appreciation. But as the first waltz ended, Cat could tell many pairs of eyes clung to her to see who would dare to dance with Lady Farrell.

When Rand appeared, bowed, and tucked her gloved hand in his, Cat knew her trials were over, her triumph complete. She could feel the gossip mongers shrivel like prunes as Rand and she talked idly and he took her in his arms. When they began to move to the music, Cat knew that she and Rand made a superb impression. His expertise doused her fears, and she gave herself up to the blend of man and music—and relief. Gratitude wended through her, adding a long-forgotten euphoria. But as the waltz died and Rand took her to the edge of the floor to introduce her into a little group, their conversation—by its very novelty of warmth—soon had her longing for solitude to recapitulate.

Making polite excuses, she left them to thread her way through the crowd toward one fat pillar and one huge fern partially concealing one appealing chair. *Here* she would rest, recover her breath and her equanimity, and begin the formation of that public persona she longed to cultivate from tonight forward. To those who mattered, she would become that venerable oddity: the School Headmistress. To her students, she would become the Battle-ax. The Harpie. Their Bad Dream.

Ugh. Just her image.

She gathered her train to her left and sank to the chair with a whoosh of her skirts. A footman appeared with a tray of champagne flutes, and she gleefully divested him of one. In satisfaction, she sipped the bubbles and felt the effervescence ripple into her bloodstream.

No one had hurt her. No one had looked at her unkindly. No odd sensation of being watched had crept up her spine. This was Dorrie's, for heaven's sake. Not the tunnel to Farrell Hall, where she had felt the sinister sensation of being observed days ago. Billington Manor was *safe*.

After tonight, she would have her students, her school. Jess would have her dream of helping others. The past would be forgotten.

She shifted, suddenly feeling other eyes on her.

"The champagne *is* reviving, isn't it, Cat?"

This was not like the other day when she'd thought someone observed her in the tunnel. *That* incident verged on . . . malicious. This felt warm and sounded . . . husky. Seductive. *Terrifying.*

"Then again, you always did adore the stuff."

No, no, no. Her eyes fell closed as a haunting bass tantalized her senses, stirring memories of passionate moments to life. *This cannot be happening.*

"Of course, I much prefer something stronger. Like the way brandy tastes from your lips."

She clutched the flute so hard that she stared at it, amazed it didn't shatter. Scenes of one dinner party and one delicious man reconstructed fragments of one unforgettable ecstasy brought by her introduction to brandy. How he had poured it and swirled it in a bowled glass, sipped a draught, and then given her a taste of the liquor by pressing his mouth to hers and letting her taste the essence from his own tongue.

She strangled a gasp and dragged her mind to this time, this ballroom, this reality. "Oh, God in Heaven, Spence, go away!" It was a whisper, an order, a horror that he—of all people—should be here now.

She glanced about the room. Courtesy of the fern, no one seemed to notice that Spencer Lyonns stood in back of her, spoke to her, conversed with her as if . . . as if this were normal, as if nothing had ever passed between this woman and this man. "How did you get in?"

"Don't panic, Cat. I arrived the same way you did. Dorrie and Blanding invited me."

"You *can't* be serious." She swallowed painfully, knowing she had to temper the outrage from her voice. If she weren't careful she'd be seething, and that wouldn't win her any friends or any students.

"I am quite honest with you, darling."

"Oh, please," she groaned. "Go away, Spence. Don't do this to me. *Why* do this to me? Why would Dorrie and Blanding—"

"I'll tell you everything, Cat. Just dance with me."

She caught herself before she hooted. She scanned the room like a trapped animal. "I *can't* dance with you. Not ever. You're mad."

There was a long pause, then a whisper. "Yes, *very.* I never knew just how far gone I was until I looked at you a few minutes ago. Dance with me, Cat."

"No. You know what they'll say."

"I know what they're beginning to say now as they see us talking."

She set her shoulders. Dug her nails into her skirts. "They're saying what a curious sight. Isn't that Spencer Lyonns speaking casually to the woman he left at the altar of St. Paul's? I do wonder that the man has the nerve, don't you? He must be ready to be committed."

"Ah, yes, Cat. He is *that.*"

"Walk away from me, Spence."

"Or you'll do what? Deliver me the telling blow? By every social rule, I admit I deserve it. But the truth is, you can't do it. It's not your nature to be cruel, darling. Nor is it theirs to think beyond what you show them. Tonight, everything you want depends on you acting according to code."

"Yes. Yes! How could you come here, knowing that?

How could Dorrie and Blanding do this when they understood that I needed respectability so much?"

"Don't castigate your friends. They have your best interests at heart. Mine, too. They knew so much. More than I gave them credit for." She felt his hand on her bare back, discreetly restraining her from rushing from her chair. *"No!* God, Cat, don't leave me looking furious. This crowd would gobble it up. You've got to calm yourself, please. I knew there was no easy way to do this. So did Dorrie and Blanding. But we're here, so are all of the people who matter to you and me, and I'm asking you to wipe the past from both our lives. Dance with me."

She took another drink, but frozen terror far surpassed cold alcohol for raw power. "I cannot imagine how waltzing with you could possibly help me."

"It would show the world we are friends."

"But we're not."

"We could be."

"We won't."

"We should."

"That's your view," she shot back, "and you're wrong. We can't ever be friends."

"How do you know if you've never tried, darling?"

"I don't *want* to know, Spence. And I don't want to be called *darling.*"

"But you *are* mine."

"Do you mind if I laugh hysterically?" She shook her head in disbelief. "You come to me in a room jammed to the chandeliers with English society, shock me, regale me with simple arguments to supposedly, *blithely* end three years of—of ostracism by *dancing* with me?"

"It's impulse, born of watching you. As before, you unveil violent needs in me. Besides, you know I never enter those bloody receiving lines." He took a step to her side and dropped his hand from her fevered skin. "I knew you'd never come if you thought I'd be here. So did the Billingtons. You *must* listen to me. In the meantime, please take that startled look from your face. Despite this obliging potted forest we have about us, people are beginning to notice and whisper. Smile, will you?"

She ground her teeth. "Why don't you?"

"I am. I have been all this while. You should, too. It makes the heartache lighter."

What would you know about heartache? she wanted to blurt. But thank God, she didn't. She let her eyes drift closed and then opened them, forcing her mind to notice how others perceived this encounter between the notorious two London's *Tattler* dubbed, 'The Cat and the Lyonn.' Some stared. One openly. Others intermittently.

She turned her face to her left and saw the precise black crease of his trousers. She dare not glance up at him. She need never have to look at him to visualize him. Nor did curiosity hold any allures that might complement her recollections of him. She was positive he still appeared every radiant inch the man who made her heart skip and her mouth water and her eyes hurt with his blinding handsomeness.

Till the second she died, she would recall his features. His blond hair as pale as the noon sun, with platinum streaks as dazzling as a solar glare on desert sands. His green eyes, black and moist as jungle foliage. His mouth, with its deep bow in the upper lip and the pouting wealth of his lower. His broad, bronzed face. His skin, smooth as a god's. His body, big and bold and brawny. His heart, which he had said was hers, only hers. His life, his happiness, which he said he would surrender to her keeping. Until the one day when he would have given all and vowed his troth forever—and instead he had disappeared.

"You return so easily, Spence. Wanting things I can't give you. You ruined me once. I won't let you do it again. If you are not gone by the count of five, I swear I'm rising from this chair and leaving this room."

"Cat, hear me out."

"The time for listening to you is three years gone, Spence. The night before we were to marry, even the morning of the ceremony, you could have come to me and told me you didn't love me. Didn't want me. You could have explained and I would have accepted it. I would have *had* to. But you chose to leave me in the most hideous circumstances in which a woman can discover herself. No. I cannot find it in my heart to dance it all away. Nor do I think anyone here would believe that I could." The one thing she felt she could do, would do any moment, was sob. And if she did, she'd never survive society again, much less her own self-ridicule. "I can't. So if you'll excuse me—"

"I say, Cat—" Rand Templeton sidestepped the foliage. His dark blue eyes narrowed at Spence and then smiled down at her with sweet remorse. "You look like you could do with an escort to the buffet table. Hungry?"

"Starving." She rose, restraining the urge to turn and let her eyes devour the other man whose delicious virility always sated her.

Rand tucked her hand firmly on his arm and cast a rueful look at Spence. "Valiant display. The crows ate every morsel. Let us see if any scraps remain."

Chapter 2

*H*e wanted to snatch her back, make off with her and—God, what a fool he was! He'd lost her once again because of his own rash behavior.

He balled his fists and wheeled about.

Some people had noticed what he'd done. But no one would dare to look him in the eye.

Of course, he deserved their ridicule. Just as he deserved Cat's.

But no other guest was as brazen as he had been. Each discreetly glanced away, returning to their dancing, drinking, and milling. No one deigned to allow mere emotions to rule their eternal decorum.

Sweet heaven, if only *he* had! He reeled in a red rage.

Yes, he thought he'd armed himself against seeing her once more. Certainly, he'd thought the years apart would have conquered the violent tenderness she aroused in him. But he hadn't bargained for the contrast of tonight's experience with the first time he'd seen her. That glimpse of her four years ago illustrated for him the essence of what she was to him: laughter. Rich, natural, abundant. The sight of her tonight showed him plainly that she didn't do that anymore.

Perhaps, chided his conscience, she couldn't.

That made him clench his fists.

Damn society! Damn the rules. Damn *him* for what he'd done in the name of family pride—and suffered for in the fairness of justice.

But evidently, he hadn't suffered quite enough, had he?

Tonight to look at her sitting there alone, silent and aloof amid the greenery, had gored him. He'd watched her all evening from any convenient corner. Her brave efforts told him more of the total story of her degradation these three years past than he'd allowed himself to consciously consider. Everything that had happened to her had been caused by what he'd done and by what he had tried to forget: that no matter time nor distance nor family differences, Catherine Farrell was the only woman who had ever made him laugh. One of the few people with whom he ever felt natural in his skin.

The first time he'd encountered her, he knew it. He had stood in this same room at another ball beside a similar potted palm, the sound of her laughter curling around him, warmth in a forbidding atmosphere. Touched, he had turned.

She looked even richer than she sounded. With hair like brandy, lashes of cinnamon, and skin of new cream, she was a luscious combination.

When he asked someone who she was, he grinned to himself that she'd been so precisely described to him already—by his brother, Merrick, who'd glimpsed her and termed her "that intense creature." Her father's accountant. Naturally, Spence had expected a bookworm, a mouse, a mole.

She was a bird of paradise. Exuberant, sleek, a flurry of motion. He could watch her till he died. But more than that, he could *listen* to her contralto and *feel* her to the roots of his hair, in the quick of his nails.

Instinctively, he sensed danger. Because for a practical man who at twenty-seven found bone-rattling laughter foreign, he was drawn to a woman he knew he shouldn't want. But he firmly ignored their family antagonisms for the delight of being near her.

Though she and he had not been introduced, he tried to find an opening for it for hours. She had been surrounded by attentive men who filled her dance card and took her away. He'd followed her every move, like a green boy biding his time and observing her with one man after another, until one leering ox possessed of two left feet became smoother off the floor than on it. The man had the audacity to grab for her dance card and she had the politeness to tip her fan and suggest a stroll to the dining room.

Amused by her, Spence drained his champagne and swallowed the urge to applaud her. The man's eyes lit. Hers fired in friendliness. The man detoured Cat into the garden before she understood his deftness.

Spence feared for her instantly. She was young, a novice at guarding herself. The man was a fox. So with his eyes on the man's overeager hands, Spence followed the couple at a discreet distance, tracing their steps past the roses and tulips. Spence stood apart in the moonlight, reached inside his coat for a cigar, and muttered to himself about some people's appalling manners. Then he saw the man put his hands on her arm, and she sidestepped him.

The fellow took few cues well and soon pressed his dishonorable intentions with a bear hug. At that opportune moment, Spence stepped from the shadows, pitched his cigar in the yews, and bounded up the steps.

"There you are, my dear. I've been looking for you. This is our dance, if you remember." He towered over her, grinning and appearing affably offended, while the other man had no choice but to bluster and retire.

Spence felt for the first time the deep purple power of her iris-blue eyes. She examined him, measuring the breadth of his shoulders in his dress uniform, the line of his throat, his mouth, his height, as if he were a legend come to life. "How can I thank you properly?"

Fascinated by the way her lips glided over words, he came closer to enjoy the caress of satin in her voice. Avoiding the conflicts between his brother and her father, which might end their acquaintance before it'd begun, Spence declined to give her his name in favor of the comfort that was so much more timely. But for that, he had to put his hands on her, didn't he? "Thank me with a dance."

She beamed, an expression that took her beauty from striking to spellbinding. "I'm afraid I'm not able."

"I'd say you're very adept."

Her cheeks flushed with modesty, but she kept her gaze locked to his. "I meant we'd scandalize people."

If they did what he had in mind here in this garden, they'd set England to a torch in scarce seconds. Could she read his mind? He arched a brow, and her eyes glittered over his scarlet uniform and his rakish pose.

"What I meant was my mother warned me—"

"About men like me?" he asked, thinking of a thousand ways he could thrill himself and this gorgeous creature while terrifying a protective mama.

"You *and* him," she said with a jaunty look in the direction of her departed partner. "She would have been more concerned that I danced with a stranger when another man has already spoken for the next spot." She lifted her wrist to dangle her dance card, which he could have bet the sum of his captain's commission offered no blank spots.

Spence glanced about, clucking. "Poor chap, I don't see him. Must have lost his way."

He realized he had lost his own. As a man who had scouted, mapped many a military mission, and understood the strategies of many countries' armies, he had deserted his own common sense. Then, desperate he might lose her so quickly to decorum, he stepped forward and put his arm around her waist and took her right hand in his left. She was supple and strong. "I'll fill in for him. I wouldn't want you unattended, lest your previous partner takes it into his head to return."

"How do I know," she asked with beguiling eyes, "if you are more honorable than the last man?"

"Give me a chance to prove it."

She cocked her ear. "But the orchestra has stopped."

"Lucky for me that I don't intrude on another man's prerogative."

"How will we dance without music?"

He stepped as close as propriety allowed while visions of the moves he might teach her mocked his conscience. "I'll sing."

Her eyes popped. "Do you do it well?"

He chuckled. "Only when I've drunk too much."

She swayed forward, brushing breasts to chest, and inhaling delicately. "I don't think you're drunk now."

"I must be," he rasped, his body rising to her nearness. "Otherwise, why this intoxication?"

Unsure, she blinked at him, then let one of her smiles dawn. "Far be it from me to never give you a hearing."

Filling his arms with her, he gazed into her lovely eyes and did something that before tonight he would have considered outlandish. He began to hum a simple Viennese waltz that soon had her blending her sultry voice with his. She glided with him in ever more delirious circles. With every step, he wondered anew how he'd ever thought he could remain detached, impartial to life when this sweet woman summoned every raw yearning he'd been taught to control. The whim to sample her effervescence meteored into a desire to possess her not merely temporarily, but for the evening, for the season, for as long as he could hold her.

"I should never have questioned your expertise," she told him after their need to provide music for their madness had long since died. "You're very good."

He wrestled with the mania to pause and kiss her. Chastising himself but grinning at her, he concentrated on sweeping her in lazy rounds, avoiding birdbaths and sundials, absorbing only the grace within his grasp. "I take it your mother would approve of me then."

"Of your dancing technique, hmm, yes, I am sure of it. She died almost six years ago, but I am quite certain she's watching you here dancing with me now." She leaned back in his arms, and she sobered. "I'm afraid, though, my mother would not have approved of this . . . this other."

"Which?" he murmured, though he knew he shouldn't lead her on so shamelessly.

"This," she elaborated by easing them to a halt and placing her palm to his cheek. Beneath the fine leather

of her glove, he felt a fierce affection. The type a lady restrained with a man she'd just met. The kind a man sought in a mistress and cultivated in a bride. The sort he'd forever fled.

Groaning, he brought her lithe body closer and pressed her hips and thighs to his. She came easily but shook, perceiving a sensuousness he knew no man had yet discovered. Wild to nurture it but fearful of frightening her, he comprehended that embracing her so intimately was even more destructive to all his noble intentions. He had to stop.

But with her hand on his cheek, the desire to hold her compelled him to drop a kiss into her palm.

She marveled at his move. "Your lips feel so soft."

He prayed she had no experience sampling other men's lips. Instead, he'd teach her more than a whole host of men. "You must test them this way then," he breathed and bent over her, rubbing his mouth across her warm one.

Her lashes fluttered. Her mouth parted. "They're smooth and hot. Like liquid fire."

He framed her fragile face. "If I test yours, we both might go up like fireworks."

Hope burst upon her features. "Would you?"

He yearned to but chose honor instead. "Only if you allow me to call on you."

"Tomorrow?"

"Every day, any day you'll have me."

"For tea?"

"Or singing."

"More dancing?"

"More kissing," he clarified as she blushed and lowered her gaze to his chest. He raised her chin with two fingers. "To do it now would end the mystery."

She tilted her head. "Of who you are?"

"Of *what* I am to you."

"Somehow . . . ," she speculated, "I know that now."

He hugged her and said into her hair, "But you'll wonder, won't you? I want you to. In your room at night. In bed. You'll ponder what it would feel like. Perhaps you'll even dream of more than kisses, and then I'll have reached my own objective." At her inquisitive brow, he added, "I'll keep what perfection I've found only for me."

She gazed at him then with belief.

Why wouldn't she?

He had meant it. That had been the beginning of eight months of joy with her. A period in which he learned to revel in his feelings for her. A time marked by their engagement and ended by his brother Merrick's accusations about her father and Spence's conclusion that—though he loved Catherine Farrell madly—he could never marry her. So he'd left her, condemning her to unfair ridicule and himself to a black hole.

Then, after three years of feeling nothing, to see her tonight resurrected every sensitivity she'd ever uncovered, every tenderness she inspired. To watch her dance with Rand had become a torture beyond bearing. He'd been so hollowed by it he'd thought the only antidote was to speak with her—and even that brought this new hell.

God, what had he done? Gone and ruined her again?

He couldn't stand it if he had. Christ, just when he had arranged everything with Blanding and Rand so that he wouldn't fail, couldn't fail!

What had he said? That he wanted to dance with her?

He did. He shouldn't have.

But he couldn't help himself, couldn't drown his

remorse or strangle his compassion and his need to put his hands on her. Place his arms around her. Pull her close. Move with her across this floor, across the years, take her back to what they might have been, should have been. Draw her forward to what they could be again.

That made him freeze in his tracks.

Could they recapture what they had felt for each other?

His mind whirred. Why would he think that absurdity?

Because you want her.

Because he had never really enjoyed any other woman.

Never needed to make amends for his behavior to anyone the way he must to her.

He considered his options. To ignore her was impossible. They'd be together for the next few days whether she liked it or not. To court her openly . . . well, he'd tried that, hadn't he? No contest there.

But he could call a truce.

He'd help her laugh. Really laugh from the bottom of her heart. For God knew he needed to witness the gaiety that had been her hallmark—and his addiction. He wanted to soothe what pain he'd caused, make it up to her. Wasn't that one reason he'd approached Blanding with this solution to meet her here?

Wasn't the most vital reason that you were finally ready to face her with the truth of why you'd left her?

Yes, of course, it was.

But your other motive is not personal, Lyonns?

No, that other is a coincidence.

But now inconvenient?

Very. Detrimental to the point of destructive.

He silently cursed his conscience for reminding him

of his need to see Cat for reasons of state. He'd been ordered by his superior officers to find a famous papyrus. Indications pointed to Walter Farrell as the culprit. That this professional need crossed his private one roiled him. But he couldn't chance anyone else investigating the possibility that Walter may have stolen the item. He had vowed long ago to protect Cat—and never hurt her again. To hear her father accused unjustly would have gutted her, and so, Spence had taken the assignment and prayed he found no evidence that Walter Farrell was a thief.

But his priorities shifted the minute he'd seen Catherine Farrell again. How important was finding a papyrus compared to his soul-devouring need to make amends—and help her laugh?

Instead, he had hurt Cat again.

He clenched his teeth in agony.

"Here, drink this, will you?" Blanding shoved a champagne glass into his hand.

"I'd prefer something stronger."

"How about a swift kick? I asked a footman to fill a flute with whisky. Knock it back, will you? Then gather up your famous courage and circulate."

"I'm going to speak with her."

"Later. Better, do it tomorrow or the next day. Let her recover. Us, too. The best you can do now is smile." He nodded to a passing couple whose avid gazes intimated how they wished they might overhear this conversation. "Pretend everything is *normal,* as if it will ever be again. Dorrie is readying the papers to have me carted off to an asylum. She's marked *you* as my cellmate unless, of course, you can remedy this ghastly situation over the coming days. I thought you were going to go slowly. Let her see you, become accustomed to the idea of your presence."

Spence drank, tasting nothing but remorse. "I saw

her and this opportunity to have her alone and I couldn't resist. It was crazy to speak with her. But I never thought she'd risk them seeing her leave me."

"For a man who supposedly has had experience with women in every country to which you've ever been posted, you, chum, really are a dunce about women."

"Those stories are ancient history—and part fable."

He'd had many a woman in innumerable beds. English, Russian, Indian, Japanese, they'd been stimulating, satiating only his sexuality. They'd also been purely ornamental or professionally useful. Every one was also purposely impermanent. They'd offered everything he wanted—or so he'd thought.

Yet none played the piano with a pet monkey named Darwin on her shoulder. None met callers in her conservatory dressed in men's trousers with dirt on her cheeks and a geranium cutting in her hand. None marveled at the irony that *foot*men were paid according to every *inch* of their height. No one engaged him in any conversation that dispelled his fear of intimacy.

Catherine Farrell was so different. Elemental. Intelligent and untutored in suppressing it, she argued with him over the real Darwin's theory and debated the imperialist Disraeli's politics. Perceptive, she detected his disaffection with the army. Bold, she told him if she were a man and caught in a profession she questioned, she'd resign, desert if she must. He believed her. Even when she said she'd go with him. Anywhere. For any reason he declared self-fulfilling.

She was the first woman he found totally unpredictable.

The only woman he ever trusted.

But he hadn't gauged how much his betrayal had cost her. "I thought I understood her," he said more to himself than to Blanding. "Obviously, I don't have any insight there anymore."

Blanding downed a hefty draught from his own flute. "'Hell hath no fury like a woman scorned.' But there is something worse. I dare say no one has witnessed any fury like a woman bent on correct social behavior."

Spence's gaze trailed off in the direction Rand had taken Cat. A glimpse of iris silk near the arch to the dining room made him swallow fear and jealousy. "I need to see her happy, Blanding." Spence could feel his friend's body turn to granite.

"Commendable, but not something you can do. Leave her happiness to us. Perform your duty by her—and the government."

"I will accomplish every objective." *For her. For me.*

"That was not a part of our discussions, Spence."

"I didn't know then how important it was. I do now."

"You were to appear polite. Restore her to society."

"I'll do it."

"Hmm, yes, I'm certain. But have you forgotten you, too, need restoration?"

"A detail."

"You must be careful, put aside your emotions."

"I encounter obstacles each day, Blanding."

"Not like these. Cat won't even come near you."

"I'll change her mind."

"Be reasonable, Spence. She has her school. She wants students. She's built a life without you. Accept it. Your purpose here tonight is to become her friend. To ask if the rumors about her desire to publish her father's memoirs are true. To offer help with any translations so that you can find that missing item and *that* is all."

"I'll do that. As planned." Spence took another drink. "But I swear I'll make her laugh again."

Blanding sighed. "You are stubborn to a fault."

He snorted. "How true."

"Then do it with more patience. You have two and a half more days. Don't push her. Just do what you came to do and let us breathe more easily."

Blanding could have asked him to jump off London Bridge and it would have been easier.

Spence drifted away to his duty to reingratiate himself with those who mattered. Oh, certainly, everyone in the room seemed bent on cooperating with the charade his behavior became. He joined any blathering conversation he could follow with half a mind and joked with people he could regale with half a heart. He danced with two debutantes and Marietta Hornsby. He bussed one elderly lady's parchment cheek, sat down to chat, and studiously refrained from watching Cat reenter with Rand and then proceed to waltz with every other eligible man in the blasted room. He ignored the impulse to cut in, tear up her dance card, haul her over his shoulder, and escape with her. To keep her without regard to these people and their rules.

Later, he lounged against a column to survey the dance floor. Again Cat had disappeared, and he could not follow.

He spun for the garden. Restless, he took the terrace to the path past Dorrie's roses across the grass to the red-enameled gazebo, which glistened black in the moonglow.

Marching up the steps, he reached into his tuxedo jacket for a cigar and realized he'd forgotten to put any there. Hell, he'd been so eaten alive by the jitters at seeing Cat again, he would have been fortunate to remember how to spell his name.

The sound of someone whispering and then sucking in her breath made his stop. Over in the shadows, he spied the hem of a gown and the toe of a woman's satin shoe. Had he intruded on a lovers' rendezvous? Suppressing the urge to chuckle, he began to bow in apology and would have left had the color of the lady's gown not sent sparks to his brain.

He straightened and stared into the void.

She did not even breathe.

"Cat?" he whispered, wild delight coursing through his veins at such good luck.

"You followed me," she groaned. "I wanted to be alone."

He took a step forward. His hand came up as a sign of peace, but nonetheless he heard her fall back against the chaise's cushions.

A growl made him freeze. From the shadows emerged a black animal, teeth bared, head down, ready for attack.

"Bones! Be a good boy. Sit," Cat ordered the Labrador.

"Bones?" Spence asked on a lilt of laughter. "Well now, where did you get—?" He felt teeth pierce his trouser, graze his left ankle, and hold. Spence grimaced. "I say, old man, could you possibly unclamp your jaws?"

"Bones! Let him go!" Cat demanded, then in a normal tone explained, "He's mine. He used to be the game dog for the Ashford village butcher, but he pointed at everything, living or dead. Mr. Torrence was forever confused by his actions and said Bones was too old to track properly."

"Ah. The butcher was going to put the poor old

fellow out of his misery, I bet. But you couldn't hear of it."

"Yes. Now Bones lives at Farrell Hall."

"Tracking no one but you, I see." Spence felt the animal relax, then give him a little unnecessary nip as a further warning before he did as his mistress asked. Freed, Spence stepped forward but felt Cat shrink away. "Cat, I'm so glad you're here. I—"

She rose on a whoosh of silk skirts.

He grew frantic but gave her nonchalance. "I didn't see you leave. I came out for air and—"

"A cigar?" she asked on an incredulous note.

"Among other things."

"Allow me to leave you to it."

"You could share it with me," he said, recalling the time he'd handed one over for her education, and they had both been startled when she loved it, before she'd coughed herself blue. Clearly, she remembered none of that, only her intent to get away from him. But he caught her arm just as she would have flown around him toward the entrance.

The dog grumbled low in his throat.

Spence ignored him.

Cat stood paralyzed as Spence moved closer, pressing his torso to her back, feeling every tremor through her terrified lean body. "Please let me go, Spence. I don't want what you're offering."

"Not air?" he mused, his mouth trailing her temple and ear, loving her personal musk not even roses could rival.

"Not even a cigar," she confirmed with wry humor.

"Honestly, Cat, I didn't know you came out here. I came for the same reason you did. To escape a stifling room." *And boiling desire for you.*

She strained away from him, shivering as if she'd heard that last. "I'm cool now."

"Yes, cold, I'd say. Here——" He shrugged out of his swallowtail cutaway and swirled it over her bare shoulders before she had taken two more steps. "Stay," he pleaded, while he told himself he must remove his hands. "Remain and talk to me. I promise I won't be brash or forward. I was before. I apologize."

Slowly, she turned in his arms, and within the silver rays of gathering night, he could see on her enchanting face utter surprise. "You astonish me."

Not half as much as you do me. He narrowed his eyes to examine what he thought he saw in her own. He called it curiosity and gave thanks it wasn't indifference. "I am pleased to elicit more from you than the anger of before. How is it that I can do that?"

"You once told me you never apologized to anyone for anything you did. It was beneath your dignity."

"Even a Lyonns learns how to deal with failure. And mistakes."

Her shivers became tremblings. "I must go." She tried to spin away.

He tightened his grip on her. Though the dog objected again, Spence said, "Won't you stay and let me explain more?"

"No." She tugged.

He couldn't let her go. His superior strength meant he could so easily keep her body. But he needed to capture her mind more, and his voice dropped to a desperate urgency. "I could tell you how a Lyonns tries very hard to understand his shortcomings. How he wants to change——"

"Oh, Spence, *please.*" Her eyelashes drifted down in agony. "That's irrelevant now."

He stepped nearer, close enough to draw the roses from her hair, let down her curls, sink his hands into the thick golden red mass that twined into his every memory of her. "I do want to make everything up to you." He'd almost called her darling. He wouldn't make that mistake again. "Cat, I need to talk with you. Let me. That's the primary reason I'm here this weekend."

"Talking with me won't change anything, Spence. You know it won't. I don't want to be seen with you. I don't want to remember." She stared at him with determination drawn in every elegant line of her heart-shaped face. "I came here thinking I could reingratiate myself into society. I cannot do that if you persist in this—this masquerade of caring for me."

He could tell her that was no ruse, but she wouldn't believe that. He said the only thing that might make a difference. "Cat, I want to help you."

She gaped but recovered admirably. "I don't want your help."

"But if you have it, you'll be accepted much faster." That was true in that they'd show society they were rational people who could approach each other with civility. It was even more true because of how he'd vowed to protect her if indeed he did find in her father's effects the ancient papyrus the government said was stolen and must be returned to the khedive. If Spence ascertained Walter had taken the document, his discovery would finish the job of condemning her father that his brother, Merrick, had so ruthlessly begun. Dead in his grave more than a year, Walter Farrell could not defend himself, which meant Spence had to tread carefully for Cat's sake. Compelled as he was by duty to queen and country, Spence's primary goal was to protect Cat from any storm.

What a gargantuan task he set himself.

Cat frowned. She was considering his words, he knew. What he couldn't fathom was what her decision was when finally she raised her eyes to his. "Very well, since I can't escape you or snub you these next few days without damage to my own dignity, I suppose I could consent to a practical measure. We'll pretend we accept each other."

For the first time in years, he grinned and felt it to his fingertips. "It's a beginning."

"No. It's the end."

He'd change that, make it more than she expected. "You won't be sorry."

"Where you are concerned, I have ceased to be sorry."

That subdued him. "Good. You never did anything wrong."

"Spence, as absolution, your words are a little late."

"But true."

She arched one brow. "Now, will you remove your hands from me?"

"If I do, will you stay?"

"You haven't anything more you could say to me that would interest me."

His hope fell at his feet. *What if I told you I have wanted you every day for the past three years?* He knew from the way she put her eyes on him, he couldn't say that or he'd be doing the very thing he promised he wouldn't—he'd be brash and forward. But how the deuce was he supposed to get her to listen to him?

"What if I said I was saddened to hear of your father's death? How sorry I am he's gone. He was a great man, a noted scholar, and we are the poorer for his passing."

Her eyes, which she had closed at the mention of her father, opened now, and when she looked at him again, tears dotted her lashes. She stroked the lapels of his jacket absently. "You can say you admired him in spite of his behavior toward you?"

"He came to like me as I did him."

"He thought you'd make a worthy member of the family."

"I am certain when he died, he had changed his mind."

"He decried the day he ever met you—or your brother."

"I wish he were here now so that I might tell him I never meant to harm you."

"He'd say to believe that would take an awful stretch of the imagination."

"Perhaps. But it is true."

From the look on her face, she wanted to accept that as gospel. She bent her head, pressed her cheek to his jacket, and inhaled. Her eyes grew dreamy, sad, and suddenly glazed with remorse. She jerked her head up. "Thank you, Spence. If you'll excuse me, I want to go inside and dance again."

She abandoned him to his confused thoughts. He wasn't certain, but for a second he could have sworn he'd rekindled embers. So she wouldn't dance with him, but maybe—

He caught up to her as she made her way down the path, with one hunk of canine flesh separating them. "You're not going on the hunt tomorrow morning are you?"

"You know I can't bear watching those horses and hounds rabid to tear at one little fox."

"Come riding with me then."

She choked on surprise as they reached the terrace steps, and the music floating out about them seemed less sweet than the tones of her amusement, rueful though it was. "I will *not* ride with you anywhere, especially at a house party while the others are off traipsing about the countryside!"

"Then stay here and meet me in the morning room for newspapers and coffee and good conversation."

"Spence, no."

"I promise to begin your day brightly with me about."

For a second, she looked tempted—and God above, with the stars in her eyes, so very tempting.

"No. We will appear congenial, but we will never converse over coffee. I couldn't bear—I just couldn't."

He watched her walk away for a moment with her faithful canine escort plodding along at her skirts, her head high.

He caught up to her, taming a knowing smile to one less irritating to her. "There is one thing you could do though."

She spun so abruptly he walked right into her. Flush to her warm torso, his hands steadied them both, and then like the gentleman he wished he were for her, he pulled back. But not before he felt her body's instant sizzle.

Irritated probably as much with herself as him, she tilted her head and whispered, *"What* might that be?"

He let his eyes dance to her shoulders. "You could return my jacket to me so they won't think we were standing out here conversing like any loving couple would do."

She groaned, whirled off the offending garment, and thrust it at him as if it were a monster. "Take it."

He took his coat, his hand brushing hers.

She yanked away. "Spence, do me one service only."

"Anything."

"Leave me alone."

In a furl of her skirts and rose attar, she opened the door and disappeared.

Her Cerberus plunked himself down to face Spence.

He grinned at the glowering dog. "Well, old man, I see your position in this matter. But you'd save yourself a lot of trouble if you just accepted conditions as they are."

The dog shook his head, flews wobbling, spittle flying. Then he smacked his gums as if to say, We are not dissuaded.

"No? But neither am I because, you see, leaving your lady alone is the one thing I will never do again."

Chapter 3

Cat knew exactly how and when she would escape.

She'd been planning it since precisely quarter past three when sleep had eluded her for so long that she'd risen from her bed of torture, packed one traveling case—and then dutifully unpacked the thing.

With a mutter about Spence and an insomnia she'd thought she'd tamed years ago, she flung back the covers from her tousled four-poster and grabbed up her silk robe. Padding to the French doors, she went onto the balcony that swept from one end of the massive west wing around to the east. She stood there for countless minutes. Clearing her head of the memory of Spence's words and his sandalwood scent, she let the offshore breeze gentle her anxiety. She also confirmed that the last rider had cantered from the front drive with hounds yipping at his heels.

Spurred by the thought she was the only guest left in the house, she returned to her suite, bathed, then dressed briskly in a pink sicilienne morning dress and slipped along the empty hall and down the staircase. The enormous hall clock chimed up to eight as she walked into the grand dining room. As she expected, the sideboards had been laid for the usual small prehunt breakfast. She could predict what lay beneath the silver domes. The prince always took one egg—poached—and bacon—two slices—before the horn blew. Of course, his compatriots did the same. To do otherwise would be poor manners.

But the Billington staff, praised often in other people's drawing rooms for their dedication, would have survived any mess with colors flying. So well had one footman endured that he smiled at Cat as she entered and surveyed the wreckage forty people could do in scant minutes.

"'Ello, milady. Ready for breakfast, are we?" he asked as he removed the used Minton from table to tray.

"Yes, Godfrey, but not much of it. I'm afraid I ate far too much last night." Nerves at seeing Spence again caused her to eat enough that the poor of Whitechapel could have dined for a month. "I'll help myself. But a cup of coffee would do nicely when you have time."

"Aye, mum. I'm off to the kitchen with this and I'll be back in a jig with your coffee. The *Times,* if you care to see it, is over there."

Cat thanked him as he went through the double doors. She collected the newspaper, toast, and bramble jelly to sit at one end of the table. She had just bitten into her bread when she noticed this morning's lead story was once more a discussion about the khedive of Egypt's desire to form an alliance with the British government.

Her eyes skimmed down the column, wondering if her father's achievements as one of the most renowned archaeologists of ancient Egypt would be cited again as background. Instead, she found Merrick Lyonns's name and the reference to his five-year tenure as Her Majesty's special emissary to the khedive.

She flipped the page, eager to read anything but a discussion of Merrick. Merrick had been her father's nemesis. Throughout the years of planning and funding his expeditions to the Karnak temples of the ancient pharaohs, Walter Farrell had encountered the opposition of Spence's older brother. Not once had Merrick made life easy for her father. By arguing over the citizenship of her father's diggers and the legitimacy of his paperwork, Merrick had delayed many expeditions. When most of her father's Indian *kulis* began to fall ill of dysentery, Merrick ordered them deported immediately. Walter Farrell had to appeal to the Foreign Office to pull the order. Merrick and Walter had such a horrid row that her father suffered his first heart attack. He came home to rest only to face accusations of financial improprieties brought by the Historical Society.

She stared at the paper, seeing only her father's struggle to overcome the pain of breathing and watching his fondest hopes dashed by a man like Merrick whose arrogance exceeded common courtesy and good sense.

Just like this newest attacker of Father. This blackmailer who thinks Walter Farrell may have stooped so low as to steal a valuable papyrus—and who wants it or money by a week from Friday.

At the instigation of an anonymous note threatening blackmail for her father, she had searched high and low, and she couldn't find any papyrus! None she hadn't already seen a dozen times over. None that fit the blackmailer's description! What's more, she didn't have ten thousand pounds to buy this rogue's silence about Walter's supposed theft!

On a rush of outrage, she rose just as Godfrey returned with a silver pot and held it aloft. "But, milady," he called to her as she sailed through the doors headed for the stairs and her room, "your coffee!"

"Thank you, Godfrey. I need air more!"

Within minutes, she was changed, out the front entrance, and down the path toward the stables. Buttoning her new green riding jacket, she was brought up short at the first knoll by the sight before her.

"I thought I told you to go home," she crooned to the old dog who greeted her with panting tongue and a little prance around her. She patted his dense black coat and brought his face up to hers as she bent and said, "You old scoundrel, you're supposed to have gone home to Jessica. No one's going to hurt me here," she said for him. "No one watched me last night, except Spence." He growled. "I know he's incorrigible. What am I do with *two* of you?"

Bones slurped his tongue at her and glanced down the path toward the sea.

"Ah, yes, I know. You want to go on our little jaunt. I know you like them. I do, too. Maybe today we'll be able to accomplish more than last time." *When I left because of imagined footsteps.*

The huge Labrador trod ahead, then paused when she did not immediately follow. He looked back over his shoulder at her as if to say, So, are you coming or not?

"I am, I am. I'm just not up to par this morning,

Bones. Forgive me." His rheumy eyes closed as if he needed no explanation. "I didn't sleep very well."

He ruffed at her.

"You didn't either, eh?" She fell into step with him as they wended their way toward the cream-washed building apart from the mansion. Nestled in the clearing, the stable was hollow, dark, and damp. Every stall stood empty, except one at the farthest end.

"Good morning, Blue," Cat crooned as she stroked the long nose of her mare. "How did you fare last night? Happy with your company? I hope you did better than I did."

The horse whickered, but she could swear Blue laughed.

"No, I am not with the hunt this morning. You and I and Bones will have our own. We will forget about money and blackmail—and Spence." She made off for the tack room where one young groom sprang to his feet and offered to help her saddle Blue.

In short minutes, she was up on the back of the aged mare who had won her father quite a few racing rosettes—and far more pounds sterling. Today, of course, Blue Dahlia was long past her racing days and parenting responsibilities. She was good for a slow walk into town, period.

Corinth stood not far from Farrell Hall and Billington Manor at the outskirts of Dover, the larger, more famous port and the gateway to the Continent. Cat had come to Corinth with her father often as he did his research into the smuggling trade of the past two centuries. She'd been enchanted by the idea of pirates. One of them, her own ancestor, a rogue named Black Jack Farrell, had docked his ships in coves here and hidden his ill-gotten gains in underground caves. The search through these tunnels was for Walter

Farrell a diversion from his usual devotion to antiquity. Cat continued the effort he began. She visited Corinth often lately, especially when she needed diversion from her fears. Visions of swashbuckling men sailing the seas appealed to her. That the men who appeared to her as pirates possessed bronzed bodies, blond hair, and jungle green eyes was an oddity she'd learned to live with, if indeed she bemoaned her obsession with a coloring she knew was too vivid for the dark savagery the myth demanded.

As Blue approached the Tudor-style inn at the edge of Corinth, she admired its green and white gables. She dismounted and looped the reins around the post. Bones padded along beside her as she took her tiny notebook from her jacket pocket and refreshed her memory about the secret stairs and false cupboards she'd found the last two times she'd been here. Heading round toward the back door, she slipped the notebook back into her pocket and paused to admire the way the morning sun glinted off the rush of the tiny stream that flowed past the inn. She'd come here later after her research was complete for the day. She'd reward herself: she'd remove her shoes and stockings, hike up her skirts, walk in the water. She'd soothe her nerves before she returned to her social duty and . . . to Spence.

Spence. Spence. The very reason she needed to endure this dastardly weekend. The very reason she needed to leave—and couldn't. Because of her social duty. Bah!

Why think of him? How not to? Lord, she mustn't think of him ever! It was over. Done. He'd left her. Without excuses, only a note. One meager sentence to say he was sorry but he couldn't go through with this to cover a loss so gigantic she still searched for occupations to fill the hole he'd carved in her heart.

Enough! She whirled for the door, knocked, and let herself in.

"Good morning!" she called to George and stood there a minute, no answer coming from the innkeeper.

"Wonder where he's gone," she murmured to Bones. "Fishing, do you suppose? Yes," she agreed when Bones mashed his gums. "Well, we'll let him catch his dinner, shall we? You and I can go about our business."

She went to the ancient cupboard, took up a thick wax candle in its sconce, lit it with a taper from the kitchen fire George had left burning, and proceeded through the taproom to the public room. No one else was about, just as she expected. Though George Donner kept the Wild Hare open, he took no overnight roomers and offered dinner at one o'clock. A few townsfolk would come for George's scones or fish stew, but more came for the beer he brewed from Kentish hops.

She came for the adventure, the thrill of discovery in the inn, which like many others along the Cinque Ports coast, concealed a thousand secrets of pirates long dead, legends still alive. Here, amid old taverns and wayfarers' inns, she explored a universe of unearthed treasures. A keg of Portuguese Madeira. A crate of rotting Flemish laces. A tunnel that meandered from the shore to Farrell Hall where her father had stored some of his findings despite her protests about the humidity's deteriorating effects on rare items.

Today she came to take her mind off her family, her father, Spencer, the past. Far from the blackmailer who wanted a papyrus she couldn't find or money she didn't have. She came here to focus on one of her diversions—to explore the latest novelty in the inn—

the fake cupboard that led to a tiny room with a trap door operated by a winch. She loved the ingenuity of it. That smugglers would have taken the time to have created such a complicated ruse tickled her funny bone. That she had the opportunity to explore the place and add it to what she hoped would be an informative and amusing book about the thievery along the Cinque Ports gratified her immensely. No better way to teach history than to make it exciting, real, close to home and heart. And it was so very dear to hers. It meant her soul's survival of tragedy.

She stood before the cupboard, a smile wreathing her face. The last time she'd been here, she'd stood here ever so long examining the trompe l'oeil until at last she found that by pressing the handle of the main drawer of the cupboard, the wall receded precisely at the cupboard's edges. At her touch, the wall fell open.

The smell of mildew made her nostrils constrict. Bones snorted his own objection, but then sniffed the floor as if tracking a bird. He gave a persistent round of barks.

"It's just the mold. I know you hate it. Stay here. I'll be back in a bit." He whined and circled the floor in a fret. Cat shut the door behind her. At once, her ears pricked. What was there here that she sensed? Large enough only for a rush chair and straw mattress, the room without a window was stifling, thick with the odor of years in the dark and another aroma, more animal, male . . .

"I wondered when you'd come," came smooth words from the far corner.

Cat jumped. Her candle wobbled, flickering with her panic. The fragrance of sandalwood told her who stood here.

"You're much later than I expected, but now that you're here—" Her phantom came closer, his body heat engulfing her, potent evidence of his humanity, his virility. His voice, an indelible caress, surfaced reminiscences of her desire, her need of him.

"Spence!" She put her hand out, palm flat to his corded torso, touching flesh and memories. Her candle's flame illuminated the amber-drenched beauty of the man she wished never to see again. "You scared me half to death! How did you find me?"

Ignoring her fright, he went on as if she hadn't lost her temper, and he moved an iota nearer. "Dorrie told me you like to come here. I got tired of waiting by the stream," he said with that mellow bass and lavish smile that had always soothed her ravaged senses better than any sherry she'd ever sipped. "Mr. Donner was kind enough to allow me inside, give me a cup of coffee and a tour of this grand old warren. Interesting place. No wonder you like it. You always did enjoy a good puzzle."

"I do *not* enjoy a good fright, Spence. What do you think you're doing, scaring me out my skin?"

In the candle's golden glow with his onyx eyes burning into hers, he covered her hand and said, "I'm showing you how harmless I am. How I only want to talk."

Harmless? Hardly! She slid her hand from beneath his. "You've gone to great lengths. For nothing."

She spun for the door.

"I've come to go exploring with you."

"This inn is my discovery."

"It's not what *I* wish to explore with you."

She laughed, a cynical sound even to her own ears. "Whatever else you had in mind is not on my itinerary."

He came forward as he had last night in the gazebo, and as then, he pressed her back against his long, warm body. At her own traitorous volition, she pressed her lips together in denial. She couldn't go through this any more. She'd not be able to endure the day—nor sleep tonight. She had to find a way to deter him, dissuade him. To steady her wayward body, she reached out for the wall as he circled her waist. She felt his hair slide along hers, his mouth trail her ear, her throat, seeking the hollow beneath her chin where once eons ago in some dream life his lips had driven her mad with longing and—

Her hand touched the winch of the trap door. Her mind lit on the possibility of its use. So while her heart hammered in her chest and his lips tasted the first of her skin, she gathered her courage, judged where precisely he stood, grinned, and pulled the winch down.

It creaked.

Spence paused.

She yanked the last few inches of the rod into place.

Spence tensed.

The floor beneath his feet groaned.

He sucked in air. "Cat?" he asked on a thin reed of his massive bass voice.

She felt him raise his head to smell the air, test the possibilities.

At that moment, the trap door slowly sank in one smooth slide—and took Spence with it.

She turned, her candle offering a priceless picture of Spencer Caldmore Lyonns, hands at his sides, glancing about his feet—and then up at her as he gently descended to the tune of creaks and groans while he slowly disappeared from her sight.

She cupped one hand to her mouth, stifling giggles that threatened to become gales of laughter.

I—do—not—find—this—funny!" he called up, his voice resounding in the cavern below.

"I know!" she blurted and then doubled over in

glee. "Oh, I'm sorry," she moaned as she wiped tears from her eyes and burst out laughing again. "But—but—you must admit—it gives you a head start on exploring."

He cursed viciously. "Just *how* do I get out of here?"

She could imagine him. In that tone, the much-decorated colonel of Her Majesty's Coldstream Guards would have his hands on his hips, his marvelous legs spread, his dangerous eyes blazing, his body ready for battle. She loved him that way, primeval—wicked and willing to fight. He'd never fought with her, of course. Perhaps if they had, she could hate him . . . be free of him.

Sobered, saddened, she brought herself up short. "Good-bye, Spence," she whispered but knew herself unable to leave him without clues for survival. "George told me there is a corresponding winch down there somewhere. I was going to try to find it myself today. But you'll do it and hoist yourself up. In the meantime, I'm going back to Billington Manor. I've a sudden, overwhelming desire to play croquet."

He'd make sure she played croquet, by God!

As he groped in the dark for the damned winch, he cursed in Punjabi and delved into Mandarin for the mental exercise of its demanding tones. By the time he was up and out of that cobwebbed cave, he had resurrected a few misbegotten words in Coptic. But in English, he vowed by the queen's nightshirt, he'd play croquet. Whist. Billiards. He'd play every godforsaken game she wanted—and win. He had to.

He set his teeth as he untied his horse from the tree in the copse near the Wild Hare. Vaulting into the saddle, he wheeled the animal toward the shortcut to Billington Manor. Within no time, he was waiting at the road's turn for her. As she rounded the bend, he kneed his horse to step out and fall in with her.

Bones bared his teeth, and Spence frowned at him. The animal, as he might have guessed, was not amused.

Fine. He was even less so.

He looked up just in time to see a flicker of surprise and amusement facet Cat's incomparable iris eyes, and then she turned away, her demeanor cold when she spoke. "This won't do you any good, Spence. Give over."

"I'm not here to argue with you, Cat."

She trembled.

Not the reaction he wished nor one he savored from her, except in certain private situations, but at least a reaction that reconfirmed she was not neutral toward him. After a few minutes of silence in which he tried to find some middle ground, he decided on a more neutral topic.

"I see you're still supporting Old Blue. I don't know why I'm amazed. Even your father thought she should have been put down long ago."

"Old Blue is—"

"Better fit for Old Glue," he muttered.

But she heard. "Shhhh," she warned and flashed him a look of reproof, as if she were protecting someone's feelings in a private drawing room. "Blue has many years of service left. Besides," her voice dropped, "you wouldn't dream of putting down your grandmother, why would you do it to a—?" She mouthed the word *horse.*

"My grandmother Caldmore *is* a stalwart old mare. I'm positive she'll live forever."

"She's well then?"

"So I hear. She hasn't received me since the day after I canceled our wedding."

"I see," Cat murmured, unable to talk of that day. "I'm sorry. I know how you love her. She was wonderful to you after your mother died."

"At the time, she was the only sane person in our midst. She remains the first of only three truly exciting women I ever met. The second was my mother, the last you."

Cat shivered. "You needn't give me compliments," she offered with impatience, and he knew he had to get this out fast now that they were on the subject.

"Grandma Caldmore cast me out the day after we were to marry. She told me then I should have gone on with the ceremony, bound you to me, and forgotten whatever differences Merrick and your father had. 'Let them battle their own problems,' she said. I didn't listen."

Cat stared straight ahead. "We could have married, I suppose, but it wouldn't have been what we both expected or even what we wanted. To see the two people we loved most tear at each other would have eaten at the affection we found in our marriage. You loved your brother—and your family honor as you should. I loved my father. Our marriage would have suffered in the wars."

"You make it sound so reasonable."

"I've accepted it, Spence."

Carved to the marrow, he knew he lay open to the secrets he had always feared to tell. Now he had to expose them to her. Limited though he had kept those revelations, she had accepted him. Today she might spurn him.

He had to risk it. If only to give her the fuller explanation she deserved.

Part of what she said was accurate. He had loved his family's heritage and honored the wishes of the older brother when he said his own reputation was at stake for being the British official in Egypt responsible for his countrymen's actions. If Farrell had stolen a priceless ancient papyrus and smuggled it out of Egypt under Merrick's watch, Merrick would bear the blame and lose his post.

But his most potent argument was that when this matter came to light as truth always did, for Spence to be wed to Farrell's daughter when the scandal broke would have muddied the waters, sunk them all—Farrells and Lyonns alike—in a pit of degradation.

That convinced Spence the marriage could not occur. He knew how Cat loved her father. Revered him. If Cat and he did marry, they might have been so submerged in delight with each other and perhaps a growing family that he would have been unable to protect Cat or their children from scandal. Plus, he knew discord brought arguments. When he'd been a child, he had felt the effects of fighting parents, their love soured by their inabilities to be totally intimate with each other. The chaos had been ghastly, making Merrick and him feel immaterial. No. In that respect, it was best he had called off the wedding when he did.

But he'd never been totally honest with her about why he'd left. He never wrote a word in his note about a missing papyrus, her father, or his brother. He never told Cat—he'd hardly admitted to *himself*—that Merrick had no proof, only circumstantial evidence. But he had used Merrick's accusation as the means to remove himself from a situation that, though he loved Cat, terrified him. So his leaving her had been a double-edged sword. If he went to his grave never succeeding in making Cat forgive and forget what he'd done to her three years ago, he would count himself blessed and her fortunate for his foresight then. He had not been ready for marriage and would have destroyed it by his lack of self-knowledge.

But what he had learned in the interim confirmed, too, that his brother was not perfect. By accident, he'd discovered that fact as Merrick had deteriorated physically as well as mentally. Merrick had blurted some of it out himself in his mindless rages. Yes, his brother was guilty of great misdoings in this Farrell business. Spence was not quite certain the extent of it, but he had enough unanswered questions to want to investigate not only Walter's actions but also Merrick's. Though he could not recount to Cat his suspicions because she would think them flimsy—and some were—he could discuss the other portions of his thinking.

He moved his horse closer. His leg brushed hers. "Being apart from you hasn't solved anything either."

She shook her head and reined her horse away from his. "I am sorry for you. I know how deliberate you are, how decisive. That must come from your years in the military."

"Or years thinking you can do no wrong."

"That, too." She sat like a statue.

His gaze caressed her stunning profile. She exuded a luscious vulnerability that tore his heart to shreds. Her eyes glistened, and he could have bet a thousand pounds that tears stood there. Her body, tall in the sidesaddle, was strong, but her gloved hands on her reins clenched convulsively. How he longed to uncurl her hands, put them on his body, kiss her tears away, and show her a glimpse of the paradise he remembered so well.

"You survived it. So have I, Cat. But it's not enough for me. I want a real home, family, someone I care for."

"I wish you well of it." She made to leave.

He thrust out a hand. "I don't want your best wishes."

"What *do* you want then?" She was spitting mad.

Like a shot, he knew. Knew it in full joy—and horror.

She attacked. "Spence, I may have lived in the country most of my life, but I am not without connections and news. Word has it you have 'wanted' quite a few things."

"If you're referring to Barbara Keene—"

"In addition, what of the Countess Windemere?"

"You *do* know a lot. But here is what you can't know. I did try to find a woman I could marry *safely*. Someone who wouldn't threaten my independent spirit, wouldn't *touch* me. What appeared to be such a convenient relationship with Barbara died when I realized I was appalled she was not drawn to *me* but more interested in advancing my career. I didn't need to marry a batman. I already had one. After that, I simplified my goal. I cast about for bed partners."

When Cat spun away, he gruffed, "No! You opened this subject and I *want* you to know this! After Barbara, I took up with Julia Windemere and that failed, too. It had to. The loneliness I felt before the act was magnified by the hollowness during and after it. So I relearned what I'd known before I met you and what I wish never to experience again. Cat, I can couple with any willing woman. Now I want a loving mate."

Shock paralyzed her while he frantically prayed for wise words to keep her here. "What I am amazed about, kitten," he finally said with husky warmth, "is that you have found no one."

She whipped around to face him, her eyes iridescent shards of pain and pride. "Don't be silly, Spence. No one would come near me. I was ostracized."

That socked the wind from him.

She kicked the horse to a canter.

He knew he deserved her ridicule, yet he couldn't let that be the last word. He'd never see her laugh again. Not like she had—yes, she *had* minutes ago. He thirsted for it again . . . as much as he himself needed to laugh with her!

He prodded his horse, and they took off. To catch her wasn't any challenge. As he came abreast of her, she used her crop to make Blue go faster, but the aged mare couldn't do any more, and slowly, slowly, the horse drifted to a walk. Winded, the animal blew and came to a full stop.

"Sweetheart," he beseeched as he reached over to cup her chin and brought her, resisting, to face him. "I'm only beginning to realize the enormity of what I did three years ago. If I could take it back, change it, I would. I'd marry you, take you to my heart and bed, and never let you go."

"Nooo!" she gasped, broken, eyes clamped shut, tears sliding down her arched cheeks. "None of this does any good now. The hurt is there for me. Every day. Every hour." She opened her eyes, and though he'd been wounded by bullets and knives, he'd never been speared by anguish like this. "I loved you, Spence. I adored your prowess, your pluck, your jokes, even your shyness. But it's over, so don't—" She put a hand to her trembling mouth. "Don't do this to me. Don't make me lose any more sleep or dream of things I can't have. Leave me alone. Let me have what I can. My dog, my horse, my school. My dignity."

She broke into sobs. "You can't know . . . can't believe what it's like to have people treat you like . . . like a leper. Not speak to you. Not even *look* at you." She dashed tears away from her cheeks. "You can't imagine how lonely I've been . . . without friends or Papa or—"

You.

She would have said *you.*

His heart crashed to a halt.

Then with his next breath, he felt cleansed, whole. He knew he had to help her feel the same.

If over the past three years he'd learned he'd been right to leave her so that he could discover the essence of himself, he saw now with gutting anguish that the better man who appeared before her adored her for everything she'd suffered—and survived—in his name.

She stiffened. "Do not make a scene for me here at Dorrie's, Spence. I'll *die* if I can't have this."

He knew he'd die a bitter old man if he didn't help her gain what she wanted. Her school, her reputation—and him. He'd give her *him.* Children, home, protection—and all the love she'd ever desire. The intimate care he'd craved and run from so much of his life.

His gloved fingers traced her tears, and he wished he could put his naked hands on her silken flesh to tell her this. But soon he would. Quite soon. "You won't die, darling. You'll live." *You'll live with me. Love with me.* "I'll see you have everything you desire. I promise you."

From the very heart of her rose a cry of a creature in a trap. She reeled in her saddle, warning him off with agony in her gaze and veering Old Blue toward Billington Manor.

As she left him with Bones ambling behind the aging horse, Spence did her the courtesy not to follow. Instead, his mind was churning, planning how he would transform this newest vow he'd made her into a reality.

Chapter 4

She won at croquet that afternoon.

"You cheated," Spence whispered over her shoulder as they walked across the lawn to deposit their mallets.

"I did not," she fired back.

"I saw how you moved the ball with your skirts," he chided her with a lopsided grin.

His humor was infectious. Her lips curled. "I didn't want you to win."

"I noticed." He winked and then turned to stroll back to the manor.

Cat was momentarily stunned, then pleased by his acceptance of his loss. A novel thing for a man of Spencer Lyonns's background in which winning was a matter of honor and losing an issue for debate. A new development for a man who had always considered himself rational—and right.

* * *

Later, between tea and supper, she won at billiards. "You've improved," Spence told her as she returned her cue to the cabinet and the other spectators departed the room to dress for supper.

"Not that much," she confessed because she understood her opponent, the Prince of Wales, was a superb shot and few ever won over him. Today, she had and wondered why.

Spence hoisted his glass of sherry at her and downed it. "Perhaps he was being polite."

"I prefer the challenge of someone bent on winning."

"Then you're ready to play with me." He took a cue.

She stayed his hand. "No games with you."

"Sounds fair to me," he said so circumspectly that she almost believed him. But in the deserted room, he seized her breath when he stepped flush to her and raised her face with a gentle finger. "Soon you'll see I've wagered very high stakes and what I play for is very precious to me. I am a very determined man, Cat. This time both of us will win." He chucked her chin, smiled in dark green ardor, and left.

Mind-mushing desire flowed through her veins. How she wanted what he described. How she wished she could have it.

With him.

But she was rational and he was wrong.

What they had together had not been strong enough to surmount circumstances. He might be sorry about what he'd done, and he might be determined to ease the pain, but that did not mean he could waltz into her life and make the past disappear. Or create a future for them both she'd want to share. Because with him and with no one else, she had wanted and,

God help her, *needed* all the love and devotion her arms could hold. She wanted to be free with him, honest, open in word and deed and every act of love—and how could she? How could she, if she never knew when he'd leave her without adequate explanation or warning?

That night, her team won at charades.

"Very clever impersonation of Cleopatra," Spence commented to her as they wended their way behind other guests into the drawing room for coffee.

"The snake in the death scene was Dorrie's idea."

"Dorrie has some wonderful insights." He gave Cat a haunting look of regret as he maneuvered her in an alcove and others milled past.

Cat frowned up at Spence. "She knows I await a full description of her viewpoint on why you are here this weekend."

"Don't be hard on her, Cat. She was doing what she thought best. Especially for you."

"I'm not fond of the fact that I am the object of many people's discussions."

"You're the object of more than that with me. You walk my nights. Haunt my days. Reminding me what I might be if—"

She fought down a thrill, a terror. "Spence—"

Someone came round the corner and when she saw it was Marietta Hornsby, Cat knew the woman was eavesdropping.

Smooth as glass, Spence lifted his voice as if Cat and he spoke of normal things. "Well, I didn't think you were going with the shooting party tomorrow morning. But that's true to your form. See you afterward perhaps." He turned, nodded nonchalantly at Marietta, and departed.

Cat stared after him. He hadn't made any attempt to rendezvous with her as he had this morning. She was elated.

She'd won! She preened, filled with . . . despair.

She'd finally persuaded him to leave her alone. Precisely what she would forever be. Alone.

Without him.

Sunday afternoon, she walked down to the boathouse. Book in hand, she glanced about for Bones, but he must have finally understood he must go home to Farrell Hall. She wished she could. This weekend dragged on like a year. Especially this morning. Certainly, last night had. Evidence of it showed in her face. Dark circles under her eyes and a lack of light within them.

Seeing Spence in the afternoon sun over croquet and later in the oak-lined billiard room with the gaslight gilding his hair and blackening the green of his eyes, she had suffered the most stunning blow to her willpower. His dashing good looks had made her heart remember too much of what it was like to trace the platinum streaks of his hair with her fingertips and to skim the linear perfection of his mouth with her own. So last night's attempt at rest had been a failure she knew would appear this morning, which showed more on her nerves than on her face.

When the morning dawned hotter than most recent days, she'd decided on a boating expedition to soothe her fevered endeavors to forget Spence. The trickling sound of water, the song of birds—the solitude—would do the trick.

With her parasol hooked under one arm and a tome by Trollope tucked under the other, she stood on the wooden dock and investigated the boat. It was a skiff of the size she had at home, and she'd easily manage it to the center of the lake. There she could enjoy her afternoon while the others shot animals with a gusto she'd never shared.

Bending over, she placed her book on one seat and her parasol close beside it. The boatswain, enlisted as bagger for the shooting party, was not about. Now, if she could only find an oar, she'd be off.

But she couldn't find any. Odd. Finally, she walked over to the ancient weather-beaten hut and flung open the door. There, arms crossed, two oars standing in his hand, stood a statue waiting for her, grinning at her. Spence.

She burst out laughing. "Imagine, a wooden soldier!"

"Tut, tut, my dear. Today I'm a sailor."

"Oh, no." She was wagging her finger at him and backing away as he advanced, admiring his devastating boating attire of navy blazer, ivory linen trousers, and white bucks. The colors contrasted with his bronzed skin and mane of champagne hair. "You will not come out with me."

"Why not?" He pursued her across the dock until there was nowhere else to go except into the boat—or into the water.

"You know perfectly well why not." She was chuckling.

His darling dark eyes were laughing as he spread one hand and took up an orator's pose. "It is daylight. Nothing covert there. You will sit in that seat, and I will be three untouchable feet away. Nothing improper in that. You will read whatever opus it is you are carting about with you these days. I will row. We will from time to time comment on the weather or on Blanding's rather ugly and unruly geese. So the morning will pass to afternoon."

She quieted. "Meanwhile, you'll think it is quite all right to walk into my life and change my plans."

"For now, let's just say, my presence will enhance your afternoon."

Her skin tingled at the mere idea of minutes in the sun with him. Remembering the wealth of warmth and affection he always brought with him, she shivered at the blizzard her life had become without him. She clutched her wool shawl about her more securely.

"Come on, Cat. Be a sport. You know I'm a better rower than you."

"But it's dangerous to put you in control."

"Where can I go but out to the middle of the lake and back?"

"But you'll have *your* hands on the oars."

His eyes glinted in delight. "Precisely *my* point."

Rebel to her best interests, she recalled what it was like to have his hands on her. Her cheeks, her nape, her breasts . . . She cleared her throat. "But then I won't know where you're steering."

"Of course, you know where I'm going," he insisted softly. Then he pursed his mouth, pouting in that liberal way that made her bones melt to the marrow. Meaningfully, he added, "At the very least we won't go round in circles."

Her lips twitched at the memory of how, in her maidenly rush to impress him, she'd once insisted that she row them about Farrell Lake and wound up sending them in rings while he grinned his appreciation of her flustered eagerness. "Very well, you win." She let him help her in the boat. "But you must not take your hands off the oars."

"Worse than being ordered about by an army general," he muttered. "Get in here before I haul you over my shoulder."

She froze. Touching his hard, welcoming hand was bad enough—and good enough to make her blood catch fire. She had to find some objectivity. "Ah, ah, you have to promise."

His brows rose.

Instantly, she knew what he thought.

"Will you let me make you a promise, Cat, and will you expect me to keep it? Thank God, we've progressed so far."

"We haven't." She had to keep him at bay while she herself discovered why in the world she was letting down her guard with the one man who should never pass it again.

They were out on the lake for at least half an hour, her book in hand but unread, before she knew she could speak. Nor did she want to. She'd rather look at him.

He had ceased rowing long ago and sprawled his large body in repose. Sliding back in the cushioned seat, he had stretched his long legs out so that his linen trousers molded to the muscles of his thighs and hips. Over the rim of her book, she noted how the ivory fabric jutted at his hip bones and bulged at the juncture of his thighs.

She dragged in air, remembering how his hips felt against her, how his muscles used to tense and bulge, how his manly parts pressed against her in a carriage or in a dance used to make her feel breathless. Willing.

She flexed in want but could not tear herself away. Her book fell open in her lap. Her eyes went to his torso. He'd cast off his jacket, unbuttoned his shirt, exposing the smooth luster of his throat and a portion of his chest, which rose and fell with measured serenity. His tanned arms, in the soft white shirt, which he'd rolled above his elbows, were contoured with the big, bold might of him. His face with the strong, sweet features she longed to caress was still a study in perfection. His hair, gold lined with platinum, remained a wealth that she longed to comb with her fingers, bury her lips in. God, how she wished she could tell him how dreadfully handsome he was. How much the look of him pleased her, teased her. How very much his nearness appeased her ravaged pride despite everything he'd done.

"You are more devastatingly beautiful than ever."

His deep murmur seemed such a natural part of her reverie, it was an eternity before his meaning seeped into her consciousness and she blinked at him.

She blushed. She knew she did and didn't cover her reaction. She just sat there like a ninny and watched him as he slowly opened his eyes and pinned her to her spot with a promise in his jungle green gaze.

She thought he would have risen, tried to take her in his arms. But he didn't, and she was disappointed. So violent was her loss that she squeezed her eyes closed.

When she peered at him again, he was merely looking at her in that steadied way that spoke of elemental needs. A primal look of acquisition that always made her perspire—and desire him. Ever only him.

"I could feel your eyes on me from across a desert," he told her in words what his gaze declared. "Even from across a crowded ballroom, I'd know it as I have the past two days. Ahh, Cathy, don't bother to turn away. There is nowhere to run. You can't deny what we have is alive, breathing. I know it. I can feel what you do. I always have. When I left you, I knew how hard you'd take it. I expected you to hate me. God knows, I hated myself."

She opened her mouth, but he shook his head. "No, don't. Let me talk, will you?"

He slid upright, and she thought he'd reach for her, so she shrank backward, her parasol and shawl falling, the sun baking her reason. But he was as good as his word and didn't touch her. Except with his devouring eyes.

"I have hungered for you every day of the past three years. Now, since your father and Merrick have died, I predicted with every day's passing that you would feel more able to come out into society again. I didn't know about your school until recently, but I always knew that many would forget what happened, put the blame on me—where it belongs—and soon you'd have quite a few gentlemen dancing attendance on you."

"I don't want another man," she objected, angry and trapped by her honesty, propriety, and this god-forsaken lake.

Relief washed his features. "I am ecstatic."

"I don't want you either, Spence."

"I hear you say that and I see the evidence of it. But then, what am I to think of this *other?*"

Irritated with his persistence, she slapped her book shut and sat straighter. "What other?"

"The way you look at me with a yearning so palpable I can feel you in my arms."

She wanted to twist away, run, deny him, touch him. She did none of it but inhaled the essence of his cologne, the substance of his ardor.

With the grace and assurance of a compelling creature, he reached for her with a slow, steady hand that had her on his lap and his arm circling her waist. "The way you breathe with a rapid little pant so exciting I can imagine what the rest of your body is doing."

She knew. Her every fiber evaporated in liquid desire.

He sank one hand into her hair and cuddled her close with the other while his mouth, moist and murmuring, came closer. "The way you stiffen and yield. Always, kitten, you would tense and curl to me like a wild animal. Like *now*," he revealed as his fingers massaged her nape and lifted her face so that her lips might brush his. "Like *this*," he demonstrated as he bent over her, took her breath, and curved her beneath him.

The luxury of the cushion met her back, the wonders of his lavish mouth descended, and she wanted him and his kiss as she had never wanted any necessity of life. Air. Sun. Water. His lips offered sweet wonders of the universe.

But she mustn't have them or him. Ever. The hurt was too wide, too deep. Deeper than this lake.

So she arched, pushed, and finally struggled from his arms. And stood.

But he did, too.

With the ruckus, the boat rocked wickedly.

He tried to grab her arm to steady her.

She flailed.

He missed her. "Cat! Stop! I won't—The boat!"

So she did what she thought impossible before. She put her fingers to her nose, pinched, and jumped.

"Cat? *Cat!*"

She could hear him calling her as she hit the cool lake and cursing as she surfaced, spitting out water and grass.

"Cat, dammit!" He was trying to row near her to get her back in the boat.

But she refused him and swam a few strokes—with huge difficulty for her layers of clothing. Luckily, the lake was shallow, if cold, and her struggle to the shore was brief. So as she trudged up the bank, she hiked up yards of her water-laden skirts and wrung them out with a purposeful yank.

He docked the boat, tied the rope to the pier, and ran toward her. "You scared me to death! Are you all right?" He seized her arms and surveyed her face and clothes.

"Completely." She tossed her sodden hair and would never admit the act almost snapped her neck. Angry, she pivoted and staggered, her attempt at bravado weighted by tons of water rivering from her body. He caught her arm to steady her while she chided herself in mute unladylike ways.

She could feel him smiling at her and could have hugged him for not laughing at her. "I applaud you, Cat. What courage. You'd brave a houseful of gossipy servants seeing you in transparent clothes rather than let me kiss you."

She froze, stared down at her once white lawn dress, now a revealing gray, and gasped. True to his statement, it disclosed every line, every curve of her figure. Only the thickness of the corset concealed her most private places.

"Here." He shrugged out of his blazer, came close to drape her in it, and secured it up high under her defiant chin. "Wear this inside. I don't give a tinker's damn who notices you in it. I'd rather that than they see you the way only a man who loves you should."

Beyond coherent words, she stomped her foot at him, her teeth chattering, her eyes boring into his in a mixture of outrage and gratitude.

He offered a rakish smile, then touched the tip of her nose. "Go, sweetheart. Maybe no one will have returned yet and they'll never know we were out together"—his brows arched and danced down over her body—"swimming." He puckered that mischievous mouth of his. "Virtually nude."

No one did. None of the shooting party had returned, and none of the servants, thankfully, were flitting about when Cat entered the conservatory door and took the back stairs to her room. If she left a trail of water, which her maid commented on that night as she helped her with her hair before supper—well, no one else seemed to have noticed.

But her heart did.

Through the soup course that night, she ate quietly, sedately. Spence, radiant in his midnight black tuxedo, sat across from her between two debutantes, utterly absorbed, blast him. The table talk was of small consequence. Of yesterday's hunt, the fox was resourceful but, as expected, lost the competition. Of today's shooting tally, the total birds bagged was not up to par but the marksmanship of a few of the guns was.

"Reginald was wonderful," said Marietta Hornsby of the abilities of her friend the duke of Inniesfield. Ignoring her husband, Oscar, next to her, she nodded at Reginald a few seats away. "Did you see how he took out the last pheasant? No flutter-flutter. Just straight through the head. Absolutely fwump. Dead. Divine, really."

Cat winced. Instinct and hope for an ally made her glance at Spence. He agreed with her about her dislike of the Englishman's aggressive march against animals. He, too, thought it an enigma and a horror. But tonight when she sought his eyes, she found him sublimely engaged elsewhere.

She felt bereft. Deserted.

How could he act this way? Following her everywhere, seducing her in private with words and deeds, and then pretending in public they were nothing more than acquaintances? How could he act like she was nothing to him?

Curse it. She took up her fish fork and tucked into the poached salmon.

Isn't that just what you wanted, you simpleton?

Of course, it was.

What was more torture—and Cat admitted it about the time the rack of lamb came paired with a sirloin of beef—was to watch while one of the debutantes tucked into Spence. With a hunger Cat could equate to a manhunter, eighteen-year-old Lady Ione Campbell proceeded to bat her flimsy lashes, squeeze her even less substantial breasts, and squeal like a tickled mouse. In her heavy mocha satin with the totally unnecessary décolletage, the child even looked like a tiny rodent.

One moment hating the girl, the next sympathetic when nervous Ione began to show the effects of too much Bordeaux, Cat chastised herself for her less than charitable behavior. Once she too had sat next to the scorchingly handsome man whose smile and wit soon transformed him into her sun god. Soon she'd fallen so desperately in love with him she never stopped to think or analyze—or fear—what standing so close to so much heat could do to her heart or her mind.

Counting mixed blessings she owed Dorrie for this weekend, Cat gave her friend silent thanks that she was appointed to sit between Rand and Blanding tonight. At least their repartee kept her commenting and nodding.

What she learned in the discussion was nothing she

hadn't already surmised: that her father and Merrick's much-publicized efforts at unearthing ancient Egyptian artifacts had led to the hysterical interest of the British in cementing a relationship with the khedive, no matter his ruthless politics or his lack of ethics.

What she learned from Spence as he leaned across the table to join their discussion was novel: that the khedive was eager to sign an agreement with the British government to let them own shares in the Suez Canal. Interesting. Her father had said that the khedive was devoted to one thing only: Egypt for himself. Now that it appeared the khedive's politics had changed, Cat wondered why—aloud.

"Because," Spence answered her in that voice with which he could burn her rational thoughts to ashes, "the man sees a canal as a means to collect taxes and fatten his treasury. But he wants us to help protect it. He bargains more slyly than the rest of us." His verdant eyes touched hers in a personal embrace. "He doesn't reveal everything he wants initially. He places the bait, entices his victim, then pulls the trap."

What Spence said brought to mind her own trap. The requirement for her to find a papyrus before a week from Friday or come up with ten thousand pounds to assure the blackmailer did not go to Scotland Yard with the only blot Cat knew of on her father's record. He had told her himself in a deathbed confession how he had once forged a papyrus. Not the one the blackmailer demanded, but a different one. Her father rued the day he did it and lived in fear someone would learn of it and view everything he'd done in light of it.

To ensure that one mistake never became public knowledge, Cat had to find this other small papyrus, which—her blackmailer said—was the edict of Ramses II to Moses and a route to the copper mines the tribes of Israel had worked during Ramses' reign. She herself had never seen the paper and couldn't translate it if she had, but over the years she had seen every one of the other twenty-two papyri her father had found. She had even assisted him in cataloging them. But what was even more preposterous was the very idea that her father would have found such a valuable piece and hidden it from the world!

That she hadn't found it added to her belief it didn't exist. She'd looked everywhere at Farrell Hall. She'd read her father's diary, pillaged his desk, his expedition logs, even his leather pouch crammed with old receipts. When those yielded up no treasure, she'd rummaged through his chest of drawers, closets, and trunk steamers and had even gone to the tunnels and opened crates. She'd found nothing. Not one thing. Through her despair, Spence's words came to her now.

"The khedive," Spence offered, "is a very wily man. He lures, unfortunately, with great finesse but has no ethics. He'd do anything to get protection and money."

"He's very effective," offered Blanding. "He has us looking for ways to appease him while we make the major investment in the canal. Meanwhile, he has asked quite a few other favors."

The khedive had once asked her father for the return of the jewelry he had found in a Karnak temple built by Ramses II. Her father refused on the grounds he'd paid for the expedition and therefore was legally allowed to keep the items. Cat was not surprised the khedive asked for more now.

The conversation drifted from the khedive to Oriental policy in general. Cat lost interest in it and found herself resting her eyes in Spence's green ones while thoughts of blackmail died and Ione Campbell grew twitchy.

Cat tore her gaze away. To stay here too long under the green fervor of Spence's gaze muddled her mind. Agonized, she assessed everyone's plates and wondered when she might excuse herself to go to bed.

Prince Bertie shifted in his chair. "Now, now, men." He hefted his glass of wine. "Let us not bore the ladies with such weighty issues."

Ione Campbell squeaked her agreement while Cat clawed the hem of the tablecloth in frustration. Fortunately, the topic turned, and she found herself facing the dessert, peaches flambé, with ravenous delight. She had only to eat this and languish for a few moments in the main salon with coffee, and then she could blissfully escape.

She'd claim an indisposition. With a headache, a backache, a foot problem, every woman could and did complain the last night of a house party and retire early. Cat never had, but then, she'd never been in such a state before with Spence tracking her, apologizing, appealing, persisting . . .

Coffee, however, became an unusual affair. The men decided to forgo their port and cigars in private. A not unheard of change for a more relaxed Sunday evening house party event, this meant a gayer atmosphere prevailed. But it was one Cat could not share.

As she perched on the edge of a Chippendale chair, her coffee in hand, Cat set her teeth at the clamor for some of the ladies to play the piano and perhaps sing. She had never sung in public, hating the exhibitionism of it for one with a mediocre voice. As for playing the piano, she could but usually left that to her exquisitely accomplished cousin Jessica. Tonight, none of the ladies wished to display their musical talents, and so Dorrie prevailed upon Rand to do them the honor. Cat had heard of his marvelous ability and longed to hear it, though not tonight nor in these circumstances. Her heart was too sore to sit here too long with Spence so close and untouchable.

But Rand Templeton flicked back his tails, sat down on the bench of Dorrie's grand salon piano, and played a series of pieces that eroded every fine intention Cat had of pretending she never had been and never could be affected by the likes of Spencer Lyonns.

Worse, he faced her. Braced at one side of the massive marble fireplace, he stood with his port in one hand, his elegant form tantalizing, his hooded eyes discreetly turned from her. But then as Rand's first effort met with enthusiastic applause and he launched into a polonaise by Chopin, Cat prayed the floor would open and she disappear.

This polonaise she knew too damnably well. Written by the passionate composer for his lover, the tormenting and irresistible feminist novelist, George Sand, the piece spoke of irrepressible emotions and interminable sufferings. Chopin had written this as he and his beloved drifted apart. He had died not too long afterward, a victim of disease as much as of her spurning him. Turbulent strains rose from the piano as Rand offered up an incomparable rendition and Spence's eyes turned to Cat, lashing her to her chair, a woman tied to the stake of her passion.

She knew it. Her skin blazed wherever he touched. Her hair, her eyes, cheeks, lips, breasts. In the inferno, she felt herself consumed by a memory of this song and knew he remembered as she did . . .

This was the polonaise that the symphonic orchestra had played the night he'd told her he loved her.

When he'd pressed her to the magenta brocade drapes of Rand's box and whispered, "Darling, I walk the floors at night needing you. You enjoy me, want me. Marry me and let me make you happy."

Happy? Her breath caught.

Her coffee cup clattered to its saucer.

Her gaze melded with Spence's, and what she saw there made her heart crumble.

He narrowed his eyes at her. *Don't go, Cat. Not now. Not yet. Some notice your distress, how I look at you. They'll say you fled me, this!*

But I can't stay for such torture.

I promise you I won't let Rand play more.

Oh, Spence. I've got to leave!

As soon as Rand hit the last chords, she was out of her chair, excusing herself to Dorrie and Blanding, nodding to the others, even Ione Campbell. As she shut the double doors on the salon, she sagged against them, forehead to the cool wood. Then she spun in a fury for the grand staircase, her room, her bed, and her peace.

But, oh God, where to find it? *Where?*

She paced, cursed, disrobed. She let down her hair and combed the wild curls that resisted her attempt to tame them and her madness. The maid came, but she dismissed her through the door, waved off any hot chocolate, flung herself onto the chair, and rued the day she ever let Dorrie and Blanding persuade her to come here.

She rose and picked up a pillow, pounded it, and threw it across the room.

What was she thinking? That she could forget Spence? That she could stoically march on without him? Without coming to dead-end terms with what he had meant to her?

What he still meant to her.

No!

She had to stop craving him. Like thick cream desserts, he was bad for her constitution.

She had to stop dreaming of him. Like those useless fantasies she nurtured of him as a caring husband and an understanding father, he could only be a ghost to her. Part of her past. Lost to her.

She would have to shut away her tender memories of him. The only treasures she had from that time. The day he'd walked with her in the woods near his brother Merrick's estate and caught up a handful of purple bluebells to put behind her ear and tell her they were such poor wonders compared to her eyes. Or the night he'd come back from his regiment unexpectedly and surprised her with the key to a London house he'd let for the two of them so that they could get married months earlier. Or the kitten he'd brought for her when her old tabby died. The way he consoled her with kisses and caresses, setting her afire for his touch as a provider, a protector, a husband.

She beat a useless fist into the counterpane and got up to prowl.

How was she supposed to forget? How could she when he came forward now as if . . . as if he could so easily wipe every terror away with the wave of his hand.

Like some magician with instant cures for ancient woes. Like a gypsy who could dance in and out of her life.

Never.

She tore open her doors to the balcony and strode out. The night had chilled, the sky a whirl of umbers and purples with the threat of a storm. Billington Manor was dark, quiet, asleep. She shivered and clutched her arms about her waist, wishing she had stayed home where she knew what would happen every day, every hour. Where no one would hurt her, entice her, entreat her, not ever again.

The breeze lifted her hair from her shoulders and swirled it about her. The bracing night air stung her eyes. Tears pooled, and though she willed them to never flow, they spilled down and refracted her vision. The shifting clouds took on shapes of horses and chariots, a man, a pair of beguiling black eyes. The wind moaned, and she shifted closer to one of Dorrie's tall topiary evergreens. In the maze of her misery, she wandered, wondering why the tree had hands and heat—and a resonant voice like Spence's.

"God, I'm glad you came out," he breathed into her hair as his arms went round her in the most welcome warmth she'd ever known. "I've been standing here for over an hour watching you argue with yourself. Christ, you're stubborn—and very cold." He settled her into his embrace, and beneath the thin silk of her nightgown, she felt her body forge to his. She couldn't have left him if the whole bloody British army marched across the lawn and demanded it. She sighed, closed her eyes, and reveled in the taut, hot feel of him.

"That's right. This is where you belong," he murmured as his hands formed her to him and he kissed her temple. "Where you'll always be."

She shook her head, agony eroding the ecstasy she needed to savor before it disappeared again. Hating the pain, her own hedonism surfaced. "Don't speak of tomorrow, Spence. Just let me have this. I can't think beyond now."

"Just feel, darling." He turned her in his arms. If it were possible, his face in the scant moonlight seemed more ravaged than she felt. His hands cupped her face, his fingers stroked her cheekbones. His lips descended to bless her eyes, her earlobes, and finally the little place beneath her chin he always licked and then kissed madly.

She gripped his shoulders as her head fell back. He braced her, one hand plunging into her hair. "I've been crazy to touch you like this for three days. Wanting to have you to myself. Knowing the minute I could that you'd melt and moan. Do it. You want to and I need to hear you like that for me again."

His mouth went to the base of her throat as she began to purr. "Put your hands on me," he said raggedly. But when she seemed paralyzed, he led her one hand inside his satin robe where his supple nakedness seared her palm.

Frantic suddenly, she wanted to feel more of him. She straightened, not sure she could see right, uncertain she knew the difference between flesh-and-blood man and dark desperate dreams. "You are real," she marveled.

"Yes, darling. Real and here and forever yours. I don't want you tormented like this any longer. What a damn schoolboy I was to let you go, but I knew no other way to find myself. I never thought the longing for you could be such hell." He drew her close, his lips trembling against her forehead. "I never let myself believe you could have been this hurt this long."

Tears welled up then. She couldn't say if they came because of his tenderness or his confession or if she was just so exhausted from the rigors of the weekend. But they fell. Copiously, freely, and he couldn't brush them away.

"Sweetheart," he said, wrapping her close, "I swear you must stop crying. You'll make yourself ill. Besides, I want to kiss you." He put his warm lips to her ear and told her how he'd dreamt countless nights of holding her like this.

She shuddered.

He trailed a torrid path down her cheek and murmured how he'd developed the worst sleeping habits, waking from his dreams and sleeping better only in the days. Days of wanting her and never having her. Months and years of no hope of ever enjoying her.

At the litany of his agonies that sounded so like her own, she quaked.

He bound her closer. Putting his lush mouth to the corner of hers, he told her he was going to kiss her now and erase all their sordid pasts. "I want to create a place in your heart where you'll never evict me, never want to. I swear I will never let you go again."

He placed his lips on hers with the most delicate pressure, as if she would bolt from him or shatter in his arms. The light touch of his mouth to hers sent her over the edge of her control. She gave herself up to him, to what they'd been and what they might have been. Winding her fingers in his hair, she moved with him as he bent her backward, brought her up, crushed her to him and tasted and sampled, then suckled and savored her lips. She met him, kiss for savage kiss, moan for delight, succor for pain, desire for regret and need. She'd never known a kiss—a thousand kisses— could be like this, want like this, feel like this heaven. This floating paradise.

She could kiss him till eternity drew nigh.

Serenity came instead as he drew his mouth from hers in the gentlest of partings. "Darling," he called her, and her eyes opened in bliss while he stroked her spine and caressed her hair in endless endearing movements. Her lips felt swollen and moist, tasting of him and what she'd lost.

Euphoria evaporated in reality.

In despair, she clung to him. Her face to his shoulder, she let her arms encompass him and felt the wonder she'd so long missed. She inhaled his scent of sandalwood and musky man. She questioned how she'd ever gotten on without him in her arms. In her life. In her bed.

Perhaps that was what she needed to kill the pain of his loss. She'd take him to her bed. With the shock of so immoral a decision, she jerked away from him so quickly that Spence startled and searched her face.

"Cat, what—?"

But he never finished.

Instead, they heard someone say, "Pardon me."

Simultaneously they turned toward the sound to find Marietta Hornsby eyeing them.

"It *is* raining, but I see neither of you have noticed," she said in a frigid tone that reminded Cat of a schoolmistress she'd had as a child. Marietta needed only a disciplinary rod to complete the perfect picture of Proper Matron Affronted.

Cat glanced at Spence, his robe dotted with rain. She didn't need to look at her own gown to know that the front of her would show no drops, only wrinkles denoting the passion she was certain still glowed on her face.

Spence stepped in front of Cat. "What else is there you need to say, Marietta?"

"You know, Spencer. I needn't voice it."

"Perhaps not. But then, let me voice this. I was here to persuade Cat to marry me."

"It appears you were putting something else ahead of the ceremony, Spence."

"As you have, Marietta, put something else—some*one* else—between you and your husband?"

The lady shivered. "Don't be silly, Sp—"

"Don't be naive, Marietta. Your husband may know about Reginald, but what of the rest of the world?"

"You wouldn't," she hissed.

"No," he countered. "Not unless you find it necessary to make known how two people stepped into the rain at the Billingtons and became engaged."

"Again? Really, Spencer, you can't expect me to believe that twice—"

"Once, twice, a hundred times! Cat's *mine!* Will you debate that?" He was advancing, shouting.

Cat grabbed his arm. "You'll wake the world!"

Before such rage, Marietta retreated. "No, I—I suppose I won't."

"Wise." Nonetheless, Spence tracked her like a huge cat, the smell of Marietta's fear redolent in the night air. "Now take one more bit of advice, Marietta. Go back inside your room and don't come out tonight. It is raining"—he held out one palm—*"very heavily* and *you* need to be in your own bed, *not* someone else's. Isn't that correct?"

"Yes, very."

"Good night then."

Intimidated, she bit her lip and fled.

Spence watched the retreat of the one woman who could—but would now never—destroy Cat.

No one would hurt her again.

He'd take her, make her his wife, and the Mariettas everywhere could go to hell! Catherine Farrell was *his,* and he would prove it this time. He'd give her his name, his fortune, his future to her keeping and end this torture.

When he turned, however, he found not her but the slam of her door.

He stood there in the rain, wondering at her fright of Marietta. Marietta was no threat in this way. Not with what Spence knew about her and her lover. But Cat—

He took a step forward, wanting to soothe her, calm

her fears. But instinct told him Cat had had enough for one night. He'd see her in the morning.

They'd announce their engagement after breakfast. Dorrie would be bursting with pride. Blanding would be reassured he hadn't alienated his wife and his political party. Rand would be able to inform his friends in the shipping industry that their dilemma would soon be solved, the missing papyrus found and handed over to the khedive, commercial traffic back to normal.

Most important though, Spence's prize for the weekend was having Cat. To himself. Forever. A prize he'd wanted and never had the hope or heart to claim until now when he couldn't bear the agony of living without her.

Chapter 5

Where is she?" Spence didn't even wait for a proper greeting from Cat's cousin, Jessica. "I must see her."

He strode toward the lady as she sailed forward with a swiftness he knew came from anger and curiosity. Even in his own despair, a portion of his beleaguered mind noted Jessica Leighton-Curtis's unmistakable family resemblance to her older relative. The sleek body, slightly taller than Cat's. The mane of hair, strawberry gold in Jessica's case. Wide-set eyes, aquamarine . . . and blinking in confusion at him, though she held his calling card in her hand.

Suddenly she dropped it to the silver salver on the hall table as if it were poison.

"I am afraid, sir, the whereabouts of my cousin is none of your business."

"Please don't toy with me, Jess." His agonized tone and the use of her given name produced the desired result.

Her blue eyes softened but only momentarily. Her regal bearing, much like that of her cousin, gratified but also irritated him. This morning, Jess manned the bastion of family pride that had stood between him and Cat. He had to find a way beyond those walls.

Jess clasped her hands together like a soprano ready to belt him. "You barge into our home at this ungodly hour of the morning and ask for my cousin who is otherwise engaged."

"She certainly *is* engaged. To *me!*"

Jess gaped. "I sincerely doubt that, my lord." She gathered her skirts in one hand, a look of dismissal smooth on her brow. "Pool, show Lord Lyonns to the door." With that, she swept up the train of her delft blue dimity and turned.

He wouldn't let her throw him out like this! Insistence couldn't work. He'd try reason. "Jessica, you must hear me out. I was at the Billingtons' this weekend. I was with Cat. We got on! We *talked.*"

Jessica spun, her eyes sure blue fire. "Dorrie would never do that to Cat. She knows how Cat feels about you."

"Yes, and you know hate is not the word that fits how Cat cares for me."

"I can think of a few strong synonyms, my lord."

With a glance at the noddering butler who obligingly stood by waiting to toss him out on his ear, Spence moderated his voice and his stance. "Potent ones, yes. But I assure you none of those words are ones we should discuss except in private."

"Pool has been with the Leightons since my mother and Cat's were in the nursery together. He can hear all."

From the servants' stairs, a short, dark furry figure emerged to lounge against the doorjam and stare at Spence. The monkey, whom Cat had irreverently named Darwin and who considered himself a member of the family, folded his arms and waited for an explanation as if he were a brother.

Behind him, Bones came to sit and gloat.

Spence's sense of propriety snapped. He knew from past experience that servants cut an important swath with their constant snippets of information about their employers. Worse, Spence remembered this butler was an interfering sort, ready to burst into any discussion and offer advice. Spence was damned if he was taking chances with Cat's reputation with *anyone* ever again. But he was outraged that a five-year-old macaque in short pants and an aged dog who had the bad manners to *point* at him should stand in judgment of him! "I assure you I do not wish to *say* all until I know whom I can trust."

"A rather surprising word for you, isn't it, my lord?"

"Jess, I know how you must think of me. You have good reason. Let me assure you there were mitigating circumstances three years ago."

"Enough to leave Cat at the altar?" she scoffed.

"Yes! Last night, too, there were good reasons she left the Billingtons."

"She's left the Billingtons?" Alarm spread across her porcelain complexion, draining it of any pink. *"Why?"*

"My God." Spence felt his heart drop. "Then she's really not here. Where could she be?"

The aged servant muttered to himself so fiercely, Jess turned to him. "Pool? Pool," she gently urged the tall bald man who snapped his lips inside his mouth, "what do you know of this?"

The servant's sharp eyes ran over Spence with distaste bordering disgust. In the fulsome tones Pool brought with him from years upon the boards in

Drury Lane theaters, he delivered the knell that "Lady Catherine is not here."

Jess flapped her hands at her sides. "Pool, we're undone. Do tell us where she is then!"

"She was here and left again quickly. I promised my lady I would not reveal it until you'd had your breakfast."

Jess sighed. "Very well. I understand your position. Bring us some tea and toast in the morning room, will you, Pool? Lord Lyonns, if you would come with me, please?"

Adrift in fear, Spence accepted the small sign of help from Jessica. Cat had told him of her younger cousin's staunch love for her family, but he'd never seen it in action. He was only too eager to rely on her himself, and he followed her with Darwin on his heels, jabbering away at Bones. Monkey talk, Spence surmised, for "Throw the bastard out." Followed by canine replies of grumble, grumble, grumble.

As Jess closed the huge oak doors behind the jabbering party, Spence made his way across to the bay window that looked out over the gardens he had strolled so often with Cat. He paused there, at a loss as how to appeal to Jess to help him. The ruby rhododendrons would soon bloom. The roses, too. Then the irises, huge petals of deep violet, so like her eyes. Eyes filled with tears like last night.

Christ, Cat, where have you gone?

"Do sit down, Spence—I may call you that, I hope. I know of you in that way best."

He turned to see her features soften as the dog took up a post at her feet and the monkey climbed up to perch on the arm of her settee. Well guarded now, Jess was joined by a white angora cat who crept from a sunny spot near the fireplace to nestle at her side. The animal was the one he'd found outside his club one morning rummaging in the trash bins. He'd brought the rare but scraggly creature to Cat, knowing she'd take care of her, restore her to soundness as she had so many others. As she had Spence.

As she would soon again and he would her.

"Tell me what happened at Dorrie's." Jess looked pained. "Why were you there? Cat never knew of it, or if she did, she didn't mention it to me. She would have, I think. She tells me everything."

He couldn't sit. Ever since he realized Cat had fled the Billingtons', he'd become a ball of nerves, frantic to find her, knowing she was hurt, confused. "Cat didn't tell you I was to be a guest there because she had no idea. Dorrie didn't reveal it to her."

"That's not like Dorrie. Cat will be disappointed in her friend. She expects as much devotion as she gives." Aquamarine eyes sliced him, cutting him open like serrated knives, laying bare his failure.

"I know that. I have always known."

Jessica Leighton-Curtis, wherever she came from, whatever her background, had the great common courtesy to simply sit, tilt her head at him, and wait.

He breathed deeply, an act of agony amid the punishment of the morning. To think he had almost persuaded Cat to overcome the past and marry him and then to know he had lost her—again. Ah, it was a killing moment when the Billingtons' upstairs maid had announced Cat gone.

"Bag and baggage, milady," she had told Dorrie and Spence after the staff had scoured the manor for some sign of Cat. "The stable boy says she asked for a carriage at half past five. She went home, mum. Took her 'orse, too."

Dorrie had taken the blame. But Spence quickly corrected her impression, revealing to her and

Blanding and Rand what had happened on the balcony in the early hours of the morning.

"She's scared," is what Dorrie had said then, and it was now what Spence told Jessica. "With some reason." He quickly told her of events at the manor throughout the past few days and summarized in polite terms what occurred last night with Marietta Hornsby. "Looking back on that, I wonder if perhaps, in the emotional turmoil, Cat simply didn't realize that the woman had been put in her place."

As he spoke, he watched numerous emotions flicker across Jessica's pristine features. First came joy at Cat's admission—tacit though it was—that she cared for Spence, then surprise at Marietta's liaison, and finally distress at Cat's discovery in such dishabille. "You should have expected Cat would be repelled by the idea of any more scandal. She has suffered more than you know. It has taken every ounce of her willpower to recover from her father's death and to even think of opening this school."

"I can imagine. But she is very strong."

"Very stubborn."

"I know that for certain. What I do not know is where she's gone. *Where* might that be, Jess?"

Jessica considered her hands in her lap for the longest time. But a knock at the door and the entry of Pool meant she spent the next few minutes pouring tea. Even then the bug-eyed, doddering butler stood behind her, shuffling from one foot to the next and talking to himself. Meanwhile, the cat gave Spence the evil eye. The monkey delivered a piece of his mind, and the decrepit dog set his yellow teeth in full display for Spence.

The dog had his reasons, as did the others, of course. Protection was their game. Even without Cat here.

"Your tea, my lord," Jess offered. "Pool, thank you, you may leave us."

The old fellow shook his head.

"Lord Lyonns will not make any scenes and I have quite enough guards, wouldn't you say?"

Jess waited until the butler had fumed and then snapped shut the doors before she glanced at Spence. "My uncle Walter said Pool was always very loyal to the Leightons because he insisted he was one himself. Born on the wrong side of the blanket to an actress and Cat's and my grandfather."

"I see," Spence said as he accepted his cup from her hand. He took a drink of his tea, contemplating his precarious situation. "I could be drawn and quartered by a blood-lusting thespian. Or if I prefer I could be scratched, bitten, or talked to death by three animals before I learn a thing. I'm beset on each front and I've only begun. Just tell me where might she have gone, Jess. If you don't give me any ideas, I'll swear I'll hire an investigator. But rest assured, I will find her."

"How can she be that important to you after so many years with no word, no sign that you cared a fig about her?" Her question hardly disguised her rage.

He knew he had to reveal some of the intimate truth about his abandonment. "She's always been vitally important to me, so much so that I could not marry her and hurt her."

"She thought you left her because you didn't love her enough to make her your wife!"

"That may seem like the logical conclusion, but it's not."

They stared at each other. He knew she wanted to know more, but to ask for it was too invasive.

"Logical or ridiculous, she has lived with that. Can you imagine what that's like? It's . . . it's—"

"Heartbreaking. Yes, I saw it, I felt it throughout

the weekend. That's why I've got to find her. I must continue to dispel her idea that I don't care for her. I have to overcome the misery the past three years have brought her."

"Why now?"

"Because I have information now that some of the reasons I left her might not be valid." A generalization though that explanation was, it would have to do.

"Only some of the reasons?" She was confounded. "What does that mean? What kind of information?"

"Information about me"—he swallowed—"and about her father and my brother."

"Good Lord, will that conflict never end?" she whispered in horror. "Does Cat know this 'information'?"

"Not yet."

"Why not?"

"I never had a chance to tell her. She spent most of the weekend avoiding me."

"Rightly so, too. But will you tell her?"

"It might hurt her more and I am loath to—"

She was outraged. "You expect me to help you for that? You cannot tell me the important things? Cannot say *why* you would leave her the day of your wedding? Whatever my uncle Walter and your brother Merrick had against each other, you assured Cat during your engagement that your mutual love was grand enough to ignore it. How could that change in a few hours? Why was Walter's and Merrick's bitterness suddenly bigger and more awful than your love for Cat?"

"It wasn't!"

Jess reeled on that and flung out a hand. "Riddles! They are not good enough here with me, Spence. What happened? Did you suddenly learn Cat was a social disgrace? A criminal? An embezzler?"

He winced. "I had cause to believe that your uncle was involved in a nefarious scheme."

"Another one? Forgive me, I've lost count. I suppose it was Merrick who told you."

"Correct."

"Merrick," she huffed, trying to recover composure.

"His judgment was impeccable in public and private matters. I never before had reason to doubt him."

"I am so delighted for you both," she said through tight lips. "That did nothing for *my* loved ones. My uncle Walter and your brother *never* got along. The whole of London knew it. Everyone in the Historical Society. The Foreign Office, too. From my uncle Walter's perspective, your brother Merrick blocked his efforts to excavate ancient Egyptian sites from the first. Lambasting his archaeological methods. Criticizing his ideas to the newspapers. The upshot was Uncle Walter had a devil of a time even getting funding for his expeditions. Not until Cat took over the bookkeeping did the accounts ever show any black ink."

"You know as well as I that the red ink came not only from Walter's inefficiencies in administration but also because his erstwhile secretary was less than pure."

"Yes. We found that out courtesy of Merrick's interference, too, didn't we? Calling Uncle Walter before the board of the Historical Society six years ago for financial improprieties was a public disgrace of my uncle that did not need to occur. If Merrick had wanted to, he could have asked the Society to hold a closed-door session."

"You weren't living with Cat and her father then—"

"No, but they told me two years ago when I arrived, and what they said sounded sordid."

"I agree. Things could have been done differently. But they weren't. Like you, I don't know the details. During the hearings, I was posted to Japan as military attaché to the new emperor's court. I do know that Walter acquitted himself of any wrongdoing because it was clear from the testimony, from the ledgers, and from the secret bank accounts that Walter's private secretary was to blame. He, and he alone, embezzled the public funds that were to support Walter's expeditions to Karnak. But that's the extent of what I know of the incident. Before I learned any of it—or knew any more than the fact that Walter and Merrick were foes—I met Cat socially quite by accident. But from the second I saw her, Jess, I knew we were meant to be together."

His sincerity was not lost on her. Her eyes misting, she was blocked at the impasse of her own care of her cousin while he balked at his own inability to reveal private secrets that were also state matters. He had to concentrate on one at a time.

Jess sat unmoving. "You sound so convincing. But you didn't love her enough to marry her despite whatever wrong you thought her father committed."

He clenched his jaw at her well-struck arrow. "On the contrary, I cared for her too much to tear her between loyalty to me and to her father." She had been right about that the other day. Their marriage would not have survived such a war. "I chose to set her free."

"I find it hard to believe you couldn't find a better way. A better time."

"Merrick came home from Cairo the day before the wedding and told me something he could never put in writing. I was surprised, devastated—so much so that

I knew if I did go to Cat and tell her, I'd want to marry her anyway. I thought I might even try to abduct her." He laughed bitterly, then squeezed his eyes shut. "I would have made both our lives a living hell."

"But that has happened in any case," she said on a desperate thread.

"Now things are different."

"How different?"

"Merrick and Walter are gone."

"Are the issues they quarreled over?"

"I'm not sure."

She stared at him. Nothing moved except the dust motes floating in the sun. His heart slogged on until she perceived enough of what he'd left unsaid that she finally asked, "What is your role in this is exactly?"

He placed his tea on a table and strode to Jess.

Bones growled. The cat hissed. The monkey chittered at him.

"He won't hurt me," Jess crooned to the three, and Spence saw them relax but move closer to her.

Undeterred, Spence took the wing chair opposite her and leaned forward. If honesty about his emotions had drawn Jess this far, he'd show her more of them. "I still adore her, Jess. I never stopped. I tried to, I did, for her sake and mine. But now that I have some question that I may have been wrong to leave her, I also have hope that I can revive whatever happiness Cat and I were meant to have together. Don't forget, I have seen her now. Talked with her. She cares for me. I have tasted it on her lips."

His bluntness made Jess sink back in her chair.

"Yes. I kissed her, Jess, and she did more than return the passion, she doubled it. Had Marietta Hornsby not come along last night, Cat would be mine in body, if not soul, this morning and no one—

not even Cat herself—would say otherwise. I don't want to ruin her, Jess. I want to care for her in the countless ways a man can for his loved one. For his *wife.*" He straightened. "I need to have the chance. If you won't help me find her, so be it. I'll do it anyway. I have resources, Jess. Money, friends, influence, that I'll use until I'm bankrupt of them all."

He paused and then asked quietly, "Didn't you ever want a second chance? Haven't you ever needed someone who would give you an opportunity to correct a past mistake?"

She went still as stone. She looked beyond him. Whether she viewed her past or a future, he couldn't say. He only knew she returned to gaze at him with compassion. "Yes. The people who gave it to me were Catherine and my uncle Walter. That's another reason why I am reluctant to do anything to hurt them."

He took her hand and squeezed it though the cat jumped, the dog seized his ankle, and the monkey screeched in protest.

"Stop that," she ordered them sternly until they resumed their wary stances.

Spence took his seat. "I can tell you many do trust me. I have done well in the army. As an officer in my regiment, I have been decorated often for my service at home and abroad. I've won just as many citations for skill and bravery. The men under my command value my judgment. My fellow officers do. Some in the government."

"Meaning Blanding?"

"Yes. Rand Templeton and many of his friends. Others, too."

He let that sink in, unable to tell her the one other who trusted him above and beyond anyone else, but he could hope she'd understand the implication.

"Am I to conclude, Spence, that because of these certain others that you were able to persuade Blanding and Dorrie to allow you into the party these past few days?"

"If you want to know if my personal motive to find your cousin is noble, I can only claim it is. I can't prove it except by showing you. For now, I'll do what I can and tell you that Blanding trusted me enough and Dorrie, too—if that's the better test of my intentions—that they allowed me near Cat again."

"What happens to Cat if you discover that the reason you left her is a valid one? Tell me, Spence, can you put aside your affection for your brother to love my cousin as she should be?"

"I'll move heaven and earth to make it so."

Jess's aqua eyes hardened to glass. Her whole body filled with a righteous anger the likes of which Spence had seen a few times. On such occasions, he had stood on a battlefield. He braced himself for a zealous assault.

"Don't you believe the sins of the father extend unto future generations?"

"If it is so that Walter committed a crime—yes, Jess, a *crime*—I won't let his actions affect Catherine's life with me."

"Determination is a commendable trait, Spence. But how do you think Cat will feel living with a man who may have the proof to utterly destroy her father's reputation?"

"Word of what happens here will never be made public."

"How convenient to have the government sweep things under the rug. But what if Walter is not to blame for this matter you investigate? Tarnished as he must be by this very inquiry into his actions, will it be possible to make his innocence known to those concerned?

"Yes, I'll see that is done."

"Even if your brother's reputation falls to pieces?"

"Even that."

At his promise, she peered into his eyes as if she'd excise his brain, pick through for every fact, each emotion he'd ever experienced, and exhume every lie he'd ever told. This—he could finally see by the satisfied look on her face—was not one of them.

"If you hurt her again—"

"Never."

"—you may die an unpleasant death."

Hope sent his heartbeat thudding. "By your hand, I assume."

"I'd be only the first in line."

"Pool would be second." He nodded at the three animals. "With this menagerie not far behind, I think."

At Spence's amused tone, the dog woofed. The monkey frowned. The angora sent him a nasty glare.

Spence nodded. "I would deserve nothing less from all five of you."

Jess placed her tea on the small table, and he thought he'd won until she breathed deeply and said, "I suppose I won't be imparting anything to you that Dorrie or Blanding don't know or couldn't tell you. But there is a problem."

The desolate look on her face made his breath stop.

"Cat may not be able to marry you."

His heart practically leaped from his chest. "Why?"

"She has plans, Spence." Jess avoided his eyes and licked her lips.

"Are you telling me she's interested in another man? That she's run off to marry—"

"Stop, Spence. There is no other man." She fixed him with bold aquamarine defiance. "I wished often over the past three years there were another man, but there isn't."

"Then what is it?" His mind raced, finding reasons that made no sense. "She's ill? Incur—"

"No, it's not that bad. But to her, just as awful."

"For pity's sake, Jess, what?"

"She needs money!"

"Money?" The idea struck him like a bolt of lightning. Numb, he wrinkled his brow at Jess.

"She's gone to London. She must have. She was to leave here tomorrow after she returned from Dorrie's."

"How much money does she need?" Spence's head began to clear. From the lavish gowns he'd seen her in these past few days, he wouldn't have thought she needed a quid for the rest of her days. "For what?"

"A new boiler system to heat the water for the new bathrooms in Farrell Old Hall." She inclined her head across the gardens to the brick structure that had been the family residence of the first Baron Farrell. "We need it for the dormitories for the girls."

"Boilers? You'll knock English boarding school headmasters—and mistresses—on their rumps! Hadn't you heard that cold water, *frigid* water, is best for children, my dear?" he asked, incredulous but delighted.

"You know Cat. She will have this for her students. Nothing will keep her from making this school into the prime of its kind. Nothing," she said and focused on Spence.

"I understand. And believe me, I don't want to take that from her."

"It's been one of her dreams that have held the broken pieces of her heart together for three years."

"When first I met her, she spoke of this in the same exalted tones as she did her father."

"She won't let it die, Spence. Not even . . ." Jessica's eyes faceted in blue shards of agony. "Not even if the two of you do manage to find some happiness together. She's dedicated to it as her own self-fulfillment. She won't hand over control of that to a man. Can you understand that?"

He took both of Jessica's hands. "I don't want to destroy Cat's dreams, Jess. I want to help her build them into realities. You have got to believe me."

"If I do, will you promise me two things?"

He smiled at this ironic twist that the cousin would trust him after a conversation filled with scarce more than generalities. But then the cousin had never suffered betrayal and abandonment by him either. "Name them."

"You will not try to dissuade her from her need to perform each of her obligations to her past."

"Done. Whatever she wants to do—"

"Finish writing her father's memoirs."

He stared at Jessica. So the rumors were true that Cat wanted to publish such a work. It was the very thing, the perfect thing, he needed her to do if he were to gain easy access to Walter's papers and discover the truth of what had happened between the man and Merrick as well as the missing papyrus. His blood turned to ice, but then it warmed with his desperation to have Cat with him again. He'd find a way to dodge the pitfalls, solve the problems, win her back. "Whatever Cat wants to do, Jess, I promise you she can with me as her husband."

"Will you support her and protect her no matter what she needs to do to open this school?"

"Again, done. Although I am not certain I understand what you mean." The word *support,* he understood, but *protect* worried him. What was Jess implying?

"I mean if Cat needs to borrow money, take us into debt to buy that boiler and open this school, you won't—as her husband and therefore as her legal overseer of her money and estate—refuse her the ability to take a loan at a bank."

"Is that what she's doing?" Spence practically hooted in relief. Hell, he'd thought from the way Jess acted that Cat was going to borrow money from a less than savory source—or that she needed to do so.

"Yes, I'm certain she's gone to London. She was to go not only for the opening of her father's and uncle's private exhibit of Egyptian jewelry but also to keep an appointment with the chairman of her bank. Both are scheduled for day after tomorrow."

"Does she still bank in the City at Thornhill's?" At Jess's nod, Spence let his mind race. He knew the bank well. So, too, its chairman. Much of his own resources he kept within their vaults. "What time?"

"Ten o'clock."

"Did she plan to stay at Eaton Square?"

"Yes, with her uncle Dominik."

"I thought he took a house on Brompton Road."

"He did until last year. Walter left the family townhouse to him in his will. Cat told her father she'd never live in London after what happened between you two."

Spence squeezed her hand. "I understand. Social lions can be cruel."

"So can other lions."

"Never again, Jess."

"I believe you. I hope I'm not being foolish."

"Trust your instincts."

"That's what Cat always says."

"Even today?"

"Yes. Despite everything, she's never said a word against you. Yet because I have watched her in pain over this, I know that continuing to care for you has been an oppressive burden to her. I know that if I ever loved a man as much as she does you and he left me, I would hate him for eternity."

Spence leaned over and kissed her cheek. This time, no creature objected. "I think you and I will enjoy a long friendship, Jess. I thank God you are not Cat."

"Charm helps," she told him with a twitch of her lips.

Spence stood up and offered her his hand. "I'll try to remember that with you. When the right man comes along for you, my lady, I think I'll give him a few pointers on the way to your heart."

She shook her head. "You'll not do much talking. There is no such man and never will be."

He opened his mouth, the objection ready on his lips.

"Hadn't you better be packing?" She tossed her golden red curls, a young woman of meteoric moods, fire and porcelain. "I'm eager to see this over with now that I have given away her one vulnerability."

He grinned. "But I know why you did it, Jess. You knew helping her with money was one thing I could do to begin to show her how much I cared."

"You can then?" Jess arched delicate brows, not asking the horrid financial question in any forthright manner. "Thank God. Without danger to her pride, I hope?"

"Absolutely. Since I have come into the earldom, I have more money than this bachelor knows how to spend. I assure you I'll waste no time applying it—in the most palatable manner—to the best investment in young women's education I could make: in Cat's future and your's."

"Yours, too, my lord."

He grinned. "I'll start by giving Cat money for a boiler and see what I can provide afterward. It's everything to me that you gave me this information."

"See you don't botch it, will you?"

"For you, my dear, and for Cat, I shall be the most gentlemanly of men."

"You have only a short time, you realize. Our first term begins in August."

He was already headed for the door when he turned to give her an extravagant bow. "But my dearest cousin, I have even less time than that. London's most fashionable weddings are in June."

Jess beamed at him. "Two months, Spence." Then her delicate features began to shatter. "Is it enough?"

"It's more than I'd ever hoped for."

"But we can't wait until June!"

"Rand, there's no alternative. How soon or how easily did you think I would have access to Farrell's effects under the original plan of simply becoming Cat's friend?" Feeling sullied by this necessary discussion of the whereabouts of the papyrus he needed to hand over to the government and pass on to the khedive, Spence reached for his cigar case from his coat pocket and flipped it open in Rand's direction.

Rand took one and in the afternoon dimness of the lavish brougham, his striking of a match allowed Spence to examine Rand's eyes. Spence saw his wariness.

"What's different about the plan now?"

"Only that instead of becoming amiable with Cat, I'm going to marry her."

Rand sank into the recesses of Spence's coach. "You are mad as the proverbial hatter."

"Definitely."

"But I must say this variation bodes for more success."

"That's what I thought."

"Not for your marriage, however."

Spence drew on his cigar. "I'll ensure nothing disastrous happens."

"You and I know that will take a lot of doing."

"Yes," Spence said, "I am too well aware of it."

"Anyone need only look at Cat to know she hasn't forgotten what happened three years ago, Spence. If she finds out that you're trying to rifle her father's papers after you're married, how the hell do you think she'll forgive and forget that?"

"She won't."

"So?"

"I'll be so good at this she'll never know." It would be the second secret he would keep from her. Along with the first one, that her father had forged an ancient papyrus. He'd keep his promise to Jess so well, Cat need never know if her father were a forger and a thief. As for himself, if he never spoke Walter Farrell's name again, it would be too soon. He vowed he wouldn't utter Merrick's either. What was past was finished. He wanted Cat. Her happiness. He would buy it at any price. Even silence.

"Spence, damn it, you're insane."

"I'll find a way. Cat does not read Coptic nor has she any knowledge of hieroglyphics. If Walter took this papyrus and hid it, even if Cat found it, she could not decipher it herself. Cat was her father's administrator, not his assistant researcher. Be calm, Rand. Remember, I am very good at what I do."

"How the hell can I forget? Without you, we wouldn't know why the Prussians won the war against France or why the Russian general staff seems so intrigued with India."

"You have no reason then to doubt me."

"Spence, I don't. It's only that this mission is different for you. We've known it from the first."

"I said I would do it and I am."

"Christ, *I* know you're as good as your word. But this case is unique. You are very personally involved."

"Even if I weren't, the Foreign Office and your friends could not find anyone who could do the job as well. No one speaks Coptic, reads hieroglyphics, *and* knows ancient Egyptian history. No one has the vaguest reason to ask to see Walter's effects. No one knows Cat nor has any reason to introduce himself to gain access to her father's papers. I wouldn't allow anyone to *pretend* affection for her just to have entry to her home. Only I have all the qualifications required for this job. Admit it—in all its irony—and give over, Rand. I'll get the information we need."

"You and I have been friends a long time, Spence. I've watched what the last few years have done to you. Some good and some bad."

"Soul-searching has great benefits. But the extreme solitude required wears on one. It's not pretty, is it?"

"I'm relieved that you are finally able to see that. I am even more comforted that you never took up the pastimes Merrick found so habit-forming."

Spence flinched at the mention of Merrick's cause of death. "Hashish is not my idea of a beneficial cure. Nor is cocaine or liquor or prostitutes."

"No, work is. But if you can't find this letter from Ramses to Moses, *your* reputation will go up in flames."

"Small consolation, you are." Spence dragged at his cigar, hated it, and opened the window to throw it out.

"It's not my purpose to console you but to aid you."

"Then tell me things I don't already know."

"Oh, Christ. You won't let me talk you out of the idea of marriage to Catherine Farrell. I can't tell you how devastated you'll be if she ever learns of your secondary—shall we say—occupation. I am not to speak of the possibility that if the men we seek are not caught soon, they may just destroy our shipping and our entire foreign policy. I tell you it is fascinating, old man, that you are suddenly deaf." When silence strung out interminably, Rand sighed and said, "Very well, I surrender. What can I provide in the way of new information?"

"How would Whitehall and your friends view the publication of Walter Farrell's memoirs?"

"So, Cat's going to do it, eh?" Rand blew out a gust of smoke. "I hope she can keep her objectivity about her father as she writes it."

"Cat, I think, has always understood her father was a man with faults. Because others attacked him, she never did. But then I don't think she ever needed to. Walter Farrell was a very good father. But what of your friends in commerce and shipping? What of those in Parliament with Blanding? Those men are a different kettle of fish."

"Yes, God help us. At this particular moment with Disraeli positioned to take the seat of prime minister, I doubt those in the Foreign Office would jump for joy. They want the khedive kept happy by handing over that papyrus. Walter Farrell believed in stripping Egypt of its antiquities and bringing them home to the capital of modern civilization as we know it. Publication of anything faintly smacking of Farrell's imperialistic tone, even if Disraeli privately does think Farrell a saint, would not help to calm the khedive or make him sign any treaty with us for the Suez canal. Nothing must stop that or Disraeli's plan to create an empire for Great Britain."

"I didn't think so. Walter Farrell always was persona non grata. Even if his idea that it was Britain's burden to civilize the world was approved by some in high places."

"Farrell was too caustic. Too egocentric. The man spent half his time ridiculing others rather than unearthing the treasures he claimed to love."

"He didn't make friends easily."

Rand snorted. "Nor keep them."

"Still, he was a noted scholar. If he'd stuck to the first, then Merrick would not have tangled with him."

"Then we wouldn't have this conundrum."

"True," Spence said and then added in a stoic voice that belied his concern for his long-time friend, "You really do hate this, don't you, Rand?"

"How can you doubt I like order?"

Spence crossed his arms and wondered how his friend kept the facade of indifference polished at all times. "I need to see you bleed now and then to know you're alive."

"Thank you very much." Spence could feel the electricity of Rand's shocked smile. "You, too, can be dismissed!"

Laughter rumbled from Spence's chest. "Not in this case, I can't."

"No, dammit, I tried. I went to see her the other day."

Spence knew by Rand's tone whom he meant. Spence had not seen his queen in three years and likely wouldn't any time soon. At least not until after he found this papyrus. It wouldn't do to have anyone suspect his role here. "She is well, I assume?"

"Very, but concerned for you and Cat. I went to ask her to appoint someone else, you know. I told her it would be wise to enlist a man more detached from the issues."

"I'm not angry, Rand. I see your point of view. But I am very glad she didn't allow you to dissuade her."

"She wouldn't hear of any substitutes. She knows, though she'd never voice it, of course, about what happened three years ago. She wants an end to this riddle for you and Catherine as well as for her own reasons. She believes in love and marriage. So I don't doubt, chum, she approved of you being put on this case so that you and Catherine might find a way back to each other."

"I will make certain of it. Reassure her of that when you have your next audience, will you?"

"First thing." The sound of the horses' hooves clomping along the deserted road to London filled up the carriage and gave Spence a steady satisfaction for the first time in years. "She refused to replace you because she says you embody the finest elements of your regiment's motto."

" 'Second to none.' She has a soft spot in her heart for the Coldstream Guards. We've always belonged to the queen."

"She's counting on you."

"I'll make her happy," he vowed and meant another woman who deserved that and everything else he could give her.

Chapter 6

Cat put down her pen, stunned—and yet not—at the tight-lipped butler's announcement. "I'm sorry, Marsh. I don't believe I heard you correctly."

"Lord Lyonns is here to see you," declared the servant with censure in his frigid eyes.

"Absurd." Cat rose from her chair and her eternal mathematics. Beset by the need to hand over a papyrus she had no clue on how to find, she was thwarted by the plumbers to pay for her boiler before they ordered it from Manchester. She also had to decide how to persuade Thornhill Bank and Trust to grant her ten thousand more pounds than the boiler cost without them suspecting her real use of the money.

But her worries over obtaining the money had taken second place during the weekend to warding off Spence's advances. Driven insane by his persistence and her undeniable desire for him, she had escaped him yesterday morning—or so she'd thought. She had to rummage through this house for a strip of ancient paper, persuade an unimaginative banker to lend her a whopping pot of money—and avoid Spencer Lyonns completely.

Why didn't he just accept her rejection and go quietly back to his club and his regiment? Why couldn't he step out of her way and out of her dreams? "Tell him I am not at home."

"But you most certainly are."

She dug her nails into the upholstery at the sight of him, regal in umber top hat, chocolate Chesterfield, and matching kid gloves.

"Lord Lyonns," she addressed him with protocol in front of Marsh who had been her father's man for a decade until his displeasure over her monkey Darwin's dancing in the servants' quarters had him fleeing to her uncle Dominik. "I trust you will understand I am indisposed."

"But it is teatime, Baroness," Spence contradicted as he came forward, whirled off his coat, and deposited it, hat, and gloves into Marsh's grudgingly outstretched hands. "It is acceptable that a gentleman call at this hour, isn't it, Marsh?" Spence challenged the implacable ducklike creature, who deigned to offer a resentful affirmative. "There, you see?"

Cat stiffened. "I have not called for tea for guests."

"But you will. Don't you think she should, Marsh?" Spence asked as he undid the bottom button of his double-breasted chestnut glen plaid suitcoat to reveal a matching vest. It and the creamy cambric shirt beneath made his skin deliciously golden and his eyes darkly primal. "Do not, however, rush. I have as much time as necessary."

The butler, caught between his former mistress and her former fiancé, found no ground on which to stand

and so departed with a blast from his nostrils. That left Cat facing Spence with the fury of an animal cornered but not caught. When the door clicked closed, she counterattacked.

"How can you do this? Where did you leave your carriage? My uncle is not at home and I object to you coming here like this, uninvited, and barging in. The whole world will know it and once more, I will be—"

"Redeemed."

"Really? You have an odd definition of it, my lord."

"Cat, I assure you everything is in order. I left my carriage outside, but Rand arrives momentarily and then Lord Chiltern with his wife."

"Chil—" she caught herself keening. "You're daffy."

He grinned, his teeth flashing white in his tanned face. "For three years past, but no longer."

"Ugh. You're incorrigible! Why would those people come here to call when no one knows I'm here?"

"Invite me to sit, Cat. So should you, I think. It will calm your nerves."

"If we speak of nerve, my lord, I think you have it all. How could you, Spence! I am not even dressed for company. Good grief, the Chilterns!"

"Even if you had the time to change, which you don't, you look smashing in the strawberry," he said, nonplussed. "As for the Chilterns, they were delighted to accept your invitation."

"My invitation?" She stepped toward him, hands clenched. He had the devilish bad manners to chuckle, take her fists, and kiss each one. "Oh, Spence," she mourned, loving the feel of his mouth on her skin, and sank to a chair with a thud, "I am ruined."

"Breathe deeply, Cat. In a minute you'll see things clearly and rally." He took the giant white tapestry rococo chair opposite her, arranging himself in the relaxed position of a welcomed, frequent guest to her drawing room.

"I think I do already. The invitation I received this morning from Lord and Lady Marlow to attend their opening ball this Saturday was your idea, wasn't it?"

"No," he said as if it were the gospel truth, "it was not."

She wanted to believe him and yet remained ever so wary. "The Marlows have no need to court me, Spence."

"I am afraid I have little firsthand knowledge of what the Marlows might need. You'll have to ask them yourself."

She wanted to say she had no intention of going, but it would have been a lie, said just to rattle him.

"No one refuses them." His eyes searched hers for her intentions, and she knew the man who did so was the military man, the observer of detail, finite and ineffable.

She couldn't look at him for long without her heart slamming about in her chest like some crazed cricket ball. She swallowed, and his gaze fell to her throat where her pulse gave her away. She gulped while he examined her gauze cravat bow, its large cameo, and her throat.

Bold to the bone in his scrutiny, he let his focus go to her mouth and then to her eyes as he added the final caveat, "There is the fact that the Marlows do have three daughters, one of whom I understand is just the sort you and your cousin say you wish to help. She is high-strung, unmanageable."

Cat bit her lower lip. He was right.

Fearing what tales Marietta Hornsby might spread about the scene on the balcony and knowing she might see Spence at the Marlows' ball, Cat had debated accepting their invitation for hours. On numerous occasions, Cat had heard Dorrie mention Corinne Marlow, a ten-year-old with the inability to sit quietly and the capacity to drive her doting parents to hair-tearing despair. But she never thought the Marlows might consider allowing her and Jessica the chance to help them or Corinne. Now, if she went to the Marlows' fete, she was probably being summoned to be inspected, and if she passed muster, she might truly be admitted to the wider social circles she so required for the school's success. Certainly, her attendance at the Marlows' would be seen as her unconditional acceptance, a more complete avowal than she had last weekend where everyone knew she was invited by her best friend, Dorrie Billington.

With a flare of her hands, Cat admitted to herself that she was trapped between her need to have her school and her desire to avoid Spence completely. She rose and spun to stand before the fire. Curling her arms about her, she felt the flames but saw only ashes of her past. "I want this school very badly, Spence."

"I want whatever you do, Cat."

"I never doubted that but should have. On instinct, I don't even now. I never thought you perverse, only misinformed. But, for pity sake, why are you here?" She turned, and she couldn't cover or convert the tormented look she knew she wore. "Why suddenly"—she cast her hands out—"why *now* do you come to me and do this?"

The bravura he'd flaunted these past few minutes died. In its place rose a melancholy more debilitating to her composure. "Because," he said on bare breath, "I have come home to England from India after months of contemplation and searching for sound answers, and I discover I was wrong. About a lot of things."

"Finding you were wrong doesn't mean you can put things right."

"I can try."

"When it's too painful to others, it's best to abandon the project, Spence."

"I can't leave it—or you—alone any longer. Didn't what happened this past weekend prove that to you?"

"No," she shot back. "What happened only proved to me I can't trust—" She stumbled on the next revelation.

"Me."

"No," she offered with a shiver that made her clutch her elbows. Her horror at how she'd nearly suggested taking him to her bed the night before last washed over her. Her gaze wandered in misery to his. "Me."

His eyes blazed green fire. But amazingly, he remained in his chair. "I promise you I have not come today to persuade you with any physical displays of what we mean to each other. That would only blunt issues that need more refinement. Besides, that we are attracted to each other till the sun ceases to burn is a fact we have already proven." At her intake of breath, he set his too damnably assured jaw, then went on, "I have come here to do the rational thing and talk to you calmly, Cat."

She bristled at his gall, even though she welcomed his approach. "I have nothing to say."

"I do."

"Well, to you, I am deaf."

His mouth toyed with mirth. "But not totally insensitive."

"Spence, you are"—she chose the word she had promised herself to adopt—*"irrelevant* to me."

He chortled while his eyes sparkled with mischief.

"Perhaps you'd prefer to think so. Life would be simpler without me. But am I irrelevant? Quite apparently not. I'd offer a few substitute words. Let's start with *unforgettable.*" She shrank in her skin at his intimate understanding. "We'll add—from evidence of this weekend—*irresistible.*"

No. Her mouth formed the soundless lie. She swayed backward to feel the mantle across her shoulders, and her mind whirled at his effrontery—and his truths.

"Therefore, we can conclude—now that I am here and offering iron-clad restitution—with the word I find most appropriate in these particular circumstances. *Indispensable.*"

"You're awfully sure of yourself."

He went to stone. "No, I wasn't when I walked into the Billingtons' ball Friday night. But then I was the man whose tuxedo jacket you found comforting." His voice dropped. "And rather than touch me, I was the man you sent into the cellars at the Wild Hare." He let every word caress her tingling body. "I was the man who held you in his arms on that balcony Sunday night. I was the one who felt you melt through my skin while you forgot everything except me. So do not tell me of what evidence I have to the contrary. If Marietta had not come along, you, my lovely Cat, would have led me to your bed or—considering the trip might have lasted too long—you would have taken me right there, standing up, a virgin in her first time, hot to have me no matter the place or time or who might see."

She shuddered at his insight while he went on, his voice a swath of velvet silk against her ragged nerves.

"The issue of whether or not you still care for me aside, this matter of defining your nature persists. Which of course, occasions the next question: If it is

112

not to be me with whom you share your passion, it must be someone. It should be soon. So do tell me, my Cat, to whom will you *give* that sexuality—"

She stifled a moan as her whole body flushed.

"To whom will you entrust that wild desire you have inside? Is there another man you know as well or want to know? Is there a peer of the realm, a member of Parliament, a vicar, a greengrocer, perhaps, whom you can say summons feelings within you more than I?" He paused a long moment while she stared at him with tears in her eyes. "Why not share your life and your expectations with me, Cat? Because despite what's passed between us, that sea of emotion you navigate is one I helped you discover. So let us agree there is no need for less than the fullest veracity between us about this: I want you as badly as you want me. I mean to give you everything you want. Always. That said, you can watch it done—and I'll move on to the particulars of how it will be accomplished."

Overwhelmed with his objectivity and his blatant assessment, she balked. "I won't change my mind about this."

"We shall see, won't we?" He lifted one corner of his mouth in a sympathetic smile. "First, I want you to know, Cat, I have made a few decisions about my future. As the earl of Dartmoor now, I have many opportunities open to me that were once inconceivable."

"I'm sure you do." Grateful but wary of his next tactic, she recalled his frustration of being the second-born son centered on how regimented his life had been by his father. "I know how fond of Merrick you were. I'm certain his death left you with many responsibilities."

"The Dartmoor lands are so scattered over England

and Ireland, I fear I might spend half my year going round to every part and parcel."

"I recollect the day you told me if you ever had a plot to call your own, you'd administer it yourself."

"We rode down to the shore."

She strolled into a misty memory of one steamy August afternoon, wicked kisses, and one torrid man. "In your saddlebag you'd hidden champagne and Belgian truffles."

"The chocolate was already melting but more luscious for the taste of your mouth beneath." His eyes embraced hers for the space of two hot, deep breaths. When he spoke, his voice was rough. "That was the same day I confided I'd gladly give up my commission if I could afford my own land."

"I knew you would be a caring lord over any domain God granted you," she whispered, realizing how far into the harmony of their past they'd traveled. She couldn't draw away, though her tone wobbled. "You'll make the earldom the profitable estate it was under your grandfather."

His gentle gaze offered more eloquence than his description. "I hope so. My father was more interested in breeding race horses and breaking in new mistresses. Merrick devoted himself to his diplomacy and his studies and later to his investments in the China trade. I have not only land to manage but a small fortune. To do it well, I cannot remain in the army. I've submitted my resignation, Cat. Within a few months, it should be final."

Joy capped the heat waves of her emotion, and a huge grin spread on her face. "I'm delighted for you, Spence. It's what you've really wanted and needed, too."

His eyes twinkled. "Only you would know that, Cat. Only you approve."

"There are those who don't? But Merrick is gone and your father, too."

A muscle in his jaw worked. "Others would like me to remain."

"Don't listen to them," she pleaded.

"No. I learned that from you but never seized the courage to live in any other way than I was told. I've made up my mind. I'm going to become a gentleman farmer. Experiment with new varieties of vegetables and grains."

Pride blossomed in her chest. "That sounds idyllic."

"It will be. I'll retire to the country, padding about stables and dovecotes, puttering in greenhouses with flowers and seeds. I'll find myself in new territory, I'm afraid. I'll need a companion for such domesticity. Someone to share the harvests and the lean years."

She felt jarred back into reality. "Yes, you will," she said, remembering how Spence had relied on her during their engagement to smooth the way initially for him. At any garden party or reception, anywhere crowds gathered, he required encouragement to mix and mingle with the other guests. After an hour or two, he'd calm down, give over to his natural self, and glide through with colors flying.

Most never suspected his shyness. They thought him debonair, mysterious. The man with the exemplary manners and the enigmatic air. The former because his training had been so rigid. The last because he was shy, the urge to bolt ever with him, his need to find seclusion or diversion a constant companion. Until one day, he claimed the perfect partner was she herself and she believed him. As she wanted to again, God help her.

She squeezed shut her eyes. She felt him sit forward in the chair, the movement of his body like the movement of the sun approaching earth and scalding all, even reason.

"I need someone who likes a quiet life," he said in repetition of her thoughts. "Someone who craves it but who gets by in society easily. I want you," he told her in that marvelous melodious voice. "You helped me find the courage to see myself—and like myself—for what I am. I am no longer what others think I am or wish me to be. I *am* me, *for* me. But more, I want to share me with you, Cat."

Lured and hating her weakness for him, she lifted her chin and grabbed her fleeting courage. "You came with logic. I'll return it in kind. You don't know me anymore, Spence. Many of my views have changed. Living as a spinster I find I enjoy it. I now think that marriage is vastly overrated."

"You once treasured it above everything else—and so you should. You have much to give a husband and children. You saw your parents enjoy bliss."

"That doesn't mean I can or will."

He pursed his lips, considering her words but suppressing a giant smile. "Having had a good example bodes well for your own experience."

"Possibly. But it's no guarantee. Although many criticized my father as an archaeologist, he was a caring husband and parent. He adored my mother. Unlike him, some men drink, gamble. A few keep mistresses."

"Not, however, those who find their wives fascinating in and out of bed. You, sweet Cat, I find scintillating."

She lost her breath and rummaged through her mind for a rejoinder. "Marriage is an unequal relationship. No matter the current laws granting married women control over their own property, practice says the husband influences her and has a right to the proceeds from her endeavors. In my father's will, he made me sole trustee of his estate in spite of the objections of Uncle Dominik and Father's banker, Acton Thornhill. I have no desire to share that power with anyone, certainly not with a husband."

"I assure you that I have too much to occupy me with the upkeep of the disjointed Dartmoor estates to want to add to my workload. What you do with your school will be your own business and your own profit. I will have my solicitor put that in writing."

"Solicitor or not, what would it be worth?"

He paused, his raised brows drawn from affront to understanding and determination. "My honor," he rasped.

"Oh, Spence," she writhed in misery, tempted and torn. "Don't you understand? I cannot *afford* you!"

"My regard for you is freely given, Cat. I want no payment for it other than your company forevermore."

"The price is too high." She stared at him, her heart writhing, tears like a flood ready to burst into her eyes.

"Whatever it is, let me pay the debt to society."

"Men don't seem to do that."

"They do. They make mistakes. Their peers take them to task by withdrawing favor or support."

His implication made her pause while her heart ached for any misfortune he may have suffered. Her need to conceal her regard for vanity's sake fell before her compassion and curiosity. "Have you paid because of what happened between us?"

"Privately, I've walked the corridors of hell in my mind, wishing I had been able to find another way to deal with the issue between us. Publicly, I've paid prices as well. Hating England after our breakup and again after Merrick's death last September, I demanded foreign posts and refused to take on some projects. As a result, I was denied ones I would have preferred. I continued in the army in a position that I found increasingly untenable. The upshot was I did not enjoy my work, and people began to notice."

"But you've been promoted to colonel."

A rueful look graced his features. "You've kept informed of my career since we parted. I'm gratified," he told her on a soft chord. "I can tell you my promotion came in recognition that what work I performed was superior, but my heart wasn't in it. These last two months in India I found myself so despairing of a normal existence that I was tempted to disappear into the mountains and walk home. I dreamed about deserting, taking a new name, a new profession. I've come back to do it. I want to live a sedate life, Cat. In England. On my own land. In peace."

He didn't say *with you,* but she heard it nonetheless. She saw it in his sweet, beseeching eyes. Convinced, she was also seduced by what he'd just revealed. As a man whose entire life had been marked by being lonely, save for the companionship he gained from the older brother whom he idolized, Spencer Lyonns had enjoyed his own company. He was never bored. Never idle.

"I wish you well of it, Spence."

"To show you how I wish you the same with your school, I want to make a proposal. A *business* proposal."

That surprised her, appeased her, dismayed her. "How so?"

"I would like to invest in the Farrell School for Young Ladies."

"Why?" People talked. Men, especially. She wondered if Spence had heard from Acton that she needed money.

"Because I am told by many that you are accumulating quite a roster of impressive students. I need to invest some of the Dartmoor money."

She frowned. "In a school?"

"Why not? It gives me joy to see what Merrick earned do some good here at home. I can't fund just Rand's orphanages. Or Blanding's homes for the sick and elderly. And I need to diversify."

"How much?" she asked without a second thought and then realized she should have looked less hungry. But it was done, and she was stunned but eager to know.

"What do you say to five thousand pounds?"

"Five thousand." She licked her lips. Such a small sum for such a great relief. If she had this money to count on, Acton Thornhill need not lend her so much. He might even charge lower interest rates. She might also arouse fewer questions from him—and pay the person who demanded ten thousand pounds to ward off scandal for her father.

She kneaded her hands. Though she had searched this house in a few places that had been her father's before his death, she had not found the ancient letter from the Pharaoh Ramses to his friend and foster brother Moses. Her father, in his self-importance, would never have hidden such an important document from the world. He would have let everyone know that he, the leading Egyptologist of Great Britain in this or any century, had discovered something so valuable. But whatever the odds, she would again look for the paper secretly when her uncle Dominik was not around and unable to ask questions about her behavior. However, she fully expected not to find the paper and to have to pay the ten thousand in blackmail money by next Friday. Certainly, five thousand from Spence would be a godsend as a contribution to that sum.

But what price would she pay for accepting his money? Would she have to answer to Spence for how it was spent? If she owed him her independence or her integrity, she wouldn't—*couldn't*—take it. Perhaps, she needed to stick with Thornhill's as the source.

"That's quite a bit of money."

"Not really." He glanced about the blue and white splendor of the French-inspired drawing room. "Enough to support one household here in Eaton Square for six months, but a piddling contribution to a new school."

Terrible thoughts skipped through her mind then. At first blush, his offer could be a means to buy his way back into her life, but Spence was determined— and this was a decent act. Her second guess was her older one: that he not only knew she needed cash but knew why. He always seemed to know so much else. How to find the trompe l'oeil door in the Wild Hare. How to predict she'd go boating while others went shooting. How to appeal to her better judgment. Was his talent innate or cultivated? Or both?

Surely, if he were persistent enough to hear from Jess or their butler Pool that she'd come to London, then he was friendly enough to ask discreet questions here in town about her school's chances of success. But if he'd gotten wind of her request for eleven thousand pounds from Acton Thornhill, why offer her an insufficient amount? Why not make it eleven or, better yet, more? Say fifteen? Or twenty?

"What sort of terms are you expecting?" she asked in her most prim voice, examining any move that might give his knowledge away.

His features softened, though he chastised her with his eyes. "Not evidently what you're expecting."

"I apologize. That was unkind."

"To answer you, I thought we'd have my solicitor draw up the usual agreement in matters such as these. A repayment schedule, delayed for—shall we say?—two to three years. Or we could simply stipulate that the money, once realized, would be continually reinvested. In exchange, I would receive a seat on the board of directors."

"You're serious about this, aren't you?" The whole idea warmed her despite her hope to thwart him.

"Never more so," he said with a glowing smile on his lips. "I like children."

She recalled one spring afternoon when they'd gone with her father to hear him lecture at a boys' school in Sussex. After the presentation, they had participated in a reception while Spence, resplendent in his scarlet and gold dress uniform, had sat down under a tree, besieged by the youngsters to tell tales of life in St. Petersburg and Edo. Those boys had hung on his every word. When Spence had children, they would follow him about like ducklings. He would pamper them, please them, teach them to become honorable men and women.

"I remember. Children adore you."

"Just like they do you," he confirmed with every tender emotion a man could impart to a lady shining in his eyes. He moved even nearer, the heat of him seeping through the cold, lonely places in her soul. "Cat, you must need money, so what is the problem?" He watched her for an embarrassingly long time and said, "I won't make it public. I'm not doing it to shame you but to help you. I won't demand my way on the board either. That's not my manner. In fact,

I'll probably give you my proxy to vote at any meetings. I don't want power or control, Cat."

"I believe you," she said without premeditation. "I do need a boiler . . . But I . . . I must have assurances, Spence."

Triumphant that he'd secured her agreement, he sat back in his chair. "Why do I have the inkling I am about to be sorely tried?" He smoothed the wool of his trousers over his thigh as he crossed one leg over the other. "I love a challenge. Let's hear yours."

"I know it's possible to bend any rules when you want something badly enough."

He cocked a blond brow. "Obviously, you think I will. Well, I suppose I deserve that. But I have never been less than fair in any endeavor, even professionally. Yes, I wronged you once and promise never to do so again. But, Cat, for a woman who cheats at croquet and tosses herself overboard to best a man, I'd say your conjecture sounds like the proverbial pot calling the kettle black. Nonetheless, I can understand you need conditions. What are they, Cat?"

"We can be business associates," she said and watched his eyes gleam in contentment, "but you will not touch me."

His satisfaction became smoldering fervor. "You, however, touch me always, everywhere within my lonely soul."

Amazed by his compliance but overjoyed by his rejoinder, she hastened on, "You must do nothing even remotely scandalous."

"No impromptu swims, eh?" He chuckled. "I think I can manage that as long as you don't appear on any balconies in transparent silk. What else?"

His good humor over this assaulted her defenses but also tickled her, and she beamed back at him. Somehow, he was transforming this into a delight, and her heart had been so starved for some such frivolity that the novelty that struck her with joy also made her numb. "We won't speak of the past."

He stopped breathing, but his lush green eyes took her in, enveloped her, consuming her in a jungle fire of desire too long contained. "Only of today—and all our tomorrows."

Chapter 7

Since I received your letter last week, I have considered your request carefully, Catherine." Acton Thornhill extended to her a morning cup of tea with a lump of sympathy. She took his offerings with distasteful premonitions. She'd known him since she was a child, even fancied him when she was fourteen, thinking then he was the epitome of lean efficiency, a contrast to her flamboyant father. Cat also assumed—until now—he was her friend. But today he appeared hard as diamonds. Distant but dazzling. In the interest of money.

"I understand your need for the loan," he was going on. "But I question how the board of directors will view this application, especially when you could have been more prudent and avoided the need to come to us at all."

"I knew you'd think that, Acton. Unfortunately two months ago when I withdrew the last sizable sum from my savings and went to Paris, I had no indication that I would need such a large amount. I can assure you had I known I would have been more conservative with how I spent my inheritance." She would not dare enumerate to the president of Lombard Street's most influential bank that she had spent the last three thousand pounds on new gowns and a carriage. Acton would, like most men, see no value in that. "As it is, I am certain I will be able to pay back the loan within the year. Enrollments proceed, and I have been frugal. I can show you my ledgers if you like."

"I appreciate that, but I doubt the directors will require them. Up to now, you have operated out of your own capital and I have been pleased with the way you have handled the school's finances."

"Even if you did not entirely approve."

He gave her a level look. "I never thought you'd get one applicant, let alone eleven students."

"It's the type of student we say we wish to enroll. Girls who at first glance only *appear* unable to conform to the rigid social strictures. Youngsters with more intelligence and energy than their parents know how to contemplate, let alone tame. I need only two more such students, and I shall be able to meet my operating expenses for the first and second terms. Then, provided I can keep those girls next year and add a few, I will make a slight profit."

"But you will never be rich."

"I didn't do this for that. You know it, Acton."

"I do." He smiled sadly, sat back, and hooked his thumbs in his waistcoat pockets. "I think you're awfully courageous. If you had come to me for a loan to fund this, which of course you had no need, I would have had to refuse you for less than the usual reasons."

"I am well aware of it." Her father—in one of his stubborn fits of mind weeks before he died—had made her sole beneficiary and executor of his estate. If Acton had been trustee, she had a feeling she would have been persuaded by one means or another to sit home in Kent sewing and knitting her way to perdition.

"Bankers take only the most favorable risks, Catherine. I must be frank and say the possibility of success for you to open a school for young ladies was less than promising."

"It appeared to be more an act of desperation."

"But eleven thousand pounds sounds like desperation to me. One thousand or two I might be able to authorize without much clamor from my directors. But eleven? For what could you possibly need that much?"

If she took Spence's offer, she'd need only six, but pride prohibited she take it from him unless she absolutely had to. That's why she had repeated her request this morning to Acton for the full eleven anyway. To see if she could do this alone, she had rehearsed her rationale till she was blue with despair. Jess had no idea the amount of money she needed. Nor did her uncle Dominik. Apparently, Spence did not know either. Nor did anyone know the real reason why. Thank heaven.

"I need a new boiler for hot water for the bathrooms. I know it sounds absurd"—she put up a palm to ward off the usual objections—"but I want it. Then I need to dig out the cellar under the kitchen and pantries of Farrell Old Hall. My builder tells me its riddled with dry rot, and I must shore it up or see it fall in one or two years with the added wear and tear. Then one of my ponies grew ill last month and died. I need to replace her. Even if it were not for my cousin

Jessica's adamance on this, I think it foolish to train six- and seven-year-old girls to ride a horse many hands higher than necessary. Too intimidating, Acton. Surely," she said trying not to be harsh on the man who had lost his mother to a riding accident just as Jessica had, "you understand my position and Jessica's on that."

"You have as of this morning only seven hundred pounds or so in your account. Even though your students' parents are paying their tuitions and board, the current balance is insufficient to warrant me lending you eleven thousand pounds unless I have some hope of recovery."

"Thornhill's has served my family for over three generations. We have *never* defaulted on any of our obligations, few and small as they were." Except for her father's first expedition, Thornhill's had never had to back any of his archaeological digs. Walter Farrell stood alone in that. Even the great explorer Richard Burton could not show such continual votes of confidence from his admirers.

"Yes, I agree. The Farrells have always been financially responsible. If every one of our creditors were as reliable as you, Thornhill's would be infinitely richer. No matter my empathy, Catherine," he said, sharpening his gaze on her, "I cannot recommend this to the board without some other financial arrangement."

"Suppose I asked for six thousand pounds instead of eleven?" She had hoped she might be able to borrow the full amount and escape Spence's generosity and any obligations to him, but if she couldn't, so be it. She would do what she must to rebuild her life—and if Spence could help her . . . Well, he was the only one she could turn to now. Ironically.

Acton smacked his lips, fingering a crystal paperweight on his spotlessly clean desk. "Why would you change the amount now?"

"I'll take what I can get, Acton."

"One or two thousand," he shot back with more irritation than she'd ever seen emerge from that glass facade of his. "That's the sum I can persuade them to, I think. I *hope*." He looked . . . *nervous,* and Cat fought a frown as he ran on about how "the economy has been extremely troubled lately. Strikes and riots among mill workers in the north. The failure of wheat crops. Such events put strains on investors and banks. You've got to understand, Catherine, that funding schools is not high on anyone's priority list when production and distribution are vital to survival."

She could go elsewhere, but *where?* To whom? To go to the bank next door or down the street would mean others would instantly know Acton had found her lacking. This was not the sort of reputation she had sought to build for herself. Never were any of the Farrells—in the tradition of the first one, Black Jack—touted as less than completely solvent. But she needed the boiler. And she needed the other six thousand pounds before next Friday, April tenth to be exact, or else she needed the papyrus her correspondent demanded. So since she hadn't found the document in Farrell Hall and had yet to rummage through the townhouse here in London, she had to come up with the blackmail money.

"I could put up some sort of collateral." She had the triple strand of amethysts, two centuries old and the last of the first Farrell's notorious pirate chest. But the gems were considered Farrell estate property, tied to the family tradition, worn by Farrell women at weddings and christenings, debuts and balls. How could she sell a part of her heritage?

Oh, certainly, she had another option. She owned a few pieces of her father's findings from Karnak. Two rare pottery winejars. One glass necklace. A small red graphite cat that her father had given her for her sixteenth birthday. Her father's treasures were dear to her. Worth more and more over the years as museums scrambled to buy artifacts from archaeologists and private collectors drove up prices on scarce objects.

"That is one way. There is another, Catherine."

Smoothing her gloves across the skirt of her pearl gray walking suit, she fingered the crochet buttons. "Very well. Please tell me how I might do this."

"I have been approached by a person who may wish to purchase the Egyptian jewelry in your and your uncle Dominik's new exhibit."

Her brow wrinkled. "The items that are my father's findings are not for sale." To part with the necklaces, earrings, bracelets, and rings from her father's last trip with Uncle Dom felt like a betrayal. She sat, swimming in remorse—and in fear she might not be able to obtain this loan.

Acton shook his head, his hands opening. "Why not? You won't wear it. You have too much respect for such ancient pieces. If someone wishes to buy them, where's the harm?"

"I am reluctant to sell these. They are the last cache my father brought home."

"I see. If you let them go, you feel you have little left of him. Understandable, I suppose. But, Catherine, that view shows a rather shortsighted sense of business."

Stung by his barb, she stiffened. "Does it? I have not told you, but I planned to keep them, catalog them from my father's notes, and write a book about them. I will employ a photographer and illustrator.

The text, I should think, would be a welcome addition to any scholar's library or, barring that, any public one."

"I apologize, Catherine. Of course, I should have known you would not keep them for yourself."

"My intention was to lend them out to museums here, on the Continent, and in America as a traveling exhibit."

"I am duly chastised, Catherine. Naturally, it sounds like a wonderful idea, so much more profitable to everyone than what I assumed."

"You understand my position then on such a sale."

He pressed his lips in a sorry grimace. "As you must understand mine."

"This offer is that good and the board's view of my prospective school that poor?"

He began to sweat in his black serge suit so that he huffed, his face sheened. When he spoke, however, his words were haughty. "It is, merely, a school for young women. I must be blunt. You are opening a place for people to send their daughters, girls who are"—he waved a hand—"difficult."

"Active."

"If you insist."

"Sensitive. Talented. Some are very gifted. Artists, musicians, writers." She grew very angry at his indifference and his labeling, narrowing her eyes at him.

"Catherine, I do understand. Really, I do. But I am asking you to consider this offer."

She was fuming. "Who made it?"

"I am not at liberty to say."

Her suspicions blossomed like an evil flower. Was this another mystery to add to the one that had begun a few weeks ago when the first anonymous blackmail note arrived at Farrell Hall? "Why would someone come with an offer to buy? I never indicated to you I'd sell it. Why do they want it?"

"It is reputed to be a very astounding collection."

"Stunning, incomparable, but not from a pharaoh's family. The items were those meant for the ruler's administrators, the middle class, we would call them." The collection was from a glorious period in Egypt's history when pharaohs were likened to gods and ruled like tyrants. Their power extended over much of North Africa, across the Sinai, into biblical Palestine. It was the time of Moses, the parting of the Red Sea, and the delivery of the Ten Commandments to the wandering tribes of Israel.

"Why won't they allow you to tell me who they are?"

"I did not ask. It was not my place."

"I see no harm in knowing who wishes to purchase it."

"Neither do I, but they have requested this remain confidential."

They? A group? A rival expeditionary force? Critics of her father and his politics? "It must remain or . . . what? They will withdraw the offer?"

"Precisely."

She felt boxed. Afraid. Curious. "I will consider it."

"Soon, I hope."

New alarms rang in her head. "Is there some limit?"

"Six days."

"I see." She swallowed and shook her head. "Time appears to be of the utmost importance, doesn't it?" Five days to make a decision to sell her father's last major find. Ten—no, now nine days to discover a document she couldn't remember ever having seen, or else someone would reveal to the newspapers the one real blotch on her father's reputation: the damnable forgery of that other papyrus.

Acton lifted his brows in an apology. "I cannot control the conditions of the buyer's offer, Catherine."

She tugged on her gloves, irritated with the leather, the anonymous offer, and her growing coil. Snatching up her bag and parasol, she stood and sailed for the door.

Acton kept up with her. "You'll think this over and send me word soon, I do hope. It is a very sound offer, Cat. With such a fair sale, you need borrow less from us."

"I realize the good points."

She let him escort her through the crowded bank and out into the bracing morning air where sunshine streaked between the buildings. Curricles, tilburies, and broughams clogged the street while patrons hastened about their business. Cat allowed Acton to take her arm on the front steps and paused while she felt—*again*—the hair at the back of her neck stand up. She bristled, turned. Acton was chatting about the weather, while her acute sense of touch whispered someone watched her. Exactly as she'd felt in the Farrell tunnel to Corinth days ago.

A scan of the crowd told her she was imagining things.

"Good morning, Lady Farrell!"

Cat whipped around to see Norris Eddleworth, a director of the bank and a friend of Merrick Lyonns, smiling up at her and turning then to view Acton with disdain. "Finished your appointment so soon, Acton?" Eddleworth's steel gray brows rose as he gave Cat a once-over. "Did Acton treat you well, my lady?"

"Thank you, he did," she answered, examining

both men and finding no clues to the antagonism between them.

"I bid you good day then. Perhaps when you have seen Lady Farrell inside her carriage, Acton, we might have that talk I said I needed, hmmm?"

Acton was perspiring profusely, licking his upper lip furtively but grabbing her arm, shouldering aside those in their way to hand her into her uncle's carriage with more solicitude than he'd displayed in his office. "I hope to hear from you soon. In the meantime, I understand I shall see you at the Marlows' ball Saturday night."

"Word travels quickly," she said and cast him a fonder smile than she'd done so far this morning. "As I remember you were very interested in their second daughter. Forgive me, what was her name?"

"Nanette. Yes, I am," he said, relaxing with this topic. "I have been for many years, though Lord Marlow has not looked favorably on me as a son-in-law."

Cat thought of herself and Spence. "People change."

"Old attitudes die hard. The Marlows are such established aristocracy. The Thornhills are in commerce. We're upstarts compared to them, regrettably."

"Lord Marlow invests in shipping and mining ventures, doesn't he? He even contributed to one of my father's expeditions. The last one, if I remember correctly. He must be inclined toward you or you wouldn't have received an invitation. Capitalize on it. You're good at that, aren't you?" They chuckled together, though she didn't really feel any confidence that he was laughing inside. "I shall see you at the Marlows and we'll take them by storm."

He lifted her hand to kiss it. "I hope you're right."

"I am." She prayed she was.

When he shut the door, the thud put the final depressing note to the whole occasion. She stared idly out the window as the carriage lurched forward and wended its way beyond the City back to Eaton Square. And all the while, she could not dismiss the palpable feeling of horror at her situation.

Never in her life had she been so surrounded by problems at once. Before this, life's challenges seemed individually presented. Her mother's illness followed by her merciful death. Her father's melancholy. Jessica's trauma at the death of her own mother and father. Merrick Lyonns's attack on Cat's father and her uncle Dominik. The Historical Society's inquiry. Spence's desertion the day of their wedding. Her father's deteriorating heart condition and death.

Each of life's challenges had come one at a time with years in between for recovery. Each had been devastating. But now there was this . . . this barrage of problems. The need for money. The requirement of respectability. The demand for the papyrus or money or ruin. The worry over who might wish to buy her jewelry collection. The reappearance of the one man she had ever adored. His presence, his endearing words, his financial help, her only comfort amid the chaos.

Prickly with emotions, she fairly jumped from the cab when the porter opened the door and let down the steps to the street. She burst into the foyer, discarding her gloves and undoing her jacket. Marsh appeared from the bowels of the house to glide her accoutrements from her hands as she swirled to the hall mirror. Plucking at the giant ruched ties beneath her chin, she pulled off her straw hat with a fierceness that tested the security of her chignon and found it wanting.

"It did not go well, did it?"

Her uncle Dominik appeared behind her. As she wended her stray locks into place, she saw him in the doorway to his study from whence—she could tell by the intensity of lamplight and the fog of his ever-burning incense—he had come. The hall gasoliers lit his strawberry hair to sienna while his blue eyes beneath his thick glasses were opaque. His expression was lax so she knew he'd been brooding again. Today, from among his many worries, he had chosen her.

"Not entirely, no."

"I wish you had let me go with you."

She gave him a wan smile. "You have enough to do to prepare for your next expedition to the Sinai than to worry over my school finances. Weren't you to meet with a few possible financiers this morning?" she asked to divert Dom from her woes.

"Yes, I did. The meeting went well . . . I think. But I don't like you going out alone."

She had told him of Spence's visit yesterday and he had heard from someone at his club about Spence attending the Billingtons' party. He hadn't been happy that she'd kept the latter from him, but as the one to leave an argument, he had simply expressed his disappointment and let her tell him what she would about events at tea yesterday. Thrilled that the Chilterns had called, Uncle Dom expressed his distaste that they had received their invitation from Spence. Cat knew Dom wanted her reinstated in society on her own worth, and for Spence's presumption, she'd be smoothing her uncle's ruffled feathers over this far into the future.

"I was fine this morning, Uncle Dom. Really.

Spence wouldn't accost me in the street." That statement brought another frisson of fear like the one outside the bank.

"He's a Lyonns, isn't he? This one brought you nothing but misery." Dominik had never liked Merrick and had only tolerated Spence.

She lowered her head, wondering what diplomacy would be best to broach the latest development between the Farrells and the Lyonns when her eyes fell to the silver salver. In the bowl sat one calling card of sturdy vellum atop two larger envelopes. The card was that of Lady Marlow, who had obviously done Cat the honor of paying a morning visit. But the sight that seized her imagination lay to its right. Breathtaking, it was a gaily wrapped box in congo copper tissue bound by silver Venetian lace ribbons. More appealing—and more thrilling—was the distinctive envelope of ecru linen tucked beneath the lace strands that blossomed in a lavish bow and trailed to the edge of the credenza.

"The package came for you a few minutes ago. I recognize the wrapping. From Brescia's, isn't it?" He meant the Italian crystalmaker's shop on Bond Street. "Open it," he instructed with that authority so like her father's. "I'm curious. Aren't you?"

She was careful not to look at him, lest he see her elation at her knowledge that it came from Spence. "Of course. Presents could improve my day." She took it and the items from the salver, then walked around her uncle into the room where yesterday Spence had confronted her and given her the one occasion for hope she'd found lately.

As if to encase herself in the feel of it, she took the rococo chair he had chosen and toyed with the lace of the gift. The heavy envelope bore the distinctive embossing of a hawthorn bush in each corner. Extracting it from the ribbons, she turned it over and traced the vermilion wax crest seal of a lion rampant. Fragrant sandalwood wafted through the air, and she smiled to herself at Spence's persistence. Whatever his present, no matter that she would have to return it, it was precisely what she needed at this particular hour to lift her spirits.

With eager fingers she broke the wax and slid out his card. Above his engraved signature in his bold script, he offered two words. "For hope."

A lump lodged in her throat as she pressed his card to her thigh and paused for one long moment to gaze at the gaily wrapped present. Suddenly, her fingers flew, slipping off ribbons and tearing tissue. From the trappings emerged a cast bronze box, hinged. Confessing to herself that she was greedy as a girl, she flipped back the top and stared at the starry object nestled in the plush amber tussore lining. A brilliant crystal heart winked up at her with a thousand tiny facets. Meant for a lady's toilette to hold delicacies of her dressing table, the palm-sized heart was fashioned in two pieces. Inside, she saw the dancing outline of something small and indefinable. Her breath paused as she lifted the top from its base.

Tiny seeds awaited her. Mustard seeds.

Grains of hope. Reminders of his intentions to have his way, win her back, create a life both of them could enjoy—one in which they could both flourish. Finite expressions of faith that from something so minuscule might spring something substantial. Tangible.

Uncle Dom lit his pipe with a few deep draws and threw the long match into the fire. At this angle, she could see his eyes. They swam with concern.

"As your only living male relative, Cat, I feel very responsible for you. This man, my dear, can hurt you again."

She knew she owed him a reply but found not one. How could she explain to Dom who'd been ridiculed by Merrick Lyonns as much as her father and she had, that she simply loved Spencer Lyonns? That nothing had ever changed it, though she wished her pride might conquer the passion?

Recognition of his failure thinning his mouth, Dom inhaled on the pipe and shifted his bulky stance, one arm along the gold-leafed mantel. "I'll delay my departure for Suez for as long as necessary. I don't want you here in London alone with Lyonns. He's unscrupulous as ever."

"Uncle Dom, you needn't do that. I will be here only until my financial business with Acton Thornhill is concluded. That's two weeks at the most, then I must return to Farrell Hall. I've much to do before the term begins."

"My fear for you exceeds my need to sail. I can begin this trip any time, you realize."

Sweet gratitude filled her. "Thank you, but you mustn't. This is your first expedition on your own. You've worked for this for so very long. I won't allow you to postpone it. Remember, I know—as few others—exactly how much such a venture costs. It would be imprudent of you to stay here to protect me from things . . . from people"—her fingers caressed warm crystal and germs of survival—"with which I can deal."

His round face plumped in a smile as he pointed with his pipe at Lady Marlow's card and the two envelopes in her hand. "If the world continues to come to your doorstep, I should say so. The Marlows' footman said his lady would be happy to receive you anytime before or after their Saturday ball."

"She has a daughter, some say, who might do well with Jess and me."

"Then, certainly, you must pay her a visit soon. Meanwhile, those envelopes are moldering, my dear. Go on. Open them."

Relieved at his good humor, she broke the seal on the first. "This one is from the undersecretary for the Foreign Office."

"Bloomsbury?"

"Yes, and his wife."

"What in hell does he want?"

Her uncle and father had never gotten on with William Bloomsbury, whose view of a British empire was limited to Wales, Scotland, and perhaps Ireland.

"They've invited me to one of their at-homes."

"Little dinner parties with ten gossips plotting the direction of the government without Parliament's consent."

Cat compressed her lips. "It's next Wednesday."

"Don't fret," Dom offered and took a long deep drag on the pipe. "I know how important it is that you go. My personal persuasions should not deter you. Don't look at me so forlorn, my dear. I am not without knowledge of the benefits such exposure might bring you. Open the other, will you?"

She nodded and complied. But when she laid it open and stared at it, her fears took wing. Instinctively, her fingers surrounded the crystal heart.

"Do tell, Cat. Who is it this time?"

"Marietta Hornsby."

In the void that yawned before her, her mind spun black horror stories.

Dom lowered his pipe and cocked a bushy red brow. "What might she want?"

"Our presence at her first garden party of the season. Next Thursday at two."

"What cheek!"

"I'm going to accept, Uncle Dom. I know you're

not enamored of her or such frivolous engagements, but you must understand how I need to go for my social standing." But more, Cat needed to see for herself that Marietta was going to erase last Sunday night's balcony scene from her memory.

"I don't like it. She can be a viper when she wants. I'll go with you, of course. She'll not get the satisfaction of saying I sent my niece alone into her pit."

"She seems silly more than dangerous." *When she is subdued by reason.*

"A cover only." He spoke around the stem of his pipe. "You know, my dear, you are so eager to see the best in people. You tend to enjoy others rather than analyze them. Perhaps if you were more critical, you'd get farther."

As an insult, it stung. As an insight, it nettled. "My eternal personal problem, it appears. I wish I could follow your advice. I've tried repeatedly," she said, her eyes locking on the crystal while her mind focused on how she had never evaluated Spence three years ago. She had simply loved him from the start. "I will try again."

"Particularly when it is so vital to your school *and* since Spencer Lyonns seeks to reingratiate himself."

She could not bear to have a row with Dom about Spence now. Not with Spence's heart in her hands.

Her uncle came forward. "I can see we should put that aside for today. Shouldn't you be preparing for this afternoon's opening? Didn't you say you'd purchased a new gown? I must see it, mustn't I?" He threw her a smile that never reached his eyes.

He had tried diligently to replace her father. In major ways, he had failed, knew it, and withdrew from the arena. In minor acts, she accepted his efforts. A small voice whispered that her grief for her father had dwindled enough that she could and should appreciate her uncle more. Certainly, no one could take the place of the father who had soothed her hysteria after her mother died and who had then become both parents to a bereft young girl.

Nonetheless, she could make more room in her heart for the uncle who had tried to become closer to her. Though her father had demonstrated an odd disdain of Dom, Cat had never found justification for it. In truth, Cat admired her uncle's good intentions toward her, and she wouldn't hurt his feelings by displaying her own.

"Yes," she said as she rose, her fingers cradling the fragile heart and seeds of hope, "I'll change quickly. Never fear, we'll arrive before the gallery doors open to the public."

Chapter 8

*W*here could Father have hidden this papyrus?

The crush of the crowd at the Wyngate Gallery brought the temperature of the room up to a stifling degree. Cat scanned the people and told herself to enjoy the success of the reception. But the only thing she could think of was a location she might have missed.

She'd looked a few places inside the Eaton Square townhouse. Since she'd arrived Monday, she had gone through her father's trunks and one packing case in the storage rooms next to the servants' quarters in the basement. Last night when both her uncle and Marsh were out, she'd tiptoed into that foggy den her uncle Dom called his study and done a quick survey of his desk and cabinets. She'd found nothing remaining of Walter Farrell there. This was her uncle's house now. Every vestige of her father had vanished.

Sad as the lack made her, she understood her uncle.

Dominik had respected his brother and his memory enough to never breathe a word of their discord to anyone, especially her. Cat felt that Dom had really loved Walter dearly, excusing him his trespasses more easily than many a man would do for his brother. Walter's last massive heart failure and sudden passing had been a great shock to Dom. Even now, a year later, he did not speak of the older brother whom he imitated in demeanor and choice of profession.

A prickling awareness shook her. She rounded her shoulders, trying to suppress this persistent sensation of being observed. *Watched.*

She told herself she must rid herself of this hair-raising tingling at the back of her neck and her fear of being followed.

Certainly that was the cause of her unease today. For if she'd harbored any fears that people might avoid this exhibit because of her father's acerbic reputation or her disgrace, she'd fretted for naught. They came in droves. For three hours now, they poured through the front doors, past the lobby and the other rooms studded with displays as diverse as Roman sculpture and Indian art. They came from all walks of life. Young, old, peers, politicians, newspapermen. Even two of her father's critics. She and Uncle Dom had greeted every one by now, she was almost positive. Yet, throughout the first hour, she felt as skittish as she had this morning outside the bank.

"Lady Farrell."

Cat turned to find the terribly tall, elegant Lady Marlow before her, her equally impressive husband to one side. Stunned, Cat knew her mother's training had her performing the amenities. "How wonderful to see you here."

"We wouldn't miss it," Lord Marlow said with bland urbanity and offered his own hand.

Cat glanced up at his regal wife while her knees went to water at the thought that she faced one of the doyennes of London society. "Thank you for calling on me this morning. I was out on a business appointment." So many stayed in their bedrooms, fearful to go down to receive strangers calling out of some social code of courtesy. Cat had always been eager to meet new people. It had been another trait her mother had helped her to bring up to an acceptable—less gushing—polish.

"Please do not apologize, my dear." Lady Marlow's earnest expression told Cat this was no mere polite declaration. She drew herself up to her full six feet and nailed Cat with robin's egg blue eyes. "I was impetuous to arrive before the usual midday hours. I wanted to welcome you to London."

Since Cat was not sending round her own card because of her less than sterling past, the significance of Lady Marlow's actions was abundant and immense. "I am grateful. I have not been here for the season in very long."

"Quite so. I do understand how rusty one can become. For a while after our third child was born, I myself retired to the country. Children can be exhausting."

Knowing where the woman led the conversation, Cat assisted her. "I am about to discover that."

Lord Marlow, darting black eyes about the room, flashed Cat a strained smile. "Delighted to see the results of your father's last expedition here. I wonder if you might tell us more about them. Your uncle says you know as much about these pieces as even he does."

"I'd be pleased to describe what I can." Cat put down her glass, recognizing the man's change of the topic from children to artifacts. Was he, as many men with overactive offspring, ashamed of the child who preoccupied his wife's thoughts? Hopefully, Cat could help him as well as his wife and daughter. She'd do it by helping him understand more than the rarities her father had found.

Leading the way, Cat stopped before one of the many glass-enclosed displays in the room. This table, draped in red cornelian velvet, supported three torsos of female plaster mannequins dressed in alabaster linen and the adornments popular during the reign of Pharaoh Ramses II. Of the pieces in the room, the gold-wired necklace, earrings, and bracelets before them were the most intact.

"These came from the same workshop and were meant to be worn as an ensemble. We can tell by the consistency of the oblong shape of the red and green jasper stones."

"The carving on the scarabs is superb. Cats, aren't they?"

"Yes, meant to symbolize love and prosperity."

Lord Marlow looked totally absorbed. "Fertility."

Cat nodded, hiding her amazement that he should mention such a concept in mixed company at a public gathering.

Edwina cast her husband a withering eye, then turned back. "Forgive him, Lady Farrell. He loves this period and studies it on his own." She turned her attention and Cat's to a necklace. "The gold is so brilliant and smooth that it's difficult to believe a people so primitive could create something so precise."

"I think many of us assume that. Yet this jewelry was fashioned by craftsmen almost seventeen hundred years after the Great Pyramid was built."

"Where could they find such wonderful stones?"

Lord Marlow appeared indifferent to the point of irritation. "Edwina, they were expert miners."

Cat pointed to a gold-and-iris-colored lapis lazuli girdle dangling from the waist of another mannequin. "They were innovative, combining form with function."

"Blending decoration," came one smooth male voice, "with necessity."

Cat felt her toes curl at the signature sound of Spence. The rest of her body registered his heat. With warming interest, she watched him greet the Marlows and then allowed him to take her hand. "Lady Farrell," he tugged to bring it up to kiss it and she resisted mightily.

"Nice to see you, Lord Lyonns." At the risk of struggling like two wrestlers, she realized he could easily win this bout. Rather than make them both look like children, she bit her lower lip and let him do as he wished. "Did you just arrive?" This was his wont to come after the first rush. Or had he been here all along and she had sensed his presence as that which made her wary?

"A few minutes ago," he explained with aplomb. Eyes twinkling with green mischief, he beamed at her and nodded at the items before them. "I didn't mean to interrupt your viewing of the exhibit, Lady Marlow. Cat is certainly the expert on these. This belt belonged to the wife or female assistant of a physician, didn't it, Cat?"

Ignoring his familiar use of her first name and his tone, Cat fastened her attention on Lady Marlow with as much presence of mind as Spence's proximity ever afforded her. "Yes. Inside this pendant"—Cat pointed to a hand-sized gold casing that hung down the front of the linen tunic—"women often carried herbs or medicines."

"This one is carved with two lions' heads."

"The Egyptian symbol for life's rejuvenation," Cat elaborated. "Sometimes, they put these tiny cases to another use. They wrote their formulas on papyrus, rolled them up, and carried them. We've mounted here the one we found in this amulet."

"What does it say?" Edwina Marlow bent near the spread paper with faint hieroglyphs.

Cat grimaced. "It is a cure for gray hair made from the black hair of a calf and olive oil."

Edwina made a moue. "How divine. Did one drink it?"

"No. Applied it to the scalp. Very *aromatic.*" Cat rolled her eyes playfully. Everyone thought it great fun except John Marlow, who sighed and fished for his pocket watch. Cat sought something to interest him. "Most of the recipes we find in these casings were not so much medicines as charms to ward off the evil of illness."

"Superstitious sort," Marlow said, replacing his watch. "But with many rich as Midas."

"More so." Spence focused on the man's wife, who was gobbling these tidbits with enthusiasm. "Pharaoh's galleys plied the Mediterranean for spices, food, cloth, chariots. Anything the known world had to offer came to the house of Pharaoh. His granaries overflowed with wheat. His stables with horses from Babylon, cattle from the land of the Hittites. His treasury was jammed with every costly stone, silver, copper, and gold in blocks the size of your fist. His magazine was filled with shields and swords as tribute from other countries. His cities— the ones his predecessors built and ones he began—

became vast metropolises filled with temples, sculptures, and paintings. This was the period in which Moses lived in Pharaoh's house, became one of his advisers and later his bitterest enemy."

"Pharaoh used slave labor," Marlow told his wife. "Especially in the mines."

"But Moses," Spence added, "objected and led his people out of Egypt."

From across the room, Cat saw her uncle approach and froze. He was coming to rescue her from the claws of a Lyonns; she winced.

"I say, Dominik," Marlow said, perking up at the sight of him, and ignored his scowl at Spence, "do you think I might have a word with you? Excuse us, do."

Marlow's maneuver left Cat to wonder if Marlow's action were based on fear of social confrontation between the ever irascible Dominik and Spence or if the man had real business to discuss with her uncle. She knew Marlow had invested in one of her father's expeditions and wondered if he did the same for Dominik now. Certainly, he had never come round to talk or show any interest in her father's findings before this exhibit. Or at least, she didn't think he had. As her attention drifted back to Edwina Marlow, however, Cat registered the intrigued look Spence gave the two men.

"John hates these large public social engagements." Lady Marlow leaned closer and lowered her pitch. "He'd rather be home puttering through his own collection of ancient artifacts."

Spence was interested. "What does he collect?"

"Old coins, books. Anything about the early tribes of Israel. The Bible's origins are his forte. A musty lot, I tell you. I made him come today to see this jewelry, but in reality, I wanted to meet you, Lady Farrell."

"I'm glad you did."

Spence excused himself to talk with Rand. "I must speak with him before he leaves. Lady Marlow, if I don't see you again before I go, I will Saturday." He took her hand, kissed it, and swung his gaze to Cat. "I need to talk with you before I leave." With that, he gave them a blazing good-natured smile and left.

Lady Marlow looked at Cat. "Such a sweet man. One feels it, even if . . ." She cleared her throat. "I am sorry, Lady Farrell. I often overreach propriety."

"We all do, no matter how diligently we try not to."

"We can't control so much in life, I find," she said with distinct melancholy. "My husband and I have one such element to our lives. I fear that is as much as we can handle."

Cat did the unthinkable and squeezed her hand.

"I hate to let it affect so much of our lives. But often I do not know what to do."

Cat wanted to blurt that frustration with an overly active child was nothing new, nothing to be ashamed of and not the worst affliction one could suffer. But Cat knew that was a concept to teach the parents after helping the child learn it. "There are ways to cope with such things."

Edwina's gaze locked on Cat's. "You really think so?"

"I know it. My mother and father taught me how. My cousin Jessica has similar characteristics." Cat fought for the polite phrases that would let her couch the subject in the vaguest but most meaningful terms for this woman whom she had never met before but meant to help. "A set of standards, a lot of direction, and patience can do wonders."

"I'd like to know more. So would my husband, who is grateful to your uncle for suggesting your work and your school to us for Corinne."

Cat grew warm with gratification to Dominik. "I'd like to tell you more."

"Would you come for tea?"

"I'd be delighted."

"Next Tuesday afternoon?"

"Thank you. Yes." She'd see Acton in the morning, refuse him this jewelry collection sale, ask for her loan, and be gone.

"We'll have our girls come, too."

"Wonderful," Cat agreed, watching Edwina's eagerness sluice her mannish beauty with radiance.

It suddenly seemed so easy to throw herself into showing Lady Marlow more of the collection. The need to discuss the pieces in detail filled her mind. Meanwhile, she built a new relationship. She liked Edwina Marlow, handsome woman that she was with so many familiar problems.

As she listened and watched her, Cat knew she would be able to solve many of them. Through Corinne.

But so did Edwina solve Cat's. The illustrious lady stayed with Cat for such a long time that when Cat caught a glimpse of a few others, she knew Edwina added an aura of acceptability to Cat. Those women who had attended with their husbands appeared more ready to step forward and ask questions about various items in the display. By the time Lord Marlow emerged from his discussion with Uncle Dom and suggested to his wife that they leave, Cat felt that a new friendship and a finer reputation had been forged for her. She bid the Marlows good-bye with the promise of seeing them Saturday evening and again Tuesday afternoon. Hope, rich and luscious, raced through her veins.

"I told you there was nothing to fear."

At the caress of Spence's voice, she turned. Her eyes must have reflected her mood because his took on an emerald fire that sent her temperature higher. "Will you pop up everywhere I go?"

"If my sources are working as well as they should."

She grinned at his captivating smugness. "You're like a shadow."

"Mmm, that's one way to put it. From the looks we've gotten, I may also be something even closer to you."

"*May* is the operative word so do keep a proper distance, my lord."

People milled about them. Some began to leave and approached her to bid her adieu. She told them good night while Spence walked beside her, clasping his hands behind his back and matching his casual expression to hers. Yet what she wished to speak of was far from polite. She needed to dissuade him from his course and knew of few ways to halt such a determined man except by direct approach. "I received your heart."

"You haven't known it, but you've had my heart for ages."

His eloquent endearment summoned the equal truth that sprang to mind. "The crystal is incomparable."

They paused before a group of signet rings and, though he glanced over her head, he murmured, "Like you."

This close to him, nothing mattered except his scent, his power, his irresistible appeal. "The seeds were—" What could she say without giving her integrity away?

"Impressive? Symbolic?" he suggested eagerly.

"Touching."

Because she could not bear to look at his ferociously exciting eyes, she watched his sensuous mouth spread in satisfaction. "I hoped so."

"You weren't supposed to touch me."

His gaze traveled to her lips. "You didn't say how, sweetheart."

Enchanted, she had just a smidgen of sense left to be tweaked. "You were supposed to remain honorable."

"Haven't I?" One brow arching, he feigned surprise. "Your restriction said I couldn't do anything scandalous," he whispered, coming infinitesimally nearer, dropping his tones lower. "Sweetheart, you have no idea what torture it is to look at you, want you, and not put my hands all over you. Never even have any hope of it. I have to show you how deeply I care for you. What better way is there than to send my heart with every good intention I have inside it?"

Her body quickened, flooded, drowning in his magic. *"Spence . . ."* His name escaped in a moan.

He swelled with preening satisfaction, looked about, then riveted his hot green gaze on her. "Yes, darling?

He was too confident. She should change that. "You are not supposed to seduce me with presents and words."

"Then tell me what is left to me, love? I've got to convince you of my earnestness, and I'm simply using every means at my limited disposal."

"Your investment in the school went far to convincing me," she snapped with less gratitude than she felt.

"Now we're getting somewhere. I meant it to do that."

"If only I *didn't* need it or any m—" She froze.

"Any what? Cat? What's wrong, sweetheart?"

She'd almost babbled her money problems and asked him to give her more, but pride rose up like a snarling animal captured in a net. Two men walked close to comment on the rings, and Cat grew leery that they might overhear.

"What do you think of the collection?" She trailed a hand along one table and began to cross the room, headed for the doors and the hall, where she hoped they might speak more privately.

"It's superb," Spence said for the benefit of the men, then leaned closer to say, "but if you think I am letting you end that sentence of yours midway, you're wrong." Nonchalant again, he moved with her slowly toward the other gallery. "The jewelry collection certainly deserves wider exposure. Many would thrill to see it. Children, especially, would be fascinated by the stories you could tell of Pharaoh and his people."

That he saw the same possibilities for the collection as she did made her examine his sparkling eyes. "You are so thoughtful."

"I intend to be even more so, sweetheart."

"Flattery and presents cannot buy everything you want."

"No? I'm not choosing the right presents?" He stopped.

"You know you are. But there is one thing I'd like that you can't buy or send." She faced him in the display room filled with life-size sculptures. Nearer than she intended, she found her hands on his arms. In this area jammed with marble statues, the lights were dimmed to a sepia mellowness.

"Can they be as touching as my heart . . . or other parts of me?" he asked, his hands illustrating his words by drawing her to the security of his chest.

She licked the corner of her mouth in contemplation of his words, realizing too late his avid gaze absorbed her movement. "Advice," she blurted, pushing aside all thought of things she wished for from him. "I'd like some advice."

Like a sleepwalker, he blinked and trailed his eyes up her face. "About what?"

"Those." She inclined her head toward the room with the jewelry. "You know enough about the values of such items. Would you sell them?"

He made a noncommittal shrug. "Do you want to?" At her hesitation, he said, "No. I see you don't. So keep them." Then some other thought flashed in his eyes.

Hoping he couldn't read her mind about her need for cash, she tried to disengage herself from him, but he circled his arms to her back. Alone as they were in this room, she let herself enjoy the feel of him and told herself the relief and joy were temporary charms against loneliness.

His mouth rested near her temple. His breath fanned her hair. "What would you like to do with them, my darling?"

"Write a book for children. Hire a photographer to produce pictures of them and some of the other rare items in my father's private collection. Tell the story of daily life in Pharaoh's kingdom."

He hugged her closer, and his soft mouth spoke in a fevered whisper over her ear. "Then do it. No one's stopping you." When she lowered her head, he put a finger beneath her chin, wrapped her flush to his torso with his other arm, and peered into her eyes. *"Is* someone preventing you from doing this, kitten?" He kissed the end of her nose. "Who is it? Tell me. I'll help you."

Could she say, I don't know? Oh, certainly, she might. That would bring out the beast in him immediately. He'd pester her for details until she broke and told him all. Why, oh, why had she ever begun to confide in him?

Because you need him, his positive nature, his aggressiveness. His protectiveness as a bulwark from your enemies.

"No tears, darling. It can't be as bad as that. Or can it?" He took her face in his big hand and thumbed her cheek, blessed her eyes with his mouth, nestled her close to him like he'd done years ago, far away in a fairy-tale land where no one stalked her or demanded money and things she did not possess.

"Oh, Spence. Help me." She went to his care with a yearning for happiness and peace, now reclaimed . . . if only for a minute. Winding her arms about him, she buried her face in his shoulder, inhaled his sandalwood spice, and let the world go hang.

"I will. Name the ways—"

"Allow me, Lyonns," a man boomed across the cavernous room, "to interrupt you." Uncle Dominik's heavy footsteps echoed around the walls. "Take your hands off my niece."

Spence steadied Cat on her feet as he stepped slowly back from her. With regret smoldering in his eyes, he said to Dom, "Cat and I were having a discussion, Dominik."

"It looked more like seduction to me." Dom came over to inspect Cat and confront Spence with a narrowed expression. "She's not yours, Lyonns. You already tried to ruin her once. Walter didn't think it would work between the two of you years ago, and I don't now either. So I will thank you to leave." He reached for Cat's wrist.

She avoided his grasp. "No, please, Uncle Dom. You mustn't do this."

Dom froze. "His name was not on the invitation list!"

"This is a public gallery, Uncle Dom. I wanted to talk to Spence. Alone."

"About what?" He surveyed each person's expression.

Cat considered her uncle's question without answer. That she would not confide in him about this just as she had not about the bank interview hurt him. Visibly.

"Very well," he spat as he drew himself up as best a man of his girth could. "Live with whatever your reputation becomes, Catherine. You'll get no more help from me unless you ask." He pivoted and strode from the room.

It gutted her that her uncle could turn on her and in public. She had never perceived him as coldhearted.

Spence stood watching her a moment, and she could tell he understood her sorrow. When he came to loop an arm around her waist, he proved it. "I have my carriage. I'll take you home, sweetheart."

She stepped from his embrace. "No. Thank you, Spence. I'm going to talk with Uncle Dom."

Unable to risk blurting more of her feelings to Spence, she chose to ameliorate those of her uncle and she hastened to catch up with him. But he kept himself as fortified as Pharaoh's army, talking to anyone who looked the least interested. Cat felt so forlorn she wished she had taken Spence's offer but knew that would never do.

She made what chatter she could with a few people she barely knew and as the exhibit began to empty, she glanced about but could not find her uncle. She went from one darkened room to another, feeling particularly vulnerable and . . . chary. Yet not . . . stalked. Not *here*. Not *now*. The distinction gave her courage but no relief from sorrow over Dom. She might as well go home.

At the exhibit hall door, she saw the gallery caretaker shrouding the cases for the night.

When she asked after her uncle, the bull-faced little man gave a shake of his head. "Gone, mum. Through the back door. I'll show ye out. Do ye have yer carriage?"

Dying to leave here, she nodded that she did. She'd hail a cab two blocks over on Great Russell Street.

Making her way to the cloakroom, she found that hers was the only coat remaining. Uncle Dominik had deserted her. He must be so angry. So hurt. She'd never intended that. She'd try to explain, make it up to him.

"Come along, mum!" the caretaker called to her from the foyer. Now with the patrons gone and lights out, the gallery grew cold, eerie. She clutched her bronze wool cloak about her, secured her hat, and hurried to the huge ironwork doors. Outside, dusk had become a purple evil. Rain was falling. She'd brought no umbrella. She never thought she'd need it, having come with Uncle Dom. Pushing her collar high, she plunged out onto the street.

It poured down in sheets suddenly. Lightning flashed, and pedestrians scurried for shelter. Two hailed the only cabs available for hire. Cat scurried on. Try though she did to keep close to the buildings, she was getting drenched. Across the street, a shop with a huge overhang afforded more shelter, and she sprang into the cobbled road.

Gaslight flickered uneasily in the lamps, and the refractions on the stone pavement dappled and darted in startling shadows. Always a good runner, she sprinted into the street to make the shop's awning when she slipped on an uneven stone and went down on her hands and knees. Surprised at her clumsiness, she stared at her fingers splayed on the road.

A crack of a whip made her lift her head. Her skin prickled.

A carriage took the corner of the Wyngate Gallery at a high speed, careening around the curb with such fury that the horses whinnied. The driver lashed the animals—and headed them straight for Cat.

She scrambled to get up, but fear and the bad road conspired to make her footing infirm. She wobbled, rose, but got only a step or two when she heard another carriage.

This one approached from the other side of the gallery. With the driver bellowing instructions to the team, the shiny black brougham headed straight for the first coach. Cat stood, paralyzed between the two. Wild, the second coach swayed and blocked the other from its path to mow Cat down. Only by mounting the sidewalk did it avoid collision. It missed Cat by scarcely an inch.

Stunned, speechless, she stood in the middle of the road, hands limp at her sides as the second coach ground screaming wheels to a halt.

A giant figure of a man emerged, enveloped by an ebony Inverness cape, its points flying on the night wind like bat's wings.

Terrified, Cat spun and began to run as she sobbed. But he called to her, darting after her and lunging for her. "Cat, sweetheart. It's Spence!"

Two strong arms circled her and made more sense than words. "Spence," she breathed and sank into him.

He picked her up and carried her back to the brougham. She clung to him, fingers like talons in his coat. When he needed her to use her legs to climb inside the conveyance, she accomplished it with more eagerness than grace and fell into the supple squabs like a heap.

In seconds, Spence was beside her, coursing his hands over her and reassuring himself of her safety. "Thank God, thank God. You're not hurt." He put his lips to her forehead, shifted, and took her up across his lap. Settling a few loose cushions behind her, he propped her to face him as he delved into her eyes. "You're fine, love. Just frightened. That was such a scare."

She clutched the butter-soft wool of his cloak with two trembling hands. Her teeth chattered loudly.

He kissed her brow and undid the ties of her cloak. "You're soaked. Get this off. I have a blanket. Here . . . There," he crooned as he drew it about her shoulders and draped his coat over her legs. Settling her head into the crook of his shoulder, he took out the pins from her hat and let down her wet hair. "You're shaken. It will cease. I'm here and no one is going to lay a hand on you."

Loving the feel of his succor, she squeezed her eyes closed as he dried and cared for her. "You waited for me."

His hands enfolded her and rhythmically stroked her back. "I wanted to make certain you'd get home."

She shook her head, sniffles giving her away.

He held her like that for some interminable time while his horses clomped their way through the beating rain. "You didn't have a chance to talk to Dominik, did you?"

"No." Her tone was ragged.

He sighed and leaned over to open a drawer beneath the seat. Fishing inside, he extracted a flask, had her hold it in one hand so that he could twist off the gold cap. Upending the top to use as a jigger for something that smelled bracing, he poured and told her to drink it. "Slowly." At her question, he replied, "Anisette. You need it. I don't want you down with pneumonia on top of a bad case of fright."

"When Marsh sees me coming home like this, he and Uncle Dom will make conclusions that might be worse than death."

"Don't say that!" He gripped her arms and gave her a hard little shake. "I'll speak with them!"

Coming more to herself, she straightened. "You most certainly will not."

"I'll not have them lighting into you tonight, not after what you've just been through!"

Her whole body sang with gratitude for his vehement care. "They won't. They have never yelled at me. *I'll* tell them. The two of them are not prigs, just . . . Well, they are more aloof than my father. Surely, you understand."

He frowned. "If I say I do, then you'll take it that I agree with you. Which I don't. Dominik and that butler of his can be morbidly determined, I tell you."

"Why do I have the feeling that if I were a man you would have said something slightly more . . . colorful?" Her eyes twinkled and the anisette, she knew, reached so many formerly cold places, some of them corners of her heart.

"Because you're instinctive, kitten." He lifted one forefinger to twine about a wet escaped curl and tuck it behind her ear. In the process, he brought her chin up and brushed his lips across hers. "I would have died if anything had happened to you."

Her breath slowed. He lifted the jigger from her fingers. Freed, her hand grabbed a fistful of his coat and cravat, bringing his tempting mouth to hers more firmly.

But he spoke on it. "I have only just found you again and begun to win you back. I couldn't lose you

now. Not when we can have everything we wanted—
and more."

Lulled by his care of her and the liquor, she pressed
closer. "You say the most appropriate lovely things."

"All true." He crushed her up to him. "I swear." He
tantalized her with a sheer whisk of his lips across
hers.

Scared tonight by her uncle and the near dance with
death, she wanted his kiss for the serenity, the excitement his lips gave her. "Tell me more," she pleaded
on a thread of sound.

"Better, I'll show you. Always," he promised and
gave her what her starving soul had craved for days,
years, eons, of her life without him.

His lips met hers like a prayer. Gentle, reverent,
searching for the key to survival. Warm, liquid satin,
his mouth pressed hers. Opening, sighing, she let him
have his way. Nibbling her upper lip and sucking her
lower one into his mouth. Mesmerizing her with his
ardor as he took his infernally good time.

She mewled, jammed her fingers in his silken hair,
and pulled back to see his eyes glisten as he swept his
arm around her waist and took her under him. She
reveled in the luxuriance of his weight pressing her
down, of his careful hands lifting her face, and his
lips—his two firm lips—slanting, commanding, devouring, hers.

He offered paradise, barely glimpsed so long ago
and spread before her now in the splendor of a primal
Eden.

"Spence, darling," she called to him between kisses,
"I missed you so." Her hand elaborated as she defined
the man so long denied her, his cheeks, his throat, his
chest, his pounding heart.

He pressed her palm there while his mouth spoke
on hers. "Let me give you what we never had. I

promise I'll make this wonderful for you, sweetheart. Better than before. So much fuller. Richer. Perfect." He took her hand and led it inside his shirt to his bare skin. Buttons popped. Their mouths met.

Jungle fires spread.

Consuming reason, pain, and untold grief.

Roaring in a storm of desire so long ignored, nothing could halt the assault on the past. Forgetfulness, blessed and fierce, rose up with the passion in her body.

She gave a sob of acknowledgment and he caught it, transforming it into a moan of mutual need. His kiss this time left no portion of her mind uncertain of his infinite meaning to her. He gave her sweet fulfillment and took primitive possession. Together, they reached past torment to satisfaction and insatiable desire for more and more.

He raised his face, leaving her swollen lips parted and cool. "I wish to God I could have you now." His eyes adored her breasts and face as his big hand splayed over her ribs. "But I won't make love to you in my carriage for just a minute or two. When you and I come together for the first or the thousandth time, it'll be slow and deep and last forever. Oh, Cat, I want to show you how I'll take such good care of you. How I'll be the very best husband."

She writhed against him in splendid agony of thwarted desire. Her breasts ached and her loins throbbed. She dug her nails into him, avoiding the greater issue of marriage for the immediate one of desire. "What am I supposed to do now? Go home and gnash my teeth in frustration?"

He winked. "I know the cure and I want to give it to you, but first you must do something for me. For us."

Pleased, she nuzzled his chin. *"What?"*

"Marry me."

Her eyes fell closed. Her heart paused. What she wanted was within her grasp. She need only take it—and trust he would never change his mind. If only she could learn to believe in him again with every part of her mind, the same way her body instinctively declared he was meant for her.

He stroked her hair. "It's so fast, exactly like the first time. Love beyond reason or propriety."

For a response, she could only wrap him close.

"I know," he whispered into her hair. "It's even harder to come to terms with it this time, isn't it? The way we want each other is fierce. But we've seen how life is so desolate alone. Without you, I haven't laughed. I don't cry. I'm a machine. I hate it. I can't live without joy. Not any more. I can't—*won't*—live without *you.*"

The carriage had stopped. The rain thrummed on the rooftop, creating a tattoo she could interpret as a dirge to purge the past—or a hymn to the future. She could choose.

He arched back to look down at her, and in the lamplight, she could make out the savage loneliness in his eyes. "I have watched you, darling. Since the moment I laid eyes on you last Friday at Dorrie's, I saw what your life's been like. Before you knew I was there, you were desolate, too, my love. Then when I came to you, you came alive. Fear, anger, sorrow, desire, you felt it all! And you couldn't hide it. Not from me."

He was so right. Why—after her infinite sorrows over him—did she just simply *know* they were meant for each other?

"You need me, Cat. You have to share the joys and tears of life with me, the same way I must have you. There's no escape. I thought there was and that's why I left you. My main reason wasn't the conflict between

Merrick and your father. I let you think that because it was convenient and saved *my* pride. The barest truth is, darling, that I left you because I feared what being so close to you day after day and year after year would do."

I would only have loved you more, her mind screamed.

"I had lived so long fulfilling others' expectations for me that when we planned our life together I suddenly realized I had never fulfilled my *own* expectations for me. My father used the reason that I was too active and needed a firm hand. I'd never gone to a school I wanted or taken a class, never decided on my own profession or even rented a house without asking someone else if they liked it. Clothed in other people's views of me and what I should do, I suddenly felt naked when you and I began to make decisions about our future. I couldn't marry you and give you a man *I* didn't even know."

Compassion rolled over her. Her hand cupped his cheek. "I knew you. Saw to the heart of you. You were and are a good man."

He groaned and jerked her close. "You thought I left because I loved you less than a man should love his wife. But that's so wrong, Cat. I left because I loved you more than reason allowed and I dreaded the day you'd discover I was not my own man. Hated the time that I thought would surely come when you would see me as a creature of necessity and habit, a man who had enormous holes in his self-knowledge."

"Do you know this man now?"

"He knows so much. What he likes and what he hates."

"Tell me."

"He likes the country in springtime. Strong black beer. Indian curry. Japanese bushido arts. Chinese opera. Cats. One cat with hair the color of brandy. Eyes like huge flowers. Heart of gold. Laugh of sunshine. Oh, Cat," he swallowed, "I'm more my own man than I ever was before. Now I know what I lack, too. You. I need your vibrance, your joy, your love. I saw that at the Billingtons'. I want to live again. I want to live with you. I've surrendered to the fact that I'd have to risk you knowing me to the core."

Palm to his pounding heart, she asked gently, "What would I possibly see there?"

"That my love for you has made me *think*, but more, you make me *feel*—the very thing this man had been trained not to do since childhood."

Thrilled by such an intimate admission, she was paralyzed by equal measures of hope and fear. "Spence, I have tried to be logical about this . . . this attraction I still have to you. But I can't get beyond my emotion. I want to be with you—" There, she had admitted it, but what good did it do her? "I need to hear why you think this time can be different from the last."

"What's different is I am becoming the man *I* want to be for me. And I know I am the man who—against the worst odds—you still find lovable. I count myself the luckiest man and then swear to you I'm not running from me or you ever again. I'm here to stay. Refuse me now, it matters not. You'll see me forever. At balls and teas. At the opera. On your doorstep. Eventually, you'll become my wife because you are and will remain my only love, the mate my soul requires."

She caught back a sob of joy.

He cupped her jaw. "Think about this. Fast. I'm so lonely without you. Say yes soon and in the meantime, go inside and see me in your dreams."

"Oh, I always have, Spence."

His eyes went limpid.

"But there's been a terrible recurring problem with my dreams," she explained, smiling at him when he tilted his head in question. "In the flesh, here and now, you surpass any fantasy, my darling."

With two hands of steel, he scooped her up and kissed her swiftly. "Leave before I lose my mind and carry you home with me," he rasped. "I'll see you soon. Everywhere."

She rearranged her hair and attire as best she could, then shot him an imp's grin. "If your sources are good."

"Where you are concerned, if my sources aren't sufficient, I'll rely on my instinct. Wherever you go, I'm right beside you." He flashed a wicked look. "Soon, I'll be so close—so far inside you—you won't be able to banish me. You won't want to."

She vibrated with his sensual promise but flung her hair back in bravado. "So much for not touching," she muttered as his driver swung open the door and the last thing she heard was Spence chuckling.

Darting inside, she sank against the front door with her body singing hosannas that neither Marsh nor her uncle appeared. If they wanted to make a point of ignoring her, that was fine with her. She didn't want anyone to dilute this extraordinary elation.

Running upstairs to her room, she cast off the sodden clothes and rang for the maid to bring her a tray up for supper. She took a hot bath, turned in early, fell asleep instantly to watch Spence walk into her fantasies. Kisses as hot and free as the ones in his brougham had her tossing and disrupting the bed linens. By dawn, she admitted aloud she could never again deny him or the future he offered.

The next morning, as she secured her hat before the hall mirror, the front door bell rang.

Two men stood there. The postman handed over a stack of mail. On top was a letter addressed to her. The foolscap was similar to that first one demanding the papyrus. She quavered as she placed it in her pocket. Then she tried to smile at a perky delivery man who handed over a plum parchment–wrapped package from Roxwell's Stationers.

She closed the door on both men. Like a glutton taking refreshment first, she tore open the purple package. Inside ivory damask sat a fine fountain pen and matching inkwell.

Spence's card read simply, "For great expectations."

The foolscap letter said, "The day draws nigh. Have you found it yet?"

Chapter 9

Where was she going *now?*

Spence muttered an oath and felt his driver lurch the hired cab forward through the streets of Mayfair to wherever Cat wandered next. Certainly, she had a right to visit Dorrie Billington. He grimaced, thinking what that conversation must have resembled.

But where else could Cat possibly head? Without a maid? Riding in a hired hansom instead of using her uncle's town brougham?

Those were his initial inklings that something was terribly wrong—and that Cat was responding to it. Coupled with his suspicion that last night's runaway carriage was no accident but an attack on her life, her behavior this morning worried him.

Her first stop had seemed innocuous enough. She'd gone to her milliner's. For precisely eighteen minutes, she had debated feathers, lace, or straw with the proprietress. Watching her from his carriage through the shop's bay window, Spence caught her infectious élan. It stood him well when next she called upon her father's long-time friend and dealer a few blocks away at Christie's Auction House on King Street. Confounded as to why she would want to spend forty-three minutes with one of the few people whom she had never liked, Spence was clearer about one thing: he was right to follow her. He ordered the driver to trail her carriage at an even more discreet distance. And so had he tracked her to Dorrie's.

Now, it seemed she headed for the older part of the City.

Spence frowned. Was she returning to Thornhill's? According to what Acton had revealed late last night over a game of cards, Cat need not return until next Tuesday when they would award her a small loan. But just when her dingy cab would have turned for the bank, Cat popped out, paid the driver, and hoisted her parasol. Like a woman who knew exactly where she wanted to go, she dodged every obstacle to cross the street. In the crush of people, Spence lost sight of her for frightening minutes only to see her reappear at the corner. A vision in a walking suit of salmon sprinkled with creamed lace, she sedately walked up to another hack, spoke with him briefly, and climbed into *his* cab!

Now, Cat, you're making my life too intriguing.

Spence fumed at her ingenuity. What was she doing, parading about town? Wait till he got his hands on her. Then she'd know she was never supposed to go for . . . the Thames? The docks? Why in hell was a woman alone at half past eleven in the morning going to the river?

He soon knew.

This time when he cursed, he did so out loud as he saw her alight from the rickety brougham.

He himself had come here only last night. He knew why *he* had skulked about her father's old factory.

But what was *her* reason?

Immediately after he'd left Cat at her uncle's doorstep last night, he had decided the wayward coach in front of the Wyngate Gallery was no accidental threat. Something about the stillness of the night before she tripped in the street spoke to him of a planned attack. Someone had waited for her to emerge from the gallery, of that he was instinctively certain. Then when she fell on the slippery cobbles, that someone had taken full advantage of her vulnerability.

Thank God he had been there, waiting and watching for her, hoping he might make it up to her for the trouble he had caused her with her uncle. If he hadn't been there, he could not bear to think how she now might be maimed, or worse, gone from him forever, taken by maliciousness. He had lost his brother to the vice of opium. He vowed he would not lose another loved one to any evil if he could help it.

She was too precious.

Too *bold,* dammit, to be out here by herself! Opening that door that was so old it almost fell off its rusted hinges. Entering to traipse about in the dark past cobwebs dangling from the leaking roof.

What in creation was she after?

He had not found a thing. Though he had hoped for a trove of Walter Farrell's findings, he knew he'd settle for a few baubles. But the three stories were virtually empty. The only items he had discovered were six wooden boxes so long and wide he thought them coffins. He'd retrieved a steel rod he'd spied on the first floor and pried up the top of each container only to see rotting papier-mâché-backed books from Kashmir. He'd opened every one over his cape spread upon the dusty floor, careful lest the lacquer bindings cracking on his gloves flake over the floor and leave telltale signs of tampering. The books were faded and, even when newly printed, had obviously been poor reproductions of the famous Indian treatise on love by a third-century Brahman. Nonetheless, Spence knew such a nefarious product could have found a lucrative market in the London underground's appetite for erotica. Whatever the reason Egyptian archaeologist Walter Farrell had acquired them and left them here, he had not hidden a mysterious papyrus in the lot.

The entire search of the factory had consumed less than thirty-two minutes. Dashed by his failure to find anything, he had ordered his hack to return him to the door of White's, where he joined a game with a very morose—and very drunk—Acton Thornhill. He had queried Acton, hoping in his sodden state the man might reveal his woes. But he wouldn't. So promptly at one o'clock, when Spence's own driver had appeared with his brougham, Spence had learned only "how terribly sorry, awfully bereft" Acton was for some act he had committed that very day.

Eerie as Acton's words were, Spence found himself reviewing for the rest of the night the odd happenings of the evening while he paced his chambers in growing fright for Cat. With each new minute had come the stronger belief that some force conspired against her—and that the assault on her last night had been planned. At the edge of that horror arrived the conviction that if he had been presumptuous to follow her before, he was terrified of what might happen to her if he didn't now.

So here he sat, tapping his foot, cooling his heels, when he could merely march himself inside and tell her that she'd find nothing. Of course, that would be like inviting a Fury to dine on his carcass. She would be entitled to, certainly.

He fished for his watch, then noted the time. She'd been in there for twenty-two minutes. He recrossed his arms. Flexed his legs. He considered the spare lines of the Georgian brick warehouse that was her father's and then examined its duplicate next door. The painted sign above it read, Ball and Bull: Importers of Fine Tea. He snorted. The name was *all* balls and bull. It should have read, Ball and Chain: Smugglers of Pure Opium.

Merrick had known of it. Spence's contacts in the Foreign Office had often pulled their hair out over how to end William Ball's and Rupert Bull's insidious operation, which was a sore point in relations with the Chinese government. They'd even called on his own talents to put these two out of business. But Spence had found nothing substantive. Not in Calcutta or Shanghai and not here in London. It was a bitter pill. Merrick had noted how it vexed him and pleaded with him to increase his efforts. He had, but he never could best them with any substantial proof. That too he told to Merrick and should never have. Merrick used the information against Spence. In a drug-induced haze, his older brother had ranted on about how Ball and Bull ran opium for Walter Farrell and how these two had to be stopped. That was before Spence knew anything about Merrick's complicity.

Spence sighed, remembering old disappointments in Walter and Merrick. Old hurts caused him and Cat by the same two who supposedly loved them both . . .

His eyes skimmed the skyline—and halted. From a top-story window of Farrell's warehouse emerged one thin figure.

A man.

Spence bolted upright.

Cat! Christ above—He grabbed the door handle, his eyes glued to the stick who moved like a snake along the window ledge. Confronting a drainpipe, the intruder was not deterred but simply began to climb. At the roof, he swung himself up and over. Headed for the Ball and Bull roof.

"'ey, guvna!" The hackney called down through the thin floorboard of his perch. "She's off agin, she is! Shall we 'ave after 'er?"

Spence barked his answer and leaned toward the window to check the lithe female form for any disability. She appeared hale and hearty, if nervous, as she locked the front warehouse door and turned for her own carriage, her eyes surreptitiously surveying the yard and street. Satisfied she wasn't hurt, Spence sank away so that no one might see in but he might watch the thin man finish his walk atop the roof and disappear.

The cab lurched into motion. Jarred against the tough leather seat, Spence retrieved his hat from the dirty floor. He craved a whiskey and a bath, and not necessarily in that order, once this little jaunt of Cat's was finished. Then he was going to inject himself into her presence, run his hands over her elegant little body, and shake some sense into her before he hauled her over his shoulder and made off with her. Permanently. Legally.

To a safety *he* devised and *he* controlled. His name, his house, his arms, his bed.

"Are you following me?" Cat asked him after he'd finally caught her alone between dances with half of the eligible men of England. She stood to the other side of a giant palm plant, blithely gazing out onto the Marlows' ballroom floor.

He choked down his champagne. No one had ever detected his game. "Why would you think that?" he said, congratulating himself that he sounded more serene than he felt.

She turned slightly, obscuring even her profile from his view, and fanned herself in languid camouflage. "I feel your eyes on me."

"How encouraging." He swirled his drink and lifted one corner of his mouth in appreciation of her awareness—and then, of course, came the crushing fear just behind it that the gaze she felt upon her was not his but the lingering sensation of that thin man emerging from her father's factory. No one else followed her. Of that, he was quite positive. She had run him batty these last three days.

She'd gone to the offices of the Oriental Historical Society, the British Museum, *and* the Victoria and Albert. That was only Thursday afternoon. Moreover, she had done it in what appeared to be the best humor—and in great innocence, for she had taken her uncle's brougham.

Friday morning found her puttering about in a booksellers' shop in Finsbury Square. When she emerged—an unnerving two hours and forty-eight minutes later—she had no books in hand.

Wild to know her purpose, he had followed her back to Eaton Square before returning to talk with the proprietor of the Temple of the Muses. He'd fabricated a story of looking for a lovely lady dressed in teal, indicating he was to have met her there and asking if the man might possibly have seen her.

Indeed he had, said the molelike fellow. He wished she didn't return any time soon, too. She had stripped his shelves of any book referring to ancient Egypt, leading him on a merry chase up and down the ladder, and hadn't bought a thing. He'd pointed to a pile on a reading table.

"And those are the ones I haven't yet replaced!" He gamboled off, arms chock full of books, sputtering about the ingratitude of patrons.

"You must stop this, Spence."

He blinked, his attention consciously engaged by her lush form in the outrageously low-cut *poult de soie,* held up—it appeared—by a string of blush roses round her shoulders—and her merest breath. "I'm performing a public service, my dear. I'm tracking you so that when those rose petals wilt and fall, I can place my coat about you and save your reputation."

In gales of laughter, she looked even more provocative.

He grinned, lounging one shoulder against the malachite marble column, knowing she would converse—and laugh—and society go begging. "How full is that dance card?"

"Fuller than last Friday's, thanks to Dorrie and Blanding and Rand. You, too. All of you conspired to have me readmitted to the fold, I think. I owe every one of you so much." Her eyes traveled in the direction of the three who conferred together across the floor.

"Then give me a dance as payment."

"The same as last week?" she teased. "I would love to, Spence, but this waltz is my one vacancy and it's too late to begin."

He nodded to Marietta Hornsby as she sailed by in the arms of her lover, the duke of Inniesfield. "Not for us."

Cat inclined her head to acknowledge Edwina and John Marlow as they made their way through their guests. "People know we are friendly."

"Friendly!" he fumed. "I want to be partners."

She glanced down at her hands. "I know," she offered. "I was thrilled with the pen and inkwell." She faced him, ripe gratitude in her passionate purple eyes. "It means much to me that you approve of my efforts. *All* of them. That you don't try to control me either, like my father used to at times. I know I have so many interests. It's one of my challenges that I must make priorities, and more than others, I must keep them."

"Each of us must make choices, sweetheart. You're an active woman. You like to have many projects. That's no negative, Cat. Not for me. I adore you as you are: wild, free, full of the energy of life!" Her lovely lips parted in delight as he lowered his voice to a passionate depth. "I praise God you're who and what you are and not sitting home crocheting doilies for the Ladies Home Society bazaar!"

She blinked, innocence incarnate. "Oh, do they need help?"

He threw her a warning look. "I have other ways to keep you busy. Other places. Say the word. Name the day."

"Spence." She closed her eyes. "Please don't distract me. I can't talk about this right at the moment. You are too . . . pervasive, determined. I have problems."

He inched closer, her blush of desire driving him insane. "Yes. You were going to tell me at the gallery the other night." *Explain why you need money from Acton if you have five thousand pounds from me.*

She shook back her hair, a cascade of burnished ringlets emitting the fragrance of roses. "The school."

"What else?"

Bright with anxiety, her sweet eyes met his. "That's enough, isn't it?"

"Yes. It should be. But there is more, isn't there?" He went nearer, the warmth of her body drawing his, the coolness of her fright chilling him, spurring him on. "Confide in me, Cat."

She set her teeth. Swallowed. "I need more money."

He scowled. "How much?"

"Six thousand pounds."

"I'll give you a bank cheque in the morning."

"You don't ask why but simply do that for me?" she asked on a ghost of a whisper.

"I know why I do it—and so do you, darling. What good is money if I can't give it to my future wife?"

"Spence, Spence. I can't accept it!"

"Why not?" He plastered a nonchalant look on his face as Rand, Blanding, and Dorrie approached them. "I want nothing more nor anything different than what I asked for as compensation on Tuesday. Look relieved, will you, darling? I told you I'd help you and I will . . . Well, hello, Dorrie." He took her hand and kissed it while the men greeted Cat. "Have a vacancy on that card of yours, do you? It seems I need to dance for a round or two." With that, he joined a conversation about which he knew not one of them cared a whit. They were rallying round to do their social and political duty as well as their friendly service to Cat. He couldn't wait to get her alone.

That became the rack over which he was stretched for the rest of the ridiculous evening. Hating protocol, despising the circumlocutions of such events, he threw himself into the melee with rabid finesse.

Rand and Blanding joined him for repartee, noticing with arched brows his intensity. Soon after, Acton Thornhill left Nanette Marlow long enough to stroll with him to the billiard room.

Minutes later, Spence took himself back to the

torture of the ballroom and the sight of Cat dancing
in the arms of a captain of Her Majesty's Horse
Guard. As Spence cheerily contemplated wrapping
the man's ribbons round his throat and hauling Cat
over his shoulder, Dorrie stopped to comment that he
should really cease consuming Cat's every move for at
least five minutes. Edwina Marlow understood as well
and gave witness to it when she rescued him from a
magpie matron who made his eyes glaze with her
vacuous view of British–Indian relations.

"Why aren't you monopolizing Lady Farrell's company?" Edwina scolded without prelude or excuse.

"That obvious, am I?"

"My dear Lord Lyonns, a billboard would be re-
dundant."

He felt vindicated, edging toward ruthless, yet
rueful. "For the sake of us all, Lady Marlow, I am
obliged to pretend indifference for at least a few
hours. Not every one is as forgiving as you."

"As long as Lady Farrell has forgiven you, the rest
of us shouldn't matter a fig."

She was so right. "Yet one must pay the piper."

Ione Campbell maneuvered her way through the
guests, and both Edwina and he predicted her destina-
tion with a quick congress of eyes.

"I leave you to your piper," Edwina said as she
tapped his arm with her fan. Doing her duty by Ione,
Edwina soon removed herself to perform her hostess
requirements.

Spencer endured idle talk with the petite young
woman whose virtues could have been improved by a
solid meal and a mother who might have done her
poor child an immense favor to advise that prune was
simply not the best color choice to trap a man. Instead
of appearing gruff or downright boorish, Spence put
on a show even Ione believed. Recognizing that the

child intended to remain here until the orchestra again took up its instruments, he devoted himself to the task of making the heiress Campbell *the* subject of tomorrow's breakfast conversation. Rather than see her served up as dregs, he decided she'd crown the menu.

Astonishment that Ione had half a brain should not have hit him so hard. But when Ione commented with some prudence about the current state of British–Indian affairs, he engaged her in earnest. So as he led her out to the floor for their second waltz, he knew he had not only enjoyed their discussion, but he had succeeded in two efforts. By ten tomorrow morning, Ione would be so well reviewed that she would be dubbed this season's "Success." But before this dance was through, he would be murdered.

By Cat. Her huge hurt iris eyes yelled it at him across the gilded gaslit room.

He had all he could do to summon his renowned restraint and finish the Strauss. But it wouldn't have mattered if he'd prematurely departed the arms of Ione anyway. One glance at the girl told him she was already walking him down the aisle of some lily-bowered chapel. And by the time he had extricated himself and deposited Ione with her mama, Cat— damn his soul!—had disappeared.

Where *was* she?

He stomped inside the ballroom from his fruitless search of the garden. A check of the guests told him she had not returned.

Had she left?

Not likely, since her uncle hung about. Why Dom came to such events he and Merrick had never known. Just like his brother, Walter, who attended to perform his social duty by Cat, Dominik usually sat scowling in a corner or gaming. Tonight was no exception.

Ripping fine with him. Dom could glare at Spence from his perch till kingdom come. Spence wanted Cat.

Making his way through the crowd, he saw Dorrie reenter from the main hall. Spurred, he took her aside and asked if she'd seen Cat.

Dorrie's green eyes bored into his. "Only Thursday morning, I was forgiven my sin of omission from last weekend. Now you ask me to commit a greater one."

"If you've just come from her, I venture to say that you know how badly I need to talk with her."

Dorrie snapped her ivory fan open and tore her attention to the dancers. She lowered her voice, her lips tight with determination. "If you botch this, Spence, I'm going to personally and very slowly dispatch you by pulling out your toenails one by one."

"Christ, Dorrie, take any part of me you want! Without Cat, I'm useless anyway."

That melted her frost. "She's repairing her rather ravaged heart in the library."

"Where is that?"

"From the reception hall, take the left wing. The library is the last door on the left."

He squeezed her elbow. "You won't be sorry."

"Mmm. See that you're not."

It was more than he could do not to fly through the mansion. But the place was more a gymnasium, jammed with females to politely acknowledge and dodge, men to postpone, and corridors longer than his increasingly short patience.

But at the library door, he paused, hand upon the brass knob, and prayed. If she was still in here, he had to make certain that when she came out she was his— as he had always, only been hers.

He turned the handle, slipped inside, and sank against the closed door, the smell of good books, beeswax, . . . and ripe roses smoothing the feral edge of his fears, honing his hunting skills.

In the gloom, a tiny intake of breath told him he'd found his prize. His nostrils flared, filling with the scent of her. His eyes, so used to black, absorbed and assessed every shelf, table, ladder, globe, stained glass window. Above, the catwalk was empty, as vacant of life as here below. Or so it seemed. He knew better. He could feel her inside every portion of his brain, atop each pore, with every beat of his very lonely heart.

Yet nothing moved. Only a mild spring breeze wafted from an inglenook with casement ajar. Shadows slid across the walls of the reclusive retreat, accenting the hollows of bookshelves, the contours of a chintz-covered chair and the arm of its matching sofa, hidden from his sight but not his probing mind. The night was dark, soft, his.

With practiced stealth, he moved forward. His eyes on the nook, he found his way illuminated by the compliance of moonbeams. They shot across the chrysanthemum chintz chair, darted along the swell of the overstuffed sofa and defined the grace of pink *poult de soie* blanched to pearl in the moonglow. His eyes traveled the curve of gown, the nip of waist, the glory of her breasts, her roses, heaving with her fear and, now, her outrage.

For the merest of moments, so brief he would have ever after sworn it never existed, her eyes met his. She gave him her fright.

He offered comfort.

She sent him insult.

He returned consolation without apology.

She sprang to her feet. Headed around him, she

misjudged his tolerance and the number of inches she had in which to escape him. His fingers clamped over her wrist like iron over silk. Fresh to her feet, her balance was not what it could have been. Predator unbroken, he easily caught her with the other hand, spun her to him and forced her arms behind her. The move brought her flush to his form but offered him no clear victory. He felt it dramatically as she lifted her foot and ground her heel into his toes.

He oofed.

She kicked his ankle.

He cupped her firm derriere, attempting to show her his body's best intent, when her knee came up and would have disabled him from that possibility if he'd not thrust his leg between hers.

She managed to gouge her thigh to his groin, if only in weak imitation of the harm she would have done had she full sway.

"Stop that!" he yelped and clutched her so hard he heard her breath scythe through her teeth.

"Not"—she struggled left and right—*"bloody"*—rubbing her breasts across his chest—*"likely!"* She set his body ablaze.

In the red flames that burnt his reason to ashes, his anger rose with his need to tame the sweet animal in his arms. He caught her to him and let his weight bear her beneath him down to the couch. Trapped.

"Now, my naughty kitten"—he spread her arms wide and settled his torso along hers in the most satisfying position for his conquering state of mind— "we'll talk."

"Talk!" she scoffed and squirmed beneath him. "I wouldn't converse with you if—"

He captured her delicate face with one determined hand. He went to stone. "You're right."

She blinked, eyes behind lacy lashes stunned and wary. "I am?"

"There is no need."

She twitched her brows. Delved into his gaze.

Before her instincts served her, he kissed her.

Surprise accelerated the speed of surrender. One instant she was taut and breathless, the next she was sinking into the cushions with the pressure of his mouth on hers. Relentless, he claimed her lips with the command of a man denied, starved, dying. He took his sweet time, satisfied his need for justice and reward, claiming her as hostage to his ravaged sense of pride. He adored her mouth, following his first exploration with a groan of delight and endless new positions, slanting across her mouth in expressions of how he wanted her madly, sanely, delicately, any goddamned way he could get her. Going up on his elbow, he curled one hand around her nape to bless her lower lip, her jaw, the tiny curve beneath her chin he loved to lick and then anoint with the benediction of his mouth. He kissed her cheek, her brow, her earlobe, and let his tongue outline the shell of her ear. She shivered, her hands, now free of his, flowing up his arms across his shoulders, her fingers tangling in his hair. With a tug and a moan of need, she brought his mouth back to hers and spoke with words he'd dreamed of for three years and would have robbed heaven to hear again. Now they were his.

"I don't want to," she whispered in an achingly beautiful sound, "but I love you," and pressed her open mouth to his.

Astonishment did much to spike his ardor. He groaned, took her offering, and returned her passion a hundredfold. He ran his tongue inside her mouth, probing and meeting her own in hot response. Her hands wound inside his tuxedo, tugging at his shirt at the waistband of his trousers. As her hot fingers met his skin, he trailed fiery kisses down her throat across fevered satin to roses now wilting for him and breasts standing high and full in expectation. He nestled his lips into her voluptuous cleavage and nudged at the fabric of her décolletage. She undulated back to the couch and then stunned the hell out of him as she stretched upward, a feline arch of grace and sexual desire. Her breasts slid from the roses with an easy rise and fall of petals that made him pant. He smiled at the sight before him.

Round as coins, her nipples blossomed at the touch of his eyes. Pale, they were much larger than he'd ever imagined. "How did God make you so damn beautiful?" he asked as his eyes met hers and one finger circled the circumference of one breast and then the begging, hardening other. Fluttering her lashes in confused ecstasy, she swallowed and must have begun to think twice of what she'd done or even said, because she shut her eyes and tried to roll away.

"No!" he rasped and caught her back. "Look at me." She wouldn't, so he placed his palm to her cheek and said, "I swear I'm not letting you leave me until I say this. Catherine Farrell, dear heart, I love you."

Her eyes swam with tears, and she squeezed them out to trail her temples.

He traced them with the backs of his fingers. Tenderness could lure her, strength could subdue her, but what could convince her? "What words can tell you how sorry I am for years ago and how innocent of wrongdoing tonight? What I did in there just now was nothing more than good manners. No other woman— no other person on God's green earth—surprises me, inspires me, moves me. Oh, Cat, let me spend my life showing you how you touch me and how I can and should touch you. Won't you end our mutual misery and marry me?"

With a cry that socked the breath from him, she wound her arms around him. "I want to."

"Try harder."

"I'm in agony, dying to trust you."

"Then forget the one bad memory and remember only the good days. Do it with your heart, love."

On a gasp, she rose against him. "I do."

He brought her to his body as if she were made of the crystal he'd sent her. He brushed her mouth and said, "You won't be sorry, darling. You'll be thrilled, treasured, mated, *mine.*" He heard her cry, took her lips, rolled the areola of one breast between his fingers and felt her harden to a diamond, rare and priceless, in his hand. When she put her own hand atop his, he knew he could continue and bent. With reverent care, he lifted her breast to his mouth and prepared her with two hot swathes of his tongue. She clutched his hair. He sucked her into his mouth in one swift pull to paradise.

She arched like a bow, clamped his nape, his shoulder, writhed. She tasted of roses, sandalwood, and musky need. He loved her satin skin, the gossamer feel of her nipple inside him, as soon—so very soon—he must be inside her.

A click pierced their moans.

A whoosh of air drifted across their mingled heat.

A footfall and then more tore them from rapture.

"This had better be important!" a bass voice cursed.

Spence went to stone. Cat opened her mouth and he caught her with his lips to hers. With delight pulsing through his bloodstream, his loins raving for release, he eased Cat back to the cushions, his manner shouting his hope that she not make a sound, move a muscle. He stroked her as she shuddered in sexual need, deprivation, and fear.

If someone discovered them now, like this, half naked and halfway to heaven, they'd both have the devil to pay. He kissed her cheek and shook his head while he held her and let her body drift back to some state of normality. Remembering how he had glimpsed the couch from the door, he eased her ever so slowly—mindful of any dangerous rustle of her gown—to the far corner, which was totally obliterated by the hook of the wall.

As clarity of mind returned to him, his anger fed his curiosity about the two men who had so summarily intruded on his affirmation of love and devotion.

"I tell you I don't know what to do now!" a baritone told the bass.

"Why?" replied the elder of the two, gruff and bored. "What's happened?"

Spence consoled Cat with a tiny smile and a huge hug. She came, shaking but easy, to his care. He placed his lips against her temple. When she would have struggled back into her bodice, he waylaid her with a finger across her lips and warning look. In compensation, he brought her close to his chest, her bare breasts securely hidden by the cut of his jacket as he spread it around her and pressed her ever so near. His body raged from denial while he forced it down by concentrating on the sound he heard in the next room.

"She is not cooperating."

The words gave indication of a woman rebuffing a suitor, yet Spence detected another implication.

"How can she not? We have her."

"No, *you* do not!" the younger man asserted.

Cat's fingers stole around Spence's cravat and

gripped it tightly as the older man replied, "Don't be obtuse. You are as much involved as I."

Cat muffled a gasp in his shirt. Spence massaged the nape of her neck and let her calm, then took a finger to her chin so that in the moonlight he could view her face. Her terrified face.

What are you afraid of? he asked her with his eyes.

The younger man answered for her.

"I said only I would do this small favor for you. You cannot make me do more."

"Watch me."

"It's not worth it!"

"No? That was not your attitude weeks ago. What has changed your mind?"

"My conscience."

"Past time to claim it," the older ruminated.

"She refuses the loan. A few minutes ago she told me she doesn't need it."

Spence watched Cat's expression as these words began to make some sense to him. Her startled eyes beseeched him to understand now that these two men discussed *her.*

The younger man continued with, "She says she has a lender."

To Spence, voice blended with vocation. *Acton?* Christ, the younger man was Acton Thornhill?

"Furthermore, she says she won't sell the jewelry. She wasn't inclined to before and she doesn't need the money now."

"I told you to make that offer as a ruse. I didn't want the jewelry. It's a relief she's not biting on that fish. Would have made this whole affair more difficult."

"But . . . *how?*"

"She would have had *money* then, lots of it. I don't

want her to have money to give us, Acton. Christ! I want her to be desperate!"

Cat gulped, terrified practically out of her skin.

Spence wound his arms around her like bands of steel. Pressing his lips to her eyes, he sought to soothe her, keep her quiet while his own mind whirled. What the hell was this about that Acton Thornhill would behave so unprofessionally and Cat would die in his own arms of fright because of it? Was this jewelry Walter Farrell's Egyptian collection at the Wyngate? What did talk of selling jewelry have to do with . . . God in his heaven . . . *blackmail?*

He glanced down at her and asked her with his eyes.

She squeezed her own shut in confirmation.

It was true.

He sought to keep track of what the two were saying.

The younger, Acton, was pacing by now, exclaiming that he'd acted horribly. His rhetoric reminded Spence of what Acton had said the other evening when in his cups at White's. But Acton went on, saying how Cat had found a benefactor, probably Lyonns, who was—from the indications here tonight—hot to have her though he had cast her aside years ago at the behest of his brother, Merrick. "If it is him, I wish him well. She never stopped caring for the man, it's plain to see. But if it's Lyonns or not has no bearing. Someone is helping her, and I am out of my mind with worry that she will discover my ploy."

No problem, there, chum, thought Spence. *You've cooked your goose right here in this library.*

The older man assured Acton there were other ways to deal with her.

Oh, such as?

Cat froze against him.

"You need not know."

"I must. She is important to me."

"Oh? Really?

"Not that way, for heaven's sake. Her family has always banked with us. Her father was very kind to me. I know the world thought him a prig and a trifle too imperial for his own good, but he was kind, generous. Often brought me gifts from his travels. The perfect doting father and family friend."

"I see. So in the interest of trinkets Walter Farrell gave you, you will abandon this project, is that it?"

"No! I just don't want Cat Farrell hurt. Tell me she won't be!" He strode to the older man and from the sound of it, must have put hands on him. "Promise me!"

"Acton, really. I shall do everything in my power to see that Baroness Farrell gives us what we want first." He took the few steps to the door and opened it. "Then we shall consider your request. Good evening, Acton."

Excruciating minutes later, Spence held Cat as they were once more alone in the thick cover of dark. His hands in her hair, he tilted her head back and adored her bewildered eyes. "You have a lot to tell me, don't you?" She nodded and he gathered her nearer. "I must know everything. Rearrange your gown, sweetheart. I'll get your cape."

She groaned. "I can't leave with you. My uncle—"

"I'll take care of your uncle Dominik. I'll enlist Dorrie. I don't know what to have her say, but I'll think of something. You and I are going where we can talk freely and without interruption. Kitten"—he crushed her to him and kissed her hard and swift— "don't argue with me. It's as good as done. You're coming home with me."

Chapter 10

Spence held his hand out to her. His green eyes gleamed in black triumph in the faint light of a lamp he held aloft inside his carriage house. "Come along, sweetheart. No one will notice."

Scant minutes ago, he'd ordered his coachman to stop at the front door of Dartmoor House and deposit him in the flickering street gaslight as if nothing were amiss. Two other carriages passed by, the horses' hooves a hollow staccato in the foggy thoroughfare. Spence's driver had then taken his usual trek to the end of the row of Park Lane townhomes and down the alley to the family carriage house. Though the ebony brougham entered in plain view of every other such garage and many a servants' entrance, the Dartmoor family compound was bordered by a privacy fence and a profuse garden that avoided the prying eyes of the world. Spence had entered his own house by the front door and exited by the back to meet her and lead her to the shelter of his study.

She went with him, past the tulips and crocuses, beyond the kitchen and pantry. Up the back stairs, like a thief in the night, like a woman who had something to hide. God, if that were only true, then she could hand over the papyrus and be done with this mess!

Spence took her cloak and gave it to his butler, whom he dismissed as soon as the man set the fire. Cat stood in the center of the umber Axminster carpet, watching the flames rise in the ceiling-to-floor chalk maw of the fireplace. Spence turned up the gas in one wall sconce. The sparks licked the deep wood paneling with amber and fell over the symmetry of face and form of heart-stoppingly handsome Spencer Caldmore Lyonns.

She tore her eyes away from him to the rest of the room. The shelves contained the classics and a few tomes that weren't. *Boyle on Steam* and *Burnet's Theory of Conflagration* would have made her laugh out loud at any other time. But tonight, her curiosity was dampened by her fears and her memories of the house.

She had never been to the study, of course. Unmarried ladies, even engaged ones, never entered such male sanctuaries. Her visits to the mansion had been to the public rooms for a few ordained occasions. Her first was a supper party in the severe Wedgwood blue dining room. Merrick acted as host with his and Spence's maternal grandmother Caldmore as hostess for fourteen guests, including her father, Uncle Dom, Spence, and her. Weeks later, she'd come to a ball after their formal announcement with half of London congratulating Spence—and her father cursing some latest private insult of Merrick.

"You're freezing!" Spence wrapped his arms around her and drew her forward. "Come here."

He deposited her in a plush brown leather sofa while he stepped away to a coffee and gold japanned cupboard. He unstopped a decanter, poured liberally, and stood once more before her, a snifter outstretched. "Drink this."

She took the Waterford idly and put it down untouched. Spence sank beside her. Tears clogged her throat. All the emotions of the evening—frustration, jealousy, love, anger, sorrow—tangled in knots.

"Sweetheart." Spence tucked her face beneath his chin. "Relax. No one knows you're here. No one will. Dorrie fabricated a story for your uncle about you being upset and deciding you needed to go home with her and Blanding. She said she'd send you home in her carriage to Eaton Square whenever you wished to go. Dominik accepted the explanation easily."

"Though I venture he wasn't happy I chose to confide in Dorrie and not him."

Spence gave her a sad smile for answer.

She would have pulled away, but he kept her securely in his arms. "I'll make you feel better," he promised with determined whisper. She nestled her nose into the silky wool of his coat, smelling the mix of sandalwood with the natural essence of this man who meant the world to her. He tilted her head back and smiled at her as his mouth granted other sensations. Firm lips, warm and tender. Satin tongue, newly flavored with brandy, bathing hers in the intoxicating allure of passion and comfort. His fingers wound into her curls as he drew away and adored her eyes.

"I have never taken a drop of brandy in the past three years but what I've remembered the first time I shared it with you as we did just now. I need to know," he said as his eyes glinted in pain, "that no one else will ever do that for you, with you."

"No one"—she moved toward him—"ever." Tracing the tip of her tongue over his mouth, she admired contours and tasted needs she wanted to savor but knew she couldn't now. Not for a long time. Not until she solved this particular dilemma of money, dishonest bankers, and a missing papyrus. She broke away from him. "I have no right to do this," she told herself more than him and made to rise.

His hand gripped her wrist, pinning her to the sofa. "You have every right. You said you love me. Do it again."

She shook her head, weary. "Spence—"

"I let you go once to face the world by yourself and I was wrong. I *learn* by my mistakes, kitten. I am not going anywhere and neither are you, until you come back here and kiss me again."

A tiny part of her peeked out behind her misery, wanting to come out and play. A chuckle rose from her throat and she tossed him a grin. "I'll do it after you take another sip of brandy."

"Ah, to savor spirits and your skin."

She watched him reach for his glass and drink, holding the liquid in his mouth, tempting her closer with pouting lips and hot eyes. She slid against him, her hand to his thumping heart, her mouth brushing his. "For the many lonely years I've dreamed of doing this, I'm afraid you're going to have to endure my obsession," she teased.

He rolled the liquid around his tongue while his eyes narrowed and focused on her mouth.

"You are my every wish," she said as she trailed her nose up along his, glided her mouth across to his ear, and bathed its tip in the moisture of her mouth. When he vibrated, she felt satisfaction bloom and told him how "I've hungered for you every day you were gone from me, wanting this." She tipped his head down to bless his eyes, his other cheek, his jaw, and return to his lips. "Needing this." Then she indulged every one of her solitary erotic desires and placed her mouth to his. Quaking now, he seized her with iron might but let her lead. His restraint gratified her, feeding her confidence. She glided her tongue along the seam of his lips, moving inside, touching his, tasting the essence of exhilarating liquor and man.

Then he broke.

Gathering her up, taking her back to the leather, he groaned as he thrust his tongue inside her own mouth, warm and wet from him. "I adore you," he chanted between kisses that flamed higher, brighter, hotter, with each new one. Sating himself with her, he fed her, too. A feast of endless delicacies came to her, sweet, spicy, thick, drenched in the rich sauce of love. "Say you're going to marry me."

She laced her fingers in his soft champagne hair and smiled in lazy joy. "I'm going to be your wife till I die."

"I'm going to love you beyond that."

"God, I hope so," she whispered and reached up to spread little affirmations of it across his jaw. "I couldn't bear to be alone in eternity without you. These past three years have been hell enough."

He kissed her hard. "You're going to marry me soon."

"Hmm," she crooned as she let her hands splay across his incomparable shoulders and enjoy the rigid might of his arms. Every inch of him, she thought with a shiver, would soon be hers. "Next season. First thing."

He dragged his mouth to her ear. "I prefer June."

"June?" She pushed back. *"This* June?"

"June fifth to be **exact**."

Her brows knit. "That's not possible."

"Anything is."

"How can you be so sure?" She was wary, amused.

He was not. "I reserved St. Paul's."

Her eyes widened.

"Yesterday."

She gaped.

He looked pleased with himself and too damn nonchalant. "It's one of the smaller chapels, of course. I couldn't get the main one. You can imagine how many of last year's engagements are being consummated this year. But I thought it best, considering the circumstances."

She gripped his lapels.

He seemed nonplussed as he added, "I also have the license. Acquired yesterday as well."

She gulped. "You mean to say you *planned* this, set a date for our wedding, and you never consulted me, never *asked* me? Spence! People will talk how—"

He jerked her to him and her head fell back, the only way to view him at this proximity. "Listen to me, darling. I'm finished playing cat and mouse with you . . . Appropriate that, I suppose," he said with a rueful twist to his mouth. "Marry me, you will, properly but as quickly as custom allows. After the carriage accident and tonight this business with Acton, you need me more than ever. So I care not if you rant and rave at me for presumption, because you must admit that this which is between us"—he glanced down with lecherous intent at her ravaged rose décolletage and she knew he also implied that steely portion of his anatomy that pressed against her thigh—"*this* becomes much harder to deny the longer we wait." He punctuated his double entendre with a devastating kiss that made her moan. "I need only touch you for you to melt like butter in the sun. I could have you on this couch and make you mine without benefit of church, darling."

Despite his temper, she knew him more intricately than that. "But you wouldn't."

He grinned, the knowledge of his power over her raw in his features. However, if his anger was appeased, it was not disarmed. "At this particular moment, I am more than sorely tempted. But I regret to say I require something else first. You must tell me about Acton Thornhill."

"I do need a confidant."

"That I am to you and more."

"Everything," she confirmed, then sat back, her hands in his. "Two weeks ago, I wrote to Acton for a loan. An eleven-thousand-pound loan."

"On Tuesday, you said you wanted to buy a boiler, which cannot cost eleven thousand pounds, darling."

"I know. I . . . needed other things, too. So I asked a lot of Acton. But I was green at it. It was the first loan I personally have ever asked of the bank, and so I thought nothing of asking them. I remember my father asked for a loan once when I was young. He used items from Black Jack Farrell's booty as collateral. Such heirlooms meant little to him compared to the treasures he could find in Egypt. In that one loan, he emptied the old pirate's coffers over my mother's objections. Thank God he never needed any loans again because the only thing the Farrells have left of Black Jack's are these amethysts." Her fingertips grazed the gems at her throat. "Some sixth sense—or call it family pride, if you will—told me not to part with them."

He shook his head. "I don't understand. Are you saying you offered the Farrell amethysts as collateral on a loan?"

She rose from the sofa to go to the fire. "No, though I was tempted. You see I have spent most of my capital on transforming the estate into a school. Old Farrell is now a dormitory. The stables needed a new roof. The kitchen needed more pots and pans. I had to have globes, microscopes, telescopes, scales. For the younger girls, I needed additions to the library. For all of them, I had to acquire items for a gymnasium. Golf, tennis equipment. The list never ended!"

"So you've almost bankrupted yourself to start this."

"Yes. I wanted to do it so very badly money didn't matter. My mother and father enjoyed my behavior, nurtured it, calmed it with their tolerance and encouragement. But you cannot imagine what it's like, Spence, to grow up as such an active child and a *girl* and—even with kindly disposed parents—to be shut off from so many endeavors simply because of your gender. And then to have this boundless energy, this *need,* this *wildness,* to move through life, sample everything, taste everything before . . . before it changes or disappears."

Across the emptiness separating them, his gleaming green eyes went black, meeting hers with desire and compassion. "Sweetheart," he rasped, "you are not alone in that or in anything else. My nature is the same, and I want you precisely as you are. I am so proud of you, darling, that you would want to help others understand their innate selves and flourish. Come what may, I will spend my years on earth helping you do what you know to be your mission on earth—and making certain you're happy."

She believed him. "I always hoped you would."

"My promise on it, love. My vow, too, to help you with this coil. What happened with the loan then?"

"Acton said eleven thousand was too much. The

board of directors would not approve of a loan for a girls' school, owned and operated by a woman with a blemished reputation."

While he cursed, she threw wide her hands. "I was *furious!* I'd never asked him for a loan before and had spent down my family fortune to fund the school, yet he would not agree. In the meantime, the day before, you had offered me five thousand pounds. Though I was not inclined to take your money, I reveled in your kindness and your generosity. I let hope for us bloom in the desert my life had become without you. Soon after, my need canceled pride. My hope multiplied. You became essential to me. Again. I wanted you to be my business partner."

He grimaced. "By that time, I imagined you thought more dearly of me than that."

"I did, though I wouldn't have cared to admit it. Not so soon after that amazing scene on Dorrie's balcony."

His appealing mouth curved in a sultry smile. "I have fond memories of it, despite Marietta's unpleasantness."

"She was certainly on her best behavior tonight."

"She had better remain that way, too."

The grin Cat wore faded.

Spence saw it, and remorse stole over his features. "I don't think she's as important as Acton and this man with him tonight."

Cat wrapped her arms around her waist. "Yes. Did you recognize his voice?"

"No, I'm appalled to say, I found it muffled but familiar. Could you place him?"

She shook her head. Licked her lips. "Whoever he is, he knows an awful lot about my financial affairs."

"What was that about buying up jewelry?"

"When I was with Acton the other morning, he said

there was another way for me to raise money for the school. He told me someone had offered to purchase the jewelry collection on display at the Wyngate. At first, I refused to sell it but left saying I'd consider it and tell him Tuesday when we were to meet again. That collection is my father's last cache from Karnak and I've no intention of parting with it. I felt odd about the offer anyway. It made my skin prickle." She rubbed her arms. "I let him know tonight I definitely wouldn't sell the jewelry." She beamed at Spence. "Your pen and inkwell convinced me I was right to want to keep them and write about them. It turns out I was right to object to the sale. That man with Acton tonight said it was simply a ruse. They didn't want the jewelry anyway."

"But when he first came in, Acton was angry not so much about the jewelry but about the fact that you told him you didn't want the loan. Why, Cat, after going to the trouble to get the loan did you tell him you didn't want it at all?"

Knowing what her reply would mean to him, she paused to smile into his eyes. "Because you told me tonight on the dance floor that you would lend me any amount I needed."

His face filled with joy. "You took me at my word!"

"You said in the library to trust you with my heart, not my memory. I had already minutes before—and acted on it."

"A sound beginning for partnerships," he affirmed as his bass voice stroked her, "but vital to grand love affairs and happy marriages. So tell me the rest, darling. Then we can begin with another aspect clear."

That made her quake. She spun for the fire again. She barely understood what was happening. How could *he?* She had thought so long and hard about this and searched everywhere for the papyrus, finding nothing. How could he help? He wanted to, and two heads *were* better than one. She had told him everything else. Everything except the suspicion she had that the runaway carriage of the other evening was an attack on her life—which he too worried over obviously. "God, Spence, it's such a muddle."

"Cat," his voice cut into her misery, "turn around and look at me." When she finally did, he was staring at her with an inscrutable misery in his face. "Word has it you have enough students to open your school. If Edwina Marlow adds her Corinne to the roster—which seems likely from the way you two get on—you will be set with the proper social circles. Students and money will flow into Farrell Hall. Meanwhile, a boiler costs about a thousand pounds. So what in this green earth do you need ten thousand more for?"

She opened her mouth to blurt it out and choked on the words. It took her another try before she could tell him and even that was a whisper on the night air.

He sat, gone to granite. When finally he breathed again, he declared, "I thought so, but it's worse to hear it confirmed." He shifted. "What do your blackmailers want?"

"I'm to hand over a papyrus that my father found. And do it by next Friday. Either the papyrus, ten thousand pounds, or . . ."

He urged her with a look of pain.

"Or an impropriety of my father's will be exposed. He . . . he forged a document years ago. A papyrus. He told me as he lay dying. He admitted defacing a faded papyrus when he was young and his career unimpressive. He committed the forgery by writing hieroglyphs over the old markings. He did it, he said, to build his reputation. He confessed that he had done it, hated it afterward, but that Merrick had found out when Father sold the document and someone took it to Merrick to translate."

"So that's how Merrick discovered it!"

"Merrick knew of it?"

"Yes. It's a small world, darling. Smaller yet among people interested in the same subjects, like ancient Egypt." Spence frowned. "Is it the forged papyrus your blackmailer wants?"

She wrung her hands. "No, but I *can't* find this other papyrus, and *everyone* will learn of the forgery! Father's reputation will be damaged further. Oh, Spence, whoever this is must think I know how to read hieroglyphics. I understand a few of the cartouches, but I cannot translate entire documents! Even if I did, I don't believe Father would keep *any* papyrus a secret. He'd want the world to know he'd found something so rare. He was"—she hated to admit this about the man who had been so good to her—"terribly proud. Too much so."

Spence sat, mesmerized. "Do you know what this papyrus is supposed to reveal?"

"The blackmailers were quite specific." She swallowed hard. "It is a piece from Karnak, a finding from the last expedition my father made. The one with Uncle Dom. The one in which they found the jewelry. The papyrus is a decree by Ramses II to Moses before he crossed the Red Sea."

Spence shook his head, aghast.

"Utterly fantastic, isn't it, to think my father could find such a significant paper?"

"Even more so to think he would keep it a secret— and that someone would blackmail you to get it. But then who could know the letter from Ramses exists?" He scowled. "Who would want something so rare that it could be identified by anyone with half an interest in the subject?"

She whirled in frustration. "God, if I could find the infernal thing, I'd give it to them! I'd never feel comfortable owning something like that. It would be the crowning jewel in a lifetime of my father's work. I would write about it in his biography, but I am not so addlepated that I would hoard a papyrus of such importance and not show it to the world! It is—by all that's holy—priceless!"

"Therefore, since you have not found this, you must hand over eleven thousand pounds."

"Actually, ten thousand. By next Friday."

"I see. And the other thousand is for the boiler."

"Of course."

He smiled sadly. "Come here."

She went into his arms. Cradling her nape in his fingers, he brushed his jaw across the crown of her hair. "I know much of papyri and Egyptian hiero-glyphics, even the later language of Coptic. Fear not, I'll help you. We'll find it. I can translate it and then we'll know what we've really got." He stroked her back. "Who have you talked to and where have you looked?"

She told him how she'd searched Farrell Hall, the tunnels to the shore. She recounted her London rounds to her father's dealer at Christie's Auction House and friends of his at various museums in town and finally of a fruitless rummage of Farrells' Ware-house on the docks. "Each step I took, I was terrified, Spence. Everywhere I went I felt someone's eyes on me. I can't explain it."

She pulled away to examine his expression as he struggled with some private torment. Finally, he broke the spell by tracing a gentle finger over her brow. "You don't have to, love. You have sharp senses, and you've used them. You need not explain such things to me. I use my own to advantage, too. I have followed you since the gallery opening. I feared for you and wanted to protect you. I've seen only one fellow track you, darling."

"Oh, Spence—"

Before she could ask a thousand questions, Spence told her how he had feared for her after the carriage incident. "Then when I saw this man crawl from the window of your father's factory, I'd be damned if I'd frighten you by going to you and revealing it. I wanted answers about who he was and why he was there before I did that. But I will tell you now. He came from the Ball and Bull factory next door and he came as quickly as he went. Nor have I seen him since. In truth, that man has been the only one I've seen spying on you."

She hugged him, grateful for his care of her and relieved, if vaguely. "You don't think he'll begin again?"

"No. If he was going to, he would have by now. It was a fluke. You must have surprised him in his own foraging activity and then, by your presence, scared him off." When she accepted that with a sigh, he urged her to describe the way the blackmail came.

"In a letter on foolscap."

"Was it posted?"

"Yes. It came through a London letter drop."

"Does anyone else know of it?"

"No. Neither Jessica nor Uncle Dom. I couldn't tell them. Jess needs fewer strains in her life, she's had so very many for so long and I couldn't worry her. Uncle Dom is the same."

"He might be able to help you find the paper."

"True, though I didn't ask."

"Why?"

She avoided his eyes.

"Why, darling?"

"Some inner sense told me not to. Uncle Dom and Father were not getting along ever since their last expedition together and definitely not after our engagement."

"Could they have been feuding over us?"

"Somehow, I don't think so. Not in any direct way. I would say it was a number of older resentments come to one crisis, if you know what I mean."

"Define them for me."

"Father wanted to run the expeditions his way. Over time, Dom wanted independence to perform his own separate investigations. Father refused to back him and threatened to prohibit it. He could be as brutally imperious to Dom as he was to others. Sad to say, though my father was a sweet husband and parent, he was not the kindest brother."

"I, too, have experienced the hegemony of an older brother who thought he knew best about many things." Spence stroked her shoulder with one hand as he remembered Merrick. "I thought the world of my older brother and invested him with many sterling qualities that as I matured somehow tarnished. My major regret is that I did not learn this until after I had left you. I misplaced my trust in him. I shall pay for that naïveté until the day I die."

She cupped his jaw and brought his remorseful green eyes to rest in hers. "Not with me."

"You are forgiving, darling. I thank God you are. For I shall never quite excuse my own insensibility."

"Your loyalty was to him. As mine was to my father."

"My loyalty will now be with you forevermore."

She smiled. "And mine to you."

He kissed the drops from her cheeks with the delicacy of a butterfly sipping nectar, then adored her face. "I have found in you my ideal."

She gripped him hard. "You must not hold me up so high. I am human and *very* imperfect, darling."

"You've given me leave to be the same, love."

She wrapped her arms around his powerful shoulders and drew him close. "We'll be the better for it. Individually and together."

He told her then how they'd start anew. "In love."

"With hope," she confirmed.

"With the greatest expectations," he crooned, accented by kisses and caresses as poignant and diverse as those of hummingbirds from bees.

"I'll take you home," he said at last as he struggled to remove her arms. "Blanding should have sent their carriage round by now. Tomorrow I'll be at Eaton Square at twelve for brunch. I'll bring Blanding and Dorrie with me so that it looks like a courtesy call. We will dig in to find this document of Ramses and be done with this."

"What do you think I should do about Acton? I canceled my appointment for Tuesday because I didn't need to go, but now I wonder if I shouldn't make up some excuse and see if I can get him to talk."

"True. You could say I reneged on my offer."

She made a wry face. "We've had a falling out?"

"Mmmm," he nodded, having fun with this. "Another lovers' quarrel, I'm afraid."

She tsked. "We're riddled with them."

Chuckling, he grabbed her close. "This will be our last, public, private, real, or false."

She ran a hand through his hair that dipped over his brow. "June fifth may be too far away."

"How *do* you read my mind?"

"Where you are concerned, it is my second nature."

He took a devastating kiss from her. "We must go before I forget every one of my best intentions."

They rose but paused as a knock came on the door. The tenor of it denoted its urgency.

"Come in!" Spence called, his hand holding Cat's.

"My lord, forgive me." It was his butler, blanched to the bone with worry. "Lord and Lady Billington are downstairs. I said you were unavailable, but they insisted. In fact, they—"

"Demanded," finished Blanding as he stood in the doorway with Dorrie before him. Both remained in their formal attire.

"Oh, Cat!" Dorrie rushed to her and took her in her arms. "I was so worried!"

"I'm fine, Dorrie," Cat soothed, embracing her friend who must have known she needed no rescue from Spence, especially since he had arranged the cover of their departure with Dorrie. "Really," she said, worried.

Spence curled one hand around Cat's waist, his eyes on Blanding. "No, sweetheart. They're not here because of that. They know I didn't intend to seduce you but only talk with you. Something else is wrong."

At his tone, Cat separated from Dorrie and scanned her friends' faces. The chill drove any warmth from her heart.

Spence settled her back to his torso as if bracing her for a blow. "What is it, Blanding? You look like hell."

"Dorrie and I have come to warn you both."

"Of what?"

"Spence," Blanding bit off, "something dreadful has happened, and you both need to know of it."

A presentiment of lightning force hit Cat. "What?"

"Acton Thornhill has been found murdered."

If Spence had not held her, she would have sagged to the floor.

Blanding looked forlorn as he curled one hand around Dorrie's sobbing form. "He was shot twice in the chest. Death was probably instant."

Cat shuddered. "When? Where was he?"

Spence held her more tightly. "How did you find out?"

"We were at the Marlows'. We were among the last of the guests. Edwina Marlow discovered the body about an hour ago. In the library. In a nook."

"No." Cat wanted to scream as destruction stalked closer with each word.

"I'm afraid so, Cat. Spence, I know you told me tonight you had reason to suspect Thornhill was up to some skullduggery. But this act of violence against him bodes no good for Cat."

"Why Cat, Blanding?"

"Because when the body was discovered, it revealed something significant—and incriminating." Blanding's eyes strayed back to Cat. "Scotland Yard was called in. The inspector now searches for any ladies who wore roses. Pink roses." His gaze drifted down to Cat's décolletage. "Acton Thornhill gripped numerous pink petals in his hand. Every indication points to the conclusion that it was the woman wearing them who killed him."

Chapter 11

Cat stared at Blanding as if he spoke some dead language. Instinct had her turning into Spence's arms, closing her eyes, clutching his shirt.

"Get me smelling salts, Daniel," he ordered his butler as he swung Cat up into his arms and took her to the sofa. Nestling his lips against her temple, he reassured her that no one would hurt her. "No one will take you away. Nothing will separate us. I promise you, never again."

"Who could have killed him?" she murmured, astonished at her outer composure when she only wanted to wail. "The man he spoke with in the library?" She met Spence's eyes, green dying to black with speculation and concern for her.

"Good God, Spence!" Blanding lamented. "You talked with Thornhill in the library?"

"No. Cat and I were together in the inglenook when two men entered. We overheard a conversation between Thornhill and someone else. The second man sounded vaguely familiar to both Cat and me, but we couldn't identify him. They had their discussion, which became a chastisement, really, of Acton. Then our unknown man left. Within seconds so did Acton. Cat and I were gone from there in minutes. But Acton must have returned, whether alone or with someone. It was then he must have been shot."

"Holding my roses," added Cat.

"Since the two of you were together," Dorrie said thoughtfully, "you, Cat, are in the clear. But to tell that to the inspector—"

Spence shook his head and tightened his arms around Cat. "Is impossible. I would never admit I'd met Cat in the library nor spirited her away from a public ball to my home. I've come back to correct what wrongs I did her, not make them worse."

Dorrie thought on it. "I like that but—"

Cat did, too. She kissed Spence's cheek, undone by his noble admission and unrelenting protection of her.

"But in the long run," Blanding objected, "that approach does no good. It leaves Cat without an alibi."

The butler scurried back into the room, a small glass vial in his hands. Spence took it, checked Cat's eyes and the shake of her head so that the salts went unused, and he just as summarily returned it to the man. "Thank you, Daniel. No, don't go yet." He glanced at Blanding. "I need your help."

"Anything."

"Find out precisely what this inspector has discovered. Rose petals are implicating, but you and I know there must have been other evidence at the scene of the crime. Someone may have seen others enter the library. Those others must possess stronger motivation than Cat."

Cat frowned, mulling over who that might be. Customers of the bank. Peers, MPs, any man with the social standing to have been invited to the most prestigious affair of the London season. Spence implied that Acton had enemies. Of course, he must have. The man was dead by someone's foul deed. But for Blanding to discover what the inspector had gleaned meant that he had friends who might transgress normal boundaries. She knew men had means among themselves to discreetly offer information. But this was an infringement on the sanctity of the Yard, hallowed ground not easily breached by gentlemanly inquiries, but by other requests, more demanding. She beheld the endearing man within her embrace in a blazing new light.

"I dare say that this inspector," Spence went on, lost in his own thoughts, "once he investigates Acton and the bank, must find more suspects."

Blanding raised both dark brows dramatically. "So while I am doing this, you will be . . . ?"

"Foiling the inspector."

"By?"

"Removing the only suspect he does have." Spence turned to Cat to give her the fullest consideration with his eyes. "Sweetheart"—he was pleading—"this is not what I would have wanted for you or us. But it's the only prudent thing to do in the circumstances. You've said you trust me now." He took one hand, opened her palm, and placed a kiss there. "Prove it to me just as I now prove my devotion to you. Come away with me."

Overjoyed by his offer, she felt propriety stay her. But fear stood close beside, repulsing her with the threat of a trial and a cage called prison. Nearby loomed scandal, repelling her, compelling her to reach forward. Yet when she touched Spence with two fingers to his mouth, she did so in affection, appreciation, and love. "I want to. But I wonder if I should."

Spontaneous fires lit in his eyes. He took her hand again and squeezed it, pressed it to his heart. "Leave the details to me. You won't be sorry. Daniel," he said to his manservant though he kept his gaze on Cat, "I need you to take the paper on my desk there."

The butler stepped to the oak expanse, clean save for one long document. "This, my lord?"

A glance confirmed it. "Yes. Pocket that and some petty cash. One hundred pounds will do."

Cat sat straighter in his lap. One hundred pounds was far from 'petty.'

Spence trained one errant curl behind her ear. "Go down to the Fleet and bring me back a respectable vicar. Get a Methodist if you must at this time of morning, but fetch me someone who will marry us within the hour."

Marry? "Oh, Spence—" Cat felt her heart leap into her eyes. Faced with what she had wanted most, she wondered if she dared take it now. Was Spence offering this now in love or recompense?

"I told you, darling, I paid the archbishop for a special license yesterday. We can be married at any time or any place. Under the circumstances, I can use it to best advantage. I want to take you from London to keep this inspector on the track of the murderer. Too often, Scotland Yard ends an investigation when the evidence appears complete but is nonetheless circumstantial. I cannot allow them to stop. If you come with me, though, I won't take you anywhere without blessing of church and state. Then if it ever has to come to light that you were with me alone, we can honestly say we were married. What do you say, love? Will you have me? Now?"

She flung her arms about him. What words could possibly impart how very much she wanted to share whatever moments she could with him? Her sense of impending doom equaling her desire for a tiny taste of heaven made her ignore the major question of his motivation. "I'll have you, Spencer Lyonns," she whispered to his ear. "For now and forever."

The minor elements of any ritual seemed insignificant, though combined, created an aura that colored events far beyond the reach of the particular ceremony. So, too, was it with his wedding, Spence concluded.

He brought Cat closer in the night shadows of his coach, and she settled against him with a ragged sigh. His lips went to her unbound hair, a benediction meant to keep her within his care, away from harm. His eyes fell to her wedding band, his gold signet ring with lion rampant. It was a far cry from the Dartmoor earls' traditional diamonds, which currently sat in Thornhill's vaults awaiting the newest countess.

Even Cat's bouquet on the seat opposite them made him rue the haste of this event. A melange from his conservatory, the spray consisted of no proper lilies or orchids but of pink hydrangea blossoms, irises, and Queen Anne's lace. Dorrie had done a superb job of arranging them. But if the flowers spoke of the need with which they had met this hour, so too did his wife's traveling suit, splendid azure frothed with an ecru *canezou*. Her clothes, like the few items in the portmanteau strapped in the boot, were borrowed from Dorrie. No corsets or trains or bustles, no morning gowns or lacey nightgowns for a new bride came with them. It was far from the extravagant trousseau Cat deserved nor what he violently wished her to have.

Nor had the liturgy, which gave grace to the sacrament blessing their love, done everything he wished. It had not eradicated every injustice. Certainly, not those he had done her three years ago. Only, ironically, had it put fine polish to an action meant to help him hide Cat from the law—and its tangled ways of justice. The minister had gone far to lighten the occasion. A refreshing surprise, the stubby cleric was jolly for that hour of the morning, acting as if this were a normal occurrence. Though it probably was for him, that very fact for Spence veiled the atmosphere in a lurid haze. Try though he might, Spence could not lift the carnal curtain. Even the fact that they climbed into his coach, his horses put to with speed, and their hooves wrapped to muffle their sound on the city's cobbles cut him to the quick.

No, this wedding was not good enough for her, forgiving and joyful soul that she was. He prayed she would not sense his mood nor view the event with like mind. For that way lay greater disasters that reached far into their future.

Agonized over events of past and present that he could not control, he shifted in the voluminous squabs of his brougham and clutched his bride closer. With mute oaths, he condemned the aspects of the evening that had gained him the one treasure he wanted on this earth—and brought her to him under less than the ideal conditions for which he yearned. Beyond this hurried event, he would reveal everything to her, good and bad, about Merrick and her father. He would tell her what he knew, suspected, wished to God were not so. He had to be honest with her. Only then could he see things set aright for her. He must.

Quickly. This afternoon perhaps. Or tonight. Yes, tonight when she might expect a bridegroom's ardor, she'd have a husband's total honesty.

For him, they could not reach Richmond fast enough.

But of necessity, they took obscure roads to Richmond, where one of his father's London retreats was situated in a little dale. The house had been a favorite haunt of Merrick's. His, too—until the last time he'd gone.

Once, Spence had favored the Red House above any of his father's holdings. As a child, his mother had often packed them up to summer there. Frances Lyonns, ever sickly even as a child, had at an early age taken to books for amusement. The result was that as an adult and doting mother, she garnered tales from near and far, embellished some, amended others, in the interest of her offsprings' entertainment and her own. She'd even written the best within the pages of two small bound books and given them as presents to Merrick and him one Christmas.

The stories Spence loved to hear the most were those of his ancestors, the Caldmores and the Lyonns. The fables that leaped to life at the Richmond house were those of Henry Tudor's page, Stephen Lyonns. This man had served his monarch long and well until one day he abandoned his intended bride to wed an heiress too rich for his station—if not too high above his illegitimate but nonetheless very blue royal blood. The two lovers had defied the objections of the king— and married in haste. When the young woman's parents and brothers found her months later at the Red House, Catherine Fletcher—who was the sole heiress to her mother's De Vere marquessate—was well along with child and her sire, the Earl Fletcher, would do nothing to remove her from her husband's arms. The story resounded with small similarities to the necessities of his own situation here with Cat—even unto her given name, another Catherine to shine among the family riches. The thought brought the only satisfaction Spence had felt in hours.

But the closer they came to the Red House, the more inescapable was his memory of the last time he had come here two years ago when Merrick, then the new earl, had sent to London for him. Spence responded quickly as he always did for Merrick.

However, on that occasion, Spence arrived too speedily. He entered the house to find displays of debauchery brought on by a prolonged and liberal dosings of opium. Numerous women, from their demeanor, prostitutes in various states of physical and emotional disarray, splayed themselves over the antique furniture, along the stairs and carpets. Men serviced them—and themselves—in exotic variations. Most of the males Spence recognized as Merrick's employees in his Indian import business. Stock boys, accountants, managers, ran amuck in the throes of an addiction Spence had witnessed in the gutters of Calcutta and the Floating Pleasure quarters of Tokyo. A sickness he despised.

Merrick, who had tested the ends of his own body's limits, begged Spence to help him. Within the same fairy-tale walls where once Spence had dreamed in childish innocence of knights and damsels doing anything for love and family, he found a brother who spent himself in excess.

Merrick's blue eyes were bloodshot; his skin an abused gray beneath his stubbly copper beard as he faced him.

"Get them out of the house for me, will you, dear boy? I told them they could stay only until Wednesday. But one of my clerks brought another supply from my factory and handed it round." He plunged both hands through his filthy gold hair. "I expect some chaps up from London from the Foreign Office. They want to talk privately, you know, and I can't have this group here."

"Why ask me, Merrick?" Spence was outraged at his brother's inability to cope—Good Christ! His inability to *stand* without trembling!

"You are the only one I can call on, Spence. I don't dare get anyone from the village. I couldn't abide the talk. Help me. It's worth my next appointment. I must return to Egypt. I have work yet to do."

He had work to do for certain. Merrick had received another term as emissary to the khedive, during which time he did nothing but condemn and attack the next attempted expedition of Walter Farrell and his brother, Dominik. Merrick had succeeded, too, in blocking it. Farrell died months later. The expedition had been canceled. The last journey Farrell had taken had been the one in which he and Dom found the jewelry.

Now, Spence returned to this house he avoided. The house where his mother had taught him to revere his family as men and women worthy of legends. The house where she had died after learning her husband was no hero. Where Spence had discovered his brother deserved no respect. Ah, if Spence had only detected such tendencies in Merrick before that day, he might have been more circumspect about his accusations against Cat's family, less inclined to uphold his own family honor that was destroyed by Merrick himself.

God above, he had tried to think of an alternative to the Red House to hide Cat. But none of his holdings was as close to London and his contacts, should he need to return. None was so free of the prying eyes of servants either.

At the Red House, only two remained in the Dartmoor pay. The caretaker, originally a retainer of Spence's mother's Caldmore dower, kept his overseer position along with his wife, who acted as housekeeper and cook. The man had gained a greater share of Spence's affections when he helped Spence bundle up Merrick's "guests" that hideous afternoon. The man nor his wife had never talked of what they had seen.

Their proven trustworthiness was another reason why Spence had chosen this site to sequester his wife. Add to that his need to make Cat feel cherished, and he knew of no finer jewel in his collection of country estates. He'd see her happy here, transformed into the glowing bride she should be, with the trappings he could command for a few days of bliss . . . and meanwhile clear the way, God willing, for an eternity of it together.

Two golden fingers spread a lavender dawn across the sky as his coachman stopped the conveyance before the iron gates to the gray stone manor house. Spence's driver climbed down from his perch and banged the knocker on the caretaker's door.

Before the third bang against the wood, Spence could hear the hinges creak open as Charlie Blowes flung it wide. "Hold there, Diggins! I heard ye! Gi' a man leave to get 'is *pants* on!"

Spence felt laughter bubble from the murk of his discontent. Nothing like burly Charlie to cure whatever ailed you. He heard his coachman, a more restrained urban man, declare they'd come for a few days and "expected Mr. Blowes had the house in order."

"Diggins, me and me wife always 'ave the place

ready." He must have turned away, for his booming voice faded as he called out, "Hettie! Diggins is 'ere with Lord Spencer!"

Time lapsed until a woman's lighter tone drifted on the morning air. "Good morning, Diggins. Yer looking well but worn a bit with that trek. His lordship must be tired, too. Now, no need to grope like a fish, Diggie," she warded off the man's peckish tendencies. "The sheets are fresh. My pantry's stocked. I'm right behind you to lay on breakfast."

Diggins cleared his throat and offered up the polite news that would double Hettie's portions.

"Married?" she gasped, definitely flabbergasted.

"To who?" blustered Charlie, outraged.

Diggins, who was by now so sorely tested he began stammering, revealed in an agitated whisper that it was "La-lady Farrell. Who else would it be-be?"

"Thank God for that," said Hettie.

"It's about time," proclaimed Charlie with finality. "Well, take 'em up, man! Get 'em settled in! We'll be along in a shake and see to his lordship's needs."

Cat stirred and spoke in the muffled voice of sleep. "They're happy for you." She stretched a little, rubbing her languid body against his own as Diggins resumed his seat to usher them up the drive.

"They're delighted I have married you, love," he reassured her, his servants' joy radiating to him and her, too, judging by the lambent light in her eyes.

Cat relaxed against his shoulder, her glance wandering out the window. Over the crown of her head, he, too, spied the gray stone Tudor mansion sprawled across the grassy knoll. He was frowning at its pastoral beauty when she turned to him again and confided, "I've often wanted to see this house. Your grandmother Caldmore and you told me so much about it." She beamed lazily, her lush lips spreading in mirth, an alluring young woman who left her troubles behind. "I'm glad we're to begin our marriage here. It bodes well for us, I should think." She pressed a kiss to his cheek. "Smile, will you, darling? No one knows where we are."

"I thought I was supposed to say things like that to you." He grinned, feeling her satisfaction with small things surround his cold logic with warmth.

"You have. Now it's my turn to calm your fears. Isn't that what wives do?"

"None so well as you, I wager."

She took his hand. "Show me the house, will you please, or I'll survey its wonders by myself."

He detected in her appeal not only curiosity but also a diversionary tactic born of bridal jitters. Was she concerned about what might happen here between them, wedding night—or morn—as it was? She needn't fret. Though he would claim her in every way, the fact that he had married her in so unmentionable a manner meant he had no plans to make her his any time soon.

Not until June fifth. He'd keep that part of the ritual to its order anyway. Then she could never wonder if he had taken advantage of her or her circumstances. Besides, if anything happened to her, if they found no other culprit and Scotland Yard's inspector came to take her away, then she might not hunger for comforts they had never shared . . .

That would not happen. He hugged her fiercely. None of it. He would not permit it. Must not.

"Spence! Darling? Where *are* you?"

He shook himself from his reverie and gazed into eyes that rivaled the irises in her bouquet for dark splendor. "Here, love. With you. As for the house, well, naturally, it's a gem. Better than any description. At least that's what people say whenever they see it for the first time. And so this shall be your first exposure, which—I shall guarantee—you will adore. Come, I'll show you one of your many new homes, Countess!" Then he stepped out into the crisp air and caught her under the knees to carry her up the stone steps over the threshold.

What he showed her thrilled her. But it was not what she had expected.

She stroked the Venetian cut lace curtain lining her bedchamber window and stared out onto the endless gardens, crammed with crazed gypsophilia and impatiens, nodding daffodils and tight tulips. She acknowledged the house her husband had displayed was superlative, bar none she'd ever known. But it was not what she would have wished for on such a day as this. Far from it.

Meriting its name, the rambling three-story structure presented a spectrum of reds. The great hall, now the reception hall, welcomed any stranger in a blaze of Flemish rusts and gilded tapestries hung upon the massive walls. Behind, what in medieval times had served as the minstrels' and servants' hall now passed as the drawing room. But here the earls and countesses of Dartmoor had papered the walls in a cut Utrecht velvet of startling blackberry, then chosen furniture of ebony lacquer limned with gold.

Cat had thought her breath stolen until Spence worked his way beyond to the newer wing with the dining room of apricots and cream, the morning room of peach chintzes and bold brasses, and even a kitchen and pantry of cheerful pinks. After Hettie laid out a breakfast of gargantuan proportions, Spence took her along the visitors' wing where countless bedchambers awaited her appreciation in every shade from claret to garnet, geranium and rose, salmon, titian, burgundy and wine. There in the largest suite, swathed in blush hangings spilling down oak linenfold paneling to plush ivory Aubusson carpets, he had left her.

In the middle of the day. To a bath, he said. A nap, he suggested. Although she had done the first and was too much in want of him to do the second, clearly he had gone without intent to return. He meant her to be utterly alone.

Except for her there was no peace.

How could there be?

The sun was high. The world forbidding beyond the confines of these radiant walls and mammoth gates. Her husband, who had pledged to love and cherish her scant hours ago, was far from her, repairing his own body and mind somewhere.

Without her.

Removed from her for some obscure reason of which she had not the vaguest notion . . . or perhaps, one nagging idea.

A tiny three-year-old memory pierced her sadness and try though she might to ignore the arrows of abandonment, she couldn't. The collective barbs ripped her thin composure and had her swirling from the window and heading for the hall.

Long corridors of despair had her searching for a back stairs, a way out, relief. The servants' exit was not difficult to find, but with tears faceting her vision, the circular narrow steps were the very devil to maneuver. By the last one, she pushed open the door to the gardens with angry agony. She stood, pulling air into her lungs, viewing the myriad paths away from the house, from him.

She did not walk but paced.

If Spence thought to bind her to him, tuck her away, then desert her—*again*—he was wrong. Wrong!

She had never been a terribly biddable child. Why

should she be a compliant wife? A cipher. Someone he could run to—and run from—at will.

Arrogant man to think she'd sit back, let him control her. Let him leave her. *Forget her.*

Ahh, God, no, not *again!*

She couldn't.

How could he? Hadn't he—just this morning in his drawing room—declared before God, the minister, and the Billingtons that he loved her, honored her, would keep her? How could he do that and then leave her alone? How could he when he had so sweetly, so diligently worked himself back into her life in so permanent, so undeniable a way? How could he be so heartless, so much hers by everything that was holy, and then forsake her?

Why?

Was he too frightened of commitment? Terrified of intimacy, even though he thought he'd conquered it by a self-knowledge he'd been *proud* to proclaim?

She had no answers.

Only heartache.

She whirled for the path through the forest.

But no relief came there either.

Cooler shades of late day shrouded her. The budding leaves, the fragrant pines assaulted her senses, making her want to share them with Spence. A surge of fresh grief conquered her. She choked on torment. No idea where comfort lay, she picked up her skirts, ran, left the path, and pushed at limbs and vines. Haste tested her coordination. Emotion made her clumsy. She stumbled on a bramble, caught her foot on a root, and sank against a tree.

Arms across the jagged bark, she felt memories hit their target. Pinned to the dawning horror that misery comprised her wedding day, she thought of the only solution to save her pride.

222

She could *leave* him. Desert him. Forget him.

Couldn't she?

Never! came the reply that made her quake.

Her knees went to water. Her sobs burst hot and furious.

"Cathy—"

Her head jerked up. Had she imagined him or truly heard him?

"Sweetheart."

This time, his warm hands upon her shoulders told her he was real.

"Love, don't cry," he whispered as he pressed to her.

She turned on him, her body flattened to the tree, her eyes wild in his. "Do *not* touch me!"

"Cat—" He gripped her to bring her to him.

Suddenly, her vision cleared. So did her head. And a tactic that had worked before inspired her. She stomped on his toes.

He oofed, grabbing for his injured foot. *"Cat!"* he called to her, then muttered to himself, "Why don't I learn?"

She seized the opportunity, spinning away like the wind. But the forest was dense, her speed no match for twigs and brush—or him.

He caught her in four strides and twirled her toward him, backing her to another trunk, wrists cuffed by his iron fingers.

"You are not supposed to touch me. Our agreement—" she reminded him of the stipulations long forgotten in her recent joy of him.

"To hell with that! Tell me what's the matter. Why are you out here when you're supposed to be—"

"Napping?" She knew she was virtually screeching at him. "I do not sleep in the middle of the day!"

"Not even when you've been up all night?" His

green eyes took on primeval brilliance as his arms bound her.

"Especially not after I've just been married!" She writhed to be free of him, the act increasing a torture that accentuated her wanton need.

"I hoped you would." He clasped both her wrists in one hand to free the other and smooth curls from her cheek.

"I don't conform to your expectations? How reassuring," she murmured, torn at his objectivity while she was withering from lack of him.

He lifted her chin with his fist. "Look into my eyes and see how well you do fulfill my expectations."

She couldn't. "Just let me go, Spence. It's fine. I do understand, you know. I'm older, wiser than three years ago, but you didn't have to be so gallant. Let me save my pride. Let me go. You didn't have to marry me to protect me from—"

Air scythed through his teeth. The words that slipped out were profane. "You want to leave me? *No! Look at me and tell me it's true!"* He took her chin between two fingers, and this time when her eyes flew to his, tears stood in his own. "I wouldn't hurt you for the world! You think I married you to keep you from harm? I did it—"

"To repay me for a slight—"

"Among other things—" He was roaring with grief. *"You're damn right, I did!"*

"Well that's just dandy! You've paid your debt to me, now leave me alone—" she was wailing, wrenching to get free, hating her admission of how she needed him and recognizing how impotent she was against her love for him. Lolling her head on the tree, she squeezed her eyes shut.

"Oh, Christ," he groaned. "You think I didn't come to claim you because I don't *want* you? Cat." His lips descended to bless her closed eyes. "Darling of mine, how could you think such a thing of me when I have wanted you every minute since the night I first saw you?" His mouth caressed her cheeks, her ear, her throat and then returned to speak on hers. "I love you, sweetheart of my life, and I want you. Badly. But not as much as I want something else more."

"You *have* restitution."

His nose trailed patterns on her cheek. "Bitter without you and not what I had in mind."

"You *had* forgiveness from me."

"Then give it back to me, love. I'll need it many more times before we're old." His hand cupped her throat as he rasped, "Open your eyes, kitten, and let me show you how you'll need to forgive me again now. For I do want you, my wife, in spite of my better judgment."

That confession tore her wide open and she cried, her arms trying to flail but powerless in his.

"Ahh, Catherine Lyonns," he crooned, "stop fighting me at least long enough to let me explain how I wanted this wedding to be idyllic for you. I wanted us married, but not in the dead of night with some anonymous cleric pronouncing the vows! I wanted you made mine in a sunlit cathedral in full sight of the entire world. Anyone, everyone who mattered I needed to know how I adored you and how very sorry I was I had ever hurt you—" He swallowed and whispered, "Or so callously disgraced you."

His words evaporated her agony like the sear of morning sun on dew. Dazed, she stared at him. Slowly, he freed her hands. She rubbed her cheek against his palm while his other hand combed her unbound hair down her shoulder and his eyes poured into hers with a thousand endearments she'd never thought to know from him.

"I couldn't protect you without carrying you off from London. But I couldn't spirit you away without a wedding. Nor could I make you mine totally without the benefit of pomp and circumstance. I wanted this wedding, this marriage to be so right for you. I wanted to wait to take you to bed. I wanted you to feel cherished by me but also affirmed by everyone in the world in your right to give me your love and your body. The way it should have been and should be for you. As wonderful for you"—he brushed his mouth across hers and she opened for him, assured, delighted, ravaged with a three-year-old desire that set her blood to flame—"as perfect for you as I could make it, my sweet wife."

"You're perfect for me," she told him, casting pride to the winds while she flung her arms around him.

"Am I, darling?" he gave her a peck that passed for a kiss. "You'll have to come and sample first." He was teasing as he avoided her lips and swung her up into his arms. "Then, when we're finished if you need more time—"

She chuckled as he walked with her deeper into the forest. "Or more samples?"

He arched a blond brow in speculation. "Or that," he said in a light tone, but then grew grave. "Afterward, you can decide whether to stay with me or not."

That drained her joy. Though he continued to walk, she turned his face to hers and the look in her eyes gave him pause. "I would never leave you," she vowed in hushed fury.

"God above," he breathed, "I hope not. I'll be such a doting husband, you'll never consider it for a second." His features grew savaged by some fleeting pain she could not define. "I'll be by your side through every event of life. I'm never going away without you and I need to show you the wonders of the world. Paris. St. Petersburg. Tokyo."

She pressed a grateful kiss to his cheek. "Show me only you, ever you."

"I will. Now." He stepped from the trees into a small clearing where a lime-washed thatched cottage stood with its little lavender door beckoning. "I came here when I left you. I wanted more wood for the fire and was headed up to the main house when I saw you running through the copse."

"I see. What is this house then?"

"My mother's and father's honeymoon cottage," he told her as their eyes met. "Later, her retreat from reality."

He crossed the clearing and stepped into the oval one-room abode with cherry moiré satin walls and ivory furnishings. Before the fireplace, where flames consumed the spring chill, stood a four-poster bed draped in creamed eyelet with satin counterpane the color of good butter. Turned back—probably by Hettie Blowes—the covers lay undisturbed. Cat's excitement had her eyes dancing to the rest of the room, a contrast of passionate reds to the purity of whites. But evidence of Spence's preoccupations sat here beside one scarlet chaise lounge where upon one table lay a crystal glass with a draught of liquor and a ruby leather book, its golden-edged pages spread open.

Cat's gaze went to his. "Is it your retreat, too?"

He nodded, solemn in his admission.

"Away from me?"

"From temptation."

"But now?" she asked on bare sound.

"It's ours. If you're sure."

Sure? she mouthed. "This morning I said I'd have

you and I meant it. I have wanted you—" she told him with desire in her heart, in her eyes and voice and hands, "since time began and will until the rivers of the world run dry."

He groaned. "I'm going to make love to you at least till then." He let her slide down his body. "Maybe through eternity."

"Oh, do, please."

His arms shook as he embraced her. "Whatever we had before, my darling, will be nothing like what we're going to share from this day forward. I promise you."

"Just show me before I melt here in a puddle."

"Let's see then"—he glided his lips over hers—"if we might possibly"—he caught her to him—"do it together." He brought her mouth to his in one hot declaration. "Properly."

He wreathed her face with a garland of kisses until the need for his mouth on hers again drove her to madness. She drove her fingers into his hair and sought to bring him closer. "I don't care about propriety."

He chuckled. "Though I care about that, too, I won't whenever we're behind closed doors. Make no mistake, my darling, I want you openly, honestly, completely."

She moaned in frustration. "I'll give you that, but if you don't have me soon, I'll swoon from inattention."

He threw her a roguish grin. "Swoon away, darling. It's how I want you. But lack of attention is not what this is called."

She clutched his shirt. *"This* is delay!"

"This is something far different." He slid out the pearl buttons along her *canezou*, his palm branding her breast as he skimmed inside atop the andalusian silk of her chemise. "This," he offered as he ran the

pads of his fingers around the crest of her nipple, "is anticipation."

He glided the blouse and chemise from her shoulders and unhooked her skirt to have it pool at their feet. Expectation had her swaying to him, but he caught her with big hands wide around her ribs, holding her apart from him and making her object with a sound of frustration.

"When I saw you last night in the library, naked and reaching for me, I thanked God how fortunate I was," he said, his eyes on her bare breasts. "I wondered how I could wait for weeks to show you heaven." He ran his tongue around his mouth. "Now I wonder if I have the strength to stop myself from ravishing you. You simply cannot imagine, my darling"—his eyes circled her nipples reverently— "how gorgeous you are."

Flushed with need and not a little embarrassment, she cupped his neck while she reached up and gave him a kiss that had her viewing joy and him quaking. As if she walked a dream, she separated their lips and licked her own, her eyes closed.

"Satisfied?" he asked so quietly she thought his voice came from her own body.

"I don't think so," she told him.

He snorted and caught her up in his arms. "I hoped not, because neither am I." He put her kneeling on the bed and reached around to toss her shoes to the carpet. "But we will be very soon," he said avidly as he sent her petticoat and drawers slipping down her thighs. Naked now except for her gartered stockings, she dared not move, but cherished the look of enchantment on his face and his intake of breath that told her she pleased him.

"You are incomparable." His gaze flashed up to hers. "Eyes more lush than iris petals. And breasts as bounteous as hydrangea blossoms"—he weighed the fullness of her, his thumbs brushing her nipples to ripe bud—"with skin"—his mouth trailed across her shoulder—"as smooth as milk. And hair"—he laced his fingers into the curls at the juncture of her thighs—"as downy as angel's breath."

She arched into his care. "Love me," she pleaded, her forehead dropping to his shoulder.

"I do. I have. I always will." He punctuated his words with nuzzling kisses against her crown and the insertion of a gentle finger between her nether lips.

"I want you in every way a wife can have her husband."

"All ways, always, so shall we have each other, my love. But I mean to make this so easy for you that you will ever remember from the first time I took you, I showed you paradise."

"Please," she urged, flinging her hair back and moving with the rhythm of his fingers sliding in and out of her.

"So polite, my Cat," he said hoarsely, then gave her an open-mouthed kiss of swirling abandon. "I mean to make you forget every propriety, every rule the world has ever taught you." He eased her back to the soft cool linens. "Here in our bed, there'll be no room for anything except the love I have for you. The need." He ran fingers down her body as he straddled her. "The passion I mean to give you and have you return to me."

She undulated beneath him, her hips meeting the steely evidence of his body's desire for her. But he wore too many clothes, and her fingers flew to his shirt buttons to correct the error. She managed to open one before he stayed her hands and spread her arms wide.

"No," he warned with narrowed eyes, his blond

hair falling over his forehead to make him look like some golden god in the throes of need. "This is your first time and you will come first." His green eyes blazed with jungle fires. "In so very many ways."

His eyes dropped to her breasts. "First, I'll show you how beautiful you are here." He focused on her so intently, she felt her skin contract, tighten, fill. Anticipation made her rock her hips. He sat more firmly on her, rubbing his hard shaft along the apex of her thighs. Then he descended, his moist lips claiming her left nipple in one hard dark tug to rapture. Inside the cavern of his mouth, his tongue laved her, sending memories of hours ago to her brain and her blood.

She shot her head back, lifted off the bed in ecstasy as he shifted to the other breast and washed it with the same exciting ministration. His talents pulled her from any conscious thought into a bright whirlpool of delights. His teeth nipped at her, his fingers shaped her to wet points, his lips traveled to her navel as his thumbs drew patterns on her hips and her desire built to a turbulent storm.

Suddenly, he rolled her over. She rubbed herself against the sheets, her embarrassment a fleeing impediment to the chaotic need she had to feel him everywhere. But scarcely had she done it when he caught one arm beneath her waist and brought her up on her knees and elbows, her body shaped to his, molded, melded in a writhing passion.

He bared her neck, his teeth holding her but not hurting her, his hands pressing her against him. "That's right," he soothed, his hot breath in her ear. "This is how well you want me." She arched, her head dropping back along his shoulder. One of his hands smoothed her nipples, stroked her belly, and delved into her hair, then her lips, parting her to elicit her body's fluent declarations of her desire.

"My love, what are you doing to me?" she asked airily as his fingers sluiced her with unutterable delights.

"Petting a kitten," he assured her. When she gasped at the endearment, he explained with a growl, "Taming a cat." His fingers sank inside her, and she spasmed backward into his encompassing embrace. She felt a furious pressure pound inside her loins, and he encouraged it with gentle thrusts of his fingers.

She wanted to groan in joyous agony but whispered, "Tell me what to do to make this right."

"Follow your instincts. Enjoy me. Let me take care of you." His fingers began to swirl on some point that made her buck and moan. "I need you to be happy."

"I need"—she thought she was keening, knew she was digging her nails into the mattress—"a thousand things . . . your words, your lips and—and—"

"Sheath your claws, my puss. *This*"—he swirled her to her back and pinned her again, though this time she contorted with sensual torment—"is what you crave."

He kissed her then. Cupping her nape, he slashed his mouth across hers in an act of possession that had her mesmerized, her hands flying down his too well-clothed body. But he seized her wrists and held her captive as he gave her nipples two brief signs of homage, then dipped to her ribs and her waist, her hips, and the insides of her burning thighs. There, he spread her wide.

Beyond the propriety he'd kissed from her, not even modesty could make her resist him.

"Lord above," he intoned, "you are so pretty, my sweet wife. Pink with passion." One fingertip defined her cleft, sending hot shivers up her spine as he placed a tender kiss in her curls. "Giving up a fragrant ambrosia that says you must have me." He spread her fevered lips with two tender fingers and stopped to admire her. She thrummed with hope and dangerous erotic ideas. "How much do you want me, my beloved? Let me taste you and see . . ." His mouth sank to her.

At the touch of his lips, she groaned loud enough to shake the rafters.

His tongue darted about the craven point of her desires and then, in one torrid eddy, he sucked her into his mouth. She shot up like an arrow. He gentled her with an arm beneath her hips and the tender madness of his flagrant kisses. He licked her, nibbled her, devoured her. All nature halted. The world paused. Airless, she felt him bring her up to the astral summits of a new universe where her existence focused on him and every divine thing he did to her.

The storm inside her, around her, surged, throbbed, and when lightning struck, she pulsed in the meteoric chaos of it. Crying to him, she praised him, explaining in some celestial language how she loved him. She loved him. How could she ever think of leaving him when he only was the man she adored.

Through the euphoria, he held her, crooned to her, soothed her to him. She vibrated, thrashed, crushed sheets, and twisted his clothes. Still he gave no quarter. Only endless, brazen kisses.

She returned them, grasping him, beseeching him, urging him to come to her when he pulled her up to a sitting position, brushed her hair back from her eyes, and brought her flowing, burning body to him, opening her legs and winding them up over his thighs. With tender hands he circled her thighs, slid his fingers inside her garters and rolled them and her silk stockings down her legs. As he went he caressed her to her toes, then did the same to the other leg.

"Every inch of you is wonderful," he crooned as his

splayed hands drifted up her legs. "I've dreamed of having you draped around me. Your hair, your arms, your legs. Did you dream the other night of having me inside you"—his fingers dipped into her and she arched nearer—"hard and wild—like this?"

"No," she shook her head, ecstatic as his touch brought her peace again and yet more whimpering torment. "Never as sweet as this," she moaned, and he extracted his fingers to put her hands to his shirt. His eyes and his intent were unwavering.

She understood. In deft flicks, she had his buttons undone, his bronzed chest bared for her. She mewled and fanned her hands across the masculine beauty of him. Fascinated, burning, sated but not, she dropped her nose into his tightly curled blond hair and licked her way from one of his nipples to another. For reward, his fingertips stroked her breasts, then descended to capture her hands and lead her to his trouser flies. But as she worked the intricate things, his hands spread her legs wider. Knowing what glories he'd brought her before, she made no objections, only slid closer.

Her trophy was three fingers massaging her swollen lips in an slow circle ending in submerged possession. Surprise was not equal to the ecstasy he brought her as he scooped her nearer and murmured, "Darling, I'll never have enough of you. Kiss me."

No request could have been more sweet. More molten. More fantasy than the bold musky taste of him—and her. Upon his lips, she savored the beginnings of what they were to each other, what they could now become. And the banquet spread before her became a feast of succulent new dishes.

She gave him her mouth, her tongue dancing along his, her lips nurturing him, while he tended her with reverent fingers into a flowing, glowing core of need.

Then when throbbing delight cast her once more to the winds, she clutched him in mad joy. Floating, she fell back to the bed as he stood to discard his trousers. Her eyes glued to him, her husband. Her dream come true.

Her perfect man. Her large, lean animal. With broad shoulders and trim waist. Strong hips and thighs. With one huge attribute standing high in declaration that he desired her.

She bit her lower lip, her eyes racing to his, the first shyness within minutes making her hesitant. "I want you near me, with me," she pleaded and put out her hand.

He grasped it, nuzzling a kiss into her palm before he put a knee to the mattress. "You'll have me. Now. In any way you need me." He settled over her, taking her hand to his silken length of rigid manhood. "I want you, too. See how much," he said as he instructed her how to pleasure him.

A mother's blithe explanation of the act of married love had Cat wondering about facts she'd obviously not been told. Like how beautiful her husband was formed. How hard he was. How hot and silken. How impossibly long and wide.

"Am I to have all of you?" she whispered, wishing it were possible to have him fill the yearning cavern of her body, yet wondering if it were truly the way of things.

"Every part of me, my love," he rasped and gave her a quick buss on the cheek before he shivered at her touch. "God above, I mean to give you every part of me and make you delirious to have me evermore." He snorted and shook his head, a rueful twist of humor to his handsome mouth. "But you are too precious to me for me to hurt you. I won't stretch you beyond your comfort. If"—he reseated himself in her hands and

touched her cheek with a finger—"if we can't do this
at first, I want you to remember we have a lifetime."

"Eternity, you promised." She soothed him with
her words, her eyes and the persuasion of her hand.

He collected himself and smiled at her. "Nothing
less." He came closer, his darling green gaze sweeping
her skin and hair and eyes. "Now I'll make my cat my
lioness."

Chapter 12

She wound herself around him with the assurance of a woman adored. He called himself blessed that he had proven it to her finally. Now he'd affirm it for her completely.

Arms behind his neck, legs draping over his hips, she offered herself up to him. All love for the taking. The giving.

Her smile, a feline satisfaction in the glow of day's end, filling his vision, bursting his heart with the tenderness he'd hidden away inside himself for three lonely years. As if she had kept the key, she kissed him and turned the lock to his buried hopes. From this horde of undiscovered wealth floated up those buried emotions he had shown few. Only she called forth the love and doubled it. Only she took his fear in hand and defeated it. Only she comprised his family, his pride, his purpose in life. He shuddered with his need to express it to her in every act from this first declaration to the end of time.

Inching closer to her, his manhood brushed her mound of curls, her cauldron of heat. With the temperance his years of rigid self-control imposed, he eased himself into her. At the gates to paradise, he paused with desire drenching him. She was so slick, so swollen with her earlier expressions of her need of him that to glide inside was not so difficult as the necessity of restraining his burning urge to plunge into her welcoming shelter.

But he had promised to go slowly, savor her, serve her—and their entire future depended on his constancy to keep his word. With the tip of him barely submerged in her lithe warmth, he could hardly breathe, let alone think. But she rocked against him and took him closer to their mutual goal. Summoning his will, he pulled away to watch himself sink into the creamy depths of her, the liquid sound of his claiming her now music to his ears. Suddenly it seemed so very natural for him to move a bit closer, deeper.

He groaned, his eyes clamping shut with the ecstasy she brought him.

Her hands drifted over him. One to his nape, she pulled him down for a kiss, while her other hand wended to the part of him still beyond their union. Fascinated, he watched her revel in her newfound splendor. She stretched, mewled, writhed in want.

"Oh, darling," she whimpered, "I need every bit of you. Haven't we waited long enough?"

With those words, he moved up inside her to the only barrier left to their completion. The wall was a strong hindrance, but she had been so well prepared, she moaned at his delay. "Please, darling. Am I not yours?"

He caught her close, held her tight, and moved like a man in a sea of heaven—and found it more chaotic, more euphoric than tales in storybooks. She traveled with him, whispering how she loved him and spreading kisses down his throat.

He drew away, gripped her arms, and stared at her. With a sensual lunge, he demonstrated how he'd move with her if she could bear it.

"Mmmm," she sighed like a cat in heat, "do that again."

"Like this?" He gave her a small stroke she beamed over. "Or this?" He reared back and offered her much more.

She answered with silent nods and undulations.

At core, just a man in need of his mate, he advanced with such determined care that the shield between them split with ease and groans from both of them. She shivered as he sank into her fully, and he stopped to thank God for her.

She curved upward in a bowman's arc, her eyes closed, her breasts rounded up for the ministrations of his mouth. He gave her the succor she craved, and in response, her hands fluttered from his back up to sift through his hair as he waited before resuming what would be, he knew, the first of many hours, days, years, in their mutual bed of pleasures.

"I adore you inside me. I don't want this to end and yet—?" He saw her battle embarrassment with the need to ask something further.

"It won't. There is so much more," he said, smiling into her glowing eyes as he dropped into her until his flesh could offer no more. "This"—he drew out in a careful glide—"is only the beginning."

"Oh, yes," she exulted as he gave her all of him again with stunning power, "I can feel it."

"Feel this," he said as he showed her an increased tempo and perceived her purr rumble up from deep inside her where their bodies joined.

With reverence born of gratitude, he murmured how he cherished her, then proved it with controlled ferocity. She was his by God's design. Now he made her his by purpose. He gave her kisses, each a seeking, yearning affirmation of his right to her. She returned them in kind, her need to claim him wild as his, her delicacy a thrilling complement to his passion. When she met once more the completion that told him he might now take his own, he carved the moment on his conscious mind. Throughout the years he'd live with her, he would remember this unique time he had loved her—and their souls entered their own Eden together. He swallowed, unclenched his teeth, and let his body surrender to his beloved the substance of his earthly need of her. She held him, crooned to him, kissed him in the consummation of what they became to each other. Husband. Wife. Lovers. Trusted friends.

Careful lest he crush her, he sank to her side. He curved an arm about her shoulders, and she curled to him with a sigh.

He brought the covers up to warm them and glanced about, chuckling at their circumstances. Her head fell back, her hand to his chest, her eyes questioning his.

"My love, I'm amused that for my intense planning, we've begun this marriage in a tiny cottage rather than a suite in Paris or Venice." She arched a delicate brow. "But I am not dismayed."

"Or disappointed?" she barely added sound to her words.

"Darling wife of mine, I am thrilled." His voice dived as he threaded his fingers through her lustrous brandy hair and smoothed it down her pale shoulder across the tip of one enticing breast. Dying to bring her nipple to ripe bud again, he thought better than to take her too soon. He wondered if he'd been careful enough, if she'd bled too much, and if she'd become chagrined to allow him see to her. Rather than press too much, he took another route. "Are you hungry? You didn't eat much breakfast."

She shook her head, a bashful smile dawning on her features as she hid her face in his shoulder. "I had no appetite for food."

"How interesting. You should have told me what you craved," he crooned, massaging away her maidenly confusion with tender fingers to her scalp. "I would have been more than pleased to indulge you, starving as I was myself."

She nuzzled his chest, plucked at his hair with playfulness, and looked up at him. "I have everything I want. Here," she elaborated with a trail of her hand up his shoulder to his cheek and hair. She gave him a kiss that rattled his senses and had him hardening again, the charm of her so pervasive he marveled that he had summoned the delicacy to treat her like the exquisite creature she was.

"Do you hurt?" he asked, brazenly needing to know.

"No, not anymore," she whispered in a husky tone.

Panicked, he hugged her. "I'll make it up to you. The first time can be painful—"

She put a finger to his lips. "Shh. I meant that whatever pain I had because you left me years ago is gone, forgotten with your sweetness of the past week, last night, this morning—and now." She put her mouth to his and spoke, "You have eradicated every bit of it."

"With love, I hope."

"With ecstasy." For clarity, she kissed him.

Torn between showing her greater realms of marital bliss or a bridegroom's solicitude, he chose prudence and dampened his raging need again.

He let her go, sat up, and gathered the pillows from the floor where their passion had scattered them. With a few plumps, he piled them high against the headboard and patted the seat beside him. She smiled and slid backward, the movement slithering the sheet from her rosy body. His eyes—traitorous fellows—wandered over wonderful breasts and small waist to womanly hips and burnished hair. Her thighs glistened, but only a small streak of red marked her as his own. He said a quick prayer, swallowed, grabbed the sheet, and brought it up to her chin.

Clearing his throat, he avoided her gaze and walked to a cabinet where he extracted another glass. As he decanted Armagnac for her, he measured how far he might go to accustoming her to their new state of man and wife. He had gone far to initiate her into their act of passion, but he had done that to prepare her virgin's body to more easily accept his own. That accomplished, he would never pass the outposts of good sense to enthrall her to his sensuality. His instinct told him she and he were capable of locking in a loving lust that teetered on the boundaries to erotic fantasy. He would not take her too fast, too soon into a foreign land lest he frighten her. So he stood there, debating long after the liquor grew warm in his hand, what to do about his damnably persistent erection.

"Is that for me?" Cat asked and made him whirl in surprise that once again she had read his mind. Her eyes met his but instantly traveled down his form to widen and blink. "I think so."

He froze, aching harder from her appreciative gaze.

"My sweet lion," she beckoned with a deliberate toss of her mane over her shoulders to bare her beckoning body, "why not come here and give it to me?"

Mute, undone, he jerked his head from side to side.

"Why not?" she mouthed.

He jammed the glass down on the table. Gulped.

Like a female who began to understand her potential, she took the first steps to employing it. Sliding her creamy legs over the edge of the bed, she stood. Hints of modesty traced her features. But when she saw his eyes narrow and his nostrils flare, she pressed her thighs together, plumping the flesh he longed to please with hands and mouth and tongue. With a secret smile of satisfaction, she strolled toward him. Her breasts swayed with her natural gait. Her arms flowed at her sides, letting him view his fill of a healthy female on the prowl.

She wrapped herself around him like a creature of instinct. Her skin was humid. Her eyes hot. Her hands—oh, God—her hands flowing over him and then finally there where he needed her—any part of her he could get.

She twined around him like a temptress of fables. Her breasts teasing his chest. Her legs rubbing his. Her mouth skimming over his. "You said I could have samples. I need more," she whispered and reached around him for the glass while one of her legs circled his, leaving her furry nest feathering against the muscles of one burning thigh. The feel of slick flesh open for him, to him, made him tremble—and he could not move. "Perhaps, *you* need to taste more, my husband."

She put the glass rim to her lips with a lowering of lush lashes that limned his senses with fire. She closed her eyes as she tilted the glass. Her lips pressed flush to the crystal made him imagine how her other lips fit him like that when he was inside her. So pink. So wet.

"Want a taste?" she asked him, licking the corner of her mouth and making the glass disappear beyond his realm of comprehension. She made a pout, her mouth near his.

He smelled the liquor on her, but more, he smelled himself on her. Rare, musky, and sweet. She personified temptation. She came near, put her lips to his, and nudged open his mouth. At his surrendering groan, she sent her tongue to stroke his, releasing liquor and the languid taste of ardor to his own.

Plunging his hands in her hair, he immobilized her. "I want to consume you. Eat you up. Drink every emotion from you."

She ground her body against him, the look on her face almost pain. "I am yours. Do it. Have me!"

"No! I fear—"

She closed off his objections with a declaration of her own. Hands to his nape, she kissed reason from him, then drifted away, panting. "How can you fear anything when you can kiss me like this?"

"Oh, sweetheart." He tried madly to explain what his body attempted to prove in spite of him. "I'm afraid I need you repeatedly. Constantly. In wild ways!" He pressed her back along his arm and laved her breasts in demonstration of all his insatiable desires for her. "I don't want to frighten you away by how much and how often I must have you."

Her palm found him. "You never frightened me. So take everything you want," she offered as she pleasured him nigh to the bursting point and he ground his teeth. "I'll never turn you away."

Her invitation and admission tore a cry from him that had him taking her down to the chaise. Fanning her satin hair upon the velvet and opening her supple body into a primal pose, he stood and set her legs up around his hips. He was inside her in half a heartbeat.

His eyes fell closed, his head fell back. This was the heaven he'd ever seek.

Her hands drifted from his waist to that place where every cell in his body conspired to have her again, have her now, have her sure and long and in primitive unmentionable ways.

Like two of God's creatures, they moved in a synchrony, a harmony that resounded in his soul and made him seek hers. He heard it in her glorious cries. "My darling mate," he called to her before he pounded, then throbbed into her with a crescendo of joy that sent a duet of delight floating about the little cottage.

Peace descended like a warm blanket, taking him down to her, around her, cocooning her in a love never ending.

"I didn't think—we could—do that," he said among the efforts of his body to recapture normal breath, "so soon."

Her laughing eyes held no chagrin as she skimmed his features and slid to the place where his flesh possessed hers. "I thought it was sublime."

He chuckled and pulled her up to a sitting position, which changed the way he fit her. The sensation had him closing his eyes, and he wound his arms around her to soothe the sleek muscles of her slim back. She shifted, wiggling nearer and so summoning a groan from him. "You surrender beautifully, darling," he told her.

"I pleased you?" she said, muffled in his shoulder.

His laugh this time was an incredulous grunt. "Hardly the way I'd define what we share but good for a beginning."

Her fingers intruded between their heated flesh and

she circled the base of his manhood with gentle fingers. "Then show me the rest." When he pulled away and lifted her chin to see if she truly wanted what she asked for, she elaborated, "I want to learn." Her hand massaged him, and he caught his breath even as he flattened his hand over hers.

"We have here a man who wants you to distraction even though he has just enjoyed you twice. We have here a beast who could become unpredictable if you do not cease your explorations." He dropped his voice to a growl. "We have an animal who wants you in any way he can have you."

She pursed her mouth and said, "Then he should."

"You'd tempt a saint."

She narrowed her eyes at him, beneath his hand, her own urging his body to full ardor. "I don't want one. I want my lion."

In one swift claim, his hands lifted her sleek buttocks, fit her over his thighs and onto the straining part of him that wanted her more than any other joy on earth. He slid deeply inside with the boldness of one who claimed what was his. Indisputably. Completely. So that when he touched her womb, they both knew it. Her breath left her, her head dropped back. His hands hooked beneath her thighs to ease her and please her as he spread her wider to feel the power of his need. In a flash fire, they gave and took with no mind left after the conflagration.

She nestled to his chest, her breathing staccato. He planted kisses in her tangled hair. His body—sated heathen—shrank from the force of the storm but, in brief moments, rose to fill her flooding passage yet again. Devastated lest he show her lust beyond her capacity, he squeezed his eyes shut and beseeched his God for help.

She seated herself more firmly on him and let her

eyes meet his moments before her lips did. "Again?" she marveled.

He could tell her lies, but why? He swallowed.

She curled herself about him, so lambent with the moisture of her body overflowing with the mutual essence of their care, her face pressed to his throat, her lips murmuring incoherent things.

But he knew what she needed.

What he wanted.

Summoning some superhuman strength, he stood with her locked about his hips and swirled to press her to one cherry silk wall. Braced there, she arched up, receiving and giving with as much artless grace and boundless love as the first time. With an ecstasy that he would show her every time he loved her, he felt his body pound to emptiness, and afterward, he gathered her close to fill his arms with the only love he'd ever need.

She was gasping, writhing, mewling in his arms as he scooped her up and took the three steps to the bed to lay her down carefully as if she'd shatter into a thousand pieces. This time, he'd learned his lesson and withdrew his body before his insatiable need began to build.

This time, she let him go with a tender hand trailing his arm. "Come back," was what she seemed able to manage.

"In a minute." He kissed her palm. "I promise."

When he did return, he stretched out beside her and said, "Do you think you can drink this?"

She sighed, her arms flung up, her palms open in fatigue. Her lashes fluttered, and her incomparable purple eyes focused on him in extravagant adoration. She robbed his breath when he recognized in her gaze the fact that her universe revolved around him. "I love you," she told him.

He had never felt such radiance in a smile, and he returned it with his own declaration. "I love you, too," he admitted and kissed her in swift abandon. "I have for so long and now have every right to prove it to you. I will every day, beginning now. Here. Drink this, sweetheart. You need something substantial." He grinned, good humor wrestling wicked delight. "I won't have you fainting on me."

"When you're inside me," she confessed, "I feel faint."

"God, I'm glad." He filled with the primal urge to swagger. "But I'm thrilled you haven't. I'd feel worse to see you suffer when you make me so very happy."

"Do I?"

"Beyond my wildest dreams."

She came up on an elbow. "Mine, too." The sheet slipped. Her breasts swayed before him, and he fought to train his eyes on hers.

"Take this glass, will you, love, before my best intentions are gone again?"

She laughed lightly and grasped the thing.

He chucked her under the chin and swirled to get his own from the table. When he returned to her, she had reclined like a pagan goddess on his bed, her elbows supporting her, one knee bent, her iris blue eyes admiring him.

"To Mr. and Mrs. Lyonns." He clinked glasses with her and took a hearty draught of the liquid, which tasted the better now for the elixir of their passion. After a delicious swallow and just as fine a dose of the sight of his lovely wife's charms, he said, "To our happiness, many children, and long life."

"To eternity." She said, drank, watched him do the same, and then—for the first time since he'd brought her here—her eyes fled his.

His heart tumbled over in pain. He could have been so certain she had enjoyed their ecstasy so well that she would not regret it. Yet obviously here it was—a brazen creature called Propriety come to take his mate away.

He eased himself closer to her. "Cat." He reached out a hand to stroke her thick hair.

She curved a shoulder from him and slid from the bed. He wasn't surprised to see her lift a crocheted afghan from the bed and twirl it about her, nor did he feel anything when she went to the chaise, stood before the table, and ran a finger over the binding of his mother's collection of short stories. Numb, he barely heard her when she did speak.

"I want to be with you for always, Spence. I want to be with you as we were now, here, completely." She whirled to face him, her pink skin peeking through the loops of the afghan, her brandy and cream coloring a portraitist's ideal study of ravishing woman. "My nature is satisfied by what we just did. My mind needs to understand why you left me years ago. I don't want to hear what Merrick said about my father because I know whatever it was, it will be a slur against the only other man I have ever loved. But for us to go on together as gloriously as this"—she indicated the room with a few nods—"I must know what you felt, thought, assumed. Tell me, Spence, so that I can set it behind me and put my hope and heart to building a solid marriage."

Relief that her problem wasn't excessive sex made him giddy, but terror lest she find his explanation too simplistic or too unbelievable made him turn to stone.

How had he thought to avoid this? He couldn't. This was his price for pride—and misplaced trust.

Resigned, craving a reprieve to save his marriage, he put his glass aside and took himself back to the headboard, draping the bedclothes up about his hips.

"I am not proud of this story. It reveals my woes. My weaknesses."

"But if you cannot share those with me as well as your strengths, the intimacy between us will not grow."

"But wither. Die," he said blankly, his eyes on hers. "Yes, I know, darling. I have known that since I saw you last week on the dance floor at the Billingtons'."

"At least we agree."

"Sweetheart, if I tell you parts of this, it won't make sense. You'll have to hear everything.

"I couldn't bear to talk of my father—"

"No, darling. You'll have to because I want to have you, more of you, again. Soon."

She lifted both brows in slow amazement.

"Yes," was his response, shifting to make himself more comfortable and his erection less prominent to her, less demanding of him. "Sit down . . . Yes, there." She was delicious looking anywhere. But he tore his gaze away to the business at hand.

"I never spoke of this before to you. I couldn't. Though I told you there was nothing extraordinary to tell, in truth, I was too uncomfortable with it to reveal it. But you will know now. I have come to terms with my past and so too, will I hope in the telling, you can.

"From an early age, I loved strongly and completely. I was, I fear, born that way. Like you, I was overly active. I was a fireball that drove my parents and my nannies to distraction. I was not the only problem in the house. My mother was a beautiful wrenlike creature, kind, full of laughter—and so very heartbroken. I didn't see it at first. What child does? But I had Merrick, as younger siblings do, to clarify whatever I thought—and he was good at it. Very good.

"My parents had known each other since childhood. This Lyonns estate borders the Caldmores'. My grandmother Caldmore remains in their Dower House not half a mile from here. So when my father was eighteen, he asked for my mother's hand. Though they were still quite young, their families approved of the match and let them marry. But love—as you and I know bitterly—is often no guarantee against tragedy. Theirs came slowly.

"My mother had been prone to illness since a child. After they married, though my father took her often to Italy and Greece, she did not flourish. Nor did she conceive. My father, who was an only child, had been reared by a man who placed great importance on inheritance and family. He had warned my father about marrying a woman who might not be strong enough to bear the Lyonns heir—but when have such mundane objections ever stopped two people in love?"

The moment he said it, he deplored it. Cat sank back as though he'd speared her. Suddenly, he understood—as he never had before—to the finite ends of his being how he had hurt her years ago. Now he had to explain to her the ways that—beneath his own tough skin—he had injured himself by leaving her.

His mouth ran dry, fearing he might lose Cat even now. He rolled his tongue around his mouth, wracking his brain for the right words to heal the sorrow and allow them happiness.

"Despite my father's efforts, my mother was constantly ill, and she remained childless until five years after their marriage. That child was Merrick. He, too, suffered many childhood illnesses, and both my parents worried he would not live. The need to produce a second child led my father to continue relations with my mother, though her doctors advised against it. My grandmother Caldmore strongly objected as well.

"But it did no good. There were a succession of babies after that, each of whom were delivered stillborn or died soon after birth. My mother grew weaker with each pregnancy until finally I came into the world."

He sighed, impatient to have done with this agony of what he was about to reveal. "I was far healthier than any of the other children, including Merrick. My delivery, feet first, was a trial of two days, which nearly killed my mother. But my father at last had two sons. So from the day of my first birthday, my father finally took the doctors' advice and left my mother's bed.

"She was hysterical with grief. What could she do but hope he would remain faithful? He didn't. He became the worst libertine. Drinking, gambling, piling up debts, ignoring the running of the estate. Amid that were women. Many of them. Whether my mother heard of them, I do not know. What she did do was seek refuge in her own occupations. She was a perfect mother, doting and creative in her attentions. She wrote that book on the table."

Spence watched Cat run her elegant fingers over the ruby leather and along the gilt-edged pages. "It is a collection of family fables, if you will. The stories of the Lyonns. Noble men and legendary ladies, each full of rectitude and pride of place. Each worthy of a tale. At least so far as we know. So much as collective conscious lets us tell of our ancestors—and what we remember of them. So much as we, in our pride, will admit we became as much because of them as independent of them."

Cat clutched the book to her bosom, her head tilting in compassion. "What do you admit of yours?"

He pursed his lips. Steeled himself for the gutting act of verbalizing one truth of his character. One that defined him and from which many other aspects of his personality derived. "I loved my father in spite of his uncaring behavior."

He watched her delicate brows move to mark the question but no surprise. He smiled, praising God for the wisdom of this woman whom he adored with every fiber of his being. Was she not the same as he, caring for her own parent despite the man's flaws? Spence shook his head in wonder at how similar he and Cat were.

"Beneath my father's gruff exterior and the weakness he showed for—what shall we call it? his addictions?—he was a man who wanted love, ideal love. When he could not have it, keep it, rather than accept the things he could not change, he turned away and acquired preoccupations to fill the void. I feel very sorry for him now. But I hated him then. *Loathed* is probably the more exact word." He let that admission sink into her. Yet on her lovely face, he saw no revulsion. He could continue.

"He left us. Repeatedly. Never permanently. Always in a rage. He would find reasons to blame others for his abandonment. Hettie's meals were too bland. My mother was too distracted. Merrick, too simpleminded. I, too active and arrogant. We became his torture. He became a dervish in search of new delights, going from one preoccupation to another, meanwhile holding us in bondage to him emotionally and financially."

"What was your mother's reaction?"

"She retreated. Here." He circumscribed the room

with a hand. "Anywhere. She wrote an extensive diary from which I read this about her relationship with my father. She also wrote stories. Painted watercolors. Collected dolls, shells, buttons, laces, Christ anything! She hoarded the stuff everywhere, even in her handkerchief drawer, as if she meant to keep whatever she could since she couldn't keep her husband. She drove us all berserk! Asking us to rummage about, looking for this missing item or that. The maids were constantly finding more bits of some new obsession and complaining to my father of the mounting clutter. But he could do nothing to stop her, only hide *her* away. That he did, here, for the last five years of her life. She was, by the time she died, quite insane. Gone, dithering day in and out, in a fantasy world where no harm could reach her."

Cat absorbed that until she asked, "What of Merrick?"

"He seemed unaffected. In fact, he looked strong because of the hardships. Tried, tested, fired to an iron temperance in the furnace, if you will. I saw him as my older brother, wise and sure. He, as the first son, had the power to sway our father as no one else could. Often Merrick saved me as a young child from the verbal and physical assaults of the man. For that, I returned to Merrick a devotion that needs no reason. Just gratitude and uncompromised acceptance of the other person and his own foibles. I made him into a hero."

Spence shifted, inhaled, roiled by the ending. "But I was blind to what Merrick really was. I thought him self-sufficient. Earthy. At ease with his fellows. Enterprising in business. Lucky at cards and women." He smacked his lips. "Not with any woman he wanted to marry, though. I should have taken that as a clue to his real nature. But I loved him. I excused it or ignored it."

He paused, but Cat's voice called him back.

"You were young and he was your protective older brother. It's reasonable that you should imbue him with qualities brighter than he might possess."

Gratitude blossomed in his chest. Peace beckoned. If only he could show her his greatest vulnerability.

She came to him then as softly as repentance. She sat before him, took his hand, and when that summoned no words, she slid up against him, inspiring confession with a kiss. "I love you. Nothing you can say can change it."

"Merrick's reaction to our homelife was to show our father a personality. Seemingly accomplished, polished, educated. An expert on Egypt. A collector and a connoisseur of wine and women. But among his friends, he became something else he hid from us—from me. Merrick was a swell. A braggart. A hedonist. An addict."

Once he'd said it, this part suddenly didn't appear so monstrous. His brother, with all his imperfections and delusions, was dead.

But what of he himself? He allowed himself the ecstasy to examine his patient and forgiving bride. Ah, yes, he definitely was another matter.

"I was quite different from Merrick. I was raw, unaccomplished at artifice. Unnerved by my parents' constant wrangling, as a child I would cringe and hide. I would seek shelter with Merrick, who was so much older and so much more in control. He comforted me, but he also saw my exuberance for everything"—he smiled with sweet sadness at Cat—"so much like yours, my love—and he showed me how to tame it, put a veneer to it that didn't make our father critical and our mother wail. Merrick taught me how to avoid the confrontations and the constant callings on the carpet. Suddenly, I was a compliant child. The house became quieter for all my feigned lassitude. But my need to do things and to be everywhere was like an acid in my blood. I was fifteen before I went to Merrick one day and told him I lived a lie."

The memory made him wince and bring his wife closer to the circle of his arms. "Do you know what he told me?"

She shook her head.

"He said I could stop complaining and get on with my life. I could continue to pretend I was what everyone wanted me to be and in my private times do whatever I wanted. When I told him I felt that was squandering one's nature in the name of society, Merrick laughed. He *laughed!* I was fifteen, innocent of Merrick's pastimes, and I was appalled at his duplicity. I loved my family independently of each other for everything they were. Including an intemperate father who appeared not to care about me, about any of us. It tore me open. I went back to school and vowed to find a way to deal with what the three of them had become. A roué, a madwoman, and a callous brother."

He examined Cat now, knowing that with this next she might well vanish from his life. "I learned that to tolerate the pain of loving them it felt so much better to stay away from them. I would go home, but my visits were short, insignificant. After I joined the army, I traveled everywhere, anywhere."

She stared at him. "So when you met me, that changed?"

His breath snagged. She saw him for what he was. All of him.

"Yes! I wanted to be with you every minute. I enjoyed your laugh and your perpetual motion, your energy! It matched my own, and with you I learned I didn't have to hide it. For a man who had done that, baring my being to its core was not a fond prospect. Though I adored you and couldn't bear to be parted from you, I couldn't reveal who I was in my entirety, could I? Rather than see you discover my own faults and watch you transform before my eyes—like everyone else whom I had ever cared for—I took Merrick at his word. I believed that your father had forged that papyrus and done ever so much else." He paused, dismissing the need to detail Merrick's accusations now, saving such a discussion for its own time and place. "I used that as a cover for my real reason! I left you! Because it would be better to leave you than to have you discover what a fraud I was! To stay and watch as you eventually *left me!"*

She just sat there, watching him breathe.

With each second, he awaited the death knells to their marriage. Until she reached up a hand and curved it to his cheek.

"My beloved husband," she said with such sweetness his hope had to stop and wait, "you have told me your secrets. Now I'll share mine with you." She swallowed pain, her eyes bright with the tears from it. "You are no actor. Everything you are—honest, courageous, charming, and funny—shines in what you do. I saw it, knew it from the first night I set eyes on you. From that time I also knew such love of you that I could never leave you."

His fingers dug into her shoulders.

"Do you know what else I know, my lion?"

He shook his head, unable to see her clearly for the facets of his tears.

"I never hated you."

"Oh, *Cat!*" He crushed her close, understanding how such an admission exposed her deepest self to him, the man who had left her.

"I didn't!" she cried as he felt her tears dribbling down her cheeks to mingle with his own. "I knew, dear man of my heart, I *felt* that whatever reason compelled you to leave me was one you had to conquer by yourself. While I"—she twined her arms about him—"I could only pray you'd do it before we died and that if you came to me with an apology, you could love me."

She broke apart in his arms then, sobbing out the sorrows of her soul that in solitary agony had become hostage to his cowardice. His arms bound her to him. If he could take her suffering, he'd absorb it into himself, sound punishment for his failures to deal with his faults.

Valiant yet, she tried to collect herself, fingers to her lips, eyes streaming tears. "Do you think," she finally managed as she shook, "you could possibly find it in your heart to do me a great service?"

He smoothed her cheeks. "My heart belongs to you. Any service you want, my darling, is mine to give. What is it?"

"Could you make love to me again now, my husband?"

Trembling, he caught a breath. "Your merest thought is my greatest joy." He drifted the afghan from her gorgeous body. "I'll show you how I'll never leave you."

"I will give you plenty of reasons to stay."

"You have already." He contemplated rosy breasts, a willow waist, strong hips, a garland of treasures beneath.

"These are additional ones. These will live in your

house, spend your money, test your will, try your patience."

He grinned, scooped her under the arms to hold her high above him, kissed her belly, then swirled her to the sheets. "You'll give me a family?"

"I'll give you so many children, you'll pray for silence, diversion. They and I will run you ragged with a lifetime of responsibilities—tears and laughter. Our life will be no ideal, but *ours,* the better for its novelty. Down through the years, my darling, I won't let you go ever."

"I won't want to." He loomed over her, a scrumptious feast awaiting him. "God has granted me the one wish I would have robbed heaven to gain."

She threw him a wink. "Best demonstrate that vow, my lord earl."

"Come examine the evidence, wicked cat," he whispered as he opened her with reverent fingertips, felt her liquid paradise, and slid into her welcoming slickness. "I mean to keep you busy for at least ten decades."

"Or more."

The second after they found reward, he told himself the time had arrived to reveal the two secrets he had left. That he was a spy who had tracked her father and uncle would not endear him to her forgiving heart. That he suspected both men of smuggling would shock her worse.

He hated to do it, but he would do it now. After a bath, during lunch. *Now!* his aching heart demanded. Before any more catastrophes occurred. Before any other event happened to hurt his darling wife, who was now his very breath.

Chapter 13

*Y*ou want to do *what?*" Spence had caught himself from spitting his coffee across his bath chamber.

Cat rose from the mauve marble tub like a goddess from the sea. Water sluiced her delicate muscles with a flow that made him envious of every droplet. He fought to train his sights and his mind to Cat's words. But when he heard them again, he didn't know whether to gape or guffaw.

So he did both.

She captured the thick terry towel about her body but strolled the white carpet to rub against him in a now familiar caress, even more intoxicating for the liberality with which she offered him his heart's desire. Indeed, in the past three hours of the first ten of his marriage, he'd lost count how often they'd celebrated their union. Their baths had restored them, placed time and space between them. Though he knew he had to keep a semblance of normality, he could not ignore the insatiable appetite his wife aroused in him. So naturally at her request, he would startle.

But not balk.

He grinned, the idea of hers spreading a pressure to his already well-primed loins. "Why would you want to make love in each of the bedrooms, darling?"

Her hand ran up inside his unbuttoned shirt. "I want to see how amber your skin becomes in different shades of red." Her eyes narrowed, an ageless pleasure in their purple depths. "I like you in red."

"I love you in anything," he assured her, ready to forget his coffee and his less than hour-old abstinence for the sake of enjoying bliss again. "Best of all, nothing."

But a knock came to his bedchamber door and stopped up that ambition.

He arched a brow at Cat in resignation, closed the bath's door, and bid Hettie enter with her planned luncheon. Spence needed time to talk with Cat about their other problems. The bridge they had built this morning in the cottage had taken them from painful love to ecstasy. He hoped what they now found in this new land of their mutual trust could help them solve the mysteries of a missing papyrus, blackmail, and a murder. Their happiness, their future, depended as much on those as on the basic understanding of their personal motives. Spence prayed he could find the right words to tell Cat of his occupation and his questions.

He strolled across the carpet to open the door and find Charlie instead. With a rare frown, the caretaker added to Spence's woes with an unwelcome announcement.

"My lord, ye must come quick like. The drawing room's bursting at the seams. Lord and Lady

Billington 're downstairs." He hitched up one corner of his mouth and made a smacking sound. "So's yer grandma Caldmore."

The first set of visitors struck fear in his heart. The last perplexed him. He put down his cup and saucer. "Gran?"

"Aye, and she's none too happy either."

"Charlie, I haven't seen her smile since I was six, pretended I was a musketeer, and cut down her gladiolas to use as swords."

"Aye . . . well . . ."

The man's shuffle told another story. *"What, Charlie?"*

"Lady Caldmore's come with her usual basket of goods. Hettie and she trade produce from the gardens, ye see."

"Yes. *And?"* Spence jammed his hands on his hips.

"Well, sir." Charlie scratched his beard in wincing consideration of Spence's stance. "Hettie told 'er ye were married. Well, sir, ye know how your grandma is."

"She began recounting my past sins."

"Plus yer father's and brother's."

"So now she's taken over and—"

"Not letting Hettie or me a word in edgewise."

"Demanding an explanation." Spence was summoning his forces to deal with the matriarch whom London admired and the queen adored. He himself wished to call a cease-fire with the woman.

"Then please, Mr. Blowes," came Cat's reassurance as she emerged from the bath chamber wrapped in Spence's emerald brocade robe, "announce to her that her grandson and his wife will be down directly."

"How wonderful to see you, Lady Caldmore." Cat gave a curtsy to the reedlike woman, who presided in the drawing room chair. An empty flower basket and discarded gardener's straw hat sat on the deal table.

"Come closer, child," she beckoned with a deliberate curl of her gnarled fingers, ignoring Dorrie and Blanding. "Contrary to opinion, I do not bite . . . unnecessarily."

Cat grinned at the lady who had clipped speech and unruly white hair. Her serene countenance, which most found imperious, Cat had always thought haughty by training more than predilection. She strode forward, Spence on her heels, when his grandmother pointed to her weathered cheek and said, "You may kiss me. There. Good. Now—" Sharp blue eyes the color of a flame's sure center took in Cat's attire, a day dress of Dorrie's that fit loosely. "This looks like no trousseau to me. Nor would it be for an elopement." Her gaze cut to Spence. "Why have you done this, Spencer? Why have you married this innocent girl—as you should have done years ago, I might say—but *why* have you done it in such a way that *still* does not rectify her place in society? If you have damaged her further, I'll *not* find it in my heart to offer you the comfort of my forgiveness. You *know* my position on this."

Spence curled an arm around Cat's waist. "Yes, Gran, you've made it quite plain. I can explain."

She harumphed. "This outrage cannot continue, Spencer."

"It ends, Gran, as soon as I can arrange it."

Electric blue eyes whipped to Cat's. "He speaks in riddles. You tell me, Catherine. Have you married Spencer willingly?"

"More so than I would have years ago, Lady Caldmore."

The elderly lady pillaged Cat's expression. "What

earthly *reason* then do you have for such haste and secrecy?"

Cat knew she asked if Cat and Spence had created a child. Though they might have here this morning, that was not the motivation for their action last night. "No, ma'am. Not the usual one you'd think of in such circumstances."

"Gran, I hate to tell you the real story, but I will." Spence checked Dorrie and Blanding's wary stances and then drew Cat to the sofa near his grandmother. He stood behind Cat, one hand to her shoulder.

Lady Caldmore tapped her tiny foot on the carpet. "I'll not take any prevarication on this, Spencer. You disgraced this young woman before, and I won't hear any foolishness now. Merrick, may God find it appropriate to rest his soul, is gone. So is Walter Farrell. Although I think that alone bodes well for the two of you getting on, I will not condone anything less than the truth here. I have seen too much heartache in this family to let you hurt this woman—and I *do not care,* Spencer, how much she says she loves you. Love only survives in total truth. Give it to me as you had better have given it to her or I *swear* to you, I will see Catherine Farrell from your life permanently. Well you know"—she gored Spencer with her uncommon bright gaze—"I can summon the best of forces to do it, too."

"Yes, Gran, I do." He licked his lips.

Blanding froze. Dorrie wrung her hands.

"I'll tell you what I can."

"Everything! Or I take Catherine with me this very morning!"

Spence would have spoken, but Cat cut in. "Let me," she said and took his hand, winding her fingers through his and facing the lady with the wild hair that matched her wrath. "Lady Caldmore, Spence married me late last night to protect me. He offered and I accepted. He made the proposal in honor, and I agreed because I love him dearly and because I know he loves me."

"He said that before. It meant little compared to the accusations of Merrick."

Though Cat would never reveal to anyone Spence's intimate reason for his desertion, she could show his grandmother that her grandson was no ogre. "But he understands now why he did that. So do I."

Blue eyes shot to Spence's. "I hope you count yourself most fortunate, my boy, she accepts you so readily."

"I do. I'll make the best husband for Cat, I promise you as I have her. She believes me. I wish you would. To make that a possibility, I want you to know why she is here today as my wife. You see, my dear"—he gripped Cat's hand tightly—"Cat may be accused of murder."

A credit to her breeding, the woman did not even blink but stared. Panned the silent group assembled before her. Then opened a palm in summons.

Spence complied. "The president of Thornhill Bank was found shot to death in the library at the Marlows' annual ball last night. He clutched flower petals in his hand, roses that had fallen from Cat's gown. The Yard inspector called in to investigate at first assumed that the woman who wore those roses was the one who had killed him."

"What possible motive would the inspector say drove you to such a deed, my dear girl?"

"Anger. You see last week Acton Thornhill refused me a sizable loan of money for my school. He said I could have one or two thousand but no more unless I advanced collateral. I have none. He suggested I sell the last of my father's findings owned by me—a collection of Egyptian jewelry on display now at the Wyngate. Last night when Spence and I were alone talking in the Marlows' library, Acton came in with someone else whom neither Spence nor I could identify. Acton and the other man did not know we were there, and we overheard their conversation. They spoke of me, my loan, and . . . my father."

Spence added, "Within minutes, I had talked to Dorrie to explain Cat's departure to her uncle, and Cat and I left the Marlows' for my house."

Victoria Caldmore gripped the arms of her chair. *"Why?* If anyone saw you both, you realize society will shun you again! To say absolutely *nothing* of how guilty it appears!"

"I took her there only to talk, Gran. No one knew. I made certain of it."

Lady Caldmore scowled. "But when did the crime occur? Before you left?"

"I doubt it. Probably soon after."

"Then you have no proof that you were there or *not,"* she ruminated. "Oh, *what* have you done?"

Spence raked his blond hair and strode to the window. Hands thrust into his trouser pockets, he set his jaw. Cat had seen him this roiled on few occasions. Her heart went out to him, but suddenly he whirled to face her—and when he looked into her eyes, her heart stopped. "We've had so little time, Cat," he said it like a prayer. "I haven't had any to tell you this, but I will now. I must."

Cat swallowed. What was he leading up to?

"I should have done this days ago," he began, "but other issues were more important. More urgent." His green eyes, so full of bereavement, faded to black as they met Blanding's. "Surely you see what a royal mess I'm in here, chum? Pardon me while I cut a length of rope with which to hang myself."

Cat frowned.

Dorrie grimaced at her husband. "What is Spence talking about?"

Blanding rose to say, "A matter of state," then began to pace as if he mulled a gargantuan matter.

Cat shook her head, bewilderment leading only to an understanding that she needed to touch her husband. "Spence, I'm confused."

"Stay where you are, darling, and let me get this out quickly. It's not a pretty story."

"Spence," Blanding interjected, "you must discuss this, but first allow me to reveal something. Everyone of you must know what Dorrie and I came to tell you. The Yard arrested someone this morning for the murder of Acton Thornhill."

Cat shrank to the sofa, relieved, terrified, turbulent.

"Who?" Spence asked the obvious for all of them.

"One of the bank's directors. Norris Eddleworth."

Victoria muttered. "That thief."

"I'd hasten to agree, Lady Caldmore."

"I've met him," reflected Spence, "but only briefly."

"Distasteful fellow," his grandmother rattled on while Cat covered her mouth, feeling deathly ill but light-headed with her vindication. "Lovely wife, sorely put to the test of his character. He was always in debt. Been selling off his lands for years. For gambling, women, and sloth, too. Nevertheless, he was a director of Thornhill's. Shameless man."

Cat could make no sense of it. "Why would he kill Acton? How? How did they discover it was Eddleworth?"

Blanding raised dark brows. "John Marlow had evidently overheard them arguing in the library, which of course I did not know when I came to you last night. The inspector also found the gun in Eddleworth's pocket."

"Who told you?" Spence asked Blanding.

"Rand came to me at dawn to tell me. The inspector and two bobbies arrested Eddleworth early this morning. Dorrie and I set out for here immediately after Rand brought word. Norris's motive, Rand says, is a dispute over use of the bank's funds." Blanding zeroed in on Spence with a desperate look. "Thornhill Bank has been investing in two import businesses. The directors have been squabbling for years. Norris leading one faction; Acton, the other. But—as you and I know, Spence—Thornhill's has also earned quite a lot of money on one import business in particular."

"Merrick's China trade."

Victoria Caldmore snorted. "Merrick's *opium* trade."

Spence gaped at his grandmother. *"You knew?"*

"I'd be deaf, dumb, and blind to live a stone's throw from this house and *not* know. I *watched* it happen, my boy! First your father with his addictions; Merrick was just like him and fated to follow suit. Of course, your brother would become involved with people who would import it! He needed the constant supply. I've known for years. How long did it take the government, Blanding? As for you, Spence, how many years have you lived in the dark, my darling boy?"

"I never suspected"—his bass voice was a rasp on the morning air as he stared at Cat—"until just before he died. He sent for me to help him disperse an orgy here. Afterward, I went to Blanding and Rand with questions. Blanding said he had suspicions. Rand had connections in the import trade who could ask about. Only a few months before Merrick died did we know for certain that Merrick used his position and influence to cover the trade."

"We?" Cat asked for clarification.

"The government," Spence told her on a rasp. "The Foreign Office to whom I report. To whom I have secretly reported for five years. That association ends when I leave the army in a few months."

Cat nodded calmly while her mind asked how long she had known Spence was a spy. *Forever,* came the crisp reply.

Blanding groaned. "Christ, Spence, tell her the rest."

"Yes." He said it as if it were his own damnation. "I will. I'm the one who discovered it. You see, Cat, Merrick used his influence to help control the opium trade—and suppress any rivals."

Somehow this was not quite all she feared. "There are rival smugglers of opium operating out of London?"

"Through Shanghai, Bombay, and Alexandria," he added.

"Can't you track the sources?" she asked Spence.

But he had frozen.

"Regrettably not," Blanding looked none too happy to say. "To add greater problems to it, we are pressured by the khedive who will not allow us to invest in the Suez Canal until he has two things we are unable at the moment to deliver."

"An end to the opium trade through his port of Alexandria," Spence explained. "The second is something else we thought your father possessed."

Her heart sank. "The papyrus."

"Yes," he nodded. "The letter from Ramses to Moses."

"So you came to me at Dorrie's and Blanding's last week to see if you could get close to me and perhaps find it." When none of them moved a muscle, she knew it was true. "I really don't blame you. All of you helped me in the process and I am grateful. You convinced me finally to come out into the world again . . . And you, Spence, did act so honorably you made it easy. You each gave me something I could not gain alone." She bit her lip, close to tears she'd rather not shed. "So now the khedive wants the papyrus my father found. The same one I'm to turn over, isn't it, Spence?"

"Yes, the khedive wants it to keep as a national treasure of Egypt."

Blanding came to frown down at her. *"You* are supposed to find a papyrus? *Why?"*

Dorrie shot from her chair. "What are you three talking about?"

Victoria Caldmore fumed. "Precisely my thought."

"I'm being blackmailed for a papyrus. A decree from Ramses to Moses as he took the tribes of Israel from pharaoh's kingdom to wander in the Sinai. My father found it and hid it somewhere. But I *cannot* find it!"

Blanding cursed like a madman.

Dorrie froze. "Why would anyone want to blackmail you for a historical document?"

In the hushed room, Spence offered, "Possibly, the blackmailer is a collector, adding to his private store."

"Perhaps," said Blanding.

"But," Dorrie said, "if no one's ever seen it because Walter Farrell kept it well hidden, the only worth it can have is historic."

Cat felt a terrible truth rush through her like the first gust of a hurricane. "Certainly, my father must have told others what the papyrus contained." Her eyes went to Spence for elaboration.

"It was too significant to keep secret, love."

"Especially," added Blanding, "for a man of his pride."

"Meantime," Spence said to the others as he caressed her shoulder, "someone has attempted to frighten Cat."

Everyone else gasped.

Cat watched Spence tell them of the attack of the runaway coach the other evening outside the gallery. "I was there and took her home afterward. For the next few days, I followed her. But I am relieved—and damned confounded—when I say I have found no one tracking her. The only person I ever saw was a man who climbed from Farrell's factory top floor across to the roof of Ball and Bull Importers next door. Yes," he said at her surprise, "he did. But he didn't hurt you and I've seen no one since."

"A deuced mess," mourned Blanding.

Dorrie squeezed Cat's hand. "When must you produce the papyrus?"

"Friday. I'm to deliver it or ten thousand pounds by eight o'clock that night."

"Where?"

"They're to send me instructions in the mail."

Victoria Caldmore slapped her hands on her armrests. "Well then, you must return to London." Her blue gaze whipped to Spence. "But there is no need to reveal this marriage."

Spence turned apologetic eyes on Cat. "Gran is right, darling. You can go back. You should."

She knew she must. To find the papyrus or hand over money. Or something else terrible might happen . . .

Spence took her in his arms. "Everything will be fine. I'll see to it. I have only just found you, claimed you again. I won't let anyone hurt you, darling. We'll find this papyrus."

"We would also stop whoever it is from damaging my father's integrity, wouldn't we?" At his nod, she put a hand to his cheek. "In the process, we might destroy Merrick's reputation."

"We'll do what we must. For the truth. For us. The world can go hang."

"Not entirely, Spencer." His grandmother rose on shaky limbs. "I want a real wedding for you two."

Spence wrapped his fingers around Cat's nape and massaged her tensed muscles. She felt none of his consolation, only a recurrence of the wrenching loneliness of the past years, a solitude that had only so recently, so briefly been converted to joy by her husband's touch. Spence spoke into her hair as he agreed with his grandmother. "So do I want this for you, Cat. Oh, sweetheart," he whispered, "don't look at me like that. I'm not deserting you."

Why then did this plan make her feel so damned desolate? She bit her lip and snatched a measure of bravery from some hidden trove. "I know you're not. I was just getting used to this idea of marriage, and now—it's over."

His green eyes flowed over her like a benediction. "It's only just begun. We'll have this wedding, before everyone. The way it should have been. You and I will be apart only a little while, and in the meantime, you'll have those things we want for you." He chucked her under the chin. "Even Gran."

At Spence's sardonic brow, his grandmother grimaced. *"Gran* will ensure it. I'll come to London. We'll have a formal engagement party. We'll set a date."

Spence laughed. "We have one, dearest. June fifth."

"I see." Her wizened face fought a grin. "Do we also have a church?"

"St. Paul's."

"Admirable. My opinion of you edges up a notch."

Spence gave his grandmother a rueful look. "When will you forgive me entirely?"

"A year or two. A child or more." She shot up a bony finger. "But first things first. I'll stay with you in Park Lane, Spence. My house has been closed up for too long to prepare properly anyway. I shall act as chaperone although . . . I would wager from the looks of you both that such a function is required only for public consumption. Well"—she reached down, grabbed her straw hat and planted it on her white wisps—"if I can borrow Diggie and your carriage, dear boy, I'll go home to pack. But I return within the hour. Mind you while I'm gone, I want no regrets of what's past."

Cat watched the lady leave and wondered if she herself could fully face the future without reexamining her father. The fact that Walter Farrell had hidden a famous document was so antithetical to his egotistical nature meant his reason to hide it had to be more powerful than the lure of fame.

What motive could he have for that?

To be wildly famous had been her father's singular goal. He was never enchanted by money. Never thrilled by any woman other than his wife. Nor had he fallen victim to someone's offer of power. Walter Farrell was, first and always, an archaeologist. The only throne he ever coveted was that of the most renowned in his profession.

Therefore, the thing he feared most would be someone else becoming more presitigious than he.

Yes, Cat acknowledged with wrenching sorrow. Jealousy qualified as the only reason her father would ever hide a papyrus from the world.

But jealousy of whom?

Chapter 14

*M*y dear Cat." Edwina Marlow embraced her with a shaky expression. "I am thrilled you have come. We have quite a few other guests today," she said as she looped her arm through Cat's to lead her from the grand foyer to the Marlows' drawing room. "You know most of them. As promised, I've summoned Corinne. We shall endeavor," the lady said with rueful winsomeness as she paused before the double doors, "to put this latest unpleasantness behind us."

Cat nodded but shivered inside at the thought of murder . . . and smuggling, forgery, and blackmail. God knew, she hadn't felt up to this tea but knew she had to go to continue her march back into society's good graces. In the past two days, separation from Spence had chafed her nerves while the unproductive search for the papyrus made her fret and pace the house deep into the lonely nights. But mixed into the brew of her distress was the ironic question of her father's character that she had so long avoided. How could a man who had been so good to his child be a liar, a forger, . . . a criminal?

Edwina stared at her. "You don't, do you?"

"I'm sorry. I'm not myself these past few days, Edwina. What did you say?"

"I hope you don't think I'm gauche to bring Corinne to you this way. But she does do well at tea."

"I will be pleased to meet her anywhere," Cat reassured her but knew it was odd to invite children—especially girls younger than debutante age—to take formal tea with guests. In some ways, Cat thought it frighteningly improper that Edwina had done so at a time like this. But then again, she was marshaling her forces to defend the family fortress.

Much besieged it certainly was. By the newspapermen hovering about the door. By headlines that screamed of Acton Thornhill's murder and Norris Eddleworth's arrest. By the two bobbies stationed at either street corner. The Marlows, as a slice of the upper crust, were going to ignore the blot upon their family esteem, this horror that someone had committed a crime on their hallowed ground.

This was so much like what Cat felt about her own family. Her father. She admitted to herself now fully that her father had acted unethically. She had also ignored the shame of it. To deal with the pain, she told herself that if she could but find this damned papyrus, she would get on with her life! Her school. Her marriage.

She rubbed her left hand where once Spence's signet ring had proclaimed her his countess. She had removed it on the return journey to London Sunday and tried to give it to him. He had curled his hand around hers and told her to keep it as a symbol of what they were and would be soon again. She wore it when she was alone, when she read his mother's storybook, which Spence had also given her for the journey home, or when she slept. Her memory of their hours as man and wife made these last few days without him misery, and she pined for his presence, his voice, his touch. His reassurance.

Edwina spun, opened her doors . . . and there amid a dozen others, like a vision conjured from mere wish, stood Spencer Caldmore Lyonns. Resplendent in steel gray and snowy shirt, he smiled in welcome—and desire—for her alone.

"I think you know everyone." Edwina took Cat round to perform her introductions to those assembled. John Marlow, naturally. Victoria Caldmore, whom Cat bussed on the cheek. Spence, who gave Cat a sweet hot kiss to her hand. Rand Templeton, obviously—and uncharacteristically—unnerved over something. Blanding and Dorrie, both watchful of her, and . . . Marietta. Cat sighed. Good grief, chatty Marietta Hornsby had come with her husband, Oscar, while Marietta's lover, the duke of Inniesfield, took a chair near Nanette Marlow, too young a chick for such an old goat.

But Edwina introduced her daughter with a blind eye to the flirtation between them. "I believe you met Nanette the other evening."

The young woman smiled with no apparent effects from having had a suitor dispatched in her library a few days ago. She was totally absorbed with Inniesfield.

"Last," said Edwina, "we have Corinne, who has been trying to contain herself to meet you."

Cat put out her hand to the ten-year-old, whose cinnamon curls bobbed with her curtsy and whose blue eyes twinkled with unrestrained joy. "I am happy to meet you, Corinne."

"And I you, Baroness. Mother has told me much about you, and I have worn my best gown to impress you." She leaned over, a jovial conspirator. "My best manners, too."

Cat chuckled, while behind her she felt the powerful warmth of Spence draw near. "Well, Corinne, I'm honored. Manners make a lady—"

"But heart," said Spence to both of them, "makes a woman."

Cat gave herself the pleasure of leaning back, her shoulder to his chest. The smallest caress for a yearning that grew by gigantic proportions every moment she was parted from him. Every second she craved him. She swallowed. How was she to endure her days until June fifth?

Her eyes sought the succor she had been denied these past days when she had returned to Eaton Square, re-read her father's memoirs, and scoured her brain for where he might have hidden the papyrus that she needed before Friday.

Spence, thank her lucky stars, let her feast on him while they took a seat on the sofa across from Corinne and he discussed a thousand things. The girl, Cat could tell, thought the blond giant simply smashing. He was.

Cat licked her lips. Forced her eyes and mind to Corinne and what the child needed.

The others, who left Cat to concentrate on Corinne, pursued their own topics while Cat and Spence laughed with a child so exuberant she fairly wore the upholstery off her chair with her tales of her collections of toads and turtles and her erratic escapades over hill and dale.

"Mother says I'm much too much and need a harness," she blurted finally, then cast frank eyes at Cat. "She says you know how to help me. I know Mother is mad to contain me. I have tried, you know. But somehow, no matter what I tell myself, I *must* do, do, do! Can you possibly—"

Cat took the child's hand, which had twisted the dimity of her gown to a wrinkled ruin. "Understand? Of course I do. I am like you. Lord Lyonns, too. We are full of life and the need to discover more of it. It is inborn. We cannot and we should not change it. But others find us perplexing. What my cousin and I think we can help others learn is that this bubbling joy in life is no crime."

Corinne bit her lip. "Papa says my behavior often is."

Cat recoiled. "He doesn't really mean that, Corinne."

"Crimes," Spence clarified, "are committed by those who live outside the boundaries of human decency. An energy for living hardly equals that."

"Mother says my manners are lacking."

"Not lacking," Cat consoled the girl with a finger to her chin and a smile as she met troubled eyes. "Charm shows fully in those who possess it, Corinne. You do. What you may lack now is a knowledge of how to polish those manners so others may see through to the essence of you."

Spence whipped his head around, and his mellow green eyes drowned in Cat's, then dropped to her mouth. "What Lady Farrell is saying, Corinne, is that she and her cousin know the secret to making people whole and happy."

Cat could scarce breathe. *Oh, Spence, I want to come home with you. Be whole with you. Love you. Build a life.*

278

His foot rubbed hers. "Sometimes, you see, Corinne, we go too quickly. We don't pay attention to the little things . . . and we should. Because in the smallest details often are the most significant elements of our lives."

Cat considered him, compassionate man that he was. He was speaking generally, comforting a child who had known little of it from those who could not understand her. But something else spoke to her in Spence's words. Had she missed details? Had she not learned where the papyrus was hidden by examining evidence too quickly? Making false assumptions?

Spence caught her eye and cocked his head in question. Though he went on, elaborating for Corinne about the nature of someone like Cat and him and her, he pressed his leg full length along Cat's in comfort and query.

God, how she longed to put her hand to his thigh, to his skin. Her mouth to his lips.

She gulped.

"Tea?" Edwina held out a cup to Cat.

Yes, she needed tea. A few Devonshire cream scones. Objectivity. Clarity.

What she got was a discussion of little importance to her until they alighted on the Egyptian jewelry collection, her father, and Dominik.

"Interesting man, your uncle," offered Reginald Inniesfield. "I understand he sets out for the Sinai soon."

Cat handed over her cup for a refill. "He is to take up where he left off a few years ago with my father. Uncle Dom's special interest was always the tribes of Israel."

"Unlike your father, who only investigated the Upper and Lower Kingdoms of the Nile," Inniesfield concluded.

"My father concentrated on the power of the pharaohs through the centuries. Had he lived, I think he would have been the first to complete a treatise on the subject."

"How interesting. So am I correct to assume that your uncle Dominik learned what he knows from your father?"

"Not everything. Uncle Dom went to Cambridge, too, and has studied with some of the most well-known scholars of the ancient world. He chose to branch off from what my father did toward the end of . . . of their relationship. But even the last expedition they launched—the one where they found the jewelry"—*and the papyrus I need*—"was beneficial to them both. They studied the reign of Ramses II. The ruler who was brother and mentor to Moses."

And just like those two, Father and Uncle Dom fought bitterly. Over what?

She had never dwelled on obtaining an answer to that question. But should she have? Did they quarrel over the papyrus?

But she couldn't recollect so much in such a short time while social demands made her force her mind to those before her and say, "Ramses did spend money lavishly. He had numerous building projects and a very opulent court. To fund them, he reopened old turquoise and copper mines in the Sinai and used Moses' people for slave labor." *In the Sinai, where Uncle Dom will soon return to search for those mines.* "When Moses led the tribes out of Egypt, he took with him Ramses' means to work the mines cheaply."

"Fascinating," Inniesfield muttered, but something about his tone told Cat he could never be bored by this chat.

Marietta frowned. "I find it very mysterious. I

mean one thinks of stories in the Bible as too old to have been recorded or verified by"—she waved a hand,—"things."

By a papyrus. Cat stared at her. *A papyrus that proves that this story of the Bible was no mere fable, that Ramses really knew Moses and . . . what else?*

"Early Christians thought," offered Spence politely, "that the Exodus occurred near the village of Suez."

Rand nodded. "Where the canal is located."

When Spence agreed, Marietta's husband seemed to awaken. "Are you implying a question that perhaps Moses did not cross there?"

"There is another possibility. He might have crossed more south at a waterway so shallow that one could ford it at numerous points."

Oscar Hornsby scowled. "So this business of the Red Sea parting is folderol?"

Spence arched his brows. "No one is certain." His leg brushed Cat's again . . . to imply what? "Numerous scholars look for proof in finite details."

"I don't think that is an objective of Dominik," said John Marlow as he trained his eyes on Cat.

"No," she said and wondered if it were true. Then she told them what she knew for certain. "He does seek to find those mines that Ramses had the tribes of Israel work."

"Interesting," declared Inniesfield. "I wonder if the mines are stripped or if they hold more treasure, don't you?"

"Absolutely," said Rand, but his eyes went to Spence.

"It would be a marvelous discovery," agreed Edwina.

"Such a find would make him famous," concluded Cat.

Spence considered Inniesfield for a long moment, then turned to Edwina. "Wonderful Banbury cakes, Edwina. My compliments to your cook."

By the time the others rose to take their leave, Spence had shown his appreciation of the cook's wares with gusto. Cat could barely breathe. When Edwina and John drifted from the room to do their duties, Spence took the opportunity to ask her if she'd found any clues.

"Nothing. But I'm going to re-read Father's memoirs for details I may have missed." *To try to find out why my father and Uncle Dom argued.*

"Your uncle never questioned your so-called visit to Dorrie?" When she shook her head, he asked if anyone from Scotland Yard had sought her out.

"No, do you think they will? I canceled my appointment at the bank by sending Marsh round with a note. No one said a word about it being odd, not even Marsh."

"No one probably will. Norris Eddleworth confessed this afternoon." He rose and crushed her to him, his movement fevered in the minutes they had alone. "But still you must be careful. Do you hear me?"

He pulled her away to peer into her eyes. Then at the sounds from the foyer, he steadied her on her feet and placed his thumb atop her lips. Rolling down her lower lip, he grazed her teeth and bathed her skin in her own moisture.

She swayed into his caress.

He closed his eyes, groaned, and left her to her hot imaginings of what could have come next if he'd not gone home with his grandmother and she'd not dribbled into a pile of mush upon the Marlows' Persian carpet.

* * *

"I need to talk to you," she told him surreptitiously the next night at the Bloomsburys' at-home party as they were sitting down with much the same people as at tea the day before.

"Later," he said as he smiled at his hostess whose husband was the man responsible for foreign affairs. His wife reputedly took up her own extramarital ones.

"I *should* ignore you," Cat teased him when she could.

"Try it," he countered, "and I'll take my revenge."

She pouted and smiled to herself as the footman ladled soup into her bowl. "I'm creating my own list of tortures."

"How intriguing." He leaned over her, pretending to glance down the table at the calla lily garland centerpiece, but in reality he took in her décolleté. "I'll dispense with the items on your list our first night."

She made a little oooo with her mouth. "I'd bet you'd begin your own the next morning."

He scorched her with narrowed green eyes. "Gran says we should make an announcement soon before anyone gets wind of June fifth's reservation." When she had not answered well into the entrées, he asked, "Have you told your uncle?"

She swallowed hard. "I was going to this morning but lost my nerve. I asked him instead about the other item."

When he husked, *"What* about it?" and she could not reply, they took up their social responsibilities with the avidness of two starving people. By the time the ladies were to retire for coffee and the men for port and cigars, Cat was bursting to talk to him.

"Meet me in twenty minutes in the foyer," she whispered as she left her chair. She had no idea what excuse she'd make or how they'd escape the eyes of the servants, but talk to him—*kiss* him—she would before she shriveled up deprived of his sunny disposition and his comfort.

Minutes later, with the purpose of a hunter, he strode up to her in the foyer, gripped her arm, and practically ran with her along the corridor to some door he opened and thrust them both inside. He pressed the thing shut, shot the lock, twirled her into his arms, and seized her body, breath, lips, like a ravenous predator.

"I have hungered for you," he cupped her jaw, palmed her breasts, fused his contours with hers. "Living without you is torture."

Her hands dived into his satin hair as his own fingers ruched up her gown, past the pile of petticoats, to press her pantalets, find their slit and then the molten core of her he had so long been denied. She arched to yield him everything she was. He trailed his tongue down her throat to her breasts. "I'm a man in a cage without you. Desperate. Needing you for breakfast and—"

"Bed!"

He snorted. "Fie on June fifth!" He spread her thighs.

"It was your idea." She whimpered when her clothes foiled easy access to him.

"A bloody bad one." He braced her against the wall.

She mewled, rubbing her begging but clothed nipples against his chest. "I can't get near you."

"The hell you can't." He cursed and surveyed the room. "Here, come here." He carried her, her legs around his hips. Her forehead fell to his shoulder. Her fingernails raked his tuxedo. She groaned as her hand sought and found him. Big, hard, hers. He laid her down tenderly on some cool surface, her hips at just the right angle and height. He glided into her with a slick shock. The electricity had them pausing, panting, quaking.

"God in his wisdom," he rasped in a prayer, "gave me you. Cat, my lioness"—he thrust for the first scrumptious time in barren days—"you are such a wet, willing wife."

"I'm your complement"—she ran fingers down his shirt studs to the root of his evidence—"my lion."

He closed his eyes, bowed up in his own enjoyment. His hands splayed her wide, bringing them closer, nearer, dearer. Then he began to take her with the natural rhythm of healthy creatures in rapture. "I think either of this," he confessed between strokes, "or the damned papyrus."

She bit her lip, clasped his buttocks. "I can't eat."

"Feast on me." He came so far inside her she could feel him to her nails, to her hair, flowing through her blood.

"I can't sleep either!" she sobbed on a thrill.

"You'd better . . . do it now, darling," he said between demonstrations of their love, "because when I get you . . . in a few weeks, you won't sleep . . . for a year . . . maybe more."

She quivered with the first of tremors gone missing from her days, her nights. "Oh, Spence, I'd forgotten."

"Remember." He lifted her higher to him. "Feel." He brought them both to the first pulse of mutual pounding ecstasy. "Know."

"Now." The sun burst upon her, seared her. She dissolved in his care. "I am yours."

"Always." He showed her how much that meant to him as he lost himself in his own universe of delights.

Minutes later, he kissed her throat and licked her

there, then looked up. "A room for sport, but not the one intended." He was suddenly chuckling as he turned and smoothed her tossed curls from her cheek.

She came to and saw why. They had made love among the stuffed trophies of the master of the house who fancied himself a big game hunter. One giraffe, a tiger, and a pawing grizzly bear had witnessed the union of a lion and his cat.

"Hmmm, on an exhibit table filled with butterflies," mused her husband as he helped her rearrange her gown. "It's a wonder we didn't break the glass, darling."

Cat tapped him on the chest with her fan. "You're so adept at this. I'll avoid asking of your experience at such things to say I'm very satisfied . . . and very proud of you."

"I'll satisfy you more, Countess," he said as he tied his cravat. "Become prouder when we find this papyrus."

Her playful mood died an instant death. "I talked to Uncle Dom this morning, Spence. He's delayed his expedition. Plus I re-read my father's diary today. What was said yesterday at tea made me think about details I may have missed. I had skimmed it before, especially the end."

"Yes. And?"

"Father's description of the last expedition he and Uncle Dom made is very confusing. He writes a lot about the conflicts between them—and one argument they had over an item they found in one of Ramses's temples. He doesn't say it's a papyrus, Spence," she clarified as he gripped her arms. "Father did declare that he didn't want to tell anyone about it. Uncle Dom wanted to tell the world, but Father said he feared its authenticity . . . and so he promised Dominik to bring it back to England to examine."

Spence's eyes pillaged hers. "What do you think?"

"It could be the papyrus we want."

"Does he say where he put it? How he transported it?"

"Nothing." She dropped her gaze to his waistcoat. "Two other things disturb me. This morning I noticed the language my father used to describe the papyrus is odd. He speaks of taking it back to England and thereby curing Dom of a deadly illness, one he himself suffered."

"Was Dom ever ill?"

"As I remember, not a day in his life."

"Interesting. And what is the second thing that disturbs you, darling?"

"This morning as I tried to discuss the jewelry collection, hoping I could get Dom to talk about the expedition, he said he has postponed his departure. He said the other day he would stay in London to protect me from you, but I had a feeling there was . . . another reason."

"What could it be?"

"He doesn't know where the Sinai mines are."

"Good God! Did he *say* this?"

"No, Marsh says Dom told him. Marsh then told me after Uncle Dom left."

"Christ in his grave," Spence ranted as he began to pace. "How can a man prepare an expedition and not know where he's going? I mean what is Dom going to do? Wander the desert for forty years like Moses and his people? Looking for lost mines? That's a waste of time and money. Well, *hell!* What a mess . . . To think it could be Dom blackmailing you. I don't know why I'm surprised."

Cat froze at his conclusion. She had understood that her uncle might need the papyrus for a scholar's reasons. But Spence attributed motivation to Dom which appalled her, insulted her, angered her. "You're not surprised?"

"No. Oh, look, sweetheart. I hate to be so damnably blunt but I've suspected your uncle Dom of improper activities before tonight. I mean . . . Oh, God, Cat! Don't you see that the reason Merrick and your father never got on was because they were *rivals* in the opium trade?"

Was this the avalanche she had sensed since Sunday's revelations? Yes, yes. Was this the horror she intuited about her father . . . and his feud with Merrick? Definitely.

Spence stepped close to grip her arms. "Darling, it kills me to say **it,** but I must. Why and how would the opium trade your father began continue if it weren't controlled by your uncle?"

To hear it rocked her on her feet. Lifelong loyalties and incredulity had her stepping backward. "You *can't* be serious."

"I know this is not pretty, but . . ."

She went quite still.

He hauled her against him. His body now felt far from love, more like betrayal. *Again.* "Listen to me, Cat! I've been following Dom long before I began trailing you. As I was tracking you, Rand has shadowed Dom. Your uncle's been searching in the tunnels under the Wild Hare and—"

In her anger she bypassed this revelation for the condemnation it gave. "You've been following us?"

"Love, I swear I don't mean to insult you or your uncle."

"The same way Merrick didn't mean to hurt my father?"

"That was different."

"Really? One wonders."

"You can't. Not after what we have been to each other."

"And what *is* that, Spence? What *have* we been to each other years ago, for months, and lately for only days? What *is* that compared to what my family is to me? And how you and yours have castigated me and mine?"

His face drained of color. "Darling, you can't believe that."

"The same way you can't believe that my uncle is a scholar bent on discovering facts so that everyone may know . . ." She was shattering with this latest blow to her family, her pride, her love of him. ". . . May know the truths of history."

She spun.

He captured her round the waist, forging her back to him, his lips in her hair. "You can't leave me! Not like this. Not ever." His voice was a hollow wreck.

She withered with what he implied. "I will. Must."

"Cat! This matter is a state affair. The khedive wants this papyrus because it's a national treasure! I'm not working just for the government!" He jerked her around to face him, his eyes wide with horrible regret. "I'm working for the queen!"

"I—would—not—care," she said so carefully she could barely mouth the words, "if you worked for God Himself. You cannot ever come to me and accuse my family of criminal activities without solid evidence."

He ground his teeth, then growled, *"I am trying to protect you! You are my wife, my life, my everything!"*

"Then bring me proof."

They stared at each other for eternal moments. She gave him her resolve. He gave her a promise.

She took it and turned. Her hand to the doorknob,

she whispered, "Until the day I die, I will walk this earth wanting no one but you. But in the interim, I will attempt to prove you wrong about this, darling. And if I do—" She bit her trembling lip, unable to finish her vow, knowing that if she did, she'd deliver the final blow that would destroy them for the second time—and forevermore.

Chapter 15

At the Hornsbys' garden party the next afternoon, everyone Cat met had advice.

Rand began by taking her aside to say he had heard what had happened at the Bloomsburys' dinner the previous evening. "You must hear Spence out, Cat. There is more to this than what he could tell you then."

That brought humility, sorrow, but no succor. When she made her way to the orangery and its buffet table, Dorrie scoured her with sad eyes and offered a hurried tidbit. "Blanding says Spence has found what you required." As Cat clamped her eyes shut, Dorrie followed with, "Cat, whatever the problem is, it can be solved. He's here and looking for you." But as she scanned the lavish gardens filled with more than two hundred of London's best, Cat made excuses to find the ladies' retiring rooms.

Inside, however, she came face-to-face—and completely alone—with Victoria Caldmore who announced in no uncertain terms that she looked frightful and that Spence hadn't slept last night either. "What are you two doing, spoiling a perfect love match with family differences again?"

Cat had no simple answer that could be declared in public or without tears.

"Come with me, my girl. Now, now. I have someone to whom Spence told me to introduce you if I got the chance. He is a publisher." As Cat stared at the sprightly woman, Victoria went on. "Spence says this gift goes with the crystal and the pen, whatever that means. Come, come."

She led Cat to a gentleman who stood among the budding rhododendrons and informed her that he had heard from Spence "again just this morning" how she'd like to publish her father's memoirs and how he'd like to see the manuscript when she was ready to offer it. "I have revered your father's work exactly as Lord Lyonns so clearly does. Like him, I'd like to see others have the benefit of it."

She gave great thanks, told him she'd bring it round in a few weeks, and wandered far away from others among cascading bowers of roses, alone and stunned.

When Spence appeared in front of her, she knew she'd been expecting him. Suddenly, the air thickened with the redolence of roses and remorse. She rubbed her hand where once his ring had proclaimed them one.

"I tracked your uncle last night when he left Eaton Square at midnight," he began without preliminary. "He went to your father's factory along the Thames. Then he went next door to the offices of Ball and Bull." He advanced.

She stood her ground.

"Your uncle met with both Mr. Ball and Mr. Bull. I

saw it through the window. Cat, they argued. Violently."

"It doesn't prove blackmail or smuggling."

"But an argument with unsavory characters in the middle of the night doesn't look right. Cat—" He reached for her.

She sidestepped him. "Please, don't—"

"A lovers' quarrel?" Marietta Hornsby emerged from the path, her arm hooked in the duke of Inniesfield's. "How charming. Don't you think, Reggie?"

The man grimaced. "Marietta, leave them alone. Sorry, Lyonns. Impetuous woman." He glared at the creature who had been his mistress for months and now appeared in danger of losing her status for a moment's bad manners.

Marietta preened. "Not as wild as some, eh, Cat? I understand you and Spence have reserved a chapel at St. Paul's for June fifth. Nice time of year."

Cat choked. If this got out before she had time to tell Uncle Dom about it or discover the truth of the papyrus, they'd look idiotic when and if she canceled the wedding.

Spence came forward, and though he didn't touch her, his words did. "Catherine and I are getting married, yes. We haven't announced it yet because we wanted a few people to get used to the idea before we let the world know."

"Terribly smart. I'm sure Dominik'll need *eternity*."

"Marietta!" snarled Inniesfield. "If you will excuse us, Lord Lyonns, Lady Farrell . . ." With that he led the woman off by the elbow.

Cat felt like drizzling into a puddle. Hand over her mouth, she pivoted for the house.

Spence halted her with a plea. "Listen to me,

darling. I'm not giving up. I'll find your proof. No matter who's to blame, I will show you. Hopefully before tomorrow's delivery of the blackmail money—and you will *use* my money to pay these men, Cat." He came so close, she swore she could feel the beat of his heart. "I mean to have you, Cat. As my wife. As my lover and my trusted, trusting friend. Nothing less will do."

It took her close to an hour to find Uncle Dom who was drawing stares as he openly seethed at Reginald Inniesfield, now minus Marietta. When Dom saw Cat, he bit off an excuse to the duke, took her arm, and put a hand to her forehead. "You look hideous. What's wrong?"

When she begged him to leave with her, he never uttered a word but took her and had Marietta's porter call for their brougham. In minutes, Cat sank to the squabs.

Dom sat across from her, sullen and forlorn. His eyeglasses glinted like oval mirrors in the afternoon sun. "Do you have something to tell me, Cat?" Before she could reply, he shifted uneasily. "Marietta blurted out that you have chosen a date and St. Paul's." Instead of the fury she would have expected, he appeared resigned.

That and what she had learned about him from Spence this afternoon made her more cautious than her usual self. "I love Spence, Uncle Dom. In spite of logic and our differences. Even pride. But we have numerous problems to solve. So we haven't announced it to anyone because . . ." *because I need to know what it is you hide and . . .* "I wanted to tell you first and feared your reaction."

He whipped around, but the silver spectacles wouldn't let her read his eyes. "I'm not your father, but I do care for you. I never had children. Maybe it's just as well . . . But I do know what it's like to love someone beyond logic or family honor. I cared for someone like that once myself."

This utterly amazed her. Her heart and her hand went out to him instantly. "I am so sorry. I didn't know."

"No," he said as he considered her gesture. "No one did. Except your father." His head came up, and this time she saw tears swim in his eyes. "I adored your mother."

She fell back in her seat on a whoosh of the cushions. Was this why Uncle Dom had always seemed so cool? Was there always *this* tension between her father and his brother? Had it strained everything, including their working relationship? Had it transformed Dom into a criminal?

His next words threw terror in her heart that it had.

"I hope you don't make the same mistakes I did, Cat."

"What mistakes?" she got out.

"Failing to act on instincts. Forgiving someone their trespasses. Instead, I harbored a resentment against my brother who won a woman's affections when I obviously was not meant to do so. I destroyed my relationship with my brother from the loving thing it was, and he took up his own resentment." He grabbed a huge breath. "I couldn't cure Walter's and my problems, so this past year that he's been gone, I tried to at least help you, but I am so out of practice, I've failed. I'm the one who's sorry, Cat. I say if you love Spencer Lyonns, you'd better solve your differences and marry him. Nothing less should do."

Almost the same words Spence used. But here, was Uncle Dom saying he approved of the marriage? She could barely believe it. Dom's eyes, mellow now with remorse, told her she could. "Yes, in my heart I agree

with you. But I can't force certain matters. They are
. . . out of my control."

"Such as?"

He was inviting her to trust him? Of course, he was.
Hadn't he always? Hadn't her father been the one to
dissuade her? She rummaged through her memories
while her mind—trained to her father's will—
chanted, *Careful, Cat.*

Dom crossed his arms and gazed out the window.
"You've been ransacking the house looking for
something."

Her heart seized. Her mouth dropped open.

He glared at her. "For what?" When she shrank
back, he lunged forward, grabbed her arms, shook
her. *"Why?* What's in those godforsaken memoirs
that Walter didn't deign to tell *me?* But why should I
be surprised? *Eh?* He left me the house but only after
you said you'd never want it. He left you the estate,
the cash, the investments, and even put you in total
control of it. As much to make you your own mistress
as to emasculate me more."

He flexed his hands, and she dropped back to the
seat. He raked his hair. "Then you threw every penny
into this school. Bankrupted yourself. Never asked for
my advice or help. Meanwhile, I *die* for money. Did
you ever ask me if I needed any for my endeavors?
No, of course not. You knew my pride would not
allow me to admit I needed it. I could not ask you the
same way I couldn't ask your father either. He
thought I merited nothing. Not understanding or
forgiveness. Not equality with the illustrious Walter
Farrell, scholar, brother, torturer."

"I thought—" she managed to bring up from a
hidden corner of her heart, "I always *believed* you
loved him."

"I *did!*" he roared. "But he was so unforgiving. So

merciless. I was not *perfect.* In his eyes, I was weak
and much too human and he . . . *he* was everything,
had everything. Success, home, loving wife, doting
daughter. What did I have? What could I merit after
all I had done to hurt him?"

She had to know. "What did you do to hurt him?"

"I loved his wife, though I never touched her or told
her. It puffed up his conceit, but he used the knowledge against me. Criticizing me, containing me."

"How did he *think* you hurt him?"

Sardonic, his countenance glowed. "I introduced
him to the means of his own destruction!"

She wanted to scream in confusion.

He thumped his chest. *"I* introduced him to
Inniesfield and the man's lovely little friends!"

"Reginald and . . . Marietta?" That made no sense,
but a vision of Dom arguing with Inniesfield in the
garden and Spence's accusations of Dom smuggling
had her head spinning.

"Not Marietta! Reginald only beds her because he
knows she's after information about his activities. He,
clever man, has gotten more news from her than she
knows."

"Oh, Uncle Dom, *what are you saying?"*

"Inniesfield backed your father's expeditions, many
of them. When Walter was broke and beset by critics
of his imperialist dogma, Reginald Inniesfield gave
him hundreds of thousands of pounds. Your father
took it. Often. But what he gave in return . . . Don't
want to hear this, do you? I'm not thrilled to tell it,
believe me. But you must know so that this nightmare
ends. Cat, what your father gave Inniesfield in return
was camouflage. Inniesfield used the shipments of
artifacts from Walter's and my expeditions as the way
to hide opium transports."

She swayed with the power of his words, the progress of the coach adding pulsing torment to the painful truth. Her father . . . her *father* was responsible for her misery. How could he have done that and she never suspected? *How* could she have been so blind, so trusting? How could she have believed him so pure in heart, at least where she was concerned when she knew—had known for years—that he was so irascible, autocratic, and domineering to others? *How?* Had she ignored what she knew to be true because the pain of acknowledging it would stop her heart and deprive her of the parent she should honor?

Dom removed his glasses, extracted a handkerchief, and began to polish them. His eyebrows winged in exclamation as he spoke. "Walter's *kulis* would conceal the stuff in false bottoms of the crates in which we shipped goods home."

"So that's why Merrick attacked Father's use of Indian labor and tried to have them deported."

"Of course. How did you know?"

"Spence told me days ago about Merrick's activities."

"Then you know—as Spence must, too—that Merrick was part of an opium ring that rivaled your father's." At her jerky nod, Dom blurted, "It's for the best. You needed to know. I hated to see you pine away for the man you loved because of something so evil as two competing opium smugglers."

Voiced that way, the horror broke over her anew. "Who else is involved with Inniesfield?" *Who else has ruined my chance for a rich life with the only man I could ever love?*

"Norris Eddleworth, for one. I'm certain he killed Acton because he wanted Acton to completely cut you off from money. It was an old rivalry within the bank. Walter knew. You see Norris was in the pay of

Marietta and Oscar Hornsby, who head the smuggling ring that Merrick was involved in."

Skepticism of the logic and Dom's nature intruded. "Marietta and Oscar? That's hard to believe."

"Yes, but true."

Cat folded her arms to ward off a terrible trembling. "So Marietta's liaison with the duke of Inniesfield is merely a cover."

"Yes. Each tries to elicit information from the other about new shipments, strategies. What has followed is a war. Their ships have strange accidents. Their crews come down with odd diseases and become disabled or die."

Visions of Marietta popping up everywhere—on balconies and in alcoves—filled Cat's brain. "And Marietta is London's greatest gossip to serve her own illegal interests." *But if they are the ones who are blackmailing me for the papyrus, what good would it do to have an ancient letter from Ramses to Moses? What could it say that would compel such competition to find it that one would murder?*

Dom nodded. "Marietta has long cultivated the public image of a twit and a tart. Inniesfield decided to take advantage of it. Imagine, bedding a magpie with talons."

Cat shivered. "For money."

"Much evil has been done in the service of it."

"Is that what is at stake here?" she asked, needing to court Dom's wrath to gain the final answers that might clarify it all and set her free to love Spence.

Dom frowned. "What makes you think it isn't?"

She bit her lip.

"Cat?" He leaned across and tried to take her hand. Years of distance could not be crossed in a moment in this coach. "Fine then. Don't answer. But you must answer my first question. You must tell me what you search for. Perhaps I can help you. It must be something of Walter's. Why else would you go into my study and rifle the desk and cabinets? Unlike Walter, I am a very neat man and I know when anything has been moved. That's why Marsh and I get on so well. Cat, I also know you recently went to the factory."

"How could you know?" Had he followed her these past few weeks? Were *his* eyes the ones she had felt upon her?

"Ball and Bull told me. Yes. I see you have heard of them. Unsavory types. They were Walter's shippers. Did you not know? I thought you would have guessed. Inniesfield has always used them. One of their men saw you the other day when you were opening the crates of erotic books. Bull also knew you had been to see Acton at the bank."

Cat was reeling. "They *followed* me?"

"Your father thought Ball and Bull efficient. Yes, evidently they have been tracking you. Again, it makes me wonder why. *Why,* Cat?"

She put up a hand. "Wait. I am so shocked I—"

"I'm sorry," he said, and she stared openmouthed at him. Never in her life had she heard Dominik Farrell apologize to anyone. "I should be more direct, shouldn't I? The duke of Inniesfield heads the import ring whose smuggled goods Walter disguised with his shipments of artifacts. Norris was the banker. Ball and Bull, the shippers."

And you?

He saw the question in her eyes. "And I was never involved."

"How"—she prayed for the right words here because a part of her didn't want to believe him—"did you escape it?"

He shrugged. "Insistence. Persistence. It roiled

Walter he could not persuade me, but I kept my integrity. I foiled him at the one thing he needed of me more than anything. I must tell you, my dear, quite honestly, I *loved* resisting him. I lived, ate, and breathed defiance. Small return for his years of snobbery and indifference to me, I refused to become a part of the opium ring. Of course," he inhaled as he waved a dismissing hand, "Walter found a way to pay me back for my recalcitrance. He took the one priceless thing I found in all my digs and hid it from me."

Instinct said, *Be serene,* as she asked, "What was it?"

"A papyrus."

The words crashed down to her soul. She closed her eyes. She clutched her hands. To hear this now and know it might be the very item that she sought made her writhe. "Oh, tell me what did it say?"

"Why?" He bent nearer, and in the confines of their mutual torment, he reached out to cup her chin, and she let him lead her to look at him. His scowl turned to compassion, then fear gave way to hope in his bleary eyes. "Why, Cat?"

"My answer first."

"It is an edict from the pharaoh Ramses II to Moses."

She wanted to swoon while he went on.

"Actually, I question if it was ever sent, unless Ramses made copies of his edicts. But, of course, I'd need the papyrus itself for extended study before I could say that, and I don't have it. Walter took it from my tent." Dom's visage filled with remembrance. "It was the same day we found the cache of jewelry. I shall never forget unrolling the papyrus and beginning to read it. Even a cursory translation showed me I had found what I had long needed: proof that the pharaoh of the Bible really had existed and, what's more, so had Moses. But more than even that, the document confirmed that Pharaoh cared for Moses as a brother despite their differences.

"Ironic, wouldn't you say, that I should find evidence of such? I do. I was so stupefied by my discovery, so damned elated that I hastened to my own brother to tell him, show him, and he . . ." Dominik recoiled in his seat in agony.

"He saw straight away that the papyrus had other values. The first was political, of course. If the forces of Egyptian nationalism could use the piece to fight the British urge to imperialism, Walter knew his own views on ruling Egypt were in for trouble. The other value was the description of the route to the mines."

"The turquoise mines in the Sinai?"

"Yes, and the copper mines."

Mines. When had she recently thought of this? "John Marlow," she said without meaning to.

Dom grimaced. "You know about John?"

She shook her head. "Didn't he invest money in the last expedition?"

"Yes. In my portion of the expedition. *Mine.* Not Walter's. John has a fondness for biblical studies, and when I told him I thought I might find clues to the relationship between Ramses and Moses, he backed me. I found the proof but could not bring it to England because of Walter's treachery. John was terribly disappointed. Especially after I told him what I had found and what happened to it. He said he had never liked Walter anyway. Nor did he care for Acton Thornhill's haphazard management of the bank. John has for years suspected Walter's real activities and frowned on them."

"You never told John about my father?"

His pale eyes mellowed. "No. I would not betray

him. I could not because despite everything, he was my brother." He bit his lips white. "John Marlow used his suspicions as a means to deny approval to his daughter Nanette to marry Acton. The girl wasn't interested anyway. She has eyes only for Inniesfield, poor deluded chit."

Cat realized that she herself could not afford to be similarly duped. "But if you were not involved in the smuggling, *why* would you see Ball and Bull last night?"

He flinched. "How in hell do you know that?"

"Does it matter?" she countered quietly.

"It might."

She squared her shoulders. "I thought it was you who revealed old mysteries here."

"I need your help, though, to uncover them."

"Why would you think that?"

"Because"—he sank back in his seat—"I think you search for the same thing I do." He let that hang in the air. "Unless we cooperate, I don't think either of us can find it."

"If you were correct, *why* would I join with you to find this item?"

He cast her a wry look. "Because you want to bury our dreadful pasts. Because you want to resurrect what good from them you can. Because in your heart you are a forgiving soul, my dear Cat. Because someone is about to do you harm unless you find this item. Am I close to the truth? I think I am. What's more, I think only I can help you and only you can help me. You have Walter's papers. I remember Walter's logic, the way he thought. What better alliance? Alone, I know *I've* searched everywhere and found *nothing.*"

"Even wandering in Black Jack's tunnels."

"Yes. I've looked in every ancient crate countless

times to no avail." At her look, he sighed. "Yes, I was there when you came on one of your jaunts a few weeks ago. I couldn't let you find me. I knew you'd think I was pilfering Black Jack's wares because you had heard me maligned for years!" He sharpened his gaze. "How did you find out?"

She could not expose Spence and his purpose.

"So Spencer Lyonns *is* a spy. I always suspected he was and knew it would become one more source of trouble between him and Merrick. Spencer loved his brother too much, but his profession meant he was bound to discover the horrid truth about Merrick sooner or later."

"He did quite by accident. It hurt him immensely."

"Espionage reveals much I should think that is dangerous to body and soul. I hope to God Spence won't continue in this after you're wed."

"No," she said and smiled at her uncle for his acceptance of her love of a Lyonns. "He's resigning his commission soon and becoming a gentleman farmer."

"Thank heavens. I want you happy, Cat." He sighed and crossed one leg over the other. "So I'll give you the explanations that you want. I went to the Farrell tunnels to seek out any old crates that Walter may have hidden there. There is much but nothing from him. The reason I went to see the infamous duo of Mr. Ball and Mr. Bull is very different. They've been badgering me to perform the same service for Inniesfield's smuggling ring as Walter did. They know I need money for my expedition. John Marlow has given me some backing, but as you know these things are so costly—and I am without the one document I need to make the expedition more viable, more profitable.

"Last night, I went to see Ball and Bull at their

request. I had just returned from my club. Marsh told me you were asleep after an exhausting day of rummaging in your father's effects in the attic. I went to see Misters Ball and Bull to tell them to cease their attempts at seducing me. They, undeterred however, offered me money. A lot of it. We quarreled. I left." He spread his meaty hands wide. "What else would you know?"

A thousand things ran through her mind. How could she trust him after years of being prejudiced against him by his brother, her father? How could she fail to after a string of evidence that had her reeling but seemed so straight, so sure, she felt down in the marrow of her bones that it was truth. "Do you think . . . we could possibly . . . join forces and find this item before tomorrow?"

His features softened. "We could try."

"I want to."

A ghost of a smile appeared on his mouth only to be straightened into compassion. "Why must we find it before tomorrow, Cat?"

"Because unless I find it and give it up"—she saw him blanch—"I must hand over ten thousand pounds."

Anger made his face florid. "You don't have ten thousand!"

"But I do, Uncle Dom." She didn't tell him about the threat to defame her father with the story of the forged papyrus. That would be moot by her use of the money. "Spence gave it to me."

"He loves you." When she nodded, he smacked his lips. "The government and Her Majesty must be frantic. This Suez Canal business means the khedive wants the papyrus to house as a national treasure and it is his price for agreement to us investing in the canal, isn't it?"

"But someone else wants it as well. Inniesfield, I'd guess. But it's not useful to a smuggler."

"Yes, it *is*—as blackmail to the khedive to let the shipments continue out of Alexandria, which is the major port inside the Mediterranean."

"Ah," she said, bobbing her head. "I see. I'm not versed in the wrinkles of such lies."

"No, your rightness of character has endured so many tragedies. I am proud of you for all you are. That alone leads me to add that, in spite of his faults, Walter Farrell was an excellent father . . . and a husband."

"Thank you," she said and squeezed his hand.

He covered it in hearty warmth. "I'd like to be a real uncle to you."

"And I, a real niece."

"Wonderful," he whispered. "We shall begin with you telling me where you have looked. I shall tell you my attempts. Then I suppose we can begin to read Walter's papers." He chucked her under the chin. "We'll find this yet, my dear. Today. Tonight."

"Before tomorrow," she said like a prayer.

They found nothing.

By ten that night, they sat in Dom's study with piles of Walter's logs scattered over the desk, his receipts littered upon the reading tables, two dinner trays—so disparaged by Marsh for such untidiness—and an ever-present pot of tea donning the sideboard.

Dom removed his glasses and rubbed his eyes with his thumb and forefinger. "We've been through everything. Even my own notes. There's nothing there but the duplicate of the jewelry collection notes."

"I'll get his diary. Though there's little there but a few lines."

Within minutes she was back, standing before

Dom, leafing through the big leather-backed journal that recounted Walter Farrell's personal thoughts from his first expedition to his last, the one in which they'd found the note from Ramses and the jewelry.

"Here," she said as she wet her finger and turned the page to the entry marked September 21, 1870.

"'It is midnight,'" she read, "'and I have done what I must. Dom will be furious. He'll say I betrayed him. But I had to do it. He was ill. Getting sicker—'"

Dom sat forward. "What the hell is he talking about? I was not *ill*. He was sick with the heat that week. I remember saying to him that he should rest, let me do the work, but he forced himself. His pride, I told him, would undo him."

Cat bit her lip and went on, her fingertip trailing the handwriting. "'I tried to destroy the source, but my pride wouldn't let me. It might be false, but I doubt it. Someday, perhaps, I can bring forth this gem and let the world see it. By then Dom will be cured of my own disease . . .'"

She glanced up at Dom who wearily shook his head.

"I don't know what he's talking about, Cat. *Jesus,* if I only could!"

She went on, deflated of more hope. "'But I will do this. And then, years from now, he'll thank me that I rid him of the malady that has almost cost us our happiness and our integrity.'"

"Excessive pride," Dom snorted. "That's what he's talking about. He accused me of it after I unrolled the Ramses document and did a quick translation. He said one of us could suffer from it but not two in one family. Little did I know he was so determined to help me take a cure that he would steal from me the very thing that would give me my independence and my own recognition as a scholar. When I found it missing the next morning, he sat there in his tent looking so smug that I wanted to murder him then. He saw it. 'Wrap your hands around my throat, Dom,' he taunted me. 'Kill me. You'll pay the price.' I insulted him then in any language I could think of. He told me then he'd play physician to me, held up the belt with the amulet that stands over in the Wyngate now. 'This is the only thing the world will ever know you found, Dom.' And then he made fun of me, called me weak, sick. More names."

"What were his exact words?" she pleaded.

Dom's brow wrinkled. "What? Why? I—I *can't* remember. He always spoke in riddles, a veritable sphinx himself. Why would it be impor—? God above. Do you think it might be with the jewelry?"

"I don't know, but you nor I ever thought of it. *Did* you ever look inside the false bottoms of the crates in which the jewelry came home?"

Dom rose like a fury on the trail of evil. "No! Once we got them home and cataloged every piece of jewelry, we put them in new crates and there they stayed until they went to the Wyngate two weeks ago."

"Oh, Uncle Dom. The papyrus could be in the new crates—or in the false bottoms of the old ones!" She wanted to cry in outrage that they had come so far and failed.

"False bottoms, like hell, my dear! If I know Walter, he put the papyrus inside the physician's amulet!"

The caretaker had been none too pleased to open up the service doors at such an hour of night. But Uncle Dominik had insisted and passed a healthy ten-pound note into the man's meaty palm. That let them in with the man obsequiously turning up the gas jets. The exhibit flickered into view with a satisfied gulp from Cat and a half smile from Dom to her.

They both approached the case that held the

physician's belt and huge gold amulet, which hung down the front of the linen tunic. The two lions' heads reminded her of her and Spence and the day they had both stood here and admired this piece.

"The Egyptian symbol for life's rejuvenation," she remembered she'd told Edwina then, and now she'd evidently said the same to her uncle.

Dom grinned, suddenly a younger man despite his troubles. "A sign, I think, that we are at the end of our troubles, dear Cat." He motioned to the caretaker to help him remove the glass casing, and when the man objected, Dom countered with a gruff note of authority. "These, my good man, still belong to us. Help me remove it, I say!"

They shifted the glass up and off, then to the floor. Dom reached inside with careful hands and paused. "I'm shaking inside so badly I think I'll die. You do it."

Cat smiled at him, triumphant. "No, I can't, Uncle Dom. You do it. Take it. It was your discovery. Long denied you. Open it. Let us hear what Pharaoh had to say."

The caretaker gasped. But the look on the Farrells' faces struck him dumb.

With trembling lips compressed inside his mouth, Dom blinked away tears from his eyes and reached for the belt. With a click of the clasp, he had it off the mannequin and the amulet in his hands. The caretaker drew near. Dom flicked open the clasp and out fell a small rolled papyrus. "Pray to God," pleaded Dom, "it's what we want."

He unrolled it.

Cat did not breathe but watched her uncle's expression as he read the tiny cartouche symbols. Within minutes, his flushed face turned up, his eyes melted into hers, and he asked, "Shall I read it to you?"

She nodded like a wooden puppet.

" 'Ramses, the Beloved of the god Amun, speaks to Moses, his once dear brother, now his foe. Hear me when I say to you, the seas shall all run dry before you cease to be my brother. The world shall end for you who take your face from my sight. Because I remember your love, I shall never forget your treachery. This, I, Ramses, shall not forgive. Get you gone from my kingdom. Never return. Neither take the fruit of my land nor the bounty of my mines. Those of mine in the desert will not show you succor. My guards watch and wait for you. May you starve. May you wander for many years in punishment for your denial of my goodness and my filial affection. Ramses knew a brother, but Moses may now know no joy, ever. Thus say I, Ramses, you and yours are dead to me.' "

Dom cleared his throat, the obvious parallels to his own situation as palpable as the amulet he held. "What follows is a list and the locations of turquoise and copper mines that Ramses worked in the Sinai." He licked his lips and looked at Cat. "Oh, my dear, if this had only come to public notice years ago, then none of our tragedies would have happened. Perhaps Walter and I could have found such financial backing that he would have not needed to continue to ally himself with those men and we'd be free of our troubles."

Her own tears confirmed Dom's words, and she put a hand to his arm to comfort him.

"I sincerely doubt that, Dominik."

Cat jumped at the sound of a new male voice.

Dom squinted into the hallway and slowly rose.

Cat turned to see Reginald Inniesfield saunter in, his gloved hand firmly wrapped around a gun. "I'm delighted you finally found this. I grew weary of notes and runaway carriages. Tedious business this black-

mail." His glittering eyes swung to Cat as another
man whom she did not know emerged from the
shadows to easily bind and gag the caretaker and
assist him to the floor.

Reginald looked Dom over. "Frankly, Dom, I
thought you would find the letter sooner than this.
But now that you have"—his lips spread sardonically
and his hand came forth—"I'll relieve you of it."

"You can't have it," Cat whispered.

Reginald chuckled. "Of course I can. You think I
wanted the money? What do I need that for? What
money I have was not enough to buy a blind eye from
the khedive for my ventures. Your father usually
performed this nasty business for us, but since he's
been gone . . . Well, you can imagine my frustration. I
had great hopes you might replace him, Dominik.
But, alas"—he waved a hand theatrically—"I could
not persuade you. Now, I'm afraid I no longer need to
try. So if you don't mind, old man—" Inniesfield
waggled his fingers. "Give it to me. I would like to see
such a treasure before I turn it over to that barbarian
in Cairo."

Dom faced him, his glasses silver in the gaslight.

Instinct told Cat Dom planned something.

He stepped back toward the other exhibit room
where statues crammed the floor. "I'm afraid you'll
not have it, Reg. This, you see, was my discovery. I'll
not let you nor anyone else take it from me."

"Don't be silly, Dom. *I* have a gun." Reg walked
forward.

Dom sank back. They drifted slowly among the
marble figures. When Dom came close to Cat, she
slithered to one side. His hand shot out to bring her to
him.

But too late.

Cat slid near a statue that she thought offered

refuge. Her reward was to be caught about the waist by another man's arm!

Cat pried at his sleeve, writhed this way and that.

"Stop struggling!" growled a man who put the circle of a gun barrel to her temple.

Cat stilled just in time to see Reginald Inniesfield go down before her with a thud. Above his lax body stood Marietta Hornsby, staring at him dispassionately, a huge pistol hanging from her fingers. "Arrogant sort."

"Come, come, Dom. You try my patience," urged the man who held Cat and whose voice she now recognized as Oscar Hornsby.

Cold metal bored into her head as Cat tried to think of a way to help Dom but only writhed at her helplessness.

"Cease, I say!" Oscar seethed at her. "Dom, come forward now! You wouldn't want your niece hurt, would you? No. I didn't think so. So do come here and put the papyrus on the floor there between us, like a good man. Yes . . . yes. Now if you don't mind—"

"If *you* don't mind, Oscar—" A bass voice oozed into Cat's conscious mind as she saw an arm snake about her captor's neck, a knife piercing him in his jugular. "Release her."

In a second when there was no time for thought, she stomped on Oscar's toes, lunged away, and heard the sickening thwack of bodies hitting the floor. Scrambling to get to Dom, Cat turned to see Spence wrestle Oscar Hornsby to the tiles.

The room was suddenly alive with black-uniformed bobbies, one of whom had Marietta in a strangle hold.

"Take them away, constable," Spence ordered as he handed over a furious Hornsby. "I'll come down to the Yard to fill out the charges as soon as I see to the well-being of the Farrells."

Cat went from Dom's arms to Spence's with the speed of one possessed. For long minutes, she shuddered there while he told her their troubles were truly at an end—and their joys had only just begun.

Epilogue

*F*or the thousandth time, Cat glanced outside the coach window to see how far they'd traveled from Calais. Her hand brushed her diamond engagement ring and her two-week-old wedding band before she wound her arm inside her husband's.

"Happy?" Spence asked and squeezed her arm, his lips nestling in her hair.

"Delirious," she admitted and dropped her head back to admire her husband. "I'm grateful you indulge me so, my love."

Spence cocked a wicked brow. "How could I not give you what you want and bring you back to the Red House? Especially since you entice me with your promise of throwing open the doors to the bedrooms for certain special events."

They chuckled together while she blushed and glanced at his sleeve. "I have a wedding gift there for you."

"Really?" He was roguish now and she pinched his arm in embarrassed peak.

"I *do!* Just you wait."

He widened his eyes. "Darling, I *am* trying."

She put a palm to his smooth cheek. "One thing you could never be, my love, is *trying.*"

Efficient he had been for days after Reginald Inniesfield and the Hornsbys had attempted to steal the famous papyrus and hurt her and Dominik. Comforting he had been when everyone at Scotland Yard debated what to reveal to the public about Walter Farrell's connections to Inniesfield and the ring of smugglers. Relieved he had been, just as she had, when everyone in the Foreign Office—including evidently Her Majesty the Queen—had decided it in the best interests of the Crown and the future empire, if Walter Farrell were remembered as a noted Egyptologist and only that forevermore.

Through the agonizing days following Inniesfield's and the Hornsbys' arrests, Spence had also been charming. He had kept up appearances that he and Cat were courting again and serious enough once more about each other to announce their wedding date. To someone—perhaps God Himself—Spence had also explained the need for the special marriage license to be reissued. He told her on their wedding trip in the grand suite of their hotel how he'd asked the Methodist minister who had originally married them in the middle of the night to understand the social requirement to marry publicly. When the man of God replied that he would be most eager to see the famous couple of the Lyonn and the Cat restored to everyone's good graces, Spence whooped in joy. Later, an anonymous contribution to the man's mission made it possible to feed the poor on roast beef and potatoes for a month.

What followed was the wedding of the season. Dom threw open his house for the daily barrage of wedding gifts that arrived at the door. The social invitations poured in as well—and suddenly, Cat was universally accepted. Popular. The school's enrollment bulged. Jessica came up from Kent for the prenuptial festivities ready to discuss issues of how to deal with twice as many girls as they had planned for. Meanwhile, the newspapers spoke of the coming wedding of "the Lyonn and the Cat" with cartoons that tickled them and articles about the intricacies of her trousseau— down to the detailing on her lingerie—that made Cat balk.

"Now, sweetheart." Spence had tempered her with a stroking hand when she'd seen actual sketches of her bridal gown reproduced in the papers. "Don't fret. Let them have their share of our joy. Some people, you realize, find great hope in our story. Most lovers who have lost never regain the one they cherish. I did"—he wrapped her close and pressed hot kisses to her eyes—"and I will forever be grateful to you for such forgiveness."

"I'm thankful for your understanding that I failed to see my father for all he was."

"You saw the part of him he favored you with, and later, as adults do, you came to terms with his humanity. As we all must do with those we love."

She had embraced him then and let their torments float away upon the wind. From that day forward, she had not spoken of the past but only of their mutual future

The day she and he had for the second time become man and wife, they stood in the hallowed walls of the church where once they would have joined. Attending the ceremony were more than one hundred people they knew and loved. Uncle Dom gave her away.

Victoria Caldmore acted as hostess. Dorrie and Blanding came with relief and joy. Rand brought the wedding rings. Jessica walked down the aisle as the only bridesmaid. The Prince and Princess of Wales personally conveyed the best wishes of his mother.

Spence had given Cat a new wedding ring he had especially crafted for her. Outside were the figures of a cat and a lion rampant. Inside, he had inscribed, For Cat, with Love and Pride, This Time and Always.

She adored the ring and knew her own to him matched his in emotion: For Spencer, Who Led Me to Laugh and Love Again.

But this other gift she could not give him at the ceremony nor soon afterward.

In Paris, she had sent and received telegrams daily about its status. Finally, yesterday, she had gotten the word she wanted and almost sang in glee inside the office on the Rue Saint-Antoine. When Spence saw her so exuberant, he knew they could go home now. She insisted that they go to the Red House straightaway.

"I must give this to you there. Let's go just for a day or two more alone," she had urged. "Afterward, I know we must go south to Kent. There is so much to do for the opening of the school . . . and I feel that there may not be much time for us from now until Christmas."

He had swung her into his arms then and kissed her soundly. "Whatever you want, love, I'm here to give it. I am thrilled to have you for even a minute at a time if that's all there is. I had no hope of ever having you for so very long, my darling, that I am willing to share you with whatever pleases you. Schools. Gifts. Even taking you into each of the bedrooms of the Red House," he promised sweetly, and she promptly led him to the ecstasies of their last night in their bridal suite of the Hotel Sully.

So as ever, he was true to his word and brought her here.

At the sight of the massive iron gates and Charlie Blowes waving them into the estate, she practically jumped out of her skin.

"I hope you'll like this," she said with worry as they removed their mantles and she bounded in to find Hettie and ask her where she'd put a package for her that had arrived from London.

Hettie eyed them with glowing interest and pointed upstairs. "The master bedroom," she announced as Cat darted away. "Where else would I put anything for a new married couple?" she said to a grinning, perplexed Spence who flapped his arms and followed his wife.

"Close your eyes," Cat stopped him at the door to say.

He complied with a smile and thrust out his hands like a sleepwalker. "How am I to find my way?"

She tsked at him. "You cannot find me in the dark? I thought your instincts were better than that, my lion."

He inhaled. "I'd know you anywhere. Roses and warm, willing woman." His fingers closed around her upper arms and brought her flush to his torso. "My sweet wife." He kissed her deeply, arching her back over his arm but finding their union barred by some object in her hands.

He sighed. "What is this?" His fingers trailed down her arms to her hands. "Something else to keep you from me?" he growled playfully. "It feels like a pile of paper."

"Yes. It is and it isn't."

He peeped open one eye. "Can I look?"

"No. I want you to imagine because, you see, it is not terribly beautiful yet."

He mashed his handsome mouth in contemplation. "I'm game. What is it?"

She licked her lips and drew him to their bed. She sat him down, placed the stack in his hands, and moved next to him. "It's something you gave me when we were here, but something I want to give you, too."

He smiled. "You and your riddles, darling. You've stumped me. Tell me."

She put one hand atop his and pressed it to the paper. "This is a manuscript I edited."

He beamed. "Your father's memoirs! They're done."

"No, my love. These are not my father's."

"But you said it's a manuscript. From Dunmore's then?" He meant the publisher to whom he had his grandmother introduce her that day of Marietta's garden party.

"Right you are. But these are not my father's. They'll be done next month. These are . . . your mother's."

My mother's? he mouthed, confused.

"These are the family stories your mother wrote in her book in the cottage in the woods, my love. During our engagement, I edited them and offered them to Mr. Dunmore to publish if he thought they might be good enough. I thought they were. He says, after reading them, that they are superb."

Spence's eyes flew open, and tears stood in his eyes. "Cat!"

She swallowed hard, not certain yet if she'd done the right thing to offer his mother's works for the world to read. "I read those stories, darling, and loved each one. They kept me sane during those days when times were troubled and you were far from me. I thought they deserved a grander audience than simply me. Mr. Dunmore agrees. If you like, you can sign the contracts in this package. I meant for you to know how I value you and everything you are so that no one—not even you—would ever question how I love you."

With reverent fingers, he caressed the pages in his lap and then put them on the mattress. He turned to bind Cat to him and swirl her down to the comfort of the counterpane. His hands framed her face as his lips blessed her eyes. "My darling, my dearest wife, you astonish me. You give me so much and I think there is no more a man could ask from his God or his wife when suddenly, like a genie from a lamp, you appear with more wonders to dispense."

She got lost in his ardent green eyes. "So you do like the idea of her work—her stories—being published for everyone in the world to enjoy?"

"My heart, I adore the idea."

"They are tender stories that transform an ordinary family into legend. The stories that form a part of your identity and now mine."

"Although they may weave tales that engender pride, you and I will tell our children and theirs how to temper any excess with humility." He kissed her palm. "These stories are the perfect wedding gift from you to me. I shall value it till my last breath. But more than that, you need to know something more. For years to come, I may have wealth, land, and titles, but none equals this that I count as far and above all else on earth. It is and ever will be you. *You* are my first and my last, my most glorious and priceless, my one and my only treasure."

Author's Notes

The rush to divest other nations of their treasures was not solely a tendency of the English nor a trend of the nineteenth century. Ramses is one example—and not the first—of those who plundered other peoples' lands that theirs might enjoy more riches. Yet the urge toward nationalism did point up the need for restraint, a phenomenon still active in our hypertech world only a few years from the twenty-first century. We have just begun to understand how to value someone else's treasures by allowing them to enjoy them themselves.

In *Gifts,* Jessica Curtis takes charge of Cat Lyonns's unique treasure—their school for girls—and attempts to help one exceptionally talented student. When Jess is frustrated, she seeks help from their neighbor, Rand Templeton. But as she watches Rand give so much more than she ever thought, she realizes the greatest challenge is to her heart. Terrified, she knows that to love a man this fiercely could destroy her for all time. Look for *Gifts* in late 1996.

I love to hear from readers. Please enclose a self-addressed stamped envelope so that I can easily reply and mail to

Jo-Ann Power
13017 Wisteria Drive, Suite 384
Germantown, MD 20874

**POCKET BOOKS
PROUDLY ANNOUNCES**

GIFTS

JO-ANN POWER

**Coming soon
in paperback from
Pocket Books**

**The following is a preview of
Gifts . . .**

Chapter 1

She was the one person he didn't want.

Not here. Not now.

Not ever.

He stared down at her as she patted the old mare on the neck, handed the reins over to his butler, and picked up her riding skirt to climb the stone steps to the front door of his house. Her old black Lab plodded at her heels as the comical monkey whom she and her cousin called Darwin slid from the rump of the horse. The macaque in short pants ambled behind her. Probably reprimanding her for her speed, Rand surmised with a twist to his mouth. That monkey was a menace to society.

But not as much as Jessica Curtis is to you, old man.

Rand set his jaw.

He dropped the velvet drapes of his bedroom window back into place and jammed his hands on his hips. Of all the blasted luck to be home and have to receive her. He had avoided it so well for so long, it had become second nature.

His self-imposed injunctions to stay away from Kent and beg off from Spence and Cat's invitations over to Farrell Hall had worked fairly well for—what was it?—three years now? Ever since that June morning in St. Paul's when he'd stood with Spence at the altar, gazed down the aisle, and found a ghost gliding toward him.

The memory made him walk over to his breakfast tray and reach for another cup of coffee. The ice that had settled on him during that wedding had crystallized his entire attitude toward this one woman whom he had never met before that morning and whom he had seen only a few times since.

He had changed his routine to avoid her. Summering less in this house. Going to Cowes with the Prince of Wales instead of supervising his autumn harvests here. Seeing Spence more in London than when he was in residence next door, less than a five-minute walk away.

And now, just as he considered making an alliance that should—among other things—wipe away his preoccupation with her, Jess Curtis sent him an early morning note requesting a few minutes of his time.

He swallowed his coffee and pursed his mouth. He'd already given her more than that. Hours, to be precise. Nights, to his great dismay. But he had conquered that, hadn't he?

He barked in amusement.

No question there. He hadn't vanquished anything. He had only sidestepped the entire issue of confront-

ing her. Jess Curtis brought out more in him than
memories. She brought back all the feeling, all the
pain . . .

*Oh, Christ, you're getting maudlin again, Temple-
ton. See the woman and get it over and done!*

He spun for his morning coat, yanked it on, and
headed for the stairs.

*The better part of valor would be merely to listen to
her. Find out what she wants in the few minutes you
can spare her. Because that's all she'll ever have of you.
The smallest thing you can give her.*

She wanted so little from him.

As justification, she knew it sounded good.

If only her body heard that! Then her hands would
stop sweating. Her teeth might cease their clattering.
Her knees end their knocking.

She gave a short laugh at her silliness and resumed
her pacing, Darwin at her heels, Bones collapsed on
the floor, eyes following her to and fro.

"Stop doing that!" she reprimanded the dog, who
did as he pleased anyway. She threw up her hands,
then kneaded them.

She whirled and worried over the Portuguese carpet, stopping at one end of the thing that defined the
colossal perimeter of Randall Templeton's fabled
drawing room. Carved in an oval with the spare
simplicity of neoclassical lines, the buttercup moiré
walls gave a glow to the English Empire furniture. The
morning sun beamed through cream voile to sparkle
on the brasses and bronzes of India and Siam. The
crystals of Ireland and Paris. The portraits of the
Templetons.

But to Jess, the rays of the sun across the priceless chaises and settees shone as mere atmosphere for the real beauty in this room. The piano. His famous French Erard grand piano. Ebony and gilt rococo. Its keyboard exposed. Ivories glowing. Summoning her.

Unknowing how she got there, her hand reached out and touched the keys. A chord resounded softly in the room, definitive, crisp. The room's acoustics lived up to their reputation. She bent and tried a few more chords, a few bars from an étude she was teaching herself so that she could entice Amanda. Drawn herself, Jess put her nose in the air as if testing for possibilities. Rand might keep her waiting and this—her eyes traveled to the keys that were her irresistible temptation—beckoned. Throwing caution away, she swept aside her skirts, seated herself, and began.

The venerable piano had more resonance, more power than she'd heard from any instrument. Even though it was more than a century old, the instrument accentuated the drama of a piece by Bach—its eros, its ecstasies. Its sorrows. Its—

She felt him more than heard him.

Her back straightened. Her hands stopped. She turned.

Seized breath and courage.

She had prepared herself so well for this . . . but not for him. She never had. She knew once again she wasted her hope to have tried. But what did it matter? Every time she had ever gazed at Randall Templeton, she had been struck silly.

By his size. Taller than even she. By his coloring.

Midnight black hair and eyes as divinely blue. But the way he looked at *her* . . . Oh, now, that did make her shiver. He always gazed upon her as if she were unreal.

And that, like a shower of ice, always chilled her fantasies of him.

"Good morning, Jessica," he said with politeness as he stood in one of the few shadows of the brilliant room. The dove gray of his morning attire gloved his massive shoulders with perfection. The cambric stock he wore performed strong counterpoint to his bronzed complexion, and the manly contrasts undid her.

"Forgive me. I—" She would have walked forward.

"Don't stop," he told her with an instructive finger at the keyboard. "You're good. I remember from the musicale last summer. I wish I could have stayed to hear more. Allow me to enjoy your efforts now to make up for that loss."

"Oh, I don't think so, my lord." He was being gracious, which was all well and fitting, especially for the odd occurrence of a woman calling on a gentleman—and unescorted, too, except by her pets.

"Rand." He stepped forward into the sunlight, and she groped for the piano for support. Too close to him, she always felt light-headed. It was his extreme self-assurance, she told herself when she was alone and reminiscing about their encounters.

She managed a socially correct smile. "Rand."

He swallowed hard while his gaze drifted up from her lips to her eyes. "Can I ring for coffee perhaps?" he rasped. Then he cleared his throat, and his broad mouth firmed in a line. "Or do you prefer tea?" His expression widened as he tried to be hopeful.

He seemed ill at ease, as ever with her.

Jess found her backbone. What was she doing drooling like Bones over a tasty morsel she could not enjoy? Rand Templeton was merely being officious. *And you are being naive and featherbrained. All those qualities you rue.* A voice whispered, *Those qualities that destroy a woman.*

"I don't care for anything, thank you. But I hoped I might prevail upon our status as neighbors and ask you to see me before you began your day."

He smiled pleasantly and nodded toward a chair. "Had your note or you come later, I would not have been at home."

She swallowed her discomfort. Of course he wouldn't. "Not at home" was a favored phrase of butlers to turn out unwanted visitors. From the way Rand had always treated her as if she had the plague, Jess knew she'd never enjoy the status of one welcome to his presence. She took the chair he indicated and made much of arranging her skirts.

Darwin came to perch himself against the chair near her legs. He stood, arms folded, like a little man in charge. His gleaming brown eyes fluttered, then panned to Rand.

"I hope you don't mind that I brought them," she explained with a glance at Bones, who had fallen asleep in the sun. "They don't seem to be occupied enough. Even with all the students."

Rand settled himself opposite her in an oversize wing chair he filled admirably. His long legs in the soft gray trousers stretched out before her. As she tore herself from admiring every inch, he crossed one leg and opened a hand to her. The look on his face told her he knew she was making conversation of insignificant things. Of course she was! What else could she possibly do when the ice of their encounters now moved like a polar floe upon the sea of her distress. In such a chill, she was losing the ability to breathe and—*God!*—she hadn't even *started* to ask him anything yet!

"Let's get to it, Jess. What can I do for you?"

In the end it was so easy to grant Jess her wish.

Rand turned his black stallion down the lane to Farrell Hall from the main road and felt right about what he had agreed to do. After all, what was it but a few hours of his time?

Bah, his conscience warned him now as it had days ago when she sat so near him in his drawing room. *You know what it really means.*

He'd be spending a few hours with a student of Jessica's.

And with her.

And with her.

The very thing you told yourself you'd not do. Ever.

The very thing he found he could do. Because— after his avoidance of her for her looks and demeanor—he had discovered in that intense half hour with her that Jessica Curtis was distinctly her own person. If his interview with her had illustrated nothing else, it had shown him that.

Being so close to her, as he had never been before, had been such a revelation. She was very different from what he had expected. Strong. Yet with a resilience that put him in mind of the finest porcelain. Opal skin. Strawberry hair. Pale aqua eyes. Still, the most appealing glory of Jess Curtis was her mouth. He shifted in his saddle at the luscious memory. Her lips were the translucent pink of shells, glossy and wet.

Jess lured him, intrigued him.

So when she asked him this small favor, how could he not give her what she wanted? The beguiling answer came as another question: How could he stay away now that he knew Jess was no ghost but a delicate woman with sensitivities attuned to him?

He had felt it.

The moment he had taken her hand and raised her chin, he had discovered it. And it was as if the damn house had fallen on him. Compelled, he knew he had to touch her again. Soon.

So he had agreed to come here and help her with a reluctant student.

He noted with a start that his reverie had brought him to the steps of Farrell Hall.

The front door fell open to him.

"Good morning, my lord." Pool nodded officiously and said in his stentorian voice, "May I take your hat and gloves, sir? Lady Curtis has told me to see you to the music room. She is detained by unexpected circumstances. But she assures me she will be with you as soon as possible."

"Thank you, Pool." Despite the coolness of the April day, his ride in the sun had warmed him. In truth, most of that was really because he was eager to see Jess again. Very eager.

He followed the butler to the music room. The

sienna room was most radiant at sunset. Rand had had the good fortune to visit here often and loved its very air. Now, he would be spending a lot of time here. For days. Or weeks. As long as necessary—or as long as he could use to clarify his own attitude toward marriage, children, . . . and Jessica.

"Can I bring you anything, my lord?"

Only Jessica Curtis, he thought dryly. *Quickly.*

The war between dying to see him and living to avoid him clashed like two cymbals in her chest. Jess had been dreading or cherishing this moment for days. Now he was here playing the piano beyond that door. She could hear him. More, she remembered how it felt to touch him. Exciting. Gutting. So she closed her eyes, crossed her arms and let his music caress her instead.

This fear and enticement were so childish. She had ridiculed herself on that score for two days. Or perhaps, before that when she knew she had to see him and appeal to his better angels to help her. She'd been a goose to expect he'd reject her request. In fact, Rand had agreed so readily and without question that she was astounded. Then as their conversation became banter, she realized that she had not ever been so comfortable with a man.

That knowledge spurred her to action.

She thrust open the doors with all the authority she showed her students.

He never noticed.

She stood rooted to the floor while he continued in his rendition of a Lizst étude. Awash in sound, she experienced the same light-headedness she'd felt the first time she'd seen him at the Lyonnses' wedding and months later, the first time she'd heard his marvelously elegant hands extract emotions from a piano.

She watched him in profile. Patrician in line, stark brow and cheek and jaw. But generous mouth. Large and long of limb, sinuously hewn by a God who understood how to mold a mortal man for a woman's appreciation. But certainly, if Rand Templeton's appearance couldn't rob a woman's breath, his music did.

Enchanted by his talent, she surrendered to the aura he created. Absorbed as he was, he could not know how she admired him—no, she corrected herself—how she found him quite simply devastating. Too handsome. Too urbane. Too successful. Wildly rich. So well accepted despite a mysterious élan that attracted while it distanced.

She went to him.

Lost in his music, he had no idea for quite some time that she approached him. But when his eye caught the hem of her gown, he turned his head to consume the total sight of her from toe to crown.

Her heart crashed to a halt.

His eyes locked on hers in his only sign of recognition.

She stopped breathing.

His mouth softened. His hands continued while his eyes delved into hers.

The music he made with his body drowned in the chanting of her brain. *Don't be a fool. He's here to help you. Not entice you. Nor enthrall you.*

As if he heard her, his brows rose infinitesimally. A question sculpted his features.

She threw off her reticence and welcomed him with a smile. A polite but friendly smile.

One black brow wrinkled.

She despaired that he could so easily discern her facade. That she could so easily be undone by him.

She swallowed painfully.

He watched her throat convulse, and when his eyes returned to hers, they bore the raging heat of the other day—and the searing knowledge that he understood her discomfort.

She froze. He had burned away all her pretense. The very thing she dreaded from anyone but particularly from him.

He veered away to watch his hands finish the piece. Even frightened as she was to the marrow of her bones, she heard his artistry, perceived his wizardry, and felt his fingertips conjure melodies that spread through her bloodstream with disturbing new emotions. Loving his ability to use his body to his will, she envied the way he summoned such beauty from the instrument . . . until the last chords died. Leaving her adrift in the echoes resounding through her chaos.

Suddenly, silence filled the space between them. It loomed as a monstrous impediment to what she wanted from him. Frantic, she knew not how to destroy it.

His hands went to his thighs. He faced her, and his knowing gaze met hers. "You liked that," he had only to murmur in the solemnity of the spring morn. "Shall I play it again?"

Like a wooden marionette, she shook her head.

Those expressive brows widened. "Another then?"

With eyes alone, she pleaded with him to end this.

Compassion—that emotion she now concluded he possessed in terrifying abundance—colored his gaze in sweetness. "I need to know, Jess," he urged in more acceptable tones, "what bothers you."

As if he had cloaked her naked emotions in a mantle of propriety, she sailed toward him. Her hands to the piano, she looked at him now with the familiarity three years of genteel proximity allowed. Neighbors they were. Would continue to be. "I cannot persuade Amanda to come down."

Humor fired his features to blinding beauty. "Good God, Jess, what did you tell her about me?"

"The truth."

"Well, *that* obviously convinced her," he scoffed good-naturedly while one hand pushed back his coat to settle at his waist and he examined her face. "What was your version of the truth?"

His effervescence was contagious—and so startling that she grinned. "If I tell you, you'll be too flattered," she blurted.

He went quite still. "For a woman whom I thought eschewed coyness, you appear to be flirting with me."

No other words could have turned her to stone. "I never"—she kneaded her hands, wrestling with the urge to flee—"flirt."

"I know."

He'd watched her? Why? When?

Flattered, she battled delight. Terrified, she breathed so heavily that she thought her skin would rip the material of her dress. To show him such a sentiment was so crude, so very gauche. So demeaning. Yet she couldn't run from him. If she did, she'd never live it down. Never be able to look him in the eye. *Never* help Amanda.

She lifted her chin higher. "I told her you were the finest pianist I had ever had the honor to hear. That you were renowned for your abilities, even if you called yourself an amateur."

"That is complimentary and I thank you, Jess. But it is not enough to make a young girl stay away from someone who—according to your description—can instruct her in the very thing she seems to want more than anything else."

"I don't understand."

"Of course you do." He rose. A titan, he stepped toward her. The breadth of his shoulders in the superfine fawn wool cut off the sight of anything else, and the height of him forced her head back as he came so close she could feel his body heat sizzling her nerves. Run though she wished to, he pinned her to her spot with the wizardry of his blue eyes. And the magic nearness of his mouth. "What else did you tell her?"

Manners fled. Truth stood naked. "That Spence said you would readily agree to this because you adore children. Cat convinced me that, no matter your schedule, you would carve out the time to help me. *Amanda,*" she corrected quickly while his features spread in satisfaction.

"I *am* gratified," he declared while his gaze fell to her lips. "My friends speak well of me." With the slightest touch of his palms to her elbows, he steadied her on her feet before she registered enough to gasp—

and then he was gone from her. Across the room. Gazing at her harp. Plucking a string. Sending a note of reality into the thick air. "So then, how shall we proceed to convince Amanda I am no ogre?" He turned. "More important, how do I convince you I am safe to enjoy?"

Look for
Gifts
Wherever Paperback Books Are Sold
Coming Soon from
Pocket Star Books